EXECUTIVE INTENT

EXECUTIVE INTENT

DALE BROWN

𝓌𝓂

WILLIAM MORROW

An Imprint of HarperCollins*Publishers*

EXECUTIVE INTENT. Copyright © 2010 by Air Battle Force, Inc. All rights reserved. Printed in the United States of America. No part of this book may be used or reproduced in any manner whatsoever without written permission except in the case of brief quotations embodied in critical articles and reviews. For information address HarperCollins Publishers, 10 East 53rd Street, New York, NY 10022.

HarperCollins books may be purchased for educational, business, or sales promotional use. For information please write: Special Markets Department, HarperCollins Publishers, 10 East 53rd Street, New York, NY 10022.

FIRST EDITION

Library of Congress Cataloging-in-Publication Data

Brown, Dale, 1956–
    Executive intent / Dale Brown. — 1st ed.
        p. cm.
    Summary: When the United States develops a new, state-of-the-art missile defense weapon, it threatens global stability and pits the world's superpowers in a contest for dominance in the space around Earth's orbit.
    ISBN 978-0-06-156085-9
    1. United States—Defenses—Fiction.   2. Space race—Fiction.   I. Title.
PS3552.R68543E98 2010
813'.54—dc22

                                                                                                          2009053182

---

10 11 12 13 14   OV/RRD   10 9 8 7 6 5 4 3 2 1

This novel is dedicated to my hardworking family, who refuse to give in even during tough economic and personal times.

Remember Always the Family.

CAST OF CHARACTERS

Joseph Gardner, President of the United States

Kenneth Phoenix, Vice President

Walter Kordus, White House Chief of Staff

Stacy Anne Barbeau, Secretary of State

Marcus Colby, U.S. Ambassador to the United Nations

David C. Keeley, Deputy Secretary of State for Asia

Deborah A. Carlson, Assistant Secretary of State for Chinese
   Affairs

Conrad Carlyle, President's National Security Adviser

Miller Turner, Secretary of Defense

Gerald Vista, Director of National Intelligence

Salazar "Sal" Banderas, Secretary of the Air Force

Ann Page, Deputy Undersecretary of the Air Force for Space

Timothy Dobson, Assistant Deputy Director for Strategic
   Program Research, Central Intelligence Agency

Annette Douglass, Assistant Deputy Secretary of State

General Taylor J. Bain, Chairman of the Joint Chiefs of Staff

ADMIRAL BENJAMIN KELLY, Vice Chairman of the Joint Chiefs of Staff

GENERAL CHARLES HUFFMAN, U.S. Air Force Chief of Staff

USN ADMIRAL RICHARD COWAN, Chief of Naval Operations

USAF GENERAL ROBERT WIEHL, Commander, U.S. Space Command and USAF Space Command

U.S. NAVY ADMIRAL SHERMAN HUDDY, Commander, U.S. Strategic Command

U.S. ARMY GENERAL THOMAS GREENE, Commander, U.S. Africa Command

COMMAND SERGEANT MAJOR FRANK NAUERT, NCOIC, U.S. Africa Command

U.S. AIR FORCE LIEUTENANT GENERAL PATRICK McLANAHAN (RET.)

BRIGADIER GENERAL KAI RAYDON, Commander, U.S. Space Defense Force, Armstrong Space Station

U.S. ARMY COLONEL ALAN CAMEROTA, Substitute Space-Station Commander

U.S. AIR FORCE COLONEL GIA "BOXER" CAZZOTTO, Commander, 7th Expeditionary Bomb Wing, EB-1C Vampire-Bomber Aircraft Commander

WAYNE "WHACK" MACOMBER, "Tin Man" Commando and Cybernetic Infantry Device (CID) Pilot

U.S. ARMY RESERVE LIEUTENANT COLONEL JASON RICHTER, Commander, U.S. Army Infantry Transformational Battlelab, Fort Polk, Louisiana; CID Engineer and Pilot

CHARLIE TURLOCK, CID Pilot

U.S. AIR FORCE MAJOR ALAN "FRODO" FRIEL, EB-1C Vampire-Bomber Mission Commander

U.S. Navy Commander Scott Bream, XS-19 Midnight
Spaceplane Pilot

Air Force Major Dana Colwin, XS-19 Midnight Spaceplane
Pilot

Marine Corps Major Jessica "Gonzo" Faulkner, Spaceplane
Pilot

U.S. Air Force First Lieutenant Jeffrey McCallum,
Spacecraft Electronics Technician

U.S. Air Force Senior Master Sergeant Valerie "Seeker"
Lukas, Senior Noncommissioned Officer of Armstrong Space
Station

Petty Officer Paul Malkin, Rescue Swimmer, USS *Rourke*

Jonathan Colin Masters, Chief Engineer, Sky Masters Inc.

Hunter "Boomer" Noble, Vice President of Engineering, Sky
Masters Inc.; S-9 Black Stallion and XS-19 Midnight
Spaceplane Pilot

PEOPLE'S REPUBLIC OF CHINA

Zhou Qiang, Premier of the People's Republic of China

Tang Zhaoxing, Minister of Foreign Affairs

Zung Chunxian, Minister of National Defense

General Hua Zhilun, Commander of 11th Strategic Rocket
Forces, People's Liberation Army Air Forces

Li Jianzhu, Chinese Ambassador to the United Nations

RUSSIAN FEDERATION

Igor Truznyev, President of the Russian Federation

AIR FORCES GENERAL ANDREI DARZOV, Chief of Staff of the
Russian Defense Forces

BORIS TARZOV, Russian Ambassador to the United Nations

PAKISTANIS

AMANULLAH MAZAR, President of Pakistan

INDIANS

SHANTOSH PAWAR, Prime Minister of India

BRAZILIANS

ERNESTO NASCIMENTO, Brazilian Ambassador to the United
Nations and Temporary Chairman of the U.N. Security
Council

YEMENIS

SALAM AL-JUFRI, Employee of Yemeni Fish Company Limited

WEAPONS

AESA—Active Electronically Scanned Array, a radar system that uses pulsed radar beams instead of a mechanically moving antenna to search the sky

AIM-9 Sidewinder—American heat-seeking air-to-air missile

AIM-120 AMRAAM—American Advanced Medium-Range Air-to-Air Missile, radar-guided air-to-air missile

AL-52 Dragon—a B-52 bomber modified to carry an antiballistic-missile laser

AN/FPS/79—space tracking radar

AN/SPY-1—advanced shipborne air and space control radar

APG-79—fire control radar aboard the American F/A-18 Hornet fighter

AS-17 Krypton—Russian hypersonic air-launched attack missile

AWACS—Airborne Warning and Control System, an aircraft-based radar system used to track air and sea targets

BAMS—Broad Area Maritime Surveillance, a U.S. Navy program to use long-range unmanned aircraft for surveillance near a naval battle group

C-802—Chinese ship- or shore-launched antiship or land-attack missile

COIL—Chlorine-Oxygen-Iodine Laser, a system that uses a chemical reaction to produce laser light

Dong Feng-21 (DF-21)—Chinese submarine- or land-based mobile surface-to-surface solid-fuel rocket

DSP—Defense Support Program, a system of geosynchronous infrared satellites that detect missile launches on Earth

E-2C Hawkeye—a carrier-based long-range surveillance radar aircraft

Evolved Sea Sparrow—a ship-based antimissile defense system

FEL—Free Electron Laser, a laser that produces laser light by moving electrons freely through a magnetic field

50N8 Graza—Russian long-range surface-to-air missile

Grebe—a submarine-launched unmanned reconnaissance aircraft

Jian Hong-37N—Chinese carrier-based interceptor and attack aircraft

Julang-1S—Chinese submarine-launched ballistic missile, based on the DF-21 ballistic missile

Ka-27—Russian ship-based patrol and antisubmarine warfare helicopter

KT-3—Chinese land-based antisatellite missile based on the DF-21 ballistic missile

LADAR—Laser Radar, a system that uses electronically steered laser energy to detect ground, air, and space targets

MiG-31 "Foxhound"—Russian supersonic long-range interceptor aircraft

Mk 45—American standard shipborne five-inch gun

MQ-35 Condor—American air-launched commando insertion aircraft

netrusion—inserting damaging or corrupt data into a computer network through digital sensors

OMV—Orbital Maneuvering Vehicle, a device that can carry defensive or offensive weapons in space or through Earth's atmosphere

Orion—next-generation manned orbital and lunar spacecraft

RQ-4 Global Hawk—a large, long-range, high-altitude, long-endurance unmanned reconnaissance aircraft

SA-N-9—Russian advanced naval surface-to-air missile system

SBIRS—Space-Based Infrared System, American next-generation space-based missile launch detection and tracking system

SH-60 Seahawk—American ship-based patrol and antisubmarine warfare helicopter

SM-2 Standard—American ship-launched antiaircraft, antiballistic, and antisatellite missile

SPG-62 target illuminator—American ship-based radar that places a beam on an air target that surface-to-air missiles can home in on

Sukhoi-34 Fullback—Russian advanced interceptor and attack aircraft

thirty-mike—thirty millimeter

Tin Man—American infantryman who wears an advanced electronic protective armor system

TLAM—Tomahawk Land Attack Missile, American ship- or submarine-launched long-range attack cruise missile

***Xia*-class**—Chinese ballistic-missile submarine

YAL-1 Airborne Laser—American antiballistic-missile laser aircraft, based on a Boeing 747 aircraft

Yantar-4K2—Obsolete Russian reconnaissance satellite

ACRONYMS AND TERMINOLOGY

ACU—Army Combat Uniform, new designation of American battle uniform

ADS—Active Defensive System, American aircraft laser system that defeats enemy antiaircraft missiles with bursts of laser energy

American Holocaust—term used to describe the Russian bomber attacks against the United States

BG—Brigadier General

Boats—abbreviation for a naval enlisted man who trains, supervises, and directs ship's maintenance duties

CAG—Carrier Air Group, referring to the commander of an aircraft carrier's air wings

CID—Cybernetic Infantry Device, an American infantry combat system utilizing a manned robot to afford superhuman protection, strength, speed, and attack capabilities equivalent to an infantry platoon

CINC—Commander in Chief; former designation of the commander of a major U.S. military command (now reserved for the president of the United States)

CJCS—Chairman of the Joint Chiefs of Staff, the senior uniformed adviser to the president of the United States

CNO—Chief of Naval Operations, the senior uniformed officer of the U.S. Navy

CTF-150—Combined Task Force-150, a multinational antipiracy maritime security force

DCI—Director of Central Intelligence, the senior administrator and coordinator of all of America's intelligence services

dielectric—a hard or rigid structure that allows electromagnetic energy to pass through in both directions

Duty Officer—a computerized interactionable service linking several computer services

Electronic Elastomeric Activity Suit—a mechanical compression garment worn by astronauts that uses computer-controlled electronically compressible material to maintain near-sea-level pressure on the human body while in a vacuum

EMU—Extravehicular Maneuvering Unit, a device that attaches to an astronaut's space suit that allows precise movement in space

EPIRB—Emergency Position-Indicating Radio Beacon, a device that transmits identification and location information via satellite to rescuers

FBI—Federal Bureau of Investigation, American federal domestic law enforcement and investigation agency

ForceNet—American naval computer global data-exchange system

FSB—Federal Security Bureau, new name for the Russian KGB foreign and domestic intelligence and security force

GRU—*Glavnoye Razvedyvatel'noye Upravleniye,* Russian military intelligence agency

GUARD—international emergency radio channel

HMU—Handheld Maneuvering Unit, a device used by astronauts to maneuver in space

Hohmann transfer orbit—an orbit used by spacecraft to move from one orbit to another

home plate—common term for home base or aircraft carrier

Hydra—smaller version of a COIL laser used for self-defense

hypoxia—physical difficulties associated with a lack of oxygen (loss of sight, uncoordination, unconsciousness)

ISI—Interservices Intelligence, Pakistani intelligence agency

KGB—*Komitet Gosudarstvennoy Bezopasnosti,* Soviet domestic and foreign security and intelligence agency, now FSB

Maddie—Multifunctional Advanced Data Delivery and Information Exchange, the civilian version of the "Duty Officer"

MFD—Multi-Function Display, an advanced computer control and display system

NCIS—Naval Criminal Investigative Service, U.S. Navy and Marine Corps' chief law enforcement investigation service

NOSS—Naval Ocean Surveillance System, a system of satellites that detects and tracks vessels by homing in on radio transmissions

NSO—National Security Organization, the Republic of Yemen's domestic and foreign intelligence and security force

PETA—People for the Ethical Treatment of Animals, an American animal-rights organization

PLA—People's Liberation Army, the unified land, sea, and air forces of the People's Republic of China

PNSA—President's National Security Adviser, senior civilian military and domestic security adviser to the president of the United States

PRC—People's Republic of China (mainland China)

Ro-Ro—Roll-On, Roll-Off, a cargo ship where vehicles or equipment can be loaded on one end and driven off on the other end

SAC—Strategic Air Command, former major American military command that controlled all nuclear-capable attack and global reconnaissance and command-and-control forces

SCA—Suez Canal Authority, civil organization responsible for regulating, maintaining, and patrolling the Suez Canal

SECDEF—common acronym of the secretary of defense, the senior civilian administrator of all branches of the U.S. military

SECNAV—common acronym of the secretary of the navy, senior civilian administrator of the U.S. Navy

SECSTATE—common acronym of the U.S. secretary of state

SIGINT—Signals Intelligence, collecting, identifying, and analyzing electromagnetic emissions

Space-Based Infrared System—satellite-based system that detects and tracks missiles and aircraft

SPACECOM—common acronym for the U.S. Space Command, the major American military command responsible for space activities

STRATCOM—U.S. Strategic Command, the major American military command responsible for strategic missile defense, information warfare, command and control, and surveillance

TMO—Traffic Management Officer, the officer responsible for monitoring movements of ships or aircraft through a particular area or region

VFR—Visual Flight Rules, the rules governing aircraft operations in good weather

WMD—Weapons of Mass Destruction, referring to biological, nuclear, or chemical weapons designed to kill large numbers of people over very large areas with few numbers of weapons

REAL-WORLD NEWS EXCERPTS

U.S. PLANS FOR FUTURE WARS IN SPACE (www.Space .com, February 22, 2004): The U.S. Air Force has filed a futuristic flight plan, one that spells out need for an armada of space weaponry and technology for the near term and in years to come. Called the Transformation Flight Plan, the 176-page document offers a sweeping look at how best to expand America's military space tool kit.

. . . The CAV (Common Aero Vehicle) is an unpowered, maneuverable, hypersonic glide vehicle deployed in the 2010–2015 time period. The CAV could be delivered by a range of delivery vehicles from an expendable or reusable small launch vehicle to a fully reusable Space Operations Vehicle. It can guide and dispense conventional weapons, sensors, or other payloads worldwide from and through space within one hour of tasking. It would be able to strike a spectrum of targets, including mobile targets, mobile time-sensitive targets, strategic relocatable targets, or fixed hard and deeply buried targets. The CAV's speed and maneuverability would combine to make defenses against it extremely difficult . . .

SINO-RUSSIAN MILITARY MANEUVERS: A THREAT TO U.S. INTERESTS IN EURASIA

(Ariel Cohen, Ph.D., and John J. Tkacik Jr., www.Heritage.org, September 30, 2005): Peace Mission 2005, the unprecedented Sino-Russian joint military exercises held on August 18–25, should raise concerns in Washington. The war games are a logical outcome of the Sino-Russian Treaty of Good Neighborly Friendship and Cooperation, signed in 2001, and the shared worldview and growing economic ties between the two giant powers . . .

The Russian daily *Nezavismaya Gazeta* was more blunt about the purpose of the war games: This is above all an assault on the unipolar world that has so suited Washington since the end of the Cold War. Chinese commentators were similarly frank. Jin Canrong, professor of international relations at the People's University of China, stated that the main target is the United States. Both sides want to improve their bargaining position in terms of security, politics, and economics. As Pravda.ru announced, "The reconciliation between China and Russia has been driven in part by mutual unease at U.S. power . . ."

RUSSIA NEGOTIATES SALE OF 50 SU-33 FIGHTERS TO CHINA

(Sinodefence.com, October 27, 2006): Russia and China are finalizing negotiations for the delivery of up to fifty Su-33 carrier-based jet fighters, at a cost of US$2.5 billion.

China is expected to initially get two Su-33 jets to be used for evaluation and operational trials on the ex-Soviet carrier *Varyag* China acquired from the Ukraine in 1999. The carrier is currently stationed at China's Dalian Shipyard, being refitted since 2002. Once commissioned to service, the carrier will be able to operate the twelve aircraft of Su-33, which are included as the first-option part of the current program.

Eventually China could buy up to fifty aircraft of this type, to equip the first indigenous Chinese-built aircraft carrier expected by 2010.

CHINA'S ASAT TEST WILL INTENSIFY U.S.-CHINA FACE-OFF IN SPACE (*Aviation Week and Space Technology,* January 21, 2007): China's successful test of an antisatellite (ASAT) weapon means that the country has mastered key space sensor, tracking, and other technologies important for advanced military space operations. China can now also use "space control" as a policy weapon to help project its growing power regionally and globally.

. . . Although more of a "policy weapon" at this time, the Chinese ASAT shows that the Chinese military can credibly threaten imaging reconnaissance and other satellites operated by the United States, Japan, Russia, Israel, and Europe . . .

THE WEAPONIZATION OF SPACE (www.Stratfor.com, April 10, 2008): . . . The Pentagon intends to dominate space the same way it dominates the world's oceans: largely passively, allowing the free flow of international traffic, but with overwhelming and unchallenged military superiority. That will include not only defending assets in space, but holding those of a potential adversary at risk . . .

But the trajectory of development and the challenges that lie ahead will sooner or later dictate space-based weapons platforms. (BMD [Ballistic Missile Defense] is just one of a variety of potential justifications and applications.) And since the United States intends to ensure that its dominance in space remains unrivaled, it will move preemptively to consolidate that control. At some point, that will include actual weapons in space.

As has been said of other matters, the debate is over. Space is an integral part of U.S. military fighting capability, and therefore in all practical terms it has been weaponized.

DECADE FORECAST 2005–2015 (www.Stratfor.com): . . . Russia is the only competitor with an outside shot of actually reforming its existing space program to the point of creating a near-global, near-real-time reconnaissance system. Add this to existing ballistic-missile technology, and a space-capable Moscow would pose a genuine threat to U.S. hegemony . . .

Of course, geopolitical and military alliances between any of these rivals could accelerate indigenous programs and capabilities. It is worth noting that Russia has made a virtual cottage industry out of exporting its own space expertise and technology to countries such as India, China, and Iran . . .

THE LASER GUN TAKES FLIGHT (www.popsci.com, November 10, 2008): . . . The first successful test of a plane-mounted laser gun came on August 7, when Boeing's eighteen-ton chemical laser fired a beam from a C-130H aircraft and destroyed a three-by-three-foot target on the ground. It was the first time all of the ATL's lab-tested pieces came together to vaporize a target . . .

RUSSIA SET TO BUILD NEW AIRCRAFT CARRIER (*RIA Novosti,* March 3, 2009): Russia's state-controlled United Shipbuilding Corporation (USBC) has disclosed some specifications of a new-generation aircraft carrier currently being developed for the country's navy.

It appears that the new warship will closely resemble advanced NATO carriers also displacing sixty thousand metric tons. This revelation has been indirectly confirmed by media reports about the interest of Russia's top naval brass in the projects of France's Thales, a leading developer of advanced CVF carriers for the British Royal Navy and PA-2 carriers for the French navy.

Her dimensions will match those of the PA-2 with a standard displacement of fifty-nine thousand metric tons, while her full displacement will total seventy-five thousand metric tons. Unlike the French carrier, which will have a gas-turbine propulsion unit, the Russian ship will be powered by a nuclear reactor and will have a different air wing.

. . . The sufficiently large new-generation carrier will accommodate an air wing comprising thirty to thirty-six heavy-duty fighters, not to mention aircraft of other types.

A mixed air wing comprising twenty-four heavy-duty and twenty-four lightweight planes, including MiG-29Ks or advanced lightweight fighters, can also be deployed on-board the carrier, whose deck and hangars will also accommodate Unmanned Combat Air Vehicles (UCAVs), helicopters, and auxiliary multirole planes.

CHINA READIES MILITARY SPACE STATION; LAUNCH COINCIDES WITH SHUTTLE PHASE-OUT (Craig Covault, *Spaceflight Now,* March 2, 2009): China is aggressively accelerating the pace of its manned space program by developing a seventeen-thousand-pound man-tended military space laboratory planned for launch by late 2010. The mission will coincide with a halt in U.S. manned flight with phase-out of the shuttle.

. . . Importantly, China is openly acknowledging that the new Tiangong outpost will involve military space operations and technology development.

Also the fact it has been given a number one numerical designation indicates that China may build more than one such military space laboratory in the coming years . . .

RUSSIA BUILDING ANTISATELLITE WEAPONS (Associated Press, March 5, 2009): Moscow—Russia is working on antisatellite weapons to match technologies developed by other nations and will speed up modernization of its nuclear forces, a deputy defense minister was quoted as saying Thursday.

The statement by General Valentin Popovkin signaled the government's intention to pursue its ambitious plans to strengthen the military despite the money crunch caused by a worsening financial crisis . . .

Popovkin said Russia continues to oppose a space arms race but will respond to moves made by other countries, according to Russian news reports . . .

DOD QUESTIONS GROWING CHINESE POWER (Associated Press, March 25, 2009): Washington—China is increasing its military power more rapidly and developing new "disruptive technologies" that are shifting the military balance in East Asia and possibly beyond, a Pentagon report said.

" . . . its armed forces continue to develop and field disruptive military technologies . . . that are changing regional military balances and that have implications beyond the Asia-Pacific region," the report said. It said that included technologies for nuclear, space, and cyberwarfare . . .

CHINA ADDS PRECISION STRIKE TO CAPABILITIES (*Defense Technology International,* April 8, 2009): China has been developing and purchasing weapons for precision-strike warfare . . . The PLA's (Chinese People's Liberation Army) near-term goals appear to be greater asymmetric capabilities to target U.S. naval assets in the western Pacific and in space as part of an antiaccess strategy . . .

. . . A far less-noted potential co-orbital ASAT demonstration occurred on September 27, 2008, when the Shenzhou-7 manned spacecraft, which had just launched a BX-1 nanosatellite, passed within forty-five kilometers (twenty-eight miles) of the International Space Station . . .

. . . The U.S. and Japanese navies have long been concerned with the PLA program to create an antiship ballistic missile, by placing a maneuverable terminally guided warhead on the 2,400-kilometer-range DF-21, and likely, on the 600-kilometer DF-15. Asian military sources are also concerned that a new

3,000-kilometer version of the DF-21 may have multiple terminally guided warheads . . .

CHINESE NAVY REQUIRES SUPERCRUISING FIGHTER

(*Aviation Week*'s Defense Technology International, April 27, 2009): A supercruising combat aircraft is a high priority of the Chinese navy, the country's top admiral says in a revealing official interview that gives strong clues of perceived shortcomings and future directions for the maritime force.

Admiral Wu Shengli also says China must step up work on precision missiles that can overcome enemy defenses, and the nation should move faster in developing large combat surface ships—probably meaning the aircraft-carrier program that looks increasingly imminent.

. . . For the Chinese navy, one advantage of supercruising would be the ability to cover a large defensive area in less time—quite useful if the imagined target is a U.S. carrier group at long range.

. . . "We must develop new-generation weapons such as large surface combat ships, stealthy long-endurance submarines, supercruising combat aircraft, precision long-range missiles that can penetrate defenses, as well as deep-diving, fast, and intelligent torpedoes, and electronic combat equipment offering compatibility and commonality."

JAPAN: THE MILITARY EXPLOITATION OF SPACE

(www.Stratfor.com, July 19, 2009): The Japanese Ministry of Defense's annual white paper on defense was released July 17, making it explicit—for the first time—that Japan recognizes the need to develop space-based systems specifically for military purposes . . .

. . . This will further solidify the JSDF as one of the most technologically advanced and capable military forces in the world, and it will give it the tools to better monitor and secure Japan's global

interests. But it will not happen in a vacuum. Japan's space pro-
gram, combined with a concerted—and often clandestine—
Chinese effort, could mean that a space race is heating up in East
Asia.

CHINA DELIVERS FRIGATE TO PAKISTAN (www
.Stratfor.com, July 30, 2009): China delivered the first of four F-22P
frigates to Pakistan, *Dawn News* reported July 30, citing a Pakistani naval spokesman. Each warship will carry a helicopter,
surface-to-surface missiles, and surface-to-air missiles.

CHINA LAUNCHES LONG-RANGE WAR GAMES (Associated Press, August 12, 2009): Beijing—China's military
launched war games Tuesday aimed at deploying forces at long
distances . . .

The exercises will send fifty thousand armored troops—the
People's Liberation Army's "largest-ever tactical military
exercise"—to unfamiliar areas far from their bases for two months
of live-fire drills, state media reported.

. . . "In the unprecedented exercise, one of the PLA's major
objectives will be to improve its capacity of long-range projection,"
the official Xinhua News Agency said. It said the war games constituted the army's "largest-ever tactical military exercise . . ."

The 2.3-million-member PLA is the world's largest standing
military.

. . . The PLA has undergone a rapid upgrade in recent years in
both equipment and doctrine. Two decades of almost annual
double-digit increases in military spending have allowed the addition of cutting-edge fighter jets, nuclear submarines, and hundreds
of ballistic missiles . . . China has announced a 14.9 percent rise in
military spending in its 2009 budget, to 480.6 billion yuan (US$70.3
billion).

... The military has also taken steps to emerge from its traditional veil of secrecy and engage with other nations, most strikingly in sending ships to join the international antipiracy flotilla off the coast of Somalia this year.

COMMENTARY: PAKISTAN NUKE THEFTS FOILED

(UPI, August 12, 2009): Washington— ... Pakistan's secret nuclear storage sites are known to Islamist extremists and have been attacked at least three times over the last two years, according to two recent reputable reports.

... The first such attack against the nuclear-missile storage facility was on November 1, 2007, at Sargodha; the second, by a suicide bomber, occurred December 10, 2007, against Pakistan's nuclear air base at Kamra; and the third and most alarming was launched August 20, 2008, by several suicide bombers who blew up key entry points to a nuclear-weapons complex at the Wah cantonment, long believed to be one of Pakistan's main nuclear-weapons assembly points, where warheads and launchers come together in a national emergency ...

... While not denying the three incidents, Pakistan has said repeatedly that its nuclear weapons are fully secured and there is no chance of them falling into the hands of Islamist extremists ...

CHINA: U.S. SHOULD STOP MILITARY SURVEILLANCE OFF COAST

(www.Stratfor.com, August 28, 2009): The Chinese Defense Ministry said August 28 that "the root cause of problems between the navies and air forces" of China and the United States is the "constant" U.S. military surveillance off China's coast, Agence France-Presse reported, citing a ministry statement. The ministry said that to avoid Chinese-U.S. maritime incidents, the United States should "decrease and eventually stop" its surveillance and survey operations. The spokeswoman for the

U.S. embassy in Beijing, Susan Stevenson, said the United States "exercises its freedom of navigation of the seas under international law, while putting emphasis on avoiding any unwanted incidents."

U.S., AUSTRALIA: MILITARIES TO ASK CHINA TO JOIN EXERCISES (www.Stratfor.com, September 2, 2009): . . . U.S. Pacific Command chief Admiral Timothy Keating and Australian Defense Force leader Angus Houston met in Sydney on September 2 and agreed to ask China to hold exercises and develop military ties "at the earliest opportunity." The United States and Australia want to understand China's intentions, as both countries are concerned that China's military buildup might have purposes other than defense.

RUSSIA TO REVAMP AIR-SPACE DEFENSES (*RIA Novosti,* August 11, 2009): Moscow—Russia will create a new generation of air and space defenses to counter any strikes against its territory due to a potential foreign threat, the air force commander said on Tuesday.

"Foreign countries, particularly the United States, will be able to deliver coordinated high-precision strikes from air and space against any target on the whole territory of Russia," Colonel General Alexander Zelin said, referring to the potential for new hypersonic and space-based offensive weapons.

"That is why the main goal of the development of the Russian air force is to create a new branch of the armed forces, which would form the core of the country's air and space defenses to provide a reliable deterrent during peacetime, and repel any military aggression with the use of conventional and nuclear arsenals in a time of war," the general said.

. . . The Soviet-era MiG-31 Foxhound supersonic interceptor aircraft will most likely be used as part of the new air-space defense network, as was intended when it was designed. "We are upgrading this system to be able to accomplish the same [air-space defense] tasks," Zelin said. According to some sources, Russia has over 280 MiG-31 aircraft in active service and about 100 aircraft in reserve.

CHINA, RUSSIA: SHIPS TO CONDUCT JOINT EXERCISES OFF SOMALI COAST (www.Stratfor.com, September 17, 2009):

Chinese and Russian ships, on antipiracy patrols off the coast of Somalia, plan to hold joint exercises, called "Blue Peace Shield 2009," on September 18, testing communications links, simulating operations to identify vessels, and coordinating resupply methods, the Associated Press reported September 17.

CHINA SAYS MILITARY ARSENAL COMPARABLE WITH WEST (Christopher Bodeen, Associated Press, September 21, 2009):

Beijing—China's military now possesses most of the sophisticated weapon systems found in the arsenals of developed Western nations, the country's defense minister said in comments published Monday.

Many of China's systems, including the J-10 fighter jet, latest-generation tanks, navy destroyers, and cruise and intercontinental ballistic missiles, match or are close to matching the capabilities of those in the West, Liang Guanglie said in a rare interview posted on the ministry's Web site. "This is an extraordinary achievement that speaks to the level of our military's modernization and the huge change in our country's technological strength," Liang said.

. . . China's improved capabilities are also seen as emboldening the country's military and civilian leaders in using force to back up political and territorial claims. Chinese ships have repeatedly harassed U.S. Navy surveillance vessels collecting intelligence off China's southeastern coast, while Chinese submarines have aggressively pursued aircraft-carrier battle groups.

. . . Analysts say the odds of conflict with the United States, Japan, and other regional militaries is likely to increase as China further beefs up its arsenal . . .

RUSSIA: PRESIDENT PROMISES REBUILT NAVY IN 10 YEARS (www.Stratfor.com, September 28, 2009): Russian president Dmitri Medvedev said during a meeting with military personnel that Russia will rebuild its naval fleet within ten years, *RIA Novosti* reported September 28 . . .

CHINA: BEIJING TO BUILD LARGE DESTROYERS (www.Stratfor.com, October 9, 2009): Beijing plans to build a new generation of large destroyers as part of its effort to develop a modern blue-water navy, *South China Morning Press* reported October 9. The destroyers will displace more than ten thousand tons, according to a report by the China Shipbuilding Information Center—an institute under the China Shipbuilding Industry Corporation, the largest state-owned shipbuilder in China. According to the report, the People's Liberation Army (PLA) hopes the new destroyers—that will feature fully developed stealth technology—will close the gap in combat capability between the Chinese and Western navies.

U.S.: ADMIRAL CONCERNED ABOUT CHINA MILITARY BUILDUP (www.Stratfor.com, October 30, 2009): U.S. Rear Admiral Kevin Donegan said the United States wants to ensure that China's unprecedented rate of military expansion doesn't destabilize the region as China's spending was up almost 15 percent in 2009, the Associated Press reported October 30 . . . Donegan, commander of the USS *George Washington,* acknowledged the possibility of a Chinese aircraft carrier, stating concerns about antiaccess weapons . . .

CHINA: PAKISTAN TO BUY J-10 FIGHTERS—
PAKISTANI OFFICIALS (www.Stratfor.com, November 10,
2009): China agreed to sell Pakistan two squadrons of J-10 fighters
for as much as $1.4 billion, the *Financial Times* reported November
10, citing Pakistani and Western officials. A Pakistani official said
more sales may follow, but denied that a deal had been made to
buy up to 150 fighters. The Pakistani air force expects to buy at
least 250 JF-17 Thunder fighters in the next four to five years. A
Western official in Islamabad said Iran and Middle Eastern countries can find Western-like technology in China purchases; he
added that Pakistan's purchase is a test case for the region.

EXECUTIVE INTENT

PROLOGUE

The greatest obstacle to discovery is not ignorance—it is the illusion of knowledge.

—Daniel J. Boorstin

In the South China Sea, 500 Miles South of Hong Kong

Winter 2010

"Who the hell is this again?" the lead pilot of the formation of U.S. Navy F/A-18E Super Hornets radioed.

"Hydra flight, I say again, this is Armstrong," the unknown female controller repeated. "We have a visual on your single-ship bogey. How do you copy?"

"Stand by, Armstrong." The pilot switched over to his interplane frequency. "Lego, you have any idea who this skirt is?"

"Sure, Timber," the pilot of the second Hornet in the formation replied. "They told us they'd be on tactical freq but they didn't say they'd be talking to us. You must've been late to the briefing."

"Well, who is she?"

"It's the space station," the wingman replied. "Armstrong Space Station. Remember? The big-ass UFO—'Unwanted Floating Object.'"

"Oh, for Christ's sake, the damned Air Force," the lead pilot complained. He remembered the briefing now: The Air Force's military space station, Armstrong—what the Air Force was calling the headquarters of the U.S. Space Defense Force, although there was as yet no such thing—was conducting a test to see if its network of satellites could provide long-range surveillance data to tactical forces around the world. Instead of spying on big targets like enemy military bases, the Air Force wanted to see if they had enough capability to watch over and even direct forces right down to individual aircraft, ships, and squads. "Hey, Hydra One, is this for real?"

"Timber, this is an operational test," the CAG, or Carrier Air Group commander, radioed from the USS *George H. W. Bush,* steaming about four hundred miles away. His radio messages were being relayed via an E-2C Hawkeye radar plane orbiting nearby. "If they can't keep up, we'll terminate. Otherwise, play along."

"Rog," the leader responded resignedly. Back on the tactical frequency: "Armstrong, Hydra flight, what do you got?"

In response, the F/A-18's MFD, or Multi-Function Display, changed to show the Hornets and the single unidentified aircraft they were pursuing. The Hornet's radar was in standby, but the display looked as if the radar was transmitting and locked on. The fire control computer was using the information from the space station to compute intercepts, weapon parameters, and was even reporting ready to steer radar-guided missiles—all as if the Hornet's own radar was providing the information!

"You getting this, Timber?" the wingman radioed. "Pretty fucking cool."

"We get the same dope from the Hawkeye."

"Negatory. Select F11."

The leader noticed the flashing soft key on the edge of his MFD and pressed it—and to his amazement saw a video image of a large fighter aircraft with two immense weapons or tanks under its wings. It wasn't a still image either—they could actually see the crewmembers through the canopy glass moving about and the ocean racing underneath. "Is that the *bogey*?" he asked incredulously. He keyed the button for the tactical frequency. "Armstrong, is that our bogey?"

"Affirmative," the controller aboard the space station replied, the satisfaction in her voice evident. She seemed a lot older than most of the female Navy controllers he was accustomed to working with. "Coming at you at the speed of live. I make it as a Sukhoi-34 Fullback. I can't verify any markings, and we can't positively identify what it's carrying, but they look like antiship missiles."

Well, the leader thought, that *was* pretty cool. But it didn't replace Mark One eyeballs. "I'm impressed, Armstrong," he said, "but we still gotta go in and do a visual."

"Roger," the Armstrong controller said. "I can't give you bull's-eye vectors, but I can give you BRA picture calls."

The Air Force gadgets were cool, for sure, and the leader was even impressed that the lady Air Force controller knew the difference between "bull's-eye" vectors—bearings relative to a prebriefed reference point used instead of the fighter's own location so an enemy that might pick up their broadcast couldn't use the information to pinpoint the fighter itself—and less secure BRA calls, or bearing-range-altitude from the fighter's nose. But this was a real mission, not playtime—it was time to go to work. "Negative, Armstrong, we'll be talking to our own controller for the intercept. Break. Spinner Three, Hydra One-Two-One flight, bogeydope."

"Roger, Hydra flight, 'Wicker' Two-Zero-Zero at niner-five, medium, single ship," the weapons director aboard the E-2C Hawkeye airborne radar controller responded. The "bogeydope" call meant that the Hornet pilot was not using his radar but was relying on the Hawkeye's radar information for the position of the unidentified aircraft he had been sent to pursue. "Wicker" was the designation of the "bull's-eye" they'd use for the intercept.

Of course, the pilot already had the target's information, because the digital electronic datalink between all American aircraft around the world displayed the Hawkeye's radar data on the Hornet's primary flight display as if he *was* using his radar. The Hornet pilot was an old stick—in fact, he was the squadron operations officer—so he kept on using voice brevity codes even though his reports were all redundant. But the weapons director on the Hawkeye was a veteran, too, and he still liked the voice reports. As long as the radios weren't saturated and the situation was routine, a little chatter was allowed.

The unknown aircraft had been detected by the E-2C Hawkeye while over five hundred miles from the aircraft carrier *George H. W. Bush* and its battle group, and the *Bush* had immediately launched the "Ready-5" F/A-18E Super Hornet fighters, put more fighters on the number one and two catapults, and prepared to launch buddy air refueling tankers as well. All of the alert Hornets were armed with two radar-guided AIM-120 AMRAAM air-to-air missiles under each wing, one AIM-9 Sidewinder heat-seeking missile on each wingtip, and 578 rounds of twenty-millimeter ammunition for its cannon, plus a 480-gallon fuel tank on a centerline stores station.

By the time the Hornets caught up with the bogey it was inside three hundred miles to the carrier and still closing. "Flying less than four hundred knots, Timber—gotta be a patrol plane, not a Sukhoi-34," the wingman radioed, reading the datalinked information streaming from the Hawkeye. "It looked like a fighter, but he's flying awfully—"

Just then the radar warning receiver bleeped. "Not so fast, Lego," the lead pilot responded. "X-band radar—airborne fire control. He's tracking us. Going active." The lead pilot activated his APG-79 radar and immediately locked onto the aircraft. "Fence check, Lego, pull 'em tight."

"I'm ready to rock-and-roll, Lead," the wingman reported a moment later.

"Roger that. Take spacing." As the wingman moved away to a higher altitude and dropped back a little to be able to launch an attack on the unknown aircraft if necessary, the leader switched his number two radio to the international UHF emergency channel: "Unidentified aircraft, this is U.S. Navy interceptor aircraft, we are at your eleven o'clock position and one thousand feet above you. You are heading toward an American warship. We are maneuvering around you for visual identification. Please acknowledge."

"American Navy interceptor aircraft, this is Yu One-Four of the People's Liberation Army Navy," a heavily accented voice responded after a slight but disconcerting silence. "We have you on radar contact. Please identify type aircraft."

"Yu One-Four, this is Hydra One-Two-One flight of two, F/A-18 Hornets, United States Navy." Normally he wouldn't say how many planes were in his flight, but that was a pretty powerful radar this guy had—no doubt he already knew. "Say your type aircraft, please."

"Yu One-Four is a Jian Hong-37N, single ship." The tone was conversational and pleasant, almost jovial.

"A JH-37?" the wingman remarked. "What the hell is that? Is that like a JH-7?"

"Yu One-Four, roger," the leader responded. "Please say armament if any."

"Repeat, please, Hydra One-Two-One?"

"Are you armed, One-Four? Any weapons?"

"Weapons. Yes. We have weapons. Am not permitted to reveal type."

"Yu One-Four, you are headed directly toward an American

warship in international waters," the leader said. "We will conduct a visual inspection of your aircraft."

"Please stay well clear, Hydra One-Two-One. Do not approach." The tone now was still pleasant, like a friend gently reminding of possible danger ahead.

"If you continue your present course, Yu One-Four, we will conduct a visual inspection. Please reverse course, or maintain present speed and altitude for our visual inspection."

"Close flying is not permitted, Hydra One-Two-One." More officious now, but still pleasant.

"Hydra, Spinner, threat, ten o'clock," the Hawkeye weapons director radioed on the number one radio, advising the Hornets that they were within ten miles of an unidentified aircraft.

"Hydra One-Two-One flight is 'judy,' going in for a closer look," the leader radioed back. On the secondary radio he said, "I say again, Yu One-Four, do not make any sudden maneuvers."

"Hydra flight, this is Armstrong," a different, more urgent male voice from the space station cut in. "We got a better-angle look at his weapons, and we think they're AS-17s, repeat, AS-17s." The Russian-made AS-17 was one of the most feared air-to-surface weapons in the world, carrying a large high-explosive or small nuclear warhead over one hundred miles at speeds in excess of Mach 3. "I recommend you launch your alert fighters in case this guy is hostile."

"Tallyho, Timber," the wingman radioed. "Eleven o'clock on the horizon."

"Tally," the leader responded after spotting the target a moment later. "Armstrong, we're tied on visual, we'll take it from here, okay?" His voice was a little more irritable than he wanted, but this close to a Chinese fighter so far from the ship made things more and more tense, and the unfamiliar voices coming from space weren't helping to make the tactical picture any clearer.

The bogey was a tiny light dot in the distance, about three miles away. The lead pilot took a quick glance out the starboard side to be sure where his wingman was—high and to his right, able to watch the bogey, his leader, his radar, and his instruments without having to concentrate on formation flying—then began a slow turn as the Chinese aircraft began to pass off his left. The Chinese fighter's radar remained locked onto them the whole way, even from behind—that had to be sophisticated fire control radar to remain locked on even directly astern. That got the lead Hornet's blood pumping even faster, and he kept the power up to quicken the intercept.

It was the first time either American had seen a Sukhoi-34 fighter, one of the newest and most high-tech combat aircraft in the world. It was a big aircraft, larger than an American F-15 Eagle or F-14 Tomcat—much larger than the Hornet—with twin vertical tails and a large cockpit area with a large bulge behind the canopy. It was painted in light blue gray, making it hard to see against the sky or the sea, with large bright red numerals on the side below the cockpit and a red star with red stripes on either side on the aft fuselage—definitely Chinese naval aircraft markings. The aircraft had canard foreplanes just below and behind the cockpit, and the Hornet leader could see cooling vents around what appeared to be a very large-caliber cannon muzzle on the right side. "I'll be damned—it sure is a friggin' Russian Sukhoi-34 Fullback," the lead pilot exclaimed. "I'm pretty sure that's what it is. But it's in Chinese colors. And it's carrying those two big honkin' missiles. I'm moving in for a closer look."

The closer the leader maneuvered his Super Hornet to the Chinese plane, the more shocked he became. "Lego, he's got freaky huge missiles under the wings," he radioed to his wingman. "They have to be twenty feet long and weigh three tons each. One under each wing. No other weapons visible."

"If he's got antiship missiles, he's outta here."

"Roger that." On the secondary radio he said, "Yu One-Four,

this is Hydra flight, you are carrying unidentified weapons that appear to be offensive long-range antiship missiles. You are not permitted to fly within two hundred miles of any United States warship with such weapons. You are instructed to reverse course and depart the area. Acknowledge."

"American interceptors, you may not interfere with any peaceful flight over international waters," the Chinese pilot radioed. The friendly tone was completely nonexistent now. "Terminate your dangerous close flying immediately and leave us alone."

"Lego, get on the horn to 'home plate,' confirm they are listening in, and ask for instructions," the lead pilot radioed.

"Two."

On the secondary channel the Hornet pilot said, "Chinese warplane Yu One-Four, this is Hydra One-Two-One flight, U.S. Navy, on GUARD, this is an air defense warning in the clear, you are carrying two suspected offensive antiship missiles and are headed directly for U.S. warships in international waters." This description was for the benefit of his own ship's cockpit voice recorders, for the recorders aboard the Hawkeye radar plane, as well as for recordings made by any other nearby ships who were certainly listening in. "I am ordering you to reverse course immediately or you may be fired on without further warning. Comply immediately. This is your final warning."

"CAG says two hundred is the brick wall, Timber," the wingman reported. "Based on your description, intel says he might be carrying AS-17 Kryptons. That checks with what Armstrong told us."

"I dunno—they look bigger than Kryptons," the lead pilot responded. The AS-17 had been used by the Russians against targets in the United States during their attacks in 2004, and the whole world was now well familiar with those deadly weapons, as well as with the other supersonic and hypersonic weapons in the Russian arsenal.

"The Ready-Five is airborne," the wingman added.

"Rog. Okay, we'll climb the ladder as usual and see what he does. Light him up."

"Two." The wingman selected his "MASTER ARM" switch from "SAFE" to "ARM" and selected an AIM-120 missile. With the Chinese aircraft designated as the target, the fire control computer changed the pulse-rate frequency of the radar signal for target tracking, which would show up on most radar-threat warning receivers as a locked-on warning. No reaction from the Chinese jet.

"Two-fifty," the wingman reminded his leader.

"Rog. I'm moving to his left side." The lead Hornet quickly climbed and slid over the Chinese plane's canopy and flew beside the plane close enough to see the rank patches on the Chinese pilot's flight suit. The pilot continued looking straight ahead, but the Hornet leader could see the weapons officer staring back at him cross-cockpit, occasionally making some kind of gestures.

"You giving me the finger, buddy? Here's my reply." The Hornet pilot armed his weapons, selected the twenty-millimeter cannon, and fired a one-second burst. The Chinese pilot made a brief glance at the Hornet but then looked straight ahead again. The weapons officer stopped gesturing and seemed frozen in surprise. "Are you getting the picture yet, boys?" the Hornet pilot said. But the JH-37 did not alter course. "Okay, we'll try—"

And at that instant the lead Hornet pilot saw a brief burst of heavy machine-gun fire from the right-side cannon, the reverberations of that cannon fire rumbling through space and easily felt in the Hornet. "Bastard fired *his* cannon!" the leader reported. "Felt like a thirty-mike." He didn't need a reminder to stay away from the Chinese fighter's nose, but he got one anyway.

"Five minutes, Timber," the wingman said. "How 'bout I buzz him?"

"I don't want you within range of that cannon. It's gotta be a thirty-millimeter."

"Then how about I do a handstand on his ass?"

The leader thought about it for a moment, then said, "Okay, c'mon in."

The wingman shut down the radar lock, moved his weapons switch back to "SAFE," then descended and closed in on the Chinese fighter. The leader moved away from the fighter. "Little more . . . little more . . . down a touch . . ." the leader said, directing his wingman closer until he was directly above and slightly ahead of the Chinese attack plane. "Okay, Lego, hit 'em."

The wingman abruptly raised his nose almost to vertical and fed in full afterburner power, directing his jet blast directly down on the Chinese fighter from just a few yards away. That did the trick. The JH-37 looked as if it had completely stopped flying, and it started a drastic wobbly descent.

"How does that feel, bitch?" For a moment the Hornet leader was afraid the JH-37 wasn't going to recover, but after nearly flat-spinning and descending a couple thousand feet or so, it finally stabilized. It was off-heading perhaps twenty degrees, but its course was still aimed in the direction of the USS *Bush*. "Lego, c'mon back around, radio home plate that the bandit is still heading in and request permission to shoot."

"Two."

The Hornet leader descended slightly and slowed to keep the JH-37 in sight. It was now about thirty degrees offset, but it definitely wasn't reversing course. "Don't make me spank you, buddy," the Hornet leader said to himself. "Bring it around or I'll—"

And at that instant his jaw dropped open, his eyes bulged, and his mouth turned instantly dry . . . because the large missile on the JH-37's left wing dropped into space, the engine ignited with a tremendous tongue of yellow fire, and it shot ahead with a massive glob of fire and a trail of white smoke. Seconds later, the *second* antiship missile dropped free and launched as well!

"*Holy shit . . . home plate, home plate, Hydra One-Two-One, Vampire, Vampire, Vampire!*" he shouted on the number one radio, using the brevity code "vampire" for launch of an enemy antiship missile. "Two Vampires in the air! Lego, I'm clearing to the east and high, nail this bastard!"

"Two cleared in hot . . . fox two!" Seconds later, the AIM-9 Sidewinder missile hit the Chinese fighter, sending it out of control and spinning into the South China Sea.

"Scramble, scramble, scramble, ASM launch detected, scramble, scramble, scramble!" blared the loudspeakers aboard the USS *Lake Champlain,* a *Ticonderoga*-class guided-missile cruiser escorting the USS *George H. W. Bush.* The cruiser's AN/SPY-1B multifunction Aegis radar system detected the missile launches moments before the frantic radio call from the F/A-18 Hornet pilot was received.

Because they had been closely monitoring the Hornet intercept of the Chinese aircraft, both the ship's captain and the tactical action officer were at their stations in the *Lake Champlain*'s Combat Direction Center. Each had two large screens providing them composite information gathered not just from their AN/SPY-1 radar but also from all the other sensors in the battle group via the Cooperative Engagement Capability, which allowed any ship in the battle group to use any radar to attack a target. The Hawkeye radar plane's data feed was also giving them a look at the intercept beyond their horizon, and the Air Force space station was feeding information from almost anywhere else on the planet.

One glance at the display and it was immediately obvious that this was going to be close, because the new targets were accelerating past Mach 2 very quickly, going hypersonic, and they were descending to wave-top height. "Change engagement mode to auto special," the captain shouted.

"Changing engagement mode from semiauto to auto special," the TAO repeated. "Sir, engagement mode is set to auto special."

The speed of the missiles had already increased to over Mach

3—the Hawkeye radar's mechanical sweep could hardly keep up with the speed, and the Aegis system had to predict where the next return would appear based on last speed and track. At sea-skimming altitudes, the *Lake Champlain*'s electronically scanned phased-array radar would only have a few seconds' look in horizon-search mode.

In automatic-special mode, Aegis controlled almost all aspects of ship defense. It activated electronic radar jammers, dispensed decoy chaff and flares, slewed the Mk 45 five-inch gun and provided initial target azimuth to the Phalanx close-in weapon systems, steered the SPG-62 target illuminator, and finally issued firing and target-tracking commands to the cruiser's vertical-launch SM-2 Standard antiaircraft missiles and Evolved Sea Sparrow defensive missiles.

Using data from the E-2 Hawkeye, the *Lake Champlain*'s first SM-2 missile fired before its own SPY-1 radar locked onto the incoming sea-skimmers. The smoke from the vertical-launch SM-2 missile's exhaust motor covered the entire forward section of the cruiser as it lifted off. It climbed quickly, then dove for the ocean at a steep angle to reach its computed intercept point. Another SM-2 fired from the aft vertical launcher, followed seconds later by a volley of four Sea Sparrow missiles from the forward launcher.

"Jesus!" the captain shouted. The Chinese missiles shot past Mach 4, then past Mach 5. *"Sound collision! Brace for impact!"*

The first Chinese missile had locked onto the *Lake Champlain*, switching radar frequencies in order to maintain lock. The first SM-2 missile exploded behind and above it, unable to keep up with the acceleration. The second SM-2 also exploded behind the Chinese missile, but close enough to disrupt its flight path, and it crashed and skittered across the ocean surface like a flat stone. The Sea Sparrow missiles hit next. The antiship missile's inertia kept its disintegrating fuselage flailing toward the cruiser, close enough for the Phalanx's radar to lock on at two miles and open fire at one mile with a cloud of twenty-millimeter shells firing at three thousand rounds per minute at the mass.

The second Chinese missile locked onto the aircraft carrier USS *George H. W. Bush*. The *Lake Champlain* continued to fire missiles, assisted by missile launches from the USS *Monterey* patrolling behind the carrier, but by now the Chinese sea-skimmer had exceeded Mach 7 and completely outran the missiles. The *Bush*'s last hope was its own Phalanx cannon, which opened fire at one and a quarter miles. Even the Phalanx's high-speed Gatling gun was only able to release a total of just five rounds at the hypersonic sea-skimmer in the time it took to lock on and open fire . . .

. . . but it was enough. One tungsten shell blew through the Chinese missile's nose cap, destroying the guidance system, and a second shell hit the air inlet, deforming it just enough to disrupt the air entering the engine, blasting the engine with superheated hypersonic air that instantly tore the missile apart. The red-hot exploding engine ignited the remaining fuel, creating a massive fireball that engulfed the entire aft section of the carrier. Although the ship didn't suffer a direct hit, the hypersonic debris and fireball that slammed into it killed several crewmen on deck, injured dozens more, instantly destroyed several aircraft chained to the aft deck, and damaged others chained on the opposite side.

Over the Pacific Ocean

That same time

He said it half aloud to himself, with a feeling of joy that bordered on childlike giddiness: "I'm back. I'm freakin' back."

"Are you talking to yourself again, SC?" the mission commander, or MC, on this flight, Navy Commander Scott Bream, asked, shaking his head and smiling. Bream, twenty years older than the SC, or spacecraft commander, was a twenty-year veteran of the U.S. Navy and a ten-year veteran of the National Aeronautics and Space Administration, but he could still remember his first space flight as if it was yesterday—he knew exactly how excited the young spacecraft commander was.

"Damn straight, MC," the SC, Hunter Noble, replied happily. "It's been *wayyy* too long."

The two crewmembers sat side by side in the cockpit of a XS-19A "Midnight," a single-stage-to-orbit spacecraft, the larger sibling of the S-9 "Black Stallion" spacecraft, the first conventional takeoff and landing aircraft able to propel itself into Earth orbit. Able to carry 50 percent more payload than the S-9 and more fuel for longer and higher-altitude missions, the XS-19 went into advanced design and development as soon as the Black Stallion proved its worth. Born of the revolutionary SR-71 Blackbird supersonic and XR-A1 Aurora hypersonic reconnaissance planes, the S-series aircraft were sleek, elegantly sculpted blended-wing designs built of advanced heat-resistant carbon-carbon composites. Instead of being nearly hand-built like the Space Shuttle, Aurora, and Black Stallion, the Midnight was able to be assembly-line-manufactured, albeit by robots working inside massive autoclaves and vacuum chambers.

Although just twenty-six years old, Hunter Noble wasn't giddy because this was his first space flight—he was a veteran of dozens more of them than Bream, thanks to his own creation, which he had first conceived as a freshman engineering student: the Laser Pulse Detonation Rocket System, or "leopards." Leopards were the hybrid turbojet-scramjet-rocket engine that allowed lightweight aircraft like the Midnight and Black Stallion to take off and land like conventional aircraft but achieve low Earth orbit without the need of massive vertical-launch boosters or rocket launchpads.

Former U.S. Air Force captain Hunter Noble (nicknamed "Boomer" because of what usually happened to his early engine designs during testing) could have left the service and become a multibillionaire from his engine design, but he gave it all to the Air Force in exchange for just one thing: being allowed to fly the final product. It was an easy exchange. But now Boomer had left the Air Force and was a vice president of design and engineering for a small high-tech research-and-development company called Sky Masters Inc., which developed a range of military and commercial aircraft, weapons, communications systems, satellites, and aircraft, and he was making the money he dreamed of *and* still getting to fly his creations.

The Midnight had four larger leopard engines under the wings. For takeoff and landing, the engines performed like standard aircraft engines. The aircraft performed an aerial refueling with a specially modified tanker that topped off fuel and also loaded hydrogen-peroxide rocket-fuel oxidizer before the craft made its dash into space. This refueling was in essence the spacecraft's "first stage," since at thirty thousand feet, over half of the Earth's atmosphere was below it and the push into space was that much easier.

After the final refueling and positioning in the proper location and direction for orbit, the craft accelerated to Mach 3 on its turbofan engines. Spikes in the engine inlets diverted incoming supersonic air around the turbines to specially shaped ducts that compressed the air hundreds of times greater than the jet turbines before mixing jet fuel and ignition, quickly resulting in speeds in excess of Mach 10 and climb rates approaching that of the Space Shuttle. As the aircraft approached the edge of space, the spikes eventually closed completely and the engines converted into pure rocket engines, using hydrogen peroxide as the jet-fuel oxidizer. Laser igniters burned the fuel more efficiently, giving the engines enormous power, but the lasers had to be "pulsed" several hundred times a second to achieve maximum combustion without blowing the engines apart. As speed increased to Mach 25, the spaceplane reached orbital velocity.

Although the payloads of the S-9 and XS-19 spaceplanes were small—just six and nine thousand pounds respectively, far less than the now-retired Space Shuttle and the Shuttle's replacement, the Orion crew module, expected to be in service in three to five years—the spaceplanes accomplished what the Shuttle's designers could only dream about: quick, reliable, and frequent access to space. Orbital flights and dockings with the International Space Station and Armstrong Space Station, America's military space platform, were routine; passengers could be flown halfway around the planet in less than two hours; graduates from civilian and military pilot schools could now select "Astronaut" for their next assignment.

Hunter Noble had left the Air Force to work with private industry when it became apparent that President Joseph Gardner wasn't committed to the military use of outer space except as a support arm of the U.S. Navy. Although there was little money for space other than in satellite communications and surveillance, there was still money for research and development of other space systems, and that's where Boomer wanted to be. Today's flight was going to demonstrate one of those new technologies.

"Gipper Range Control, this is Midnight One, I show two minutes to release," Scott Bream radioed. "Checklist is complete up here."

"Copy that," the senior controller at the Ronald Reagan Ballistic Missile Test Site in the Kwajalein Atoll responded. "Range is clear and ready."

"Range is clear, SC," Bream reported to Boomer. "Release program up and running."

"Checked," Boomer said. "Counting down, thirty seconds to go."

"Select computer control to 'AUTO,'" Bream reminded his spacecraft commander.

"Nah, I think I'll hand-fly this one," Boomer said.

"The test program called for 'AUTO' maneuvering."

"I asked about it, and they said it was okay."

A moment later: "Midnight, this is Casino, select 'AUTO' maneuvering, Boomer," the chief engineer of Sky Masters Inc. and builder of the test article, Dr. Jonathan Colin Masters, radioed from the company headquarters in Las Vegas. Masters was an executive vice president and chief of design for Sky Masters. "Don't screw around now."

"C'mon, Doc," Boomer protested, "it'll be okay."

"Boomer, if we didn't have half the Pentagon watching, I'd say okay," Masters said. "Switch it to 'AUTO.' You can fly the reentry and landing."

"You're all as bad as the military," Boomer said. He sighed and configured the mission computer as necessary. "Maneuvering mode set to 'AUTO.' Where's the fun in that?" Moments later hydrazine maneuvering jets arrayed around the Midnight spaceplane came to life, which stabilized the craft during release and would maneuver the spaceplane away from the test article after release.

"Bay doors already open . . . maneuvering complete . . . payload locks released, extender arms powering up, standing by for release . . . now," Bream reported. They heard a low rumble behind them as the extender arms lifted the payload out of the cargo bay, then several short *bangs* as the thrusters maneuvered the payload ahead and away from the Midnight spaceplane. "Payload in sight," Bream radioed back to Sky Masters headquarters. "It looks good."

The payload was the experimental Trinity mission module, a twelve-foot-long robotic multimission spacecraft with a rocket booster in the rear; maneuvering thrusters; a guidance, datalink, and sensor section in the nose; and three chambers inside. Trinity was able to reposition itself into different orbits, detect and track other spacecraft, rendezvous and even refuel with a spaceplane or the Armstrong Space Station, and deploy and retrieve packages stowed in its mission chambers.

"Lost sight of it," Bream reported as the craft moved away in its own orbit. "Cargo-bay doors closed, the spacecraft is secure."

"That's the way I like every flight—boring and secure," Boomer said. He checked the flight computer. "Looks like thirty minutes to our orbit transfer burn, and then three hours until we chase down Armstrong. Wish we could be down there to watch this thing light off."

RONALD REAGAN BALLISTIC MISSILE TEST SITE, KWAJALEIN ATOLL, PACIFIC OCEAN

THAT SAME TIME

"We're just two minutes to release, everybody," Deputy Undersecretary of the Air Force for Space Ann Page announced as she lowered the headset, which allowed her to listen in on the communications between the Midnight, range control, and Sky Masters headquarters. "C'mon over here for the best view."

It was a balmy and tranquil day on the water, but that didn't prevent several observers from shakily stepping across the deck, holding on to railings and bulkheads. Ann felt as if she were on a cruise ship instead of a barge, and the heat and humidity that was obviously upsetting some of the observers felt heavenly to her. Fifty-nine years of age, auburn hair almost completely gray now, and with so many lines and wrinkles that she was actually considering cosmetic surgery, Ann Page nonetheless felt these were the best times of her life.

"Are . . . are you quite sure we're safe, this close to the target area, Dr. Page?" a pale-faced congressional staffer asked. He was sweating so badly that she thought he had fallen overboard. "How far did you say we were?"

"Four miles," Ann replied. "I won't lie to you, Mr. Wilkerson: Our previous tests were very good, but not perfect. We're launching from a platform ninety miles in space, traveling over seventeen thousand miles an hour, shooting at a wobbly target that is also spinning at nine hundred miles an hour—that's how fast the Earth rotates. The projectiles are unguided—we use mathematics to do the aiming. That's why the weapon is designed only for large-area or slowly moving targets. Only a computer can make the calculations, and if they're wrong . . . well, we probably won't feel a thing."

That certainly did not make the young staffer look any better, and he turned away as if looking for an unoccupied place to vomit into the ocean.

"It's a pretty humid day out, as I'm sure you've noticed, so we should see a very impressive sight as the projectiles descend," Ann said. "Sixty seconds to go. The projectiles are not overly noisy, but if you're sensitive to loud noises you may want to put on your hearing protectors." Most of the women put on ear protectors; most of the men did not.

"I've seen your presentations and animations, Miss Undersecretary," a Navy lieutenant commander commented, scanning the instrumented target barge with a pair of binoculars, "and I still don't see how we can invest so much money in this economic climate in such a limited, futuristic concept. It's a waste of resources."

"Thirty seconds, everyone," Ann said. "It's true it's not a legacy weapon nor very sophisticated, Commander, but as you'll see, it's certainly no lightweight. As for being futuristic . . . well, in ten years I believe weapons such as this will be commonplace. Few heard of GPS before the 1991 invasion of Iraq; by the second invasion of Iraq, it was already indispensable. Here we go."

"'Mjollnir.'" The naval officer sneered. "Couldn't you find a good ol' fashioned American name to give it, Miss Undersecretary?"

"It's pronounced 'me-ole-ner,' Commander, not 'muh-joll-ner,'" Ann corrected him, "and we do have an American name for it, although it's rather long, so we just learn to say 'Mjollnir.' And please call me Ann, okay? Stand by."

The observers stared out into the ocean. Everything was perfectly still, and the only sounds were the waves gently tapping on the sides of the barge. Nothing happened for several moments. The Navy officer lowered his binoculars and rubbed his eyes. "Did it work, Dr. Page?" he asked irritably. He looked at his watch. "It's been almost fifteen seconds since—"

Suddenly there was an impossibly loud *ccrraacckk* like the world's largest thunderclap had just erupted directly overhead. For those observers who hadn't closed their eyes, there appeared in the sky over the target several streaks of white vapor, like a searchlight beam had been turned on. The target barge disappeared in massive geysers of ocean water and clouds of steam towering several hundred feet into the sky. The white vapor streaks seemed to hang in the air for several moments, finally beginning to dissipate in the gentle tropical breezes. Moments later, another massive *boom* rolled over them as the sound of thousands of tons of seawater instantly turning to steam crashed over them.

"What . . . was . . . *that?*" someone asked, as if he hadn't listened to any of the briefings on the weapon.

"That was Mjollnir, ladies and gentlemen: Thor's Hammer, the next generation of land, sea, and space-attack weapons delivered from Earth orbit," Ann Page said proudly. "Each payload releases a spread of four reentry vehicles, but what you saw was just *one*. The reentry vehicles are guided at first by satellite but then switch to infrared or millimeter-wave radar terminal guidance; it can automatically pick out preprogrammed targets or it can be steered by operators anywhere in the world or in space aboard Armstrong Space Station. The warhead that hit the target was nothing more than a five-hundred-pound chunk of titanium, but traveling at fifteen thousand miles an hour, it had the explosive impact of two *tons* of TNT. Mjollnir is simple, inexpensive if launched from an orbiting military base, cannot be intercepted or decoyed, and does not violate any existing space weapon treaties.

"You've just seen the future, ladies and gentlemen," Ann went on, driving her point home now that it appeared the spectators were regaining their senses. "We have already established a military base and a global communications and reconnaissance network in space; we have several families of spacecraft that provide America with anytime-anywhere access to space; and now we are developing effective weapons to not only defeat America's enemies but defend our new space-based infrastructure. It's ready—all we need to do is put it all together and set it in motion.

"It's time to make the commitment to secure the high ground for the United States of America. That's why I'm spearheading this effort in Congress and the Pentagon to formally stand up the U.S. Space Defense Command and build this true twenty-first-century force. I'm asking for your help and support. Thank you very much. I'll be pleased to answer any questions you might have."

The congressional staffer meekly raised his hand. Ann smiled and pointed to him. "Uh, Miss Secretary . . . ?" he began.

"Yes, sir, what's your question?"

The staffer put his hand down, smiled . . . then his skin turned green, his eyes rolled up inside his head, and he whirled around and vomited over the side of the barge.

ONE

One must wager on the future.

—ELIE WIESEL

ARMSTRONG SPACE STATION

A FEW HOURS LATER

U.S. Air Force Brigadier General Kai Raydon expertly sailed across the command module and precisely attached himself to the commander's console with perfectly placed touches of Velcro sneakers. He still remembered what it was like to float around in zero-g—what most Earth-bound folks called "weightlessness"—for the first time. It simply took practice to get used to the fact that there was no gravity to help you orient your body—every action has to be counteracted with an opposite action. It took a lot of banging around, but Raydon, a longtime veteran of space flight and working in space, was more accustomed to moving around in zero-g than he was in terrestrial one-g.

The main screen at the commander's station showed an eight-place split videoconference view, with his image in the lower right corner, and he studied his image for a few moments to make sure he looked presentable. He knew that hair had a tendency to look tangly and get rather dirty during long tours of duty in space, so he always kept his hair buzz-cut short, even when he returned to Earth. Raydon was trim and fit, thanks to a daily resistance work-out regimen, especially on Armstrong Space Station, and he was careful to regulate his diet while in space to avoid loss of muscle tone and fluid imbalances. The schedule was demanding up here, but there was always time for exercise; that was one of the most important lessons he taught the young astronauts assigned to Arm-strong.

The other videoconference windows were still vacant; Raydon was the first to arrive in the virtual conference room. The windows were labeled with the names of where the feed was originating: PNSA, SECDEF, CJCS, SECNAV, SECSTATE, DCI, and CNO, all the national security bigwigs, and little old Kai Raydon, the only Air Force guy. He wouldn't be surprised if this meeting started late, given the shitstorm that was brewing down on planet Earth.

He checked the secondary commander's monitor, which showed the latest satellite video feed of the aircraft carrier USS *George H. W. Bush,* now motionless in the South China Sea. Smoke still covered the aft half of the carrier, although he couldn't see flames anymore. "Seeker, what's the latest on the *Bush?*" he asked on in-tercom.

"Fires are under control and the casualties have all been evacu-ated, sir," Air Force Senior Master Sergeant Valerie "Seeker" Lu-kas, the senior noncommissioned officer and chief sensor operator aboard Armstrong Space Station, replied.

"Casualty count?"

"Same as last report, sir: fifteen dead, thirty-seven wounded, nine critically. Five jets and three choppers lost."

"Damn," Raydon muttered. "Freakin' Chinese squids. They want to play in Carnegie Hall—now they're center stage."

Twenty minutes past the scheduled start time, the videoconference got under way, presided over by the president's national security adviser, Conrad Carlyle. The chief of naval operations, Admiral Richard Cowan, read the latest report on casualties and condition of the *George H. W. Bush.* "I think we were very fortunate the Sea Whiz got that missile," Cowan concluded, using the common nickname for the Close-In Weapon System, or CIWS. "If it hit at the speed it was traveling, even with no warhead, it could have possibly sunk the *Bush.*"

"Sink it?" Carlyle exclaimed. "A *single* missile? Doesn't an aircraft carrier weigh over ninety thousand *tons?*"

"But traveling at eight times the speed of sound, the momentum of that missile would be enormous," Cowan explained. "Our engineers calculated it could've exceeded a tenth of the total weight of the carrier."

"And remember, the Russian hypersonic missiles used in the Holocaust had one-kiloton nuclear warheads on them," Secretary of Defense Miller Turner added. Turner, like Carlyle and Chief of Staff Walter Kordus, was a longtime friend and confidant of President Joseph Gardner, and everyone else in the room knew that the "clubhouse cabinet's" thoughts and opinions would certainly be transmitted directly to the White House in no time. "Any evidence at all that those missiles had nuclear warheads on them?"

"None at all, sir," Cowan said. "No warhead of any kind, except perhaps a flight-data transmitter, as the Chinese claim."

"That doesn't make me feel one bit better about this," Carlyle said, shaking his head. "Why in the hell were the Chinese flying a jet with hypersonic antiship missiles near our carrier?"

"Freedom of the seas, Conrad," Secretary of State Stacy Anne Barbeau said. Barbeau, the former senior senator from Louisiana and former Senate majority leader, was a glamorous and ebullient personality who took great pride in politically destroying anyone who tried to dismiss her as a brainless bimbo, even when she played the bimbo card to the max. Everyone knew she had strong White House ambitions, and no one wanted to get in her way when she eventually made her move. "We're free to sail near their shores; they're free to fly toward our ships; we're free to intercept them, try to turn them away, and shoot their butts down if they look like they're going to attack." She turned to the chief of naval operations. "What I want to know, Admiral Cowan, is what were the American fighters doing out there that made those missiles fire off?"

"Standard operating procedures for any surface combatant, especially a carrier, is to keep unidentified combat aircraft at least two hundred miles away, ma'am," Cowan said. "In my opinion, that's too close—I'd like to make it *five* hundred miles. In any case, our intercept pilots have a gradually escalating cascade of maneuvers they are authorized to do to turn a suspect aircraft away: They fly close to the aircraft, fire guns, do high-speed passes, and do other maneuvers to show the bad guys we're serious. The last option is to attack."

"So your Hornets do this maneuver, this 'handstand' as you call it, to try to . . . what? Scare the other guys away?"

"Yes, ma'am."

"And does it usually work?"

"Very few bad guys stick around after we fire a cannon burst a few feet away from their cockpits," Cowan said. "The Chinese plane just kept on coming. They even fired their cannon in return."

"So what was this handstand maneuver that caused the missiles to dislodge from the Chinese fighter?" Barbeau asked. "Was this a deliberate contact between two planes?"

"A handstand is just a scare tactic, ma'am," Cowan explained. "It directs a jet blast down on the other guys' plane from a few yards away. It's surprising and maybe momentarily disruptive, but it's not dangerous to similar-size aircraft—and the Chinese fighter is . . . was . . . much bigger than the Hornet. It's certainly not enough to dislodge a missile from a jet—especially an *armed* missile."

"So you're saying the Chinese fighter crew *deliberately* fired those missiles at the carrier?"

"I don't know, ma'am," Cowan admitted. "But I find it hard to believe that the missiles dislodged, powered themselves up, fired off, and locked onto the *Bush* all by themselves."

"Wouldn't they need to know where the carrier was before launch?" Carlyle asked.

"Not necessarily, sir," Cowan replied. "Some antiship cruise missiles can be self-guided by radar to attack any large target; shorter-range missiles use electro-optical sensors and datalink the images back to a controller to pinpoint a particular target. Russian-made cruise missiles can do both. Such missiles can then be fired in the general direction of their targets, or programmed to patrol an area where the targets might sail into, and then lock on and attack."

Secretary of State Barbeau shook her hands and closed her eyes. "Hold on, everyone, hold on," she said irritably. "We're getting off track here. My bottom-line question: Does anybody here honestly believe the Chinese would deliberately fire a hypersonic missile at a U.S. warship in peacetime?" No one replied. "Good. I happen to agree, so we can move on from here. However it happened, I believe it was an accident. I'm going to ask the Chinese foreign minister to demand a formal inquiry and full analysis of the incident, and to have U.S. experts involved every step of the way to the maximum extent possible. China is a pretty closed society, and their government and military even more so, but I expect full cooperation. Case closed."

Admiral Cowan's eyes had narrowed into angry slits. "Excuse me, ma'am, but the case is *not* closed. What about the casualties, the damage to the carrier—"

"What about the loss of that Chinese fighter and its crew, Admiral?" Barbeau retorted. "We lost more, so they should pay? They fired the missiles, so they're the bad guys? Excuse me, Admiral, but this 'handstand' maneuver sounds to me like showing off, not defending the carrier. It's like Tom Cruise flying upside down over the MiG in *Top Gun*—he did it just because the MiG pilot was starting to piss him off. If we're all agreed it was not deliberate, then the Chinese pilot flew toward our carrier just to piss us off. Is that a reason to blast him with engine exhaust and cause him to almost flip upside down and possibly dislodge those missiles?"

"Our SOP is to do everything necessary to divert a possible hostile target away with nonlethal means before resorting to lethal force—"

"Your men have their SOPs when they're out there in harm's way, Admiral—it's for you and the national command authority to decide what they are and if they're being properly performed, not me," Barbeau said. "I know your men don't have the luxury of sitting in a nice comfy chair and calmly debating things when they're looking down the barrel of a gun thousands of miles from home, when the only dry landing strip and hot meal is a four-acre hunk of floating steel that might end up at the bottom of the South China Sea at any moment.

"But now we're in *my* battlefield, Admiral, not yours. If we're all agreed this was a tragic accident and not deliberate"—Barbeau paused, then pointed at each window in her videoconference monitor, querying each participant—"and we are all *still* agreed, are we not . . . ?"—she waited a few breaths: still more silence—"that it *was* an accident, then we investigate fully to prevent such accidents from happening again; we issue the sincerest of apologies; and we move on. You start asking for reparations, or justice, or payback, and it tells me you don't really believe it was an accident. If that's the case, Admiral Cowan, you'd better tell me right now."

The chief of naval operations looked as if he was going to continue the argument; then, like a balloon slowly losing air, his shoulders slumped, he folded his hands, and made an almost imperceptible shake of his head.

"Thank you, Admiral," Barbeau said. "Now I have something to work with. One more question: Where did that Chinese fighter come from? Was it on a patrol mission, some kind of test, or is there any possibility that it could have been launched on a strike mission?"

"I can give you the answer to that, Madam Secretary," Kai Raydon said.

"Who is this?"

"General Kai Raydon, commander of Armstrong Space Station, Air Force Space Defense Command," Kai responded. He typed in commands on his console's keyboard, and the image on a new videoconference monitor changed to another trio of naval vessels. "You're looking at live pictures of the People's Liberation Army Navy Project 190 aircraft carrier, named the *Zhenyuan,* accompanied by two underway replenishment vessels on either side of the carrier. We've been monitoring the Chinese carrier since it sailed within five hundred miles of the *Bush* and observed the fighter launch."

"Who are you again, General?" Barbeau asked. "Where are you?" She turned to Secretary of Defense Turner. "Is he one of yours, Miller?"

"General Raydon commands Armstrong Space Station, the Air Force's orbiting space reconnaissance and communications platform," Turner replied. "Where are you exactly right now, General?"

"Two hundred and twelve miles over Argentina, sir, falling eastward at seventeen thousand six hundred miles per hour."

"'Falling'? You're *falling*?" Barbeau exclaimed.

"Spacecraft in Earth orbit aren't floating, Madam Secretary, and they aren't being propelled—they are pulled to Earth by gravity like any other object," Kai explained. "At our altitude and speed, however, we never hit the Earth as we fall because we speed past Earth as we continue to fall toward it."

"I'm sure I don't understand any of that, General Raydon," Barbeau said, "so I'll defer to your expertise. You saw the fighters launch from that carrier?"

"Armstrong is the hub of an extensive network of communications-and-surveillance satellites that cover the entire planet twenty-four/seven. If any American military unit goes into possible danger, the Air Force watches it from space. We've monitored the Chinese carrier almost continuously in real time since it left port."

Barbeau nodded. "It sounds impressive," she said. "Any unit, anytime, anywhere?"

"Yes, ma'am," Raydon responded. "If we don't have a satellite constellation ready to observe, we can set one up PDQ. If a satellite breaks, we can fix it. We can tie into a network of satellites and unmanned surveillance aircraft that fills in a pretty complete picture of every carrier battle group, surface-action group, and Marine Expeditionary Force deployed around the world, plus major exercises and other deployments. And if something needs blowing up, we're developing the capability of blowing it up from here faster than you can imagine."

"Naval support is a top priority for the Air Force these days, isn't it?" Barbeau remarked with a slight smile. She knew that the increased emphasis on naval operations, especially carriers and multipurpose submarines, was a sore point with many services, especially the Air Force, whose budget was the hardest hit.

"Yes, ma'am, it is," Raydon said. "They badly need the help, after all, and we're happy to assist."

"Go on without the editorial comments, General," Turner said.

"Yes, sir," Raydon said, suppressing a smile.

The space thing was back, Stacy Barbeau thought as the space general blathered on about all the stuff his station could do. President Joseph Gardner had vowed to kill the space station and spend the money on more carriers. The carriers were indeed on order—she had procured at least two to be built in her home state of Louisiana, thanks to her intimate relationship with the president—but the Air Force's push for space was apparently still going strong. That was a very interesting development indeed . . . "Tell me about this Chinese aircraft carrier, General Raydon," she interrupted without knowing or caring what he had been talking about. "You said that's a *live* picture?"

"Yes, ma'am, that's a nighttime shot of the carrier performing a night underway replenishment—a very tricky maneuver for any carrier navy, and a very impressive feat for China's very young carrier navy," Raydon said. "The Project 190 carrier was laid down three years ago in Novosibirsk, Russia. It was meant to be Russia's second carrier and first true angled-deck catapult-equipped supercarrier—they had been using 'ski-jump'-equipped carriers before this—but China made Russia an offer it couldn't refuse."

"Russia actually *sold* its aircraft carrier to China?"

"Military cooperation between the two has been increasing over the past ten years at least," National Security Adviser Carlyle said. "I wouldn't say it's as close as it was in the sixties, but it's an easy way for China to quickly and easily build a world-class military."

"What else has Russia been selling to China?"

"You name it, Madam Secretary," Carlyle said. "Naval weapon systems, long-range precision-guided weapons, spacecraft, maritime attack, air-launched missiles—big-ticket, relatively low-tech, high-volume items."

"Is this carrier a threat to us?" Barbeau asked. "Is it like our carriers?"

"It is a monster, on a par with any of the world's carriers with the exception of America's," Raydon went on. "It is over nine hundred feet long, two hundred and fifty feet wide, and has a seventy-five-thousand-pound displacement fully loaded. It features two aircraft elevators, four steam catapults, almost thirty-knot top speed, and forty fixed- and rotary-wing aircraft aboard, including thirty-two former Russian Sukhoi-34 advanced fighter-bombers ruggedized for catapult and tailhook operations. Total crew complement is four thousand sailors, and it usually embarks a company of special operations forces. Because it was designed for 'green-water' operations, within easy reach of supply ports, it does not have a nuclear power plant, although the 190 has been deployed as far as East Africa in support of Somali antipiracy missions, which means the Chinese have gotten very good at long-range naval operations with extended supply lines."

"But it can't match an American carrier, right?" Barbeau asked. "It's smaller, and they only have one? We have twelve, plus its escort ships, and are building four more."

"The 190 is China's second carrier—they have a smaller carrier, purchased from Iran, that's been used to train crews on carrier ops," Carlyle said. "But a Chinese carrier shadowing an American carrier battle group is emblematic of a growing trend: China is building its ability to project naval power far beyond its home waters in order to protect its business interests around the world, protect shipping lanes, and counter American hegemony."

"American hegemony?" Barbeau asked with playacted southern-belle innocence. She knew exactly what that term meant, but she wanted to hear the military's spin on it. "What are the Chinese worried about? We're not at war—we don't even compete with them. We buy billions of dollars of their goods, and they buy trillions of dollars of our debt. China is under no threat of invasion from *anyone* I'm aware of, except perhaps internally, and they employ very effective anti-insurgency intelligence and interdiction forces to eliminate unrest."

"The situation is plain and simple, Madam Secretary: the U.S. Navy is the world's best, and the second- and third-string players don't like it and will do anything they can think of to bust us up," Raydon said.

"Thank you, General Raydon, but I can take it from here," Carlyle said. He spread his hands and nodded. "But as the general said, Stacy, China depends on exports—selling their goods to every corner of the globe, sent mostly by oceangoing vessels. Everywhere they go, in every ocean and sea near any major port of call anywhere on the planet, they are confronted by the same thing: the U.S. Navy. They know the Navy patrols and controls the world's sea-lanes, and has the power to deny access to anyone if they so choose.

"Therefore, China wants a blue-water navy to challenge American dominance and protect its interests around the world," Carlyle went on. "They bought themselves an aircraft carrier from Russia and are undergoing a massive crash training course to make it fully blue-water operational. Additionally, we know they're placing ground-launched ballistic hypersonic antiship missiles in their sea-launched ballistic-missile submarines' operating areas and sea-lanes near their shores as a warning to our survey ships and hunter-killer sub patrols to stay away—"

"And now they've engineered this so-called accidental launch as another warning: Your carriers are at risk, so stay away," Raydon said. "They say it was an accident, and we're buying into it."

"Thank you, General Raydon," Barbeau said irritably. "If there's nothing more you have for us, you can resume your duties up there . . . wherever you are."

"Over the South Atlantic now, ma'am," Raydon said. "I do have one more comment to make regarding China. Their new manned space station, the Golden Wing Ten, maneuvered itself into an almost mirror orbit recently. We're still separated by altitude and distance, but it clearly is a hostile move on their part."

"I don't understand, General," Miller Turner said. "What's hostile about this? The so-called Chinese space station is a couple of space capsules docked together with a central engineering and mating module. There are only four Chinese astronauts aboard."

"It demonstrates some important capabilities, sir: the ability to maneuver, to be refueled, and to track another spacecraft with accuracy," Raydon said. "Moving a spacecraft into a different orbit requires a lot of fuel, and unless the fuel is replenished, the service life of a satellite is greatly shortened when it's moved, especially to the degree this one has been. It's a relatively simple task now to maneuver within striking distance of Armstrong Space Station."

"'Striking distance'?" Carlyle remarked. "You mean, deliberately collide or attack the space station?"

"Why else would you send a spacecraft on nearly the same orbit, sir?" Raydon asked. "We don't know that much about the Golden Wing Ten. The Chinese tell us it's to expand their knowledge and experience in orbital operations, but that's about it. We speculate that it's akin to our early Gemini-Agena spacecraft docking missions, where we learned docking, handling, and equipment-transfer procedures that we eventually used on Skylab, lunar, Shuttle, and International Space Station missions, but again, we're making excuses for the Chinese that are not backed up by any evidence. We should—"

"We're completely off the topic here, gentlemen," Stacy Anne Barbeau interrupted, "so let's save this discussion for another time, shall we? We're agreed that the Chinese missile launch was most likely accidental; we want to participate in a full-scale investigation; and we'd like the Chinese to stay away from our carriers and point their missiles in some other direction. In return, we'll pledge to use less aggressive maneuvers to warn foreign pilots to turn away, in order to avoid possible damage that might result in accidental launches. Can I go to the president and recommend this course of action to him?" Kai Raydon looked as if he was going to raise his hand, but no one else said anything, so Barbeau said quickly, "Thank you for your inputs, gentlemen. My staff will follow up with each of you for details for the report to the president, and I'll call if I have any more questions. Thank you." And her videoconference window disappeared.

"Thanks for the good work, General Raydon," Secretary of Defense Turner said. "Please pass along your full report of the *Bush* incident to Air Force as soon as possible."

"Yes, sir," Kai responded, and signed off.

"Opinionated SOB, isn't he?" National Security Adviser Carlyle remarked. "Seems that flying . . . or according to Raydon, *falling* . . . through orbit in a space station gives you the right to say whatever happens to be on your mind."

"They're doing great work on a shoestring budget, Conrad," Turner said. "Every time they go out and capture, repair, refuel, and reorbit a satellite, they save us about a hundred million dollars compared to the cost of launching a satellite from Earth."

"If he shoots his mouth off at Barbeau again like that, he'll be beached faster than any rocket ship," Carlyle said. "After putting up with McLanahan for so long, Barbeau's not going to let another cocky space cowboy stay put."

"Speaking of the space station, I got the initial report from Air Force about a test of a new space weapon," Turner said. "They call it Mjollnir, or Thor's Hammer, a system that reenters titanium bars through the atmosphere at thousands of miles an hour. They hit a small ship-size target from a hundred miles in space with one big metal bar. They had a bunch of congressional staffers observe the hit—I guess it really watered their eyes."

"The 'Rods from God' actually worked, eh?" Carlyle remarked idly.

"Blew the hell out of the target. Direct hit."

"Mil, I gotta admit: The space stuff is cool, and I'm sure the Air Force's recruiting numbers are going through the roof, but there's not any money in the budget for Rods from God or any more space stuff," Carlyle said dismissively. "The president wanted aircraft carriers, Congress said yes, so there's going to be aircraft carriers."

"I know, Conrad, I know," Turner said. "Building four more carrier battle groups has sucked up every available dollar out of the next ten defense budgets. But I'm already getting queries from Congress about the space stuff. When the word gets out about this incident in the South China Sea and then the success of this space-weapon test, the obvious questions will arise: Why are we building carriers that are so vulnerable?"

"We, especially the president, have the answer: The carriers are the ultimate in power projection," Carlyle said. "You park an aircraft carrier battle group off someone's coastline, and the negotiations start soon afterward. And they're far more versatile than space-based assets. The space guys watched the incident in the South China Sea, but what could they do about it? Even if they had the Rods from God, or even that big laser they used to have up there, would they have sunk the Chinese carrier in response? The president is making the right decision, Mil."

"The Air Force undersecretary in charge of space, Ann Page, is really pushing this new Space Defense Force thing," Turner said. "Now that the Thor's Hammer project is unclassified and apparently successful, she'll be pressing a military presence in space even harder."

"That's her job," Carlyle said. "But she was brought into the Pentagon so we could monitor and control her public comments. She can talk all she wants, but she still has to support the president and the administration as long as she's in that post. If she doesn't toe the line, we'll make sure she's disgraced as well as dismissed. It's your job to make sure she stays on the right side."

"I know that, Conrad. I'm just giving you a heads-up. We may be building carriers like crazy, but space is not going away."

ARMSTRONG SPACE STATION

THE NEXT DAY

"Attention on the station, hostile spacecraft detected, all personnel to emergency posts!" Senior Master Sergeant Valerie Lukas announced on the PA system. "Time to possible collision, seven minutes! All posts, report when configured for station defense and damage control!"

Kai Raydon was on his way from the latrine cubicle when the alert came, and he propelled himself across the large command module faster than he had ever done before. "Why do these things always happen when I'm in the latrine?" he muttered. "Report."

"Pirinclik has detected liftoff of a large rocket from an unknown launch site in southern Russia, designated E-1," Lukas said, referring to the U.S. Air Force's AN/FPS/79 space tracking radar facility in Turkey. "Confirmed by DSP and SBIRS-High. E-1 does not appear to be going into orbit, but is on a very high-altitude, very high-speed ballistic path."

"Aimed at us?"

"Yes, sir," Lukas said. "Time to impact, six minutes."

"No announced launches of any kind?"

"No, sir."

"Then it's a bad guy," Kai said. "Designate E-1 as hostile. Are we tracking it yet?"

"Negative, sir. Our tracking radar and Doppler are off-line."

"Perfect. Pirinclik still have it?"

"They'll lose it in ninety seconds," Lukas responded. "Globus-2 and Diego Garcia aren't tracking. Shemya might pick it up about sixty seconds before impact."

"They attacked at the perfect moment—right where our space surveillance coverage is the worst," Kai said. "Okay, we're down to our own infrared and optical sensors. Let's have a look. We'll have Pirinclik aim the sensors for acquisition."

The large multifunction display between Raydon and Lukas changed from a radar graphic of the launch to a split-screen view of Earth. The left split showed Earth as a cool gray mass in the background, with flashes of light here and there from lightning and reflected sunlight, which computers were attempting to tune out as much as possible. The right split showed Earth through a telescope, set for wide field of view as it searched for the incoming missile.

"Four minutes to impact," Lukas reported.

"C'mon, guys, find the sucker," Raydon said.

"Too much background clutter . . ."

"Try manually tuning," Raydon said. "The computers are tuning out the background clutter—tune for the target."

Lukas switched the infrared sensor's tuning to manual, and the left side of the monitor flared almost to complete white as the energy being radiated by the Earth washed out the heat-sensitive sensor. Seeker carefully adjusted several controls until the background faded, then began tuning even more carefully. "The sensor slaved to Pirinclik's radar—it's gotta be right in front of us, and hotter than hell," she murmured. "Anything on the camera?"

"Nothing yet."

"You'll find it, Seeker," Raydon said. "Countermeasures?"

"Standing by, sir," the officer in charge of the station's active defenses replied. "All systems active."

"Three minutes. Pirinclik radar lost contact."

"Seeker?"

"It's gotta be cooler than I'm expecting," the Air Force senior master sergeant said. "Unslave the camera and search separately in case I'm way off."

"You're not," Raydon said. "Relax and find it."

"Damage control parties in position, sir."

"Copy." On the stationwide intercom he said, "All personnel, two minutes to—"

"*Got it!*" Lukas crowed. "It's cold, not hot—they must've figured out a way to cool it off to make it harder to pick up on infrared." She immediately slaved the camera to the infrared seeker and zoomed in. The visual image showed a simple black bullet-shaped object. "It looks like a payload, not the entire rocket—it must've already staged."

"Countermeasures ready?"

"Defensive systems ready, sir."

Raydon punched in instructions in his computer keyboard, then opened a red-covered switch and activated it, giving commander's authority to fire weapons. "Attention on the station, countermeasures under way. Permission to engage, Seeker. Shoot when ready."

"Radiating now." Lukas entered commands into her computer, activated her own authorization switch, and hit a keyboard button. Moments later, an alert flashed on the monitors. "Automatic tracking failed," she announced. She grasped a joystick handle on the right side of her console and squeezed the slewing lever, which brought up a set of crosshairs on her camera monitor. Adjusting the field of view with her left hand while watching the monitor, she carefully placed the crosshairs on the target and squeezed a trigger. "Targeting lasers firing . . . COIL activating."

Mounted below the pressurized modules of Armstrong Space Station, in the place where the controversial Skybolt magnetohydrodynamic antiballistic-missile laser had been mounted, was a simple boxlike structure with several articulating turrets around it. Small targeting lasers shot from the turrets began tracking the incoming target, precisely measuring distance and bearing.

When the object was in range—about two hundred miles, or just forty seconds to impact—the main weapon activated. The structure contained the Hydra, a five-hundred-kilowatt Chemical-Oxygen-Iodine Laser, or COIL, a smaller version of the two megawatt COIL aboard the YAL-1 Airborne Laser and the AL-52 Dragon antiballistic-missile laser aircraft. Chlorine and hydrogen peroxide were mixed under high pressure, instantly producing highly energetic oxygen, which was compressed by nitrogen and mixed with iodine, creating laser light. The light was amplified by mirrors and optics into a beam and sent to a beam director and through an adaptive-optics focusing mirror, which sent a nickel-size spot of intense laser light on the target.

As soon as Lukas pulled the trigger to activate the COIL, they could see tiny sparkles of light around the target—but it wasn't from the laser. "Maneuvering thrusters—the sucker's maneuvering," Lukas said.

"Stay with it, Seeker," Raydon urged her. "Nail that sucker."

"I'm not sure if I have a coherent beam without auto tracking—"

"The targeting lasers didn't malfunction, only the main turret," Raydon said. "You're the tracker now. Get it!"

Lukas released the trigger when the computer told her the laser volley had ended; she had to wait ten precious seconds until she could fire the next volley. "Sure would like to have another COIL up here," she said.

"We're lucky to have the one," Raydon said. "Get ready for a second shot. All personnel, brace for impact and report any damage to me immediately."

As soon as the computer said she could fire again, she pulled the trigger and sent another burst at the target. "It has a pattern," she said. "I've got you now, sucker." Carefully matching the target's gyrations, she was able to keep the COIL beam on target long enough for the laser to burn a hole in the target's thin skin with just seconds to spare . . .

. . . and as the beam drove itself through the target, it broke apart and showered Armstrong Space Station . . . with a cloud of paper confetti, traveling at eighteen thousand miles per hour but causing no damage.

"Good job, Seeker," Raydon said. Lukas safed the COIL and secured her station, then let herself go limp in zero-g, being careful to use a towel to wipe away the sweat before it floated off her skin and became both a nuisance and a hazard. "Telemetry says you had the beam on target for three-point-eight seconds. I'd say that would be enough to take down a real antisatellite weapon."

"Thank you, sir," Lukas said. "But I wish we could do an auto engagement one of these days so I could sit back and watch the Hydra work."

"What fun is that?" Raydon asked with a smile. On the station-wide intercom he spoke, "All personnel, exercise target successfully destroyed in a visually acquired, manual-track engagement with the COIL. Inspect your stations for any signs of damage, secure from emergency stations, and submit postexercise reports to me as soon as possible. Thank you, everyone. Good job."

"Midnight One to Armstrong," Hunter Noble radioed from the XS-19 Midnight spaceplane, which had launched the target at the space station for the test. "Just want to be sure you guys were still breathing air and not space dust."

"Successful visual-manual engagement, Boomer," Raydon replied. "The confetti was a cute touch."

"Thought you'd like it, General."

Raydon switched the monitor at his station to the constant feed of telemetry he received from all of the spacecraft under his control, including the Midnight spaceplane. "Come on in to refuel and we'll load you up for a return to Roswell." Spaceport America, located at the former Roswell Industrial Air Center in southern New Mexico, was America's first private-commercial facility dedicated to supporting manned spaceflight—many of the supply rockets sent to the space station were launched by commercial companies from there. Because of its rather isolated location and twelve-thousand-foot runway, it made a good place to land from space without disturbing too many residents with sonic booms. "Hope you don't mind doing another trash run."

"Anytime, General," Boomer said. "Any chance I get to fly the spaceplanes, even if it's just haulin' trash, I'll take it. FYI, the major will be doing this approach and docking, so don't be surprised if you feel or hear something hit the station in a couple hours."

"Thanks, Boomer," the copilot, Air Force Major Dana Colwin, interjected. Colwin was a thirty-year-old former Air Force B-2 Spirit bomber pilot and aeronautical engineer, and had completed military astronaut training only a few months ago. She still wore her jet-black hair long, and preferred Dallas Cowboys baseball caps under her headset to keep her hair under control in zero-g.

It would take almost two hours for Boomer and his copilot to catch up with the space station. "I've got a project I need you to do while we're waiting to rendezvous, Colwin," Boomer said.

"Sure," she replied. "What is it?" Boomer called up several pages of computer routines that he had downloaded from Armstrong Space Station and sent the list to Colwin's multifunction display. "All this? This'll take me hours."

"Nah. They're diagnostic programs. When the first program finishes, it'll direct you which ones to do next. The results all get beamed to the station, but unfortunately the computer won't automatically select the next program to run, so you have to babysit it. Wake me when we're five minutes out."

"Wake you?"

"I'm going to inspect the cargo bay, and then I'm going to take a nap in the air lock."

"A *nap?* Are you kidding?" But Boomer unstrapped, gave her a wink, then floated though the cockpit and entered the air lock.

The dark-haired, brown-eyed astronaut shook her head in amusement. "Okay, Noble," she muttered, and got to work running the diagnostic programs. Hunter Noble always seemed so hyper during every flight she had been on with him, hardly ever appearing to need a nap—but she thought nothing about it and got to work. He still checked in every fifteen minutes as required, but she couldn't see that guy actually napping back there. Oh well—spaceflight sometimes really takes it out of you, she thought, and Noble was by far the busiest pilot in the unit.

About ninety minutes later the intercom clicked on: "How's it going, Colwin?"

"If you don't mind me saying, Boomer, this is mind-numbing busywork," she replied. "Tire-pressure histories? Hydrazine-container electrostatic checks? A monkey can do this."

"If it seems like it's just busywork, Colwin, you're right . . . because it *was* just busywork."

"Say again?"

"I needed you distracted so I could finish prebreathing and suiting up."

"*Suiting up?*"

"You're fairly new with the spaceplanes, Colwin, but you've done several automatic dockings, observed a few manual dockings, practiced many times in the simulator, and we have plenty of fuel, so I think it's time you did a manual rendezvous with the station."

"*A manual rendezvous?* Are you *nuts?*"

"You *have* been practicing in the simulator, haven't you? I guess we'll find out shortly. I'll be watching from outside."

"*From outside . . . ?*"

"Just don't jostle me around too much, Colwin. Relax and do it nice and easy. Don't cheat and turn on the computer—I'll be checking the flight-data logs. Outer hatch coming open. Break a leg, not the spaceplane." The large red "MASTER CAUTION" warning light flicked on, and the message OUTER HATCH UN-SEALED appeared on the computer monitor.

"Where are you, Noble?"

"I'm just halfway out the hatch, enjoying the view." Armstrong Space Station was about two miles away, sunlight reflecting off its silver antilaser covering, which gave the station its nickname "Silver Tower." "Once you're down to less than three-meters-per-second closure rate, I'll hop outside on the tether and use the suit's thrusters to watch away from the ship."

"I feel like going to less than three mps right now, Noble."

"We've got plenty of fuel, Colwin, but not all day," Boomer said. "You can do this. You need to do this for spacecraft-commander certification, and you *know* you want this. Let's do it."

"This your idea of fun, Noble?" General Kai Raydon radioed from Armstrong Space Station.

"I think Colwin's ready, General."

"You're in charge of pilot training, Noble," Raydon said, "so you're responsible for these little unplanned unannounced evolutions of yours. If the major dings up my station or the spaceplane, you might as well stay out there."

"Copy loud and clear, sir. She'll do fine."

As Boomer watched from the upper hatch, one by one he saw the thrusters on the nose release tiny jets of hydrazine exhaust. Colwin used the spaceplane's control stick and trim switches for directional control to make it easier and more intuitive, but steering a spacecraft wasn't like flying an airplane because orbital forces dictated the path, not flight control surfaces or aerodynamics. Although the thrusters could make minor altitude corrections, "up" and "down" were controlled by forward velocity—slowing down always meant losing altitude, speeding up always meant increasing altitude, and you had to be ready to correct anytime you made a velocity change. There were other nuances as well. In space, there was in reality no such thing as a "turn"—you could either move laterally into an entirely different orbit, roll along the longitudinal axis, or you could yaw the nose in a different direction, with the actual orbital flight path unchanged.

Normally the flight control computer controlled all of these subtleties, but computers failed quite often, so spaceplane pilots were expected to manually fly and dock the spacecraft with control, confidence, and precision before being fully certified as spacecraft commanders. Apart from a fully manual reentry and power-off landing, manual dockings were the most difficult and nerve-racking for pilots, and they practiced doing them quite often in the simulator.

Maybe it wasn't quite fair to unexpectedly lay this on her, Boomer thought, but it was time to see if she had what it took to qualify as a spacecraft commander. A lot of pilots stayed as mission commanders, perfectly happy to be second in command and let the computers and someone else accept all the responsibilities. Boomer was determined to separate the real spacecraft commanders from the mere pilots as soon and as safely as possible.

The cargo-bay doors were open, and he did a quick inspection of the cargo bay for any signs of damage or debris from the target release. "Cargo bay appears secure," he reported. "Colwin, keep the bay doors open and I'll get into the station from the air lock after you cross over."

"Roger," she replied, her voice cracking and monotone.

He exited the cargo bay, made his way back to the entry hatch, then looked "upward" to admire the Earth. He could watch it for hours, for days. He saw Africa beneath them, thunderstorms erupting along the Mediterranean coast near Libya; the incredible vastness of the Saharan wastelands; even the little crook in the Nile River where Luxor and the Valley of the Kings were located. Then in moments, the landmarks disappeared from view, but were replaced by even more treasures: Crete, Sicily, the impossibly blue Mediterranean, Greece, the Balkans, now Anatolia.

He always made a point on every space walk to marvel at the planet called Earth. It really was a spaceship, he reminded himself: every erg of energy, every element, every resource, every life-giving and life-sustaining particle except sunlight was already *there,* on that little sphere, save for a few stray atoms sent smashing in from the solar wind or from comet dust. Since the planet's formation, the chemicals, elements, molecules, and compounds that created

life had always been there, and they would never die, just be transferred into a different element, a different compound, or a different
form of energy. Humans could probably kill all life as we knew it,
but all the elements to rebuild life would remain on that little rock
until the sun incinerated the planet in a cataclysmic supernova.

Colwin was closing nicely with the space station, now probably
five hundred meters away. When Boomer saw the forward thrusters fire, he carefully eased himself out of the hatch, using the tiny
nitrogen thrusters on his space-suit backpack to propel him forward enough to ease the strain on his tether. "About four minutes
to go, Colwin," he radioed. "You're doing fine." More thruster jets,
but this time he saw jets in one direction, followed immediately by
spurts in the opposite direction that seemed to push the spaceplane
in the opposite direction instead of just countering the first push.
"Ease up on the thrusters," he said.

"I am."

The docking cradle on the space station resembled a giant gar-
den hand spade. Colwin's job was to maneuver Midnight into position on the spade, after which a grapple underneath the craft would
gently grasp the spaceplane and a transfer tunnel would be moved
into position on a separate beam beside the main entry hatch. Since
the Space Shuttle was retired, these days the Midnight spaceplane
was the largest craft to dock on the cradle, so there was plenty of
room to spare, but if the spaceplane was not perfectly in the center
and not perfectly level, the grapple might not latch, the transfer
tunnel might not seal tightly enough on the air lock, and the umbilicals that would service the aircraft might have to be manually
attached by a spacewalker.

Boomer disconnected himself completely from the Midnight
spaceplane when he knew he had plenty of thruster fuel in his
space suit to reach an entry hatch on the station. He stowed the
tether in its reel and made sure the hatch from the air lock to the
cargo bay was secured, then eased himself away from the space-

plane. "I'm clear of the air-lock hatch," he radioed. "Clear to close the main hatch and pressurize the air lock." He watched—yes, with a little pang of panic, since now he was completely on his own—as the hatch closed and locked. "You're a solo space pilot now, Colwin."

"Roger," Colwin said in a slightly squeaky voice.

Boomer maneuvered himself toward the front of the docking cradle, where he could watch the spaceplane enter the spade, being careful to keep out of Colwin's sight so she wouldn't be distracted. "How is she doing, Noble?" Raydon radioed on the secondary frequency so Colwin couldn't hear them.

"Very slow and cautious, but I can't fault her for that," Boomer replied.

"Think this was a good idea, you leaving her alone like that?"

"Back when I was at MIT getting my Ph.D. I remember when my Aero Club instructor pilot at Hanscom Air Force Base told me to pull my Piper Warrior over so he could hop out and I could do my first solo," Boomer said. "He didn't give me any warning—one minute he was sitting there, and the next minute the seat was empty."

"Every pilot experiences that."

"I know, but I thought I was such hot shit impressing the instructor that I never thought about soloing," Boomer said. "Then when it happened so suddenly, I never felt more scared and alone. I sat there until the ground controller told me to taxi for takeoff or park it back on the ramp. I finally shook it off, flew once around the pattern, and landed. I was scared shitless, but I did it."

"This is a whole lot different."

"If she screws up, they'll say it was the wrong decision," Boomer said. "But she won't."

Boomer had his doubts as he watched the Midnight slide forward into the cradle—he thought Colwin could've gotten it a little straighter and perhaps a little lower, and she was certainly *slow*—

but eventually she got it into position. The nose of the XS-19 contacted the large docking "donut" dead center and barely recoiled as the 170,000-pound spacecraft came to a stop. "Zero closure rate, Armstrong," she announced. "Grapple ring extended, ready for capture."

"Noble?" Raydon asked over the secondary frequency.

"She's a little off longitudinally and a little high, but I'll bet she's dead in the center," Boomer said. "Grab her and reel her in slowly."

The cradle's grapple moved and contacted the spaceplane's grapple ring on the first try. "Good contact, Midnight," the cradle operator reported. "Spacecraft moving to secure position." It took longer than normal, but eventually the Midnight spaceplane was hauled down onto the cradle. "Spacecraft secure. Extending transfer tunnel and umbilicals. Well done, Major Colwin."

"Thanks, guys," she replied a little weakly. "And, General, Boomer, thanks for trusting me to do this."

"Good job, Major," Raydon said.

"You're welcome, Colwin," Boomer added. "Just don't forget to unlock the cargo-bay air-lock hatch for me when you deplane."

"Roger." Boomer watched as a deplaning module motored along the service beam beside the Midnight and a transfer tunnel extended and fastened onto the spaceplane. A few moments later: "Transfer tunnel shows secure in place. Clear for pressure test." The tunnel was pressurized to be sure it was securely in place and sealed and so there was no difference in pressure between the station, tunnel, and spacecraft. A few more moments later: "I show pressure steady."

"Checks, pressure equal and steady," the deplaning module technician responded. "Clear to open your hatch, Major. Welcome back."

"Hatch coming open," Colwin said. A moment later: "Inside the tunnel . . . main entry hatch secure, Boomer."

"Thanks, Colwin. Armstrong, I'm entering Midnight's cargo

bay. I'll depressurize the air lock, come inside, repressurize, and unsuit before I come up. You can disconnect the tunnel and bring Colwin aboard."

"Copy that, Boomer," Raydon replied.

Boomer waited until he could see Colwin through the windows in the deplaning module, took another look at the incredible spectacle around him, then floated into Midnight's open cargo bay. As the transfer tunnel began to retract back up into the deplaning module, Boomer hit a switch to depressurize the air lock, heard the pumps sucking out the air for reuse, then when completed, grabbed the hatch handle . . .

. . . and it wouldn't move. He tried again—no use. He looked up at the deplaning module. "Colwin, are you sure you unlocked the air-lock hatch for me?" he radioed.

He could see Colwin's smiling face in the window of the deplaning module as the tunnel completed retracting. As the module began moving away down the service beam toward the station, Dana Colwin waved, then replied with a question of her own: "How does it feel to be suddenly left all alone in space, Noble?"

OFFICE OF THE SECRETARY OF THE AIR FORCE, THE PENTAGON, WASHINGTON, D.C.

THE NEXT DAY

"Why do I get the feeling, Mr. Secretary," Ann Page asked as she was shown to her seat, "that this is my 'come to Jesus' meeting?"

Secretary of the Air Force Salazar "Sal" Banderas smiled and nodded as he returned to his chair. Standing in front of their chairs, arrayed around the conference table in the meeting area adjacent to the secretary's office, were General Charles Huffman, the Air Force chief of staff, and General Robert Wiehl, commander of Air Force Space Command at Peterson Air Force Base, Colorado, and dual-hatted as U.S. Space Command chief. "I guess you could say it is, Dr. Page," Banderas said. "You know everyone here, yes?"

"Of course, Mr. Secretary," Ann said as she shook hands with all the men in the room. They respectfully stayed standing until Ann took her seat, even Banderas. She noticed that copies of the two latest reports she had submitted to the secretary of the Air Force were before each of them, along with other reports—contrary opinions, no doubt.

"Dr. Page, I'll get right to it: If what you've said in these reports is even half true, I'm completely blown away," Banderas said. "Two successful back-to-back tests of space-based weapons. I'm impressed. Congratulations."

"Thank you, Mr. Secretary," Ann said. "I assure you, the results are accurate, and my conclusions and recommendations for follow-on funding, development, and deployment are as well." She looked around the table, trying to gauge the opinions and positions of the others, but they were all too politically savvy to allow their facial expressions or body language to reveal their thoughts . . . not yet at least. "My office runs out of R-and-D money for the Trinity weapon series soon. Most of the funding came from the Martindale administration, canceled programs, and funds borrowed from other areas. I'm requesting an increase in funding for 2014 through 2020 and a supplemental for the rest of this fiscal year and for the next."

"To do what, Dr. Page?" General Huffman asked. He opened her report to a tabbed page. "You want to spend twenty billion dollars this next fiscal year plus ten billion a year for the next ten years to launch forty-eight 'weapon garages' into low Earth orbit, armed with these Trinity kill vehicles? That's *twenty percent* of our current budget! Where in the world did this plan come from?"

"The plan came from a continuing request from Congress for persistent, global, rapid strike following the destruction of the manned bomber and land-based intercontinental ballistic-missile forces after the Russian bomber attack on the United States, General," Ann replied. "President Gardner's response was to add four aircraft carrier battle groups over the next ten years at a cost of ten billion dollars a year."

"It's proven technology at less cost, Ann," Banderas commented.

"But it doesn't fulfill the mandate, Mr. Secretary," Ann said. "Even with sea-launched cruise missiles, which our adversaries are better able to detect and destroy, the Navy can hold less than thirty percent of all strategic targets in Russia and China at risk. Even against those targets we can reach, even a sixteen-carrier fleet could take days to be in a position to attack, and then its ability to attack is affected by environmental conditions. And as we saw just recently, the carrier is becoming more and more vulnerable to a wider array of threats."

"The argument's been made that long-range strike is no longer necessary," Banderas said flatly. "After the American Holocaust, strategic attack was all but killed off."

"I think the same was said *before* the American Holocaust, sir,"

Ann said. The American Holocaust was a Russian sneak attack using supersonic low-yield nuclear-tipped cruise missiles on American antiballistic-missile defense launch and radar sites, intercontinental ballistic-missile launch control centers, and long-range bomber bases. The attack killed several thousand persons, injured hundreds of thousands more, and in effect destroyed America's land-based nuclear deterrent. America's counterattack took place shortly thereafter, when Patrick McLanahan led a force of the surviving B-52, B-1, and B-2 bombers to capture a Russian air base in Siberia, from which he staged search-and-destroy missions throughout Russia that destroyed the majority of Russia's fixed and mobile intercontinental ballistic missiles.

The attacks left the two countries with a rough parity of nuclear-armed long-range missiles—the United States had its fourteen Trident ballistic-missile submarines, which had not been attacked (although it was widely believed that Russia had a follow-on attack mission ready), and a handful of long-range bombers, and Russia had two dozen surviving ICBM launchers and a handful of nuclear submarines. The world breathed a silent sigh of relief because now everyone saw the unspeakable horror of nuclear war, and all nuclear nations pledged to work to mothball all of their remaining nuclear weapons and delivery systems so the nightmare was never repeated.

"And now you're proposing to create another arms race, Ann—this one in space," Banderas said. "We put forty-eight weapon garages in orbit; China launches sixty; Russia launches a hundred. They start putting nukes in their garages; we modify our garages to attack their garages; they do the same to theirs. That's a race we don't need to start."

"That race is already under way, sir," Ann said. "Both Russia and China are stepping up their space launches; China has a space station aloft that they admit is being used for military research. Every nation knows that space is the ultimate high ground, and that the United States is way ahead in space technology. They will do one of two things: cooperate or compete."

"Most countries are cooperating, Madam Secretary," U.S. Space Command General Wiehl said. "With the Shuttle retired, we rely on the Russians almost every month for spacelift to the International Space Station."

"I know that, General, and it worries me," Ann said. "What if the Russians decided not to send Soyuz to the ISS anymore?"

"They wouldn't do that, Doctor," Wiehl said. "Russia has invested a lot into the ISS, and they usually have one or two cosmonauts aboard. They rely on us as much as we rely on them." But the sharpness of his rebuttal showed Ann that perhaps the question worried him more than he let on.

"Let's get back to Dr. Page's proposal," Secretary Banderas said, glancing at his watch. "Twenty billion to put forty-eight . . . you called them 'garages'? What's in this 'garage'?"

"Each weapon platform carries an infrared sensor, a tracking and targeting radar, electro-optical surveillance cameras, maneuvering engines, control and communications systems, and six Trinity kill vehicles—a mix of three antiballistic missile and defensive missiles, and three Mjollnir reentry vehicles," Ann said. "The platforms are small enough to be placed into orbit with smaller boosters like Athena Two, Taurus, or the Midnight spaceplane, and they're designed to be reloadable from manned or unmanned spacecraft."

"Why forty-eight of these garages? Can it be done with fewer?"

"The number is based on commercial communications satellite structures that provide continuous global coverage, sir," Ann said. "At an orbital altitude of about two to three hundred miles, which makes them easily accessible by our spaceplanes for servicing, there will be at least six platforms continuously overhead almost every spot on the planet."

"So six garages with three antiballistic-missile interceptors—

assuming some aren't used to defend the garages themselves—is just eighteen interceptors able to respond at any moment to an attack," Wiehl said. "Doesn't sound like that many."

"If we're being attacked by more than eighteen enemy missiles—especially nuclear ones—we have a serious problem that wouldn't be solved by twice as many interceptors, General," Ann said with a wry smile. "The antiballistic-missile portion of the system is, of course, part of a layered system that includes boost-phase and terminal defenses."

She turned to Secretary Banderas. "Sir, you've said it yourself many times: the Air Force has to do more with less; we have to field multi-role systems. The platforms are much more than just for space-based weapons. The sensors on board each platform and the integration of their data with other space assets through Armstrong Space Station will be invaluable to operators around the world. This network will provide real-time infrared, radar, and optical imagery to all users—even the Navy." She leaned forward and opened her hands. "*That's* the way we sell it to Secretary Turner and the White House."

"This is a benefit for the Navy? That's how we sell it?"

"The president is an unabashed Navy advocate," Ann said. "He and SECDEF both believe that the Navy is the preeminent military power of the United States of America, and that every other service, especially the Air Force, is a support service. If that's the way they want to see us, that's fine. But let's design a support mission that suits *us,* not fit in with how *they* see *us.*"

Secretary Banderas thought for a moment, then, as Ann breathed a sigh of relief, nodded. "I like it, Ann," he said. "Global look, global persistence, global availability, with self-protection and antiballistic-missile capabilities—and run by the Air Force."

"I think we'll have real problems with the land-attack option, sir," Chief of Staff Huffman said. "Even though these Mjollnir space weapons don't technically violate any treaties, the whole idea of weapons raining down on top of you from space will spook a lot of people, possibly including the president."

"Then we'll downplay the land-attack thing at first," Banderas said. "The missiles—"

"We call them 'orbital maneuvering vehicles,' sir," Ann said.

The secretary of the Air Force nodded approvingly. "I like that," he said. "Not 'kill vehicles,' not 'missiles'—'orbital maneuvering vehicles.' OMVs. Okay, the OMVs are on board for self-protection and for ballistic-missile defense. The land-attack weapons are possible future development spirals. When can I get platforms upstairs, Ann?"

"The sensor packages and network integration was completed some time ago—the weapon interfaces have just completed R and D," Ann replied. "We can build and launch one, perhaps two spacecraft a month. Within a year we can have sixty percent coverage and one hundred percent coverage within two years."

Banderas nodded. "Excellent. We'll meet to discuss where the money will come from, but because we'll pitch this as a naval support system, we might be able to siphon some bucks out of the Navy. So what are you going to call it, Ann?"

"I thought of several names, sir," Ann said, "but given the way we're going to pitch this to the National Command Authority and Congress as a naval support system, I've narrowed it down to one: Kingfisher. The Navy won't be as intimidated by a more globe-dominating name. Cute brightly colored little birds—the marine variety dive below the surface after fish."

Banderas shook his head and got to his feet. "You learn something new every damn day, I guess," he said with a smile. He held out a hand to Ann, and she shook it. "Thank you, Dr. Page. You've done some incredible work. We'll see about selling this to the powers that be and get a supplemental authorization. After what happened to the *Bush,* I think they'll be responsive to a system that puts more eyes out there over the horizon."

"Thank you, sir," Ann said. "Another question: standing up the Space Defense Force—"

"Don't even go there, Ann," Banderas said. "This sell is going to be tough enough without recommending forming an entire new military entity. We'll be lucky if it doesn't turn into a Navy program after all. Let's get the thing built and in orbit before deciding what color to paint it, okay?" He shrugged his shoulders and added, "And the way the Air Force is faring these days, that color will probably be battleship gray."

TWO

Beaten paths are for beaten men.

— ERIC JOHNSTON

LAS VEGAS, NEVADA

JANUARY 2012

"You have the mind of a twenty-year-old, the bod of a thirty-year-old—but the eyes of an eighty-year-old?" Air Force Colonel Gia "Boxer" Cazzotto said, giving Patrick McLanahan a kiss on the cheek. Gia was tall, with straight dark hair, mischievous brown eyes, and a disarmingly shy smile—all of which disguised a woman who commanded one of America's few remaining heavy bomber wings. "Cataract surgery, intraocular implants—*you?*"

"'Fraid so, babe," Patrick said. Patrick was a retired three-star Air Force general and one of the most highly regarded and popular military men in American history, having led mostly secret bombing missions all over the world for almost two decades, as well as the man responsible for starting America's military Space

Defense Force. But today, he was sitting up on a hospital bed in street clothes, being prepped for surgery. "I guess they're common for astronauts, high-altitude pilots, and anyone who works where ultraviolet rays are stronger."

"No, it's common for old guys," quipped Jonathan Colin Masters, who was also waiting with his friend. "Nervous, buddy?"

"A little," Patrick admitted.

"You *are* the first guy to get the newest version of the e-lenses," Jon said. "But the other versions have worked out very well, so there's nothing to be worried about."

"I don't like anyone messing with my eyes."

"Your eyes will still be blue and gorgeous," Gia said, giving Patrick another kiss. "Heck, I might get *my* lenses replaced—if Jon lowers the price."

"No military discounts—yet," Jon said. "But in a few years, everyone will have them." In the hour Patrick had been in pre-op, nurses had been putting various drops in his eyes every few minutes, and his pupils were fully dilated, so even tiny bits of light were bothersome. He had an intravenous line put in, but the anesthesiologist hadn't put anything in the saline bag just yet. Patrick's blood pressure was slightly elevated, but he appeared calm and relaxed.

Since leaving the U.S. Air Force two years earlier, he had let his hair grow a bit longer, and despite almost-daily workouts, he couldn't keep a little "executive spread" from setting in. He still bore some scars from his time in Iraq on the ground evading Republic of Turkey fighter-bombers; the blond hair was gone, replaced by middle-age brown with a slowly rising forehead and rapidly spreading temples of gray; and the bright blue eyes were slowly being clouded by ultraviolet radiation. But otherwise he was looking good for a man approaching his midfifties.

For the umpteenth time he was asked if he had any allergies, that it was indeed his left eye they were going to operate on, and if he had anything to eat or drink in the preceding twelve hours—and finally it was time to go. Gia and Jon said their good-byes and headed for a nearby laboratory to watch the procedure on a closed-circuit monitor while Patrick was wheeled into the operating room.

The entire procedure took less than thirty minutes. After immobilizing his head and face, an eye surgeon made a tiny incision in Patrick's left cornea, and he inserted an ultrasonic probe that dissolved the clouded left eye lens so it could be flushed away. Another tiny probe inserted the new artificial lens and positioned it in place. After several checks and measurements, Patrick was wheeled into the recovery room, where Gia was waiting for him and Jon and two other engineers from Sky Masters Inc. worked on a laptop computer set up on a desk in the recovery room. Gia kissed his forehead. "Yep, they're still blue," she said. "Feel okay?"

"Yes," Patrick said. "It's still a little shimmery and distorted, but I can already see in 3-D rather than just 2-D. I never realized how bad my vision had gotten." He turned to Jon. "And no more glasses?"

"Glasses are so twentieth century, Muck," Jon said. "It'll take a while for your eye muscles to adapt to the new lens, but in a couple weeks your eye muscles will be able to flex it just like a natural lens to focus on distant, mid, and close ranges. Plus it corrects astigmatism, and it'll last four lifetimes—you can will it to your grandkids if you want. And it can do a lot more stuff, too." He swiveled an examination lamp around and aimed it at Patrick . . .

. . . and to his amazement, the glare in his left eye quickly dimmed. "Wow, the sunglass feature works great," Patrick exclaimed. "No more sunglasses either!" He concentrated for a moment, and the glare returned as the electronic darkening feature deactivated. "And it's easy to shut it off, too."

"Same haptic interface we use in the Cybernetic Infantry Devices—you think about doing something like removing sunglasses, and it happens," Jon said.

"No telescopic vision, like the Six Million Dollar Man?"

"That's a few versions in the future, but we're working on it," Jon said. He typed commands on his keyboard. "But try out the datalink next, Muck."

"Here goes. Maddie, status report, Armstrong Space Station."

"Yes, General McLanahan, please stand by," responded the computerized voice of "Maddie," or Multifunctional Advanced Data Delivery and Information Exchange. Maddie was the Sky Masters Inc. civilian version of the "Duty Officer," the computerized virtual assistant that listened in on all conversations and could respond to requests and questions, retrieve information, remotely unlock doors, and thousands of other functions. *"Data ready, General,"* Maddie said a few moments later.

"Maddie, display data." Patrick spoke, and moments later a chart showing the military space station's position over Earth in its orbit appeared, along with readouts of altitude, velocity, orbital period, number of personnel, and status of its major systems . . . right before Patrick's eyes! "I can see it!" Patrick said. "Holy cow! This is incredible, Jon!"

"The new lens is really a microthin liquid crystal display and datalink receiver, powered by your eye muscles," Jon said. A mirror copy of the display was playing on Jon's laptop. "Right now you can access information only through Maddie, so it's limited to Sky Masters facilities, but we're working on a way to link into any wireless data source. Pretty soon you'll be able to tap into any sensor, radar, satellite download, any computer, the Internet, or any video broadcast, and watch it as if you were sitting right at the console. We're working on ways to be able to control computers and other systems that you are seeing as well."

"Maddie, close the display." Patrick spoke, and the image went away. "Pretty cool, Jon. But I *am* starting to feel like the Six Million Dollar Man, though—new implantable cardioverter defibrillator, new implanted telecommunications device, and now an electronic eye."

"I appreciate you offering to be a Sky Masters guinea pig, Muck," Jon said. "We're getting approvals for the new stuff that much faster because you're a famous guy and you're already so wired for sound that we can collect gobs of data on how the new gadgets are working. Speaking of which, how about we run through a few of the display functions so we can—"

"I've got a better idea, Jon—how about I take Patrick home, make him lunch, and let me visit for a while before I have to get back to my unit?" Gia interjected. "Tomorrow you can fine-tune him all you want."

Jon rolled his eyes in mock exasperation. "Another woman standing in the path of scientific advancement," he deadpanned. Gia stood, towering over him, and gave him a friendly smile but a very direct glance. Jon held up his hands in surrender. "Okay, okay, but first thing tomorrow, we run your new eyeball through its paces, Muck. See ya."

Gia wheeled Patrick through the Sky Masters laboratory and out to his waiting car, then drove them to his home in Henderson, just southeast of Las Vegas. The air was a little cool, but Gia and Patrick still enjoyed sitting outside, so they turned on gas patio heaters, snuggled under a comforter, and sipped hot tea while looking out at the view past their tiny yard with its swim-spa and out through the wrought-iron fence across to the golf course, with Henderson Airport beyond it. "I can actually see airplanes out there now," he commented. "So you're off to RIMPAC tonight?"

"RIMPAC's not until June, but the participants are meeting in Hawaii to start the final planning," Gia said. RIMPAC, or Rim of the Pacific, was a large-scale naval warfare exercise involving Western allied navies and other invited participants and observers. "This is the first time since the American Holocaust that the U.S. Air Force will be involved."

"About time," Patrick commented. "They should get Armstrong Space Station and the Space Defense Force involved, too."

"They should, but they're not," Gia said. "Secretary Page met with Pacific Command several times and offered services, but they were turned down every time."

"They're afraid that Armstrong will smoke them—all of those carriers are vulnerable to Armstrong and its weapon garages," Patrick said.

"Ann Page needs a strong voice to help sell the Space Defense Force to Congress and the American people, Patrick," Gia said. "The defense contracting business has been slowing down since the drawdowns in Iraq and Afghanistan—maybe it's time for you to get into the defense lobbying business."

"Me? A lobbyist?"

"Who better to do it?" Gia asked. "People will listen to you, and you know all about technology, geopolitics, the military, foreign policy, and even how Congress operates."

"Go back to Washington? Prowl around Capitol Hill again?"

"You won't be a presidential special adviser, but you'll still be Patrick McLanahan, and everyone in Congress will want to meet you, get their pictures taken with you, and listen to what you have to say," Gia said. "You can make a difference. I'm sure former president Martindale can put you in contact with the right people, get you registered, and grease the skids for you. After that, you just tell them what you know. Give them a glimpse into the future."

"Be a salesman for a bunch of defense contractors?"

"Not a salesman—you'd be an advocate, a spokesperson for the future U.S. military," Gia corrected him. "You already are—you might as well get paid to do it."

"That would mean pulling Bradley out of middle school again."

Gia shrugged. "I've spent more time with him now, Patrick, and I think you're doting on him a little too much," she said frankly. "He's a tough, smart, resilient kid. He's an egghead like his old man, but I see a lot of things in him that I don't see in you, stuff he probably got from Wendy—a thick skin, a lot more outer energy, a little attitude with folks that get in his way. But most of all, he wants to be near you—not right beside you every day; what kid wants that?—

but close enough to check in on you, be a little part of whatever you're doing. And honestly, I love Vegas, but it's no place to raise a teenager. Washington will be much better for him."

Patrick frowned. "Me . . . a lobbyist," he muttered. "My dad will be rolling in his grave."

"Maybe, but he won't be one bit less proud of you," Gia said. She snuggled closer to him. "So, Mr. Bionic Eyeball, my flight leaves in a few hours. How about you and me grab an early dinner before you drop me off at the airport?"

"Sounds good."

At that moment Patrick's cell phone rang—caller ID said it was his son, Bradley. "Hey, big guy."

"Hi, Dad. How did that eye thing go?"

"No problems. I can see great. I didn't realize how bad it was."

"Cool. Hey, football team's going to meet after workouts, and Coach offered to take us out for pizza afterward. I know Colonel Cazzotto is leaving today. You going to be okay?"

"No worries. My eye is better than new." That wasn't quite true, yet, but he really wanted the time alone with Gia. "Be home by nine."

"Cool. Thanks. Later."

Patrick hung up and put away his phone, then snuggled closer to Gia. "Are they going to feed you on the plane to Hawaii?"

"Ten bucks for plastic chicken in coach? No thanks. I usually bring a sandwich. Why?"

"Because we suddenly have the house all to ourselves this afternoon," Patrick said, nuzzling her neck, "and I know of a better way to kill a few hours."

"A few *hours*?" she asked with mock disbelief. "Look at you—give a guy a fancy high-tech eye and a nanotechnology pacemaker, and he starts to believe he *is* the Bionic Man!" But despite her kidding, he didn't stop his ministrations, and she quickly agreed to his change in plans.

THE WHITE HOUSE SITUATION ROOM, WASHINGTON, D.C.

THE NEXT DAY

President Joseph Gardner somehow always seemed to look polished and alert, even after being awakened in the middle of the
night by a phone that did not stop ringing until he picked it up—
the real emergency phone, what they called the "Batphone." He
strode into the Situation Room in the West Wing of the White
House just minutes after the call; the only evidence that this was
not business as usual was the slightly loosened knot in his tie.
"Seats, everyone," he said. The men and women arrayed around
the large conference table quickly sat. "Something about Pakistan?
Talk to me."

"We detected a sudden deployment of a flight of Pakistani mobile ballistic missiles, sir," Vice Chairman of the Joint Chiefs of
Staff Admiral Benjamin Kelly said. "No movements of any missiles have been announced by Islamabad."

"Show me," the president said.

"Yes, sir." Kelly motioned to the Situation Room operations officer; the lights dimmed slightly . . .

. . . and in moments the conference table transformed into a
huge holographic computer-generated map of Pakistan. The men
and women around the conference table stood to get a better look
at the incredible imagery. As they watched, mountains and valleys
appeared out of the tabletop in three dimensions; rivers and cities
appeared, with floating names near them. Some details were mere
computer wire structures, while others were in stunning full-color
photographic detail. The map slowly zoomed in to a place in western Pakistan east of the city of Quetta.

"This damn thing always gives me vertigo," the president muttered to Conrad Carlyle, his longtime friend and national security adviser. "I feel like I'm skydiving from space. Incredible detail, though."

"The system stitches together dozens of different sources of data—satellite and photoreconnaissance all the way to simple drawings—chooses the best and most recent info, and fuses it together into one image," Carlyle said. "But we can go back to old maps and slides if you'd prefer."

"After what we just paid for this thing? Not on your life."

"Quetta, capital of Balochistan province," General Kelly said, pointing to the laser-projection map. "Three Shaheen-2 mobile intermediate-range ballistic missiles belonging to the Pakistan army's Fourteenth Strategic Rocket Brigade have been deployed to presurveyed launch points east of the city."

"What's going on?" the president asked. "What's the Pakistani army up to?"

"We're not sure it *is* the Pak army, sir—we haven't detected any other military units on the move," Kelly replied.

"We're afraid of the worst here, sir," Gerald Vista, the director of national intelligence, interjected. "Quetta has been largely occupied by Taliban and al-Qaeda forces since 2009, and it's only been a matter of time before they got their hands on a missile capable of carrying weapons of mass destruction. It could also be rogue elements of the military."

"No other deployments?"

"Standard military deployments only, sir, mostly on the Afghan and Indian borders. No other rocket deployments or alerts."

"This is not an exercise, correct?" the president asked.

"Correct, sir. If it's a Pakistani exercise, they didn't announce it to us."

"Damn," Gardner muttered. "Do we think India has detected these rockets?"

"No sign of any Indian responses, sir," Kelly answered.

"Let's hope they don't get spooked," Gardner said. "Alert our embassies, consulates, and military units in Pakistan, India, and Afghanistan—wake them up, but don't let them know what's happening, yet, in case our alerts are intercepted. Get President Mazar on the phone." Within the next few minutes, the vice president, Kenneth Phoenix, and the president's secretary of defense, Miller Turner, hurried into the Situation Room, followed shortly thereafter by the chairman of the Joint Chiefs of Staff, General Taylor J. Bain, and the White House chief of staff, Walter Kordus, and they were quickly brought up to speed. "Well?" the president thundered over his shoulder to no one in particular. "Where's Mazar?"

"An aide told us that Mazar is aware of the developments in Balochistan and he is busy getting it under control," a communications officer said.

"Shit," the president murmured. "He's either lying and doesn't know, or he knows but can't do anything about it. What are those rockets?"

"Shaheen-2 is an intermediate-range ballistic missile, sir," Admiral Kelly said. "It could have a conventional or nonconventional warhead—they've even tested a model with multiple reentry warheads."

"'Nonconventional warhead'?"

"Pakistan does have weaponized chemical and biological warheads for their tactical missiles, and they are known to have as many as two hundred and forty nuclear warheads, ranging from one- to two-hundred-kiloton yields."

"Shit. What range?"

"They can easily reach New Delhi, sir," Kelly said. "Solid-propellant motors, so once in launch position and aligned, they could fire at any time. India has an array of Russian air defense systems, but no true antiballistic-missile weapons to our knowledge."

"Christ. What do we have out there? Where are the carriers?"

"The *Stennis* battle group is in the Arabian Sea right now," Carlyle said, referring to his notes. "There is a guided-missile cruiser, the *Decatur,* making a port call in Karachi. It has the SM-3 antiballistic-missile system aboard."

"Excellent," Gardner said. But he looked at the electronic chart and frowned. "Can those SM-3s fly that far if the Shaheens are launched toward New Delhi?" He looked at Admiral Kelly and instantly knew that he had thought the same question and had come up with a bad result. "Dammit. Contact the *Decatur* and tell them to give it a try anyway. Maybe they'll get lucky."

"Mr. President," Vice President Phoenix said, "I recommend authorizing Armstrong to respond if the rockets launch."

President Gardner looked confused. "Authorize who?"

"Armstrong Space Station, sir," Phoenix said. He pointed at the electronic laser-generated chart. "Most of this video and intel is coming from the space station's satellite networks—they have almost constant watch over almost every part of the globe. They were the ones who initiated the alert." He touched controls on the edge of the table, and the image zoomed in to the Pakistani rockets themselves. Touching the screen, he turned the image until they were looking at the rockets as if hovering just over them on a helicopter. "Look at the detail—you can see the wheels on those transporter-erector-launchers." The fine detail disappeared, but only for a few moments. "The image changes when one satellite goes out of sight until another one comes in again." He returned the image to the area around the launch site. "Armstrong controls a network of space-based antiballistic-missile interceptors. I recommend authorizing a shoot-down."

"Space-based ABMs? I thought they were just experimental."

"I understand they are not fully operational, but they might have enough ready to do the job."

The president frowned at Phoenix, surprised and a little annoyed that he knew so much about the space station. He turned to

General Bain. "I want to talk with someone on that space station, *now*."

"Yes, sir." Bain picked up a telephone. "Get me Armstrong Space Station." A few moments later, Bain pressed the speakerphone button on the phone: "General Raydon, this is General Bain in the Situation Room. Report."

"Armstrong has been monitoring a number of known or suspected missile launch points in Pakistan, India, and several other countries, and we came across these three in Pakistan, sir," Raydon said. "It could be an exercise or a training session, but we're not seeing the usual deployments of security personnel around the area—anytime they take one of those things out of the garage, even for an exercise, they normally set up a lot of security. We've been looking, and we don't see any. That's why we issued the alert."

"We tried calling Islamabad—they said they're aware of the situation and are working on it."

"That doesn't sound good, sir. We're standing by."

"This is President Gardner, General Raydon," Gardner interjected. "What exactly do you propose to do?"

"The Shaheen-2 ballistic missile flies to an altitude of between sixty and one hundred fifty miles, sir," Raydon said. "That's well within the Trinity's engagement envelope. The problem is, we don't have a complete constellation of OMVs to—"

"OMVs? What the hell is that?"

"Orbital Maneuvering Vehicles—interceptors, sir," Raydon said.

"Then just say 'interceptor' and let's cut the crap," Gardner said hotly. "So can you take those things out, yes or no?"

"If we have a Kingfisher—a weapon platform—within range at the time the missiles reach apogee, we can nail them. Our constellation is incomplete, so there's just a fifty percent chance we'll have a platform in range. Am I authorized to engage, sir?"

"Stand by, General," Gardner said. He hit the "HOLD" button

on the phone. "Get Mazar on the phone again, and this time I want to talk with him directly."

"All embassies and consulates have acknowledged our warning message and are standing by," Kordus said.

Gardner nodded, scanning the map, thinking hard. "Can the *Decatur* launch cruise missiles and take those things out?" he asked finally.

Bain measured the distances with his eyes. "About three hundred miles . . . it would take the TLAMs over a half hour to hit their targets after launch," he replied.

"Half an hour . . . ?"

"The Paks would certainly see or detect the launch," Vice President Phoenix said, "and they might respond against the *Decatur* or against India."

"India would certainly retaliate," Bain added, "probably with WMDs."

"Mr. President, President Mazar's office says he will call you immediately when the current situation has terminated," the communications officer said.

"Dammit," Gardner swore. He looked at his advisers around the huge electronic map. "All right, folks, let me hear options."

"No choice, Mr. President—we have to take those missiles out," Secretary of Defense Turner said. "Mazar won't say if he ordered those missiles to deploy or not, or if he's planning on launching them, or if some Taliban gang got hold of them. A cruise-missile attack is the only way."

"I agree, sir," National Security Adviser Carlyle said. "We should launch immediately."

"General?"

"Agreed," Bain said.

"Ken?"

"Notify New Delhi and Islamabad first," the vice president said. "But I think we might have another option. General Raydon?"

"Yes, sir."

"You and Undersecretary Page briefed the National Security Council last year on these weapon platforms of yours," Phoenix said. "You said they were being armed with self-defense and antiballistic-missile weapons, but you also mentioned as a footnote the space attack weapon. I seem to remember you had a successful test of that weapon back then, so I assume you are still testing it."

"Yes, sir. It's called 'Mjollnir'—'Thor's Hammer.'" Several of the president's advisers raised their eyebrows, just now remembering; President Gardner still looked confused.

"What's its status?"

"Still in research and development, sir," Raydon said.

"Undersecretary Page and Secretary Banderas seemed to indicate it was well beyond that stage, General," Phoenix said. "What's the *real* status?"

There was a slight, uncomfortable pause; then: "Mjollnir has been deployed on all of the weapon platforms for mate, stability, and connectivity tests, sir."

"What's this all about, Ken?" the president asked.

"There's a weapon on those orbiting garages that can take out those missiles . . . in *seconds,* not minutes."

"What?"

"If a garage is in position, it can fire a precision-guided penetrator that can take out those missiles," Phoenix said. "General Raydon, when do you have a garage in position?"

"Stand by, sir." A moment later: "One Trinity vehicle carrying a Mjollnir reentry weapon with three penetrator sabots will be over the target's horizon in about two minutes, and will be in optimum launch position for about ninety seconds. The next one won't be in position for twenty-seven minutes."

"Whoa, whoa, wait a damn minute," Gardner said. "What are these penetrators? Are they nuclear?"

"They are simply titanium shapes, like a big antitank sabot round, sir," Raydon said. "They have no explosive warhead of any kind—they're designed to destroy with sheer velocity and mass. They reenter Earth's atmosphere at greater than orbital speed: thousands of miles an hour, like a meteor."

"A *meteor?*"

"Ninety seconds to go, sir," Raydon said. "Yes, Mr. President, the reentry vehicle carries three sabots through the atmosphere and then uses sensors to get a precise fix on the target before releasing the sabots at hypersonic speed. Shall I engage?"

"Just shut the hell up, all of you," the president said. He stared at the holographic map in front of him, uncertainty evident in his face.

"Mr. President, Prime Minister Pawar of India is on the line."

The president snatched up the phone. "Mr. Prime Minister, this is Joseph Gardner . . . yes, sir, this is indeed an emergency. We have detected three Pakistani rockets that appear to be in launch position. We have attempted to contact President Mazar but he won't talk to me. He—yes, sir, I'm told they appear to be Shaheen-2 intermediate-range ballistic missiles."

"Thirty seconds, Mr. President," Raydon said.

"Mr. Prime Minister, I don't have much time," Gardner said. "I am advising you that I intend on attacking these rockets . . . using cruise missiles fired from sea." Most of the president's advisers looked relieved; Phoenix looked confused. "I'm doing this because . . . yes, from a U.S. warship visiting Karachi. I don't want you to mistake it for an attack against India. I don't know who is in control of those rockets, and for the safety of the entire region I . . . they are positioned east of Quetta, at a town called—"

"Platform's over the horizon, sir," Raydon said. "Ninety seconds before we lose it."

"Mr. Prime Minister, I didn't call you so you could attack those rockets yourself," Gardner said. "I think that would spark a wider exchange between India and Pakistan. I called to advise you of our actions so you wouldn't try to attack. I'm urging you to let us take action and asking you to be on extra alert but do not take offensive action. I am asking that you—" The president's expression turned blank, then to disbelief, then to red-hot anger. "Shit, he hung up!" He slammed the phone onto its cradle so hard the holographic images on the Situation Room's conference table shimmered. "Get him on the line again, and then—"

"*Scud, scud, scud!*" a female voice shouted. "All stations, this is Armstrong, single ground missile launch detected from location sierra-alpha one-three." As the stunned presidential advisers watched, one of the holographic images of the Shaheen-2 rockets they were watching lifted off and began to fly above the conference table. "Armstrong is tracking a single ground-launched missile. Preliminary trajectory appears to be suborbital ballistic, flight time estimate nine minutes."

Ken Phoenix adjusted the display so they could see the computed flight path of the rocket—and sure enough, it was headed directly toward New Delhi, India. "Mr. President, order Armstrong to attack both the missile and the ones on the ground! The platform is in position *now*—"

"Attack an ally with a hypersonic meteor from space? Are you *crazy,* Ken . . . ?"

"Sir, if they launch all those missiles and they have WMDs on them, they could kill millions of people," Phoenix argued. "Even if the Taliban or rogue forces were involved, and not the Pakistani government, it would certainly start a war."

"I *don't* believe the Paks would allow missiles with WMDs to fall into the hands of the Taliban," Gardner said. "This is a provocation, nothing more. Someone *wants* to start a shooting war. We tell New Delhi to stay calm and not overreact, and we'll come through this."

"But what if you're wrong, sir?" Phoenix insisted. "What if they're armed with WMDs? We have a way to stop them. Order the space station to attack."

"The world will think *I'm* nuts, firing those meteor things—"

"You can't just sit back and do nothing, sir—"

"Hey, Phoenix, *shut the hell up* and remember who you're talk-ing to!" the president snapped, jabbing a finger at his vice presi-dent. The room fell silent except for the reports of the missile's flight path being relayed from Armstrong Space Station. Gardner looked at the holographic 3-D map for a few moments, his eyes darting here and there; then, his head still lowered, he said in a low voice, "Order the space station to attack those other rockets and nail that one that lifted off."

"Armstrong, this is General Bain, immediate attack commit authorized by the president," Bain ordered.

"Armstrong copies, attack authorized," Kai Raydon responded.

"All stations, all stations, this is Armstrong, attack-commit au-thorization received," the voice of Senior Master Sergeant Valerie "Seeker" Lukas said. She was at her monitor and tracking console in Armstrong Space Station's command module. "All personnel, stand by." To Kai Raydon beside her, she said, "All combat sta-tions reporting manned and ready, sir."

"Okay, kids, this is for real this time, but we do it just like we've rehearsed," Kai said on the stationwide intercom. "Line it up, Seeker."

"Roger, sir," Lukas said. "Kingfisher Zero-Niner is responding to telemetry and reports ready, sir." She turned to Raydon. "This will be a Mjollnir and ABM attack from the same platform at al-most the same time, sir—I don't think we've ever practiced that before."

"Now's a good time, Seeker," Kai said. "I want to concentrate on the rocket. Have they launched any other Shaheens yet?"

"No, sir."

"Then you can use more than one Trinity on the one in flight," Kai said. "Hopefully we'll nail the others before they launch. One

Hammer should be more than enough for the ones still on the ground, but use another if you need to."

"Yes, sir. Trinity One is counting down, twenty seconds to release. Hammer One is counting down, twenty-six seconds to release."

As the Pakistani ballistic missile rose through the atmosphere, four hundred miles above it and six hundred miles behind it, the weapon garage named Kingfisher-9 emitted short thruster pulses in response to steering commands from its tracking and targeting computers. The cylindrical spacecraft had its own radar, electro-optical, and infrared sensors trained on the rocket, but the muzzle of the spacecraft was aimed well beyond it, along the computed flight path.

At the proper instant, the fire control computers launched the first Trinity interceptor vehicle. The kill vehicle used steering instructions broadcast from the weapon garage to insert itself into its own orbit that intersected the missile's flight path. By this time the rocket motor on the Shaheen-2 ballistic missile had already burned out, and it was approaching its coasting phase at the top of its ballistic flight path. Even though it was a "tail-chase," Trinity was traveling at orbital velocity of almost five miles per second and closed the distance to the vastly slower Pakistani missile in just eighty seconds. With ten seconds to intercept, the Trinity weapon activated its own millimeter-wave terminal guidance radar, refined its aiming with ultrashort bursts of thruster fire, and zeroed in for a direct hit.

Back on Kingfisher-9, immediately after launching the first Trinity vehicle, thrusters were already turning the weapon garage in a different direction, and as soon as the spacecraft was pointed properly, a Mjollnir vehicle fired—this one aimed toward Earth. Thrusters directed the payload on course. Specially shielded to withstand the extreme two-thousand-degree heat of reentry, slowing but still traveling more than four miles per second, the weapon package pierced the upper atmosphere in just over ten seconds.

As the superheated ionized air around the heat shield subsided, the shield was ejected, exposing the millimeter-wave terminal guidance radar aboard the payload guidance bus. The radar took digital pictures of the target area, comparing terrain features to its internal database for fine course corrections, then zeroed in on the target itself. In thousandths of a second it identified the target, measured the total target area, and computed the precise instant to release the titanium sabots. Small maneuvering vanes allowed some small course corrections, but the weapon was traveling too fast for the vanes to have much effect.

Seconds before impact, the sabots separated from the guidance bus, creating a radius of destruction precisely equal to the target area. The sabots hit the Earth traveling almost two miles per second, each with the force of a two-thousand-pound high-explosive bomb, creating a crater large enough to fit a jumbo jet within it . . .

. . . but missing the target area by over a mile, completely destroying a grain-processing facility on the outskirts of a village instead. Panicked by the massive explosion that erupted so close by, the terrorists abandoned the remaining two missiles and fled.

"It missed!" Bain shouted. "The other missiles are still alive."

"But we got the one they launched," Phoenix said happily. "We won't have an interceptor to get the other ones if they launch, but—"

"What . . . just . . . happened . . . here?" President Gardner asked in a low, completely stupefied voice. His eyes looked up from the holographic imagery of the two nearly simultaneous attacks to the faces of the advisers around him. "Was that *real*?"

"Sir," General Bain said, grinning like a kid at a circus, "it looks like we just took out a ballistic missile . . . *with a weapon fired from space*." He pumped a fist in the air. "I don't believe it myself, but they did it. They shot down a ballistic missile *from space*."

The president looked at the chairman of the Joint Chiefs of Staff in utter disbelief, then with exasperation at his senior uni-formed military adviser celebrating like a kid at a Little League game. "As you were, General," he growled. "Who knows what we hit with those meteor things. This thing's not over." Bain lowered his eyes contritely, but not convincingly so. Gardner glared at Phoe-nix angrily. "I never should have fired those meteor things at Paki-stan. That was wrong advice, and I shouldn't have had to have it shoved in my face by *you*." Phoenix said nothing, but returned Gardner's glare with a steady gaze.

"Mr. President, it appears the terrorists are abandoning those remaining missiles," Kai Raydon reported from Armstrong Space Station. "They're bugging out."

"General Bain, make sure that space station stands down and doesn't fire any more meteors at anybody!" the president said, drawing a finger across his throat to order the link cut off. To the State Depart-ment representative: "Send an immediate message to New Delhi, tell them the missiles have been abandoned and will soon be recovered, and urge them not to retaliate," the president said. "Tell them the emergency is over. Get Mazar on the phone—call his office every ten seconds if you have to, but I want to talk to him immediately."

He took a breath, swallowed hard, then added, "And I want to see Page and that general on the space station, Raydon, in the Oval Office as soon as possible. I want to know everything about those weapons. Then I want to meet with Secretary Barbeau and figure out what we're going to say to the rest of the world when the news of what we've just done gets out. And someone shut this damned table off."

The room began to clear out, but just as the vice president was leaving, Gardner said, "Mr. Phoenix, a word with you." Ken Phoenix turned and returned to the Situation Room, along with Chief of Staff Kordus; the others wore expressions signifying they were happy to be leaving. "I'll meet you in the Oval Office in a few, Walter," the president said. Kordus glanced warily at the president, but nodded and departed, closing the door behind him.

"What was *that*, Phoenix?" Gardner exclaimed after the door was closed. "What the hell do you think you were doing?"

"My job, Mr. President," Phoenix replied flatly.

"Your job is to take over for the president if he is unable to serve and to preside over the Senate, not to call up whatever military units you feel like and issue orders to the president of the United States! And you did it in the middle of a damned crisis, in front of my entire national security team. You undermined my authority and far overstepped yours."

"I thought part of my job was to offer advice, sir."

"Advice, yes—then shut up and let *me* make the decisions, not pop off at me!" Gardner snapped. He looked at Phoenix inquisitively. "You did seem to know an awful lot about that space station and those weapons. Why is that?"

"I get the same briefings as you, Mr. President."

"Been keeping up on the so-called Space Defense Force? Your friend McLanahan's old wet dream, before he retired, joined up with Martindale in that illegal mercenary outfit, and screwed the pooch in Iraq?"

"I keep up on a lot of things, sir. That's my job as well, isn't it?"

"I see. You seem to have a lot of lofty ideas about what your job is." Gardner sat back against the conference table, looking Phoenix up and down, studying him. "You know, Ken, I keep hearing these rumors that you intend to resign as vice president and run for the White House. Any truth to that?"

"This isn't Paraguay, sir," Phoenix said. "No U.S. vice president has ever resigned his office to run for president. It would be political suicide."

"That wasn't a yes-or-no answer, Ken," Gardner observed. "You would at least have the decency of talking to me beforehand, open and honestly?"

"Sir, the election is in ten months. You've been campaigning for reelection since last September—"

"But there's supposed to be a supersecret campaign organization in place that can get you up and running in an instant, right? That's what I heard." Gardner couldn't tell if Phoenix's silence was an admission, a denial, confusion, uncertainty—or hopefulness. "Listen, Ken, you're a good guy. I've never said it outright, but I'm sure you've known this already: You're a formidable politician. You're very bright, folks like and respect you, your background and public record are exemplary, and you're not afraid to get your hands dirty, like what you did in Iraq. I picked you to help unite the country after the partisan mess Martindale left it in."

"And so I wouldn't run against you in the last election."

"That didn't matter, Ken," the president said earnestly— whether it was real or not, Phoenix couldn't tell, which was one of the things that made Gardner such a formidable political figure. "You're a young guy. If you want to run for office in 2016, you'll still be a young guy, in your midfifties, and with eight years of experience in the veep's office. But let me give you some advice: If you resigned to run for office, you'd be committing political suicide, like you said, public and bloody. No one respects a quitter, especially a political quitter. You'd have less than one term in office, running against your former running mate, and you'd be forgotten in the dustbin of history except as the only guy to resign as vice president to run for president. Do you really want that?"

"I never said I wanted it, sir."

"No, but you've never denied it either," Gardner said. He affixed Phoenix with a direct gaze. "Start denying it. *Forcefully*. Or you'll be spending a lot of time sequestered away in some undisclosed location. Understand?"

"Understood, sir."

"And remember, there's only one president in this country. Keep your opinions and directives to yourself unless I ask you a direct question or until you raise your right hand and say 'So help me God' with me either standing in the background at your inauguration or in a flag-draped box in the cargo hold of Air Force One. Don't interfere with my Situation Room again. Clear?"

"Clear, sir."

President Gardner shook his head and smiled. "'Blast 'em from space,' he says. 'Don't just sit there and do nothing,' he says. We're going to catch some shit for that, for sure," and he departed the Situation Room and headed back to the Oval Office.

"Had your heart-to-heart with Phoenix, Joe?" Chief of Staff Kordus asked after the president entered his office. "I know you've been looking for just the right opportunity to tell him the score, and he sure delivered."

"He came back from that nightmare in Iraq with a big head, and it needed to be shrunk down a few," the president said. He longed for a cigarette and a glass of rum, but it was way too early in the day, even for him.

"What did he say about running for president?"

"Neither confirmed nor denied it," Gardner replied. "But we know there's an exploratory committee set up. I don't know what he's waiting for."

"He's not sure," Kordus offered. "If you dropped him from the ticket, he'd go for it in a heartbeat."

"I'm not about to do that, unless he does something really, *really* dumb and there's such a loud hue and cry against him from the party or the public that I'm *forced* to drop him," the president said. "And with what he went through in Iraq, he's an action hero and rock star rolled into one."

"Well, we've leaked so many hints about a rift between you and him that today's outburst will put more pressure on him to shit or get off the pot," Kordus said. "His speeches on your behalf are less and less about you and more toward your policies—rather, *his* take on *your* policies. Everyone is guessing he'll leave. What's Stacy Anne saying?"

"She's getting real impatient," Gardner admitted. "Her campaign speeches are packin' 'em in like crazy—she's a natural, and the public loves her sass. With her actions in Iraq and Turkey, the public really got a good look at her diplomatic experience in the face of hostile action—not at the same level as Phoenix, but pretty damned close. She keeps on saying that she wished it was *her* that got shot down over Iraq."

"I heard that—and I don't think she was kidding."

"Me neither. But she wants in the West Wing in the worst way."

"So like you said, Phoenix has to be forced to resign, or do something Agnew-like to voluntarily resign, or something completely egregious that you have no choice but to drop him from your ticket," Kordus said.

"Too bad I can't fire him."

"Unfortunately he was elected, same as you, so he can only resign, be impeached, or die," Kordus said. "But if he keeps on popping off at you in cabinet or NSC meetings, the others might force him to resign for the good of the country."

The president waved a hand. "Enough about Phoenix—he'll wait four more years, and then he'll probably just waltz into the White House," he said. "I won't give a shit then—I'll be at my beach house in Florida in between seven-figure speaking engagements. My bigger problem is how to explain what in hell we just did today."

"Give it a week or two for things in South Asia to calm down," Kordus said, "and then we'll leak the existence of those Pakistani missiles—if it hasn't already been leaked by India or Russia. You'll look like a hero for taking them out. You can just tell everyone that you're not at liberty to discuss how it was done. Then you'll have to decide if you want to keep those space interceptors up there, or take them down." He saw the president's upticked eyebrows, indicating the silent question, and replied, "They sure as hell did the job, even if they missed the target."

"They sure as hell did . . . and that's what concerns me," the president said. "If people start believing in space weapons, they may not want aircraft carriers."

"There's no comparison," Kordus said. "It's apples and oranges. I remember when the so-called experts were saying carriers were obsolete because of the cruise missile and the stealth bomber. It's not true. Eventually we'll have hypersonic flying ships and laser guns and then maybe the aircraft carrier will go away, but it won't happen in our kids' lifetimes."

The president looked uneasily at his friend, chief political adviser, and idea machine. "I hope you're right," he said. "I'm not afraid to say I was impressed. That Kingfisher thing is a game changer. But we've got a lot invested in building up the fleet again, and I don't want some new cool technology to derail our plans."

"If it looks that way, we'll pull the plug on Kingfisher," Kordus said. "It *did* miss, after all, and killed a lot of innocent people in the process. It may not be ready for prime time yet."

SOUTH OF HAINAN ISLAND, PEOPLE'S
REPUBLIC OF CHINA

DAYS LATER

The sea-launched ballistic-missile tube door opened on the spine of the USS *Wyoming,* the seventeenth *Ohio*-class ballistic-missile submarine, but instead of launching a Trident ballistic missile, a missile-shaped vehicle called a Grebe slowly eased out of the missile tube and began floating to the surface as the submarine moved away. It listened for any sign of collision or interference using passive sonars, even halting its ascent at one point when it detected a nearby fishing vessel.

After reaching the surface, it assumed a semisubmerged tail-low stance while it updated its navigation system using GPS signals and continued to listen for threats. Once it determined the coast was clear, wings and skis popped out of the Grebe's body, two rocket engines fired to lift the vehicle out of the water, and a small turbojet engine started when the vehicle reached a thousand-feet altitude. It climbed slowly, using a spiral flight course to avoid flying too close to Hainan Island before it reached its cruising altitude. Once reaching twelve thousand feet, it activated its low-light television and imaging infrared sensors and set a course for the Chinese naval base on Hainan Island. The Grebe's composite structure and small size kept it from being detected by air defense radars on the heavily fortified island.

The objective of the mission was the Wenchang Spaceport, the southernmost and newest of China's four satellite-launch facilities. Because Wenchang was closest to the equator and could therefore use the Earth's spin to help shove bigger rockets into orbit, the launch facilities, seaport, and rail lines had been greatly expanded to allow launches of China's biggest boosters, including the new

Long March-5 heavy booster intended for manned lunar missions, and lifting larger parts of Tiangong-1, China's growing military space station, into orbit.

There were four launchpads at Wenchang, and the Grebe got busy photographing them in detail. It was risky using the Grebe to photograph the base at such a low altitude, but even advanced satellites could not provide the extreme detail that the large drone could; also, satellites were too easy to detect and predict when they flew over the base, making it simple for the Chinese to hide a classified project from sight.

Along with optical and infrared sensors, the Grebe also collected electromagnetic signals such as radar, radio, microwave, and cellular telephone. It would avoid any areas of greater radar-signal activity, especially the naval port on the south side of the island, to avoid being detected. When it encountered a suspected air defense radar lock, the Grebe would automatically stow the electro-optical and infrared sensor domes to reduce its radar signature, then redeploy them when the signals subsided.

The Hainan Island military complex was actually three bases in one: the naval airfield that housed long-range maritime patrol planes, air defense fighter interceptors, and the Chinese aircraft carrier's air wing; the port facilities for the six ships in China's first aircraft-carrier battle group; and an underground submarine base actually carved into the island, which hosted a dozen hunter-killer and ballistic-missile submarines. Although Wenchang was the main target of this mission, the Grebe drone also snapped a few pictures of the rest of the island superfortress when its sensors detected that any radars were no longer tracking it. The Chinese aircraft-carrier group had returned from its encounter with the USS *George H. W. Bush,* and its aircraft were safely on shore.

As the Grebe swept back to the north to take one last pass at Wenchang before returning for its rendezvous with the *Wyoming,* some new details began to emerge. Three of the four main launchpads were vacant. The fourth main launchpad held a very large rocket with an incredible twelve rocket motors strapped onto the lower section and an enormous cargo fairing atop the rocket.

A new development was the presence of two smaller launchpads situated away from the main launch complex and serviced by roads, not rail lines. These were occupied by large rockets on mobile transporter-erector-launchers, with six concrete shelters large enough to house them built nearby. That was certainly a new development—they hadn't been spotted by any satellite surveillance passes as soon as a day earlier.

Mission complete, the Grebe stowed its sensor turrets and headed northeast. It would take a wide sweeping course away from the island, turn on its transponders so Chinese air defense would spot it heading away, then go back into stealth mode, descend, and turn south for its rendezvous with the *Wyoming,* hopefully sending any pursuers off in the wrong direction. Once at the preplanned rendezvous point, it would ski-land on the South China Sea, sink itself to a safe level, and await retrieval by divers from the *Wyoming.* Although in service for only a few months, the Grebe was proving to be a very valuable intelligence-gathering tool, giving the Navy yet another over-the-horizon asset that allowed . . .

. . . and at that moment, less than two miles off the northeast coast of Hainan Island, a Type P793 mobile twin thirty-seven-millimeter antiaircraft cannon, guided by passive electro-optical and infrared sensors and therefore undetected by the Grebe's electromagnetic sensors, opened fire. The drone was cut to pieces in seconds, scattering pieces of itself across an entire square mile of the South China Sea.

THE WHITE HOUSE SITUATION ROOM

THE NEXT MORNING

"They are Dong Feng-21 missiles, sir," Gerald Vista, the director of national intelligence, said. President Gardner peered with close attention at the images on the large-screen computer monitor at the front of the room. It was an amazingly clear image of the launch-pads at Wenchang Spaceport on Hainan Island, China, transmitted via satellite from the Grebe sub-launched unmanned aerial vehicle—they looked as if they were taken from a platform just above the weapons. "In my opinion they represent a major escalation of weapons in the South China Sea."

Vista used a remote control to zoom in on two of the launch-pads. "Note the differences in the nose section of the missiles between pad number five and six, and the extra set of fins near the top of the missile on the ones on pad five," he said. "The extra fins allow more maneuvering in the atmosphere. We believe the missiles on pad five are maneuvering ballistic antiship missiles."

"So the rumors are true, eh?" the president remarked. "I remember they were supposedly experimenting with them when I was at the Pentagon. Any chance they might be fakes set up out there for us to take pictures of them?"

"Of course, sir," Vista said. "We'd need a clandestine operative, an informant, or a special ops mission to be sure. Until then, we shouldn't take the chance."

"I know that, Gerald," the president said perturbedly. "So they finally rolled the big antiship missiles out. Because of the *Bush* incident, I presume?"

"That, and I'm sure the Pakistan strike as well," National Security Adviser Conrad Carlyle said. He turned to Vista. "The missiles on pad six are the antisatellite missiles?"

"Yes. Officially called the KT-3, but still a modified DF-21 missile like the others. We estimate it can hit satellites as high as six hundred miles—plenty to reach Armstrong and the interceptor garages. It was the same missile that shot down their weather satellite a few years ago."

"You think they want to attack the space station, Gerald?" the president asked. He turned to Secretary of State Barbeau and National Security Adviser Conrad Carlyle. "That make sense to you, Stacy? Conrad?"

"I think we're seeing the beginnings of the Chinese response to our naval buildup program, sir," Carlyle said. "They know they or the Russians can't build space weapons or aircraft carriers or train experienced carrier crews fast enough to match us. So while they get up to speed on carriers and space, they bring out the antiship ballistic missiles and ASATs."

"The Chinese don't want to challenge us, Mr. President, but they don't want to be seen as being restricted at all by the U.S. Navy," Barbeau said. "We don't want to restrict free access to the world's oceans—"

"We just want the *ability* to do so if we choose," the president said. "So what about these damned Dong Feng missiles? Are they something we need to worry about?"

"The DF-21 and KT-3 are mobile solid-fuel missiles with good accuracy even with just an inertial guidance system—they get near zero-zero accuracy with a precision system such as electro-optical, satellite, or laser guidance," Vista said. "They're easy to hide, easy to set up, can be fired and reloaded quickly, and are hypersonic, which makes intercepting them more difficult. Even without a high-explosive or nuclear warhead, just one could probably severely damage an aircraft carrier enough to take it out of action just by sheer impact force."

"But it *does* have a nuclear warhead, right?"

"Yes, sir, it does," Vista said. "They can also carry a one-thousand-pound high-explosive warhead, but it has a much shorter range. The ASAT missile is kinetic-kill only—no warhead, hit-to-kill."

"The nukes are a problem, Mr. President—a very big one," Vice President Ken Phoenix said. Gardner gave him a fleeting warning glance but let him speak. "China is deploying *nuclear*-capable anti-ship missiles? What if they start deploying them in large numbers? Are they trying to restrict our movements or exclude us from certain areas?"

"The problem is targeting, sir—finding and tracking an aircraft carrier," Carlyle said. "Oceans are big, especially the western Pacific and Indian oceans, which the Chinese would want to patrol, and carriers move pretty quickly and unpredictably. But if you spot one and pass the location to the launch site, the situation quickly turns critical."

"Do the Chinese have that ability?" Phoenix asked.

"In certain regions, yes, sir," Vista said. "The South China Sea, East China Sea, and Yellow Sea are quickly becoming Chinese lakes, like the Gulf of Mexico is to the United States—open to all, but definitely under our direct control. Straits of Malacca, Java Sea, eastern Indian Ocean, the most important sea-lanes from Asia to the Middle East and Europe—not so much yet, but building quickly. They have three satellites in circular equatorial orbits specifically tasked for surveillance of the Indian Ocean and South China Sea, and they operate large fleets of manned and unmanned patrol aircraft to monitor seas closer to the mainland."

"Well, that's an awful big chunk of the Far East, and nukes in open ocean can be pretty devastating even if you miss your target," Phoenix offered. "It's a serious situation. We should demand they remove the nuclear warheads from those missiles immediately and allow verification inspections."

The president took a sip of orange juice and thought for a moment; then: "Putting nuclear warheads on missiles out in the open is a big deal, Ken, I agree," he said, "but Stacy Anne is handling China right now, and I think she's doing a good job. She closed the book on the *Bush* incident, so now we can turn to Hainan Island and those missiles."

He thought for a while longer, then went on: "We let them know that we know they're there, period. If China wants to put missiles there, let 'em; if they want to do some test launches, we'll collect even more data on what they have. Now that we know they're there, we'll be keeping an eye on them even more closely, and at the first sign of any conflict, we'll take 'em out." He noticed Phoenix wanted to say something, and gave him another warning glance. "I'm not going to do anything that will make the Chinese think we're scared of their missiles." He nodded toward the screen. "What about that big-ass rocket out there?"

"That's their new heavy-lift booster, the Long March-5, sir," Vista said. "It's an enlarged Long March-3 rocket with four solid-fuel motors strapped to the outside. It can haul twenty-five tons into low Earth orbit, fifteen tons to geosynchronous orbit, or ten tons to the moon—not quite Saturn-5 class, but still impressive. The Chinese have already announced they're going to use it to insert the new crew habitation module of their space station, Shenzhou-7. The launch is scheduled for May first. Their first lunar mission—orbit the moon, then return—is also scheduled for this year."

"China is really going full throttle on their space program, aren't they?" Vice President Phoenix remarked.

"Let's talk about our own space program—namely, Armstrong and those weapon garages," the president interjected. "Get Page and that general in here." A few moments later, Ann Page and Brigadier General Raydon were escorted into the Situation Room, along with Secretary of the Air Force Salazar Banderas. Stacy Barbeau did a double take when Kai Raydon entered the room—obviously she liked what she saw. "Take seats, folks, and let's talk," the president said. He waited until the newcomers had seated themselves, then said without preamble or pleasantries, "If I didn't know any better, Secretary Banderas, I'd say you sneaked those Thor's Hammer things on those space platforms, disguised as antiballistic-missile weapons or space experiments. Am I wrong?"

"Mr. President, I didn't try to conceal anything," Banderas said. "We revealed everything in our budgets and research plans." He glanced at Secretary of Defense Turner. "I briefed SECDEF myself on every aspect of Kingfisher."

"Miller?"

"I'd have to check my records, sir," Turner said uneasily. "Kingfisher I recognize. I remember something last year about a successful test of a space-launched surface-attack weapon, but I didn't know it had been deployed as part of the space-based antiballistic-missile system."

"I recall getting a briefing, Mr. President," Phoenix said. Gardner ignored the remark.

"Mr. President, it was a successful employment," Ann said. "A crisis was averted. We should—"

"Dr. Page, I'll get to you in a second," the president said, holding up a hand. "Secretary Banderas, I feel as if I've been deceived. I've got to explain to the world what we did in Pakistan, and I don't know enough about these space weapons to do that. That's my fault and my problem. The question is: What do we do from here?"

"Mr. President, I recommend accelerating deployment of the full Kingfisher constellation," Banderas said. "They proved they work. We were lucky we had a weapon platform in position to strike. Now that the world understands what we have, they can time their strikes to take advantage of coverage gaps. We need to fill those gaps as quickly as possible."

"Do you read the papers, Mr. Secretary?" the president asked irritably. "Do you watch the news? Pakistan is accusing us of attacking them with a conventionally armed intercontinental ballistic missile! We killed *dozens* of civilians. Pictures of that crater are being shown on TV every hour of every day. And I can't tell the world that we stopped a Pakistani missile attack—India and probably Russia would attack in a heartbeat."

"Sir, all of the nations in the region are manipulating the events in this incident to suit their own political agenda," Banderas said. "China has a space tracking facility in Karachi, and Pakistan has dozens of long-range radars; India and Russia have them, too, in India. They all know Pakistan launched a ballistic missile at India and that we intercepted it, but that hasn't hit the news yet."

"What's your point, Mr. Secretary?"

"My point is, sir, that we can't respond to international criticism and fear because people aren't being told the whole truth," Banderas went on. "The only thing we can do is make the system completely operational and respond to the next emergency as appropriate."

"And you don't feel this will cause a new arms race?"

"Sir, the race is already on," Banderas said. He motioned to Kai Raydon, who opened a folder and dropped a photograph on the conference table before the president. "Does that look familiar, sir?"

President Gardner glanced at it, then nodded and slid the photo to his national security adviser. "They look like the missile shelters on Hainan Island in China," he said.

"They are missile shelters for DF-21 missiles, sir—but they're located in Karachi, Pakistan, not China," Kai said. "We photographed them just a few hours ago. It looks like China is deploying DF-21s and probably KT-3 antisatellite missiles in Pakistan."

"That's ridiculous," National Security Adviser Conrad Carlyle said. "China deploying missiles designed to attack American warships—in *Pakistan,* an American ally?"

"China is a Pakistani ally, too, Mr. Director, as you know," Banderas said. "We've been drifting apart from Pakistan for quite some time, since Predator drone sorties were stepped up in the Afghan-Pakistan border region, and at the same time China has been increasing economic and military aid to Pakistan."

"We're scanning other Chinese-allied nations looking for more of these DF-21 launch sites," Kai said. "I'll bet we'll soon find them in Africa, the Pacific, South America, and Southeast Asia—everywhere they have military cooperation agreements or have bought basing rights."

"Again, they can build all the launchpads they want—we'll have to keep track of them and make a plan to take them out if necessary," the president said. Kai noticed the uncomfortable set of the vice president's jaw—obviously he didn't agree with that tactic. "Making this situation even more complicated was the attack from space. Why should the Chinese give up their missiles while we have orbiting killer meteoroids?"

"Sir, it's obvious China has been working on deploying these DF-21s and KT-3s around the world for quite some time—probably since we first started inserting the interceptor garages into orbit," Banderas said. "Now those things are out in the open, possibly with nuclear warheads. And remember, sir, that the DF-21 is at first a surface-to-surface missile as well as an antiship and anti-satellite one—from Hainan Island they can reach as far as Guam and Okinawa and hit all of the transit routes between the Pacific and Indian oceans. The only weapon system we have right now to hit those launchers in a timely manner is Mjollnir."

"I think a sea-launched cruise missile could do the job adequately as well, Sal—let's not lose perspective here, okay?" the president said. "I know you're an air- and space-power advocate, but let's not forget the big picture." He turned to Secretary of State Barbeau. "Stacy . . ."

She smiled and held up a hand. "I know, sir, I know . . . back to Beijing."

"I need to learn more about what the Chinese intend to do with these DF-21s," the president said. "I'm not going to force the issue or demand removal—yet—but I want to get a statement from them."

"I think I know what they'll say: It's to protect vital Chinese shipping lanes and the free flow of commerce around the world," Barbeau said. "They'll openly cite Somali and Philippine pirates; less overtly, they'll say that American domination of the world's oceans is a threat."

"Get it firsthand, and then we'll hold their feet to the fire," Gardner said.

"Yes, Mr. President," she said, taking that opportunity to look Raydon up and down again. He did the same to her, but more discreetly.

The president turned to Ann Page. "Dr. Page, you have a long and distinguished career, but to me you seem to take great delight in shaking up the system. As an engineer and former member of Congress, that's probably a good thing—but as a member of my administration, it most definitely is *not*."

"Mr. President, it's not my intention to shake anything up," Ann said. "We had the technology to build an entirely new defensive and offensive weapon system and take the U.S. military to the next level. The technology may be immature and imperfect, but as we saw, it's viable."

"Viable? You missed the target and killed a lot of civilians, Dr. Page."

"I'm sorry about that, Mr. President," Ann said sincerely. "While I don't believe that the ends justifies the means, we *did* stop the Pakistanis from launching any more rockets."

The president closed his eyes and shook his head. "I'll tell that to the United Nations: We put out a house fire by blowing up the dam and flooding the town," he said. "So we have an immature and unreliable weapon system that is controversial to say the least, incomplete, and bound to cause a major outcry if not an outright global arms race. What do you propose I do about this?"

"Resolve to win the race, sir," Ann said immediately. "With current funding, it will take another fifteen to twenty-four months to complete the Kingfisher constellation. We have a plan to draw on Air Force and Navy budget resources and complete the constellation in ten months or less, along with making improvements in detection capabilities, self-defense to counter the growing Russian and Chinese antisatellite threat, and weapon accuracy."

"Navy budget resources, eh?" Secretary of Defense Turner asked. "Such as?"

Ann looked at Secretary Banderas. When he hesitated, she replied: "BAMS and ForceNet, Mr. Secretary, among others."

"What?" Turner exclaimed. His astonished expression slowly turned into one of amusement. "You want to downsize two of the biggest and most cutting-edge naval surveillance and information networking systems?"

"We don't want to downsize them, Mr. Secretary—we want to *cancel* them," Banderas said.

"Cancel them?" Turner asked incredulously. "They're not even fully implemented yet!"

"Exactly why they should be canceled, sir," Banderas went on. "The Broad Area Maritime Surveillance program is based around old technology—"

"Global Hawk may be old, but it's proven technology."

"Global Hawk is proven, but compared to emerging space technology, it's slow, vulnerable, costly and difficult to sustain and support, limited by availability of shore facilities, and in its current configuration has no strike capability, sir," Banderas went on. "ForceNet is seven years in the making but is far over budget, is still not fully operational, and isn't fully integrated into other services' computer network systems. For network systems managed by major non-Navy commands such as U.S. Strategic Command,

ForceNet will demand an upgrade of *their* network infrastructures to mesh, with the costs estimated in the tens of billions of dollars and another ten years. That means that ForceNet would probably never be tied into other networks as it was designed to be."

"Once completed, Kingfisher can act as a global fleet communications-and-reconnaissance system," Ann jumped in. "Our systems are already tied into several services' reconnaissance and surveillance networks, including the Navy's, along with Strategic Command, the National Reconnaissance Office, and even the CIA. Everyone in Washington has accessed our imagery, used our communications relays, and taken advantage of our global Internet access and secure data network—and the system is only half finished."

"The Navy is never going to cancel two vital programs to invest in these orbital weapon garages," Turner said.

"Nor should they," the president said. "It's not going to happen. I supported maritime Global Hawk and ForceNet from day one— I'm not about to kill them, especially for an unproven system."

"It's not unproven anymore, sir," Kai said. Barbeau's eyes fairly twinkled when he spoke.

"I'm not convinced the land-attack missile portion is ready, General," the president said. "The missile defense part is impressive, but I'm not ready to cancel important programs for other services for a global missile defense shield. We spend a lot of money on missile defense for the United States already—defending India is not in our budget."

He got to his feet, and everyone else followed suit. "Good to see you, Sal," he said, shaking hands with the Air Force secretary. "We'll discuss this and let you know how it'll be."

"I've got the entire proposal ready for your review, Mr. President," Banderas said. "I know you'll be surprised and pleased with the program."

The president ignored the last-second sales pitch. "Dr. Page, good to see you again," he said, shaking her hand next. "Deploying a new weapon system is a process, as I'm sure you are very aware. If you spring it on the world all at once like this, folks put up an immediate negative reaction to it—and that goes double for something this different."

"I know very well, Mr. President, after all my work on Skybolt and in the Senate Armed Services Committee," Ann said. "But Kingfisher is what's needed now for global reconnaissance and a truly rapid-reaction ballistic-missile defense and global strike."

The White House chief of staff, Walter Kordus, could see the president's exasperation at the chatter and began herding the visitors out the door. Kai Raydon stuck out a hand before Kordus could reach him, and the president shook it. "Nice to meet you, Mr. President," he said.

"Same, General," Gardner responded curtly before Kordus finally corralled the visitors and led them outside, trailing them with a chorus of thank-yous.

"I'd be happy to talk to those people for you next time, Mr. President," Secretary of Defense Turner said after all but he, Conrad Carlyle, and Stacy Anne Barbeau stayed behind. "They're starting to sound like used-car salesmen. And I had no inkling they were going to propose killing BAMS and ForceNet for their space stuff. They must be breathing too much rare gas or something."

"I'm not about to kill any Navy programs for this Thor's Hammer thing," the president said. "It is indeed impressive—just impressive enough to offer it up to the Russians, Chinese, North Koreans, or anyone else we need to make a deal with. Otherwise we threaten to start launching more weapon garages into space, and they'll have to spend trillions to counter it."

A phone rang, and Kordus answered it immediately—calls that came in to the Situation Room during meetings were always emergencies. He handed it over to Barbeau. "Barbeau . . . what's up,

Ben? . . . What? . . . Great Lord, what in God's name? . . . Okay, Ben, call the senior staff together right away. I'll be there shortly." She hung up the phone. "Islamabad has recalled its ambassador to Washington," she said to the president, "and the ISI has arrested twenty-seven Pakistanis who work at our embassy, accusing them of spying for the United States. Further, the warship visiting Karachi is being barred from leaving port until the ISI inspects it."

"Here it starts," the president said wearily. "Walter, get Mazar on the phone for me. Stacy Anne, you talk to the Pakistani foreign minister. Ask them to reconsider those orders, or at least change the order to 'return for consultations' or something less flammable than 'recall,' and ask them to release the embassy staff. They don't want to start a diplomatic squabble over an incident that everyone wants to keep hidden in the basement. We have pictures of those missiles and a full transcript of the launch and engagement—they wouldn't want us to release those videos." Barbeau hurried away to her office at the State Department. "Conrad . . ."

"I'll see what I can do about getting that ship released," the president's national security adviser said. "We probably gave every Pakistani naval officer and local government official a tour of that ship already—they shouldn't be demanding inspections."

The president nodded. "And I want to get briefed on contingency plans in case we're barred from Pakistani ports and airfields—how do we sustain Afghanistan operations if we can't bring in supplies through Pakistan." He ran a hand through his hair in exasperation. "I almost wish we let the Paks fire off another missile. Let's get busy."

THREE

> *You will soon break the bow if you*
> *keep it always stretched.*
>
> — PHAEDRUS

MINISTRY OF DEFENSE, BEIJING, PEOPLE'S REPUBLIC OF CHINA

DAYS LATER

The conference table in the office of the minister of defense of the People's Republic of China was strewn with black-and-white and color photographs attached to larger pieces of cardboard with descriptive notes around the edges. Nothing too terribly important-looking could be discerned in the pictures by themselves, but the minister of defense, Zung Chunxian, a sixty-one-year-old career bureaucrat with thin dark hair, thick glasses, and a thick waistline, stared at them as if he were looking at works of ancient Chinese art.

"Identification?" he asked the military officer before him as he lit a cigarette.

"We believe it was an unmanned reconnaissance vehicle, sir," General Hua Zhilun, commander of 11th Strategic Rocket Forces of the People's Liberation Army, replied. Young for a general officer at age fifty-three, Hua was lean, fit, and polished. He, too, wore spectacles, but he put them away as he addressed the minister. Hua was in charge of the newest division of the Strategic Rocket Forces based on Hainan Island: offensive long-range ballistic-missile forces with targets in space and at sea instead of land. "The sensor package has not yet been recovered, but I am confident that is what it is. Most certainly American."

"Where could it have come from?"

"Most unmanned aerial vehicles today have very long-range and loiter capability, and could have come from thousands of miles away," Hua replied, "but the shape of this one suggests it was submarine-launched. The Americans and British both employ UAVs that can be launched from submerged missile or torpedo tubes."

"Ingenious," Zung said. "But why use such a device over Hainan Island, when they certainly have satellites that can do a better job without fear of being shot down?"

"A satellite's orbit and position at any given time can be predicted with high accuracy, sir, which can give one time to hide something that one does not want to be photographed," Hua said. "Unmanned air vehicles such as this can pop up anywhere and anytime."

"So the attack missiles on Hainan Island have been discovered?"

"We must assume they have, sir," Hua said. "It is of little consequence."

"Why do you say that, General?"

"The deterrent effect of the Dong Feng-21 missiles is much greater than their actual demonstrated capabilities, sir."

"What do you mean?"

"To be quite honest, sir, the DF-21 antisatellite and antiship weapons are mostly for show as of yet," Hua explained.

The defense minister's eyes bulged with indignation. "*Zhe shi shen-me yi-si?* What did you say?"

"They are reliable and effective in their primary role as intermediate-range ballistic land-attack missiles, sir," Hua explained, "but they have hardly been tested in their new roles. We were able to successfully intercept one satellite in a carefully rehearsed exercise with an absolutely fine-tuned weapon, but it is quite another matter to deploy a cold-soaked missile that has been in a transporter tube in a corrosive marine environment for a long period of time and have it successfully launch, track, and hit its target, even if the target is not maneuvering or dispersing countermeasures."

"So why have we spent billions of yuan on them?" Zung asked incredulously. "Why would my predecessor agree to such a thing?"

"Because the Americans began deploying their Kingfisher antisatellite and antiballistic-missile weapons," Hua replied, "and honored Defense Minister Chi wanted to respond in kind and as quickly as possible. We could argue that the Americans have the same problem with their Kingfisher weapon containers—space is far more hostile than salt air or terrestrial weather—but they chose to deploy them as they continue to test and upgrade them, and China had to respond in like manner."

"So it is an empty force, a hollow threat, and a waste of money?" Zung asked.

"We really do not know for sure, sir, unless we test the systems more often," Hua said. "But for the kind of tests we require to fully validate the DF-21 system, we need to launch at real satellites from real installations, not merely at simulated targets or on the Lop Nor instrumented test ranges. That means launching targets into orbit. My budget requested twenty million yuan per month for the next fifteen months just to test the antisatellite and antiship versions of the DF-21. It was turned down because the increased test tempo would certainly alert and possibly alarm the Americans."

"I think that is not a consideration any longer, General, especially now that we know that Washington is stepping up deployment of those weapon satellites and being much more aggressive in surveillance," Minister Zung said. "It will take some time to resubmit your requested testing funds, but I think this time they will be approved." He paused for a moment, then said, "But are there other targets on which to test?"

"Other targets, sir?" Hua asked. He paused as well, then shook his head. "I know of no other suitable defunct or out-of-service satellites, sir," he replied, "except the weather satellite we plan to use for the upcoming sea-launched weapon test. We could possibly inquire of our allies or commercial operators to see if—"

"What about satellites that are not defunct or out of service," Zung asked, "and do not belong to our allies or ourselves?"

"Sir?" Hua was confused . . . but only for a moment. His eyes widened in surprise, and Zung thought he noticed the beginnings of a devilish smile on the corners of the young general's lips. "Sir, are you suggesting . . . ?"

"I am suggesting, General Hua," Zung said, stubbing out his cigarette, "that if an opportunity would present itself to conduct a *very* realistic test of our antiship and antisatellite weapons, and if you notified me in a timely manner, I am quite certain both the Central Military Commission and the Military Committee of the Party Central Committee will approve it. Do you understand me, General?"

200 MILES OFF THE COAST OF MOGADISHU, SOMALIA

SEVERAL DAYS LATER

"Pan-pan, pan-pan, pan-pan," the frantic marine radiotelephone message began on Channel 16 and 2182 kilohertz frequencies, "all stations, all stations, all stations, this is the freighter *Yutian,* People's Republic of China, two hundred three nautical miles east of Mogadishu, proceeding southwest toward Mumbasa, Kenya, at twelve knots. A small motor vessel is about three miles west of us and we can see men armed with automatic weapons and RPGs on board. We believe they are Somali pirates and they mean to board this vessel. Requesting immediate assistance from any nearby Combined Task Force warships. Over." The radio operator repeated the message, adding the freighter's geographical coordinates.

Seventy-six miles to the north, the People's Liberation Army Navy *Luyang*-class destroyer *Wuhan,* part of the multinational Combined Task Force-151 group of over thirty warships and dozens of aircraft from twenty-five nations, responded to the call by launching a Russian-made Kamov Ka-27 antisubmarine warfare helicopter. As part of the CTF-151 tasking, the Ka-27 had a chin-mounted sea radar and was armed with a smoke-rocket launcher on one hardpoint and a 7.62-millimeter machine gun on the other.

Nearly an hour later, the Ka-27 approached the freighter. The helicopter was manned by a pilot and copilot plus two Chinese marines acting as observers. "*Wuhan,* this is Patrol Unit Three," the pilot radioed, "we are approaching the *Yutian,* and we have the suspect vessel in sight. It is a ten-meter open-hull motor vessel with two armed persons aboard. There is a rope ladder on the *Yutian*'s port side midships at the low-ramp gunwale and the suspect vessel appears to be tied to the *Yutian*. Four suspects are holding about a dozen crewmembers at gunpoint near the bow. We are fifteen minutes until bingo fuel. Request instructions."

"Patrol Three, this is *Wuhan,* you are authorized to fire warning smoke at the suspect vessel," came the reply. "Remain well clear of hostile fire. We are dispatching another patrol helicopter and are under way toward your position."

"Acknowledged," the pilot responded. On intercom he said, "Prepare for smoke-rocket launches from the port launcher, crew." Flying about a half mile from the freighter, the pilot armed his weapon panel, pedal-turned slightly right, and pressed the red button atop his control stick three times, firing three forty-millimeter unguided rockets ahead of the freighter's track.

"*Wuhan,* this Patrol Three, I have fired three smoke rockets ahead of the freighter," the pilot radioed. "It was clearly observed by the suspects. The suspects on the boat are not moving. The suspects holding the hostages are waving their AK-47s at me. They—" He stopped his narration in shock when he saw one of the pirates, who appeared to be no more than a teenager, turn back to the hostages, lower his AK-47 to his hip, and fire, cutting down the first row of hostages. *"The pirates are killing hostages!"* he screamed on the radio. "They are murdering them!"

"Patrol Three, Patrol Three, remain clear of hostile fire!" the commander of the *Wuhan* radioed.

But the Ka-27 pilot couldn't hear him, or ignored him if he did. Instead, he pedal-turned to the right, moved in closer to the freighter, and squeezed the trigger on his control stick. The 7.62-millimeter machine gun on his starboard-side pylon chugged to life. The pilot carefully walked the bullet hits up the side of the freighter and across the deck, killing two of the pirates and scattering the others. *"Take that,* you murderous bastards!" the pilot shouted. "Take—"

"RPG! RPG!" the copilot shouted. *"Break left!"*

But it was far too late. A pirate aboard the smaller boat tied to the freighter had immediately raised a rocket-propelled grenade launcher, aimed, and fired, and from about a hundred yards away, he could not miss. The grenade round hit and exploded, and the Ka-27 burst into flames and dove straight down into the Indian Ocean.

OLD PORT DISTRICT, MOGADISHU, SOMALIA

LATE THAT NIGHT

The pirate mother ship, a thirty-meter oceangoing tugboat captured by pirates several months earlier, had returned at flank speed to its berth at the Old Port of Mogadishu, northeast of the new port facility and east of the slums of downtown Mogadishu, after the news came that the crew of one of their pirate ships had shot down the Chinese patrol helicopter. The port's old piers had not been rebuilt after years of disuse, but had been repaired enough to service the mother ship and its small fleet of pirate assault vessels, including enough roadways and security positions to allow refueling and rearming the vessels and their crews. It was the busiest the Old Port had been in many years. The crew didn't much care about how well they secured the ship—they tied it off, threw some pieces of corrugated tin and canvas on it to disguise it the best they could, then got away as fast as they could.

Old Port had been the location of several foreign embassies headquartered in the Somali capital, all now closed, when Mogadishu was one of the largest and busiest ports in all of East Africa. Now various warlords and pirate captains occupied the old embassy buildings as their headquarters. The buildings in the Old Port district had been rebuilt and fortified with the millions of dollars of ransom money paid by shipping and insurance companies around the world to have their vessels, crews, and cargo released by the pirates over the years. The nearby Abdiasis district, with its beautiful white-sand beaches, sports facilities, and tree-lined neighborhoods, had been taken over by the pirate captains and the warlords who controlled them, creating a security buffer between themselves, the teeming squalor of the city, and the continuing civil war that kept the government nonexistent, the entire country lawless and fractured, and the economy in shambles for almost a decade. But if a visitor was transported to the area and saw only Old Port and Abdiasis, he might conclude that Mogadishu was an up-and-coming city striving for greatness.

A meeting of the mother ship's captain, six of their boarding crew-boat captains, and the local warlord was called to discuss the downing of the Chinese patrol helicopter. In the former French embassy building, across the street from the Abdul Rahman Mosque and a large madrassa, they watched news coverage of the incident on satellite TV, but there was not much yet. Discussions centered around where to move the base of operations—it was a given that the Chinese, or someone who belonged to the Combined Task Force antipiracy group, would respond.

Unknown to the Somali pirates, the Chinese response was already under way. An unmanned patrol aircraft that had been launched to assist the Kamov patrol helicopters had been diverted when the mother ship was observed fleeing the area, and the UAV followed it back to the Old Port. It was easy to spot exactly where the mother-ship crew went after disembarking, and the crew of the *Wuhan* watched as the meeting of the band of pirates commenced. The *Wuhan* had been moving toward shore, and in ten hours was now within range.

As soon as the meeting started, the captain of the *Wuhan* ordered the attack to begin, and the ship fired four C-802L cruise missiles toward the Old Port. The C-802s were reverse-engineered French Exocet antiship missiles, modified and improved for land-attack missions with greater range and speed, a larger five-hundred-pound high-explosive warhead, and a GPS satellite navigation system with an infrared terminal guidance seeker. In five minutes, the missiles crossed the remaining distance between the *Wuhan* and shore and destroyed the old French embassy and the Abdul Rahman Mosque, a suspected pirate haven.

The Kremlin, Moscow,
Russian Federation

A short time later

"Premier Zhou, this is President Truznyev calling," Igor Truznyev, the president of the Russian Federation, said on the secure telephone connection to Beijing. The former head of the Federal Security Bureau, the new name of the defunct *Komitet Gosudarstvennoy Bezopasnosti,* or KGB, Truznyev at age sixty-eight was much older than most of his recent predecessors, but was in excellent health and took great care of his body and mind. Tall, loud-voiced, and imposing, with a mane of thick silver hair, thick bushy eyebrows, and thick legs, Truznyev often walked the streets of cities, towns, villages, factories, and farms throughout Russia even in the worst weather, greeting citizens with a hearty handshake, accompanied by an impressively small and remarkably inconspicuous security detail.

Truznyev was unabashedly "old school" and a fierce nationalist, strongly believing that Russia had to be governed by a strong central government willing to do whatever it took to run the vast country and secure its mostly indefensible borders. Most Russians embraced the very same ideals and voted overwhelmingly for him, securing his second term with 82 percent of the popular vote—even without his networks of internal security officers squelching all signs of dissent or opposition anywhere in the country, Truznyev would have won the election by an overwhelming majority.

"Good evening to you, sir," Truznyev went on; then, without waiting for a response, he continued, "What in bloody hell do you think you're up to in Somalia?"

"Good evening to you as well, Mr. President," Chinese premier Zhou Qiang replied in Russian, without the need of a translator.

"It is exactly as you perceive, sir: a punitive action against Somali murderers. The people of China are tired of their killing and hijackings, and they demanded retribution against those that ordered the slaughter of our sailors."

"A simple phone call before the attack was in order, sir," Truznyev said. "We are fellow members of the antipiracy task force, and we have sailors in those waters. An accident or misidentification would have been most unfortunate."

"Your sailors were in no danger, Mr. President," Zhou said. "Our naval forces may not be the equal of Russia, but they know how to distinguish a pirate ship from a warship."

"Meaning no disrespect to the skill and determination of your sailors, Premier, but a call or message would have been welcome. After the attack on your freighter and helicopter, nerves are on a knife's edge out there."

"My apologies, Mr. President," Zhou said. "Perhaps you are correct: A message to our friends and allies in the area would have been wise. But these days it is hard to accurately determine who are China's allies or friends."

"Russia is certainly no enemy of China, Premier," Truznyev said. "Our foreign ministers and embassies have long discussed the many ways our countries should be working together. We should be putting ideology aside and joining forces for our mutual benefit and support." He paused for a moment; then: "I trust you did not notify the Americans of your attack on Mogadishu ahead of time?"

"Washington would have been the *last* capital I would have notified," Zhou spat. "If I had done so, I would not have been surprised if the letch Joseph Gardner would have notified a dozen neighboring nations, told us to warn the citizenry so as to minimize innocent casualties, and had television cameras on hand to document the attack. And all that would be *after* trying to talk us out of attacking."

"Their history in Somalia has certainly not been pleasant," Truznyev said. "I am happy to hear that we have similar attitudes about Washington and Joseph Gardner."

"I think our interests have been drawing closer and closer in recent years," Zhou said, "especially since the return of Kevin Martindale and the establishment of the American military outpost in space."

"I wholeheartedly agree, Premier," Truznyev said. "The Armstrong Space Station is a dangerous, destabilizing monstrosity, especially since the addition of their weapon satellites. They claim they are defensive in nature, but that is obviously not so, as they have recently demonstrated in Pakistan. The entire world is their target now."

"China will never stand by and become a target of American weapons, from the sea, from space, or anywhere else on the planet," Zhou said, his Russian momentarily becoming strained and garbled as he grew more and more irritated. "China's rights will be respected."

"As well they should, Premier," Truznyev said. "Russia is not sitting idly by while the Americans deploy their weapon satellites."

"Oh? What is Russia doing about them?"

"Just because they are hundreds of kilometers in space does not mean they are invulnerable to attack," Truznyev said. "While you build more and more antisatellite missiles, our scientists and computer engineers are discovering other, subtler ways to disrupt them."

"You must share these ways with China, Mr. President."

"Perhaps so, if they prove to be effective," Truznyev said. "So. What more of poor Somalia?"

"When we finish pounding the pirates' hideouts into the sand, we will return home."

"Oh? They will only return, perhaps with revenge on their minds," Truznyev said. He waited a few heartbeats to hear if

Zhou would or would not remain adamant; when he did not, Truznyev went on: "The Americans have a massive base in Djibouti from which they control the entire southern access to the Suez Canal. They once claimed it was a forward operating base for antipiracy operations. Do you think *they* would depart once you destroy the Somali pirates?"

"What of it? The Americans would not dare restrict access to the Canal or anywhere else."

"Probably not, but they *could* do so, and that alone is troubling enough for me," the Russian president said. "When Russia had access to ports in Yemen and Egypt, we tied up a great many American warships just from our presence. America wanted a ten-to-one ratio of warships in the Gulf of Aden, Red Sea, and Indian Ocean. It was fun just to watch the hapless Americans driving these huge convoys of massive warships around like chickens with their heads cut off just because we sailed a tiny frigate through the area."

"But they *did* build the ships, and they fill every ocean with them. What of it, Mr. Truznyev?"

"We will talk more of it at a later time, Premier," Truznyev said. "But allow me to make a prediction: Once China gets a taste of foreign adventure, it will be hard to stop. Russia once sailed vast fleets and squadrons of bombers all around the world. We stopped after the Soviet Union collapsed and the oligarchs robbed our country blind, and our country lost its pride and hope for the future.

"But when we took control of our government and our resources and resumed showing the flag, even though in vastly smaller numbers, the world sat up and took notice once again, and the Russian people regained hope for the future. We are not yet a superpower again as we once were, but no longer does the United States disregard our rights and wishes.

"China has always had the reputation for isolation, for staying within its own borders, for closing its ports and its very society when the pressures of the outside world create social and economic stress," Truznyev said. "You have changed that dynamic tonight, Premier. I suggest you observe the reaction of the world and decide if China might try another direction."

"What direction, sir?"

"The opposite of isolation: engagement," Truznyev said. "China's armies outnumber the next three nations' armies *combined*. That should be enough to cause any nation, even the United States, to tremble. I am not saying go to war, but make the adversary think you are not contemplating isolation any longer. If you dare take your rightful place, you will find a willing ally in Russia, Premier."

U.S. Africa Command Headquarters, Bole International Airport, Ethiopia

A short time later

"We just moved this headquarters here from Germany, Mr. Carlyle," complained U.S. Army General Thomas Greene, commander of U.S. Africa Command, one of the newest unified commands in the U.S. military. Greene, a short, rather heavyset, square-headed, and powerfully built black man in his early fifties, was sweating profusely underneath a full set of ACUs, or Army Combat Uniform. "Nothing is working right, half of my staff is still in Stuttgart and hasn't arrived yet, and you can fry an egg on the roof of my Humvee. So to answer your question, sir: No, I have not been briefed on the incident in Mogadishu yet."

"Well, what *can* you tell us about the situation out there, General?" the president's national security adviser asked from his office in the West Wing of the White House.

"Not much regarding the attack last night, sir," Greene replied. "I get a briefing on the Combined Task Force antipiracy operation every day, and I meet with the task-force commander and senior officers at Camp Lemonier in Djibouti every two to three weeks depending on how active things get."

"What about the Chinese, General?" Carlyle asked impatiently.

"The Chinese have five ships as part of the task force—the destroyer *Wuhan* is definitely one of them, along with another destroyer, a frigate, and two supply ships," Greene said. "They operate mostly out of Aden, Yemen. Two warships are on patrol at a time, with a replacement coming in every two weeks to relieve one of them; the supply ships rotate with each other every week. Every four months another group of five ships comes in, they do a little drill package together for a couple days, and they're back at it again. They keep up a pretty good ops tempo. I've met the Chinese commander in charge—he seems like a regular guy."

"You had no indication they were going to attack Mogadishu, General?"

"None at all, sir," Greene replied. "The Chinese keep a very low profile. As far as I know, they haven't been in Somalia and have had only one or two other run-ins with Somali pirates over the years. I don't think they've visited Djibouti or been briefed by the Joint Task Force–Horn of Africa, and I don't know about any other East African nations."

"You said they were based out of Yemen? Why not Djibouti, with the rest of the task force?"

"The Chinese seem to prefer to stay by themselves and not get crowded in with a lot of other foreign vessels," Greene said. "I'm told they don't really like the Yemenis, and vice versa, but it's a convenient port for resupply—the Chinese can't sustain blue-water ops as well as most Western navies can, so they want a pretty short supply line. Yemen works for them, and of course the Yemenis will be most happy to take China's cash for fuel, food, and other goods."

"So what are the Chinese up to now, General?" Carlyle asked.

"Back to business as usual, sir," Greene replied. "We've just received word that they've got a big convoy of three container vessels and one or two Ro-Ros heading for Tanzania next week, so they're setting up for that."

"'Ro-Ros'?"

"Roll-On, Roll-Off ships—you just drive vehicles in one end and drive them off at destination out the other end," Greene explained. "They'll take a dozen tractor trailers loaded with goods on one ship. Pretty impressive. The Chinese prefer to escort their own ships through the region; they say it keeps up morale. That's fine with us. Most skippers prefer to see their own flags surrounding them."

"Okay, General Greene," Carlyle said. "We're hoping things will calm down now that the Chinese have spanked the pirates pretty badly. Thank you for the update, and let us know if you get any more info."

He hung up before Greene could say "yes, sir," and the general dropped the phone back on its cradle. "Jeez, where did *that* come from?" he muttered to his command sergeant major, Frank Nauert, who was in charge of the secure communications facilities along with all of his other duties. "Hasn't he ever heard of chain of command?"

"That strike must've really spooked the White House, sir," Nauert said.

"I'd definitely say so," Greene said. "I just wished it was *us* who kicked Somali ass, not the Chinese."

"Roger that, sir."

"Well, if the White House is calling me directly, we need to have more info for them the *next* time they call," Greene said. "Teleconference the staff together and build me a situation-and-force status report. Quick as you can."

"Roger that, sir," Nauert said, reaching for the phone. But just before he picked it up, it buzzed with the distinct encryption ring of a secure call. Nauert picked up the receiver, heard the unlock tones, read the unlock routine code on the phone's display, looked up his reply code, and punched it in. "Nauert, U.S. AFRICOM, secure, go ahead, over," he said when the encryption routine was authenticated and locked in.

"Raydon, Air Force Space Defense Force, secure," Kai Raydon responded. "How are you, Sergeant Major?"

"Who is this, sir?"

"Brigadier General Raydon, aboard Armstrong Space Station. I have a couple questions for your traffic management officer if he has a moment."

"Absolutely, sir," Nauert said. "We haven't stood up this head-quarters quite yet, so I'm the TMO today and for the foreseeable future." Even though Nauert was a dedicated veteran infantry soldier, he had always been fascinated by space technology, especially these days when it seemed to be advancing in vast leaps and bounds—he definitely saw himself as one of those Robert Heinlein "Starship Troopers," dropping from orbit in delivery capsules to fight on planet Earth. He saw Greene's quizzical expression and nodded assuredly. "What can I do for you?"

"We have been tracking a large convoy of Chinese cargo vessels heading your way," Kai said. "I assume you're familiar with the convoy?"

"Yes, sir, the Chinese Ministry of Trade gave the Combined Task Force their manifest and transit plan as requested. Destination Dar es Salaam, Tanzania; part of a twice-annual aid shipment to its friends and allies in Africa. Pretty standard convoy."

"But the port call in Karachi was delayed a week?"

"Yes, sir, I believe that's correct."

"Any reason given?"

"Not that I'm aware, sir," Nauert said. "Could be any number of reasons. We usually don't get concerned about delays unless it affects the flow of traffic going through the Suez Canal or ports in East Africa—we don't want too many ships anchoring wait for passage or berths because that complicates our patrol activities—or if traffic transiting our ops area increases to the point where we can't provide enough security. In wintertime, traffic is usually less, so delays usually don't create bottlenecks."

"I see."

"Why do you ask, sir?"

"No particular reason, Sergeant Major," Kai said. "We collect a lot of data up here, mountains of it every hour, so in order to help sift through it, we look for trends and anomalies. If we see a broken sailing plan, we look for obvious reasons like weather, accidents, or civil disturbances, and if we don't see any obvious reasons, we start asking around."

"Sorry we don't have that info for you, sir," Nauert said. "I'll pass your concerns to Stuttgart and they'll take a look and report back. You may have to contact them directly for the latest info until we're fully set up here."

"Thanks, Sergeant Major, I will. If we see anything else from up here, we'll pass it along. How do you like Ethiopia so far?"

"Nice place, good facilities, decent weather, friendly locals—a lot different than Afghanistan or Camp Lemonier. And how are things in space, sir?"

"Pretty routine, like being in a submarine, I guess, looking for trouble and hoping like hell you don't find any," Kai said. "Anytime you'd like to take a trip up here to look around, we'd love to have you stop by for a visit."

"That's definitely on my 'bucket list,' sir," Nauert said. "Anything else I can do for you, sir?"

"Not right now. Nice to talk to you, Sergeant Major."

"Same here, sir. AFRICOM clear."

"That was the space-station guy?" Greene asked after Nauert terminated the call.

"Yes, sir. BG Raydon himself, asking about that convoy of Chinese ships headed our way."

"What about it?"

"They were delayed for about a week in Pakistan. Raydon wanted to know why."

"Shit, *he's* the reason why the Pakistanis don't tell us stuff anymore," Greene complained. "If he hadn't blasted that Pak village all to hell with his space weapon, we'd still be on speaking terms. The Paks aren't going to tell us nothin' about anyone's ship movements until we get back on friendlier terms."

"I'll drop an e-mail to TMO at Stuttgart and ask the question."

"Do that, but I'll guarantee we won't get an answer back from the Paks," Greene said. "If the powers that be really want to know, they'll probably have to send in the CIA to find out." He sniffed derisively and shook his head. "Raydon and the Air Force think their space station and fancy space radars are so cool, but we'll still use plain old-fashioned grunt work—some local in sandals and a turban, getting paid a couple bucks for info and maybe a photo or two—to get the *real* dope."

ARMSTRONG SPACE STATION

THAT SAME TIME

"I would sure love to have a look inside those ships," Kai Raydon said as he closed the secure telephone connection. "I have a bad feeling about those things."

"Can't the Coast Guard just pull them over and inspect them?" Boomer Noble asked. "I know the Coast Guard does that all the time, everywhere in the world."

"Pretty low odds of a Chinese ship in international waters voluntarily agreeing to an inspection, Boomer," Senior Master Sergeant Valerie "Seeker" Lukas said. "Unless there's a Memorandum of Understanding between a nation and the Coast Guard, it's up to the ship's owner or captain to allow an inspection, and the Chinese aren't likely to allow it."

Kai checked the chronometers at his computer console to get the local time in Washington—it was early, but he knew that most career bureaucrats liked to get to work early. "It'd be worth a phone call to the State Department," he said. Seeker nodded and got to work on her communications console.

"What do you think is in those ships, General?" Boomer asked.

"Another DF-21 emplacement, bound for Tanzania or Zaire—anywhere that has strong mutual defense and cooperation treaties with China," Kai replied.

"With nukes?"

"Nuclear warheads can be detected without boarding a vessel," Kai said, "but medium-range missiles like the DF-21 are allowed. If they wanted to put nuclear warheads on the DF-21s, they'd probably fly them in separately."

"State Department is on the line, sir: Assistant Secretary of State Carlson, China desk, not secure," Seeker said.

Kai hit a button on his console and readjusted his microphone. "Secretary Carlson? This is General Raydon from Armstrong Space Station, unsecure."

"You're on the space station right now, General?" Carlson asked, her voice quickly changing from young but very official to almost childlike. "Are you kidding?"

"Not kidding, Miss Carlson."

"Call me Debbie, General, please." Kai thought she was on the verge of a giggle. "Sorry we couldn't do a secure videoconference, but I don't know how to work the phone and my assistant's not in yet. How can I help you today? The senior master sergeant said something about inspecting Chinese ships for medium-range missiles?"

"That's right, Debbie. And please call me Kai."

"Okay, Kai." Her voice quickly switched back to official but friendly. "Here's the deal: China routinely allows us to inspect vessels bound for U.S. ports, and that's pretty much it without authority from Beijing, which takes about as long as it takes to sail a ship around the world. China doesn't even allow inspections of its ships in times of distress, which means the Coast Guard won't board a Chinese ship in distress unless the captain authorizes it, which in most cases he won't. And just for clarification? That's true for U.S.-flagged ships on government business, too."

"I didn't know that."

"No one wants to have foreign inspectors poking around on ships carrying sensitive or classified materials—that's pretty standard," Carlson said. "Most nations would rather have such a ship go down rather than have foreigners, even rescuers, board it and discover their secrets.

"Now, you mentioned missiles. That's covered under a voluntary protocol called the Missile Technology Control Regime, which was set up to try to prevent the proliferation of ballistic missiles and unmanned vehicles around the world. Unfortunately, China is not a signatory to MTCR, although they have several times agreed to abide by its principles. Also, MTCR doesn't automatically allow foreigners to inspect suspect vessels—that's still up to the captain, the ship's owner, or a legal authority representative of the ship's flag."

"In other words, Debbie: If China doesn't want us to inspect those ships, they're not going to get inspected," Kai summarized.

"That's pretty much it, General . . . I mean, Kai," Carlson said. "Again, it's pretty standard all over the world—it's no different than what we do. Ships on the high seas have always had a special 'hands-off' designation—don't mess with them until they come into your home waters or you observe them doing something illegal.

"Now, China is a signatory to the Nuclear Non-Proliferation Treaty, which bars countries from distributing nuclear weapons and materials or to induce nonnuclear weapon states from acquiring them," Carlson went on. "If you *knew* that those missiles were nuclear, and China was transporting those missiles to a nonnuclear weapon state, *and* you could convince the International Atomic Energy Agency of this, they could request an inspection of the ship. Not impossible, but extremely unlikely of China cooperating, unless you had a Polaroid of the nukes being unloaded in a nonnuclear weapon state."

"The ships are bound for Tanzania."

"China does a lot of business in sub-Saharan Africa, especially the business of buying oil fields and farms to import energy and food," Carlson explained. "They bring in a lot of manufactured goods in return. Nothing out of the ordinary yet. Tell me, Kai: What's going on with these ships?"

"We've been monitoring several new Chinese antisatellite and antiship missile sites being constructed all over the world," Kai explained, "and I think this convoy is carrying another one. Obviously such a site puts us in danger, and I'd like to find out if that's what we're looking at here."

"Perfectly understandable," Carlson said. "Unfortunately, all we can really do is watch those ships and watch when they start off-loading cargo to see what they're carrying."

"What if they were going to transit the Suez Canal? Can you ask Egypt to search the ships?"

"The Constantinople Convention guarantees free access to the Suez Canal to all ships of all nations, even nations at war with Egypt," Carlson said. "The Suez Canal Authority, which operates the canal, has the right to inspect all vessels using the Canal, but only for specific purposes and in specific locations—the inspections are usually limited to paperwork checks of logbooks, manifests, and crew documents, unless there's a request by Interpol. Over twenty-one thousand vessels use the Canal every year, and the SCA just doesn't have the manpower to inspect the holds and spaces of every one. It would take an army of inspectors an entire year to inspect a U.S. aircraft carrier going through the Canal, even if we ever allowed it."

"I'm impressed by your breadth of knowledge about this stuff, Debbie."

"Not as impressed as I am talking to a guy in a space station orbiting the Earth, Kai," Carlson said. "I'm a bureaucrat in a little office in Washington—you're hundreds of miles above Earth floating in space."

"Anytime you'd like to come up and check it out, Debbie, you're welcome."

"Are you *serious*?" The schoolgirl voice was back big-time.

"You don't need to be a NASA-trained astronaut to travel in space these days—just be healthy enough to withstand the trip up here, and be patient until a seat opens up on a spaceplane."

"How healthy is that, exactly?"

"Do you like roller coasters?"

"Sure."

"Think you can ride one for ten minutes?"

"Ten minutes?"

"It's not that much pressure, but it's on you for a long time," Kai said. "There's a lot of noise and shaking, but it's not too bad. And it's both positive and negative—you have to put up with the deceleration part, too, for ten minutes during reentry, like when a Metro train is pulling into a station."

"Doesn't sound like that much fun anymore."

"It's worth it once you get up here. You can't beat the view, that's for sure."

"I'll think about it, Kai," Carlson said. "You've got me very intrigued."

"Good. We'd love to have you. And about those Chinese ships . . . ?"

There was a slight pause; then: "Wellll . . . I can ask around and see if any of my contacts have trusted persons in Dar es Salaam that can give us some firsthand information on what's in those ships when they start to unload. No guarantees."

"That sounds fine, Debbie. Thank you."

"You can really get me a ride up to the space station, Kai?"

"Clear it with your boss, get me an e-mail from your doctor saying you're in good health, promise your family won't sue me or the U.S. government if you burn up on reentry, and we'll set it up."

"I can't believe it!"

"Believe it. Space travel is not just for jocks anymore. We'd love to have you."

"I can't wait! Thank you! Thank you!" And with squeals of joy still audible, she hung up.

Seeker looked at her boss with extreme skepticism. "You're giving joyrides and tours of the station now, sir?" she asked.

"To tell the truth, Seeker, I offer folks rides up here all the time," Kai admitted. "But I always hit them with the 'burn up on reentry' line. I figure if they're still excited after hearing *that,* they're ready to fly in space, but I haven't had any takers yet. Miss Carlson might be the first."

"Are we going to charge admission?"

"No," Kai responded with a laugh, "but if you make up T-shirts and coffee mugs, I give you permission to sell them. How's that?" Kai's console beeped an urgent message alert, and he called it up immediately, read it—and flushed in surprise. "Seeker, you are *not* going to believe this," he muttered, with a curse added in for good measure. "Get the sensors set up right away—this should be one hell of a show."

FOUR

*Many of our fears are tissue-paper-thin, and a single
courageous step would carry us clear through them.*

—Brendan Francis Behan

In the South China Sea,
South of Hainan Island,
People's Republic of China

The next day

The U.S. Navy had only one vessel within twenty miles of the
hastily announced launch point, the USS *Milius,* an *Arleigh Burke–*
class destroyer—and it had to run at flank speed to get as close as
possible to the launch vicinity—but it had a ringside seat for a spectacular show from the Chinese navy.

Four warships, including China's aircraft carrier *Zhenyuan,* and
an intelligence-gathering vessel, a *Dalang*-class submarine tender
that had also been modified for electronic eavesdropping duties,
were on hand, surrounding a three-mile-diameter circle of open
ocean. A tall buoy marked the center of the protected area. Three

Z-8 Jingdezhen heavy patrol helicopters from Hainan Island cir-
cled a ten-mile radius of the area, using their French-made ORB-
32 Heracles-II radars to search for unauthorized ships or submarine
periscopes peeking over the surface.

At the announced time, two of the ships in the cordon blew
horns and whistles, which continued for about thirty seconds . . .
until a geyser of water erupted from a spot about a quarter mile
from the buoy in the protected zone, and moments later a missile
burst through the column of water and ignited its first-stage solid
rocket booster. The missile was a Julang-1S sea-launched ballistic
missile, the first-generation sea-launched missile modeled from the
Dong Feng-21 land-based mobile ballistic missile. It had just been
launched from a *Xia*-class ballistic-missile submarine submerged at
a depth of 150 feet and traveling at three nautical miles per hour. A
slug of compressed gas pushed the missile out of its launch tube
and surrounded the missile in a protective cocoon as it shot toward
the surface. The force of the gas pushed the missile about thirty
feet out of the water, when the missile's first stage fired.

But this was not a land-attack ballistic-missile experiment. The
JL-1 did not adopt a ballistic flight path, but instead continued almost straight up, punching through the atmosphere at several
thousand miles per hour. Five minutes after blasting through the
surface of the South China Sea, the JL-1 flew into the path of a
Chinese Fengyun FY-1D weather satellite, orbiting 320 miles above
Earth, and destroyed it with a high-explosive cloud of shrapnel.

OFFICE OF THE SECRETARY OF DEFENSE, THE PENTAGON, WASHINGTON, D.C.

A SHORT TIME LATER

"They scored a bull's-eye, sir," Kai Raydon said on the secure video teleconference link, "and put us square in their crosshairs at the same time."

"Let's not be so dramatic here, General Raydon," Secretary of Defense Miller Turner said. With him in his office was the secretary of the Air Force, Sal Banderas; Ann Page, undersecretary of the Air Force for space; and Chairman of the Joint Chiefs of Staff General Taylor Bain. Also in on the teleconference was Admiral Sherman Huddy, commander of U.S. Strategic Command, from his temporary command center at Battle Mountain Air Force Base in Nevada; and General Robert Wiehl, commander of U.S. Space Command, from his headquarters at Peterson Air Force Base in Colorado, along with several analysts and advisers from around the world. "Every Chinese missile test isn't a direct threat to us."

"Sir, it was an antisatellite missile launched from a *submerged submarine,*" Ann Page said. "The DF-21s were a big enough threat, but at least we could see where they were placed and target them, even the mobile units. The sub-launched ones can be anywhere. The land-based missiles have a range of about fifteen to nineteen hundred miles, but in antisatellite mode the sub can be positioned within a thousand miles of a satellite's path and be able to hit it in almost any orbital inclination. It's a radical new capability that poses a direct threat not only to Armstrong, but to all American space assets."

"All right, Secretary Page, you made your point," Turner said, holding up a hand. "But let's get some perspective here, shall we? First of all: Do we know it was a direct hit?"

"As far as we can measure, sir," General Wiehl replied. "It's possible they could have faked the hit. But the satellite they destroyed was a weather satellite that we've been tracking for many years."

"We have some pretty clear electro-optical pictures of the engagement—it looks like a direct hit to us, sir," Kai chimed in.

"Let's say it was a direct hit," Turner said. "In that case: good show. But let's put this in some perspective, shall we? We were similarly surprised when the Chinese shot down their other weather satellite back in 2007, but this is the first ASAT test since then, am I correct?"

"Yes, sir," Wiehl replied.

"So two successful ASAT tests in five years? Not exactly a grave threat to national security, I'd say. Next: The Chinese have how many subs capable of launching a JL-1 missile?"

"Eight, sir," Admiral Huddy replied after checking his notes, "with two more nuclear-powered boomers in the works. But there are only four *Xia*-class subs active now—the other four *Jin*-class subs are designed to carry the larger JL-2 missiles for intercontinental ballistic-missile duties."

"So you're saying just four subs capable of launching ASATs?" Turner asked. "How many missiles per sub?"

"Twelve, sir."

"And normally only two subs are at sea at a time? That's true for us, right, so it must be true for the Chinese?"

"Yes, sir. They could surge them in times of crisis, as we would, but half on patrol and half in training, predeployment workup, or maintenance is typical."

"So we're down to two subs on duty with a max of twenty-four ASATs. It doesn't sound like much of a threat to me, ladies and gentlemen."

"Combined with the land-based antisatellite missiles, I'd say it was a very serious threat, especially in a coordinated attack against Armstrong, sir," Kai said. "They would salvo their ASATs to try to overwhelm our defenses, dilute the number of interceptors we could use for antiballistic-missile defense, and put us on the defensive to prevent us from employing ground-attack weapons."

"And if they load up their subs with antisatellite missiles they have fewer land- or ship-attack weapons to use against someone else," Turner said. "The president warned about an arms race, folks, and it looks like it's happening right before our eyes. We spooked the Chinese by firing antiballistic-missile and ground-attack weapons from space, and now they're scrambling to make up for lost ground."

"The good news is, they're forced to compromise other plans and programs to do so," General Bain said.

"Only until they ramp up production and build more subs and missiles, sir," Kai said.

"Which they certainly will," Ann Page interjected. "So I believe it's imperative to start ramping up our own space programs, such as deploying the remaining interceptor garages quicker and completing the network integration of Space Defense Force with the other services, the Pentagon, and the intelligence services. We know now that if we do nothing, the Chinese are very capable of quickly fielding a potent enough mix of weapons to seriously threaten our foothold in space. We need to deploy the remaining twenty-four garages as soon as possible. With the right funding, we can—"

"You're talking money that's not in the budget now and is not expected to be in the budget for the next three to seven years, Ann," Turner said. "We're spending billions to launch things into space that cost the Chinese only a few million to kill. That kind of fuzzy math is not going to solve the problem." He turned away from Ann to the chairman of the Joint Chiefs. "General, what's the conclusion of the Chiefs? Is this a real threat against our space assets, a warning message, or a successful demonstration that isn't a real threat to us?"

"The Chiefs had the same questions you did about the numbers of ballistic-missile-capable subs in the Chinese fleet and the number of ASAT tests over the years, sir," General Bain replied, "and they have concluded that the test was indeed very impressive, but the threat to Armstrong Space Station or any other assets would be minimal.

"True, the Chinese have deployed many of these ground-based mobile antisatellite emplacements in recent months," he went on, "and the submarine-launched ASAT is a much greater threat because it would be harder to target ahead of time." He looked at Ann Page, nodded, and spread his hands. "And frankly, I'm not *on* Armstrong, looking down the barrel of all those guns pointed at me. But the United States has declared that attacking any space assets would be treated the same as attacking sovereign American soil or a U.S.-flagged ship at sea, and the Chiefs don't believe China wants to attack anyone.

"The bottom line is this, sir: China has deployed an awful lot of these ASAT sites in direct proportion to our deployment of these interceptor garages in space," Bain concluded. "Those garages are there not to *start* a fight, but to respond in case a fight breaks out. We feel the same is true for the ASAT sites. Further, China is deploying these weapons with way below the bare minimum of testing. We looked at the same info: Two tests in five years, although successful, do not normally signal a green light to widely deploy these systems. China is doing this in response to our actions, whether or not the weapons are truly effective. They are trying to show they can't be bullied or intimidated."

"But we're *not* trying to bully or intimidate anyone here," Turner said, "so China is setting up these antisatellite weapons for nothing. It's a waste of their time and money."

"But what if China *does* have another agenda?" Ann Page asked. "We're not opposing China—we want their investments and cheap goods. But what if China has other plans that we *might* oppose? Could they take away our advantage in space if we don't respond to this escalation?"

"That's a policy hypothetical that doesn't concern us right now, Dr. Page," Turner said. "This meeting was called to explore whether this recent development constituted a credible and imminent threat to national security that needed to be addressed right away by the White House. The answer seems to be no. Am I correct in that, ladies and gentlemen?"

"I think it remains to be seen, sir," Ann said.

"As General Bain said, Secretary Turner: We're looking down the barrels of a lot of guns all of a sudden," Kai said. "The only defense against a bolt-from-the-blue antisatellite attack is with defensive weapons, and right now our defenses are borderline. We couldn't survive a direct concentrated attack without a full-up constellation of interceptor garages and a fully responsive and integrated defense data network, based from up here. China could have the capability to shoot down this station at a time and place of their choosing, and our chances of surviving an attack is low right now without more support."

"Message received and understood, General Raydon," Turner said. "Thank you for your input. Thank you, everyone." And the connection went dead.

"Well?" President Joseph Gardner asked impatiently on the secure phone line from the Oval Office, just a few moments from the conclusion of the videoconference at the Pentagon. With him were Vice President Kenneth Phoenix, Chief of Staff Walter Kordus, National Security Adviser Conrad Carlyle, and Secretary of State Stacy Anne Barbeau. "What's the word?"

"As you surmised, sir: The Air Force and the space nuts are all freaked out, but the Joint Chiefs don't think it's a big deal that China tested this sub-launched antisatellite missile," Miller Turner said. "The Joint Chiefs say it was a successful demo of an antisatellite system that's not likely to be used except to show the world that China doesn't like current U.S. space policy. They may continue to deploy more antisatellite weapons and submarines, but are unlikely to ever use them. Space Defense Force thinks they can defend themselves against all but a concentrated, dedicated assault, which everyone agrees is very unlikely."

"But of course Page and Raydon want more, right?"

"Of course. Like you said, they want to accelerate deployment of more interceptor garages and set up the fully integrated space defense network—with *them* in full control, of course."

"Apparently we haven't made it clear enough to them that it's not going to happen: The Space Defense Force is pure fiction, and it's not going to get one single dime more than what's budgeted right now to keep their stuff operating at current levels," Gardner said. "Thank you for getting that meeting put together so quickly, Miller. I'll be talking with Stacy about what our diplomatic response should be, but I'm encouraged by the fact that China gave the world a heads-up before testing that weapon, even if it was a pretty short one. I think once the saber-rattling dies down, we'll be able to work with the Chinese to ratchet the tension down. Thanks again."

"Yes, Mr. President," Turner said, signing off.

The president nodded and set the receiver on its hook. "It's as we figured: The Chiefs say the missile launch was a successful test of a new capability, but it doesn't represent a significant threat because it's immature technology and the Chinese have so few subs capable of launching the missiles," he summarized for the others in the Oval Office with him. "Not a cause for undue concern. Thoughts?"

"I still disagree, sir," Phoenix said. "We have a trillion-dollar investment in Armstrong Space Station and the other components of the Space Defense Force network. Testing that sub-launched antisatellite weapon was a direct threat to all of it. We have to respond by finishing the interceptor garages and completing integration of the space-sensor network with the rest of the military, and we have to do it quickly before China gains an advantage by fielding more of those antisatellite missiles."

"It would take an emergency funding bill costing hundreds of billions of dollars, Mr. Vice President," Carlyle said. "I don't think we have the votes in Congress, and I'm *positive* we don't have the money."

"I believe strongly enough in the program that I'm willing to lead the effort to get as many representatives to support it as possible, Mr. President," Phoenix said. "I know a group of lawmakers who would draft a bill, and I can get a number of industry groups and contractors together to explain exactly what the completed system would give us. Just say the word."

"Maybe after the elections, Ken," Gardner said flatly.

"We should act as quickly as we can, sir—"

"I think it's important not to overreact to this test, Mr. Vice President," Barbeau interjected when she saw Gardner's warning glare. "I've spoken with the premier and civilian military leadership of China, and they've all assured me that China views space as it does the high seas: It should be free for peaceful and cooperative exploitation by all nations." She turned to the president. "The Chinese say current U.S. policy toward space makes it difficult for them to back away from deploying antisatellite weapons, sir." She saw a hint of confusion in the president's face, so she explained: "Our stated policy is that travel, access, and development of space is considered a vital national imperative and we'll defend it like our own soil and shores." The confused look vanished, replaced by one of worry. "Our policies don't mesh."

"So you're suggesting we change *our* policy because China doesn't like it?" Phoenix asked. "Since when does China tell us what to say or do?"

"I'm not suggesting we change our policy because China said so, Mr. Vice President," Barbeau said testily. "I'm saying that in my opinion the sticking point with the Chinese and other nations is that our policy states America is claiming the right to space and will go to war to protect that right. China and other space-faring states want a guarantee of free access for all. If they don't get that assurance, their only response is to build and field weapons that can at least threaten our systems."

"If they want an arms race, we should give it to them," Phoenix said. "That's how President Reagan took down the Soviet Union and ended the Cold War: He forced the Soviets to invest more and more in weapons until their economy finally collapsed. China may have a red-hot economy now, but if they're forced into a space arms race with us, we can bankrupt them just as easily as the Soviets. We should—"

"All right, Ken, all right," President Gardner interjected. "My main objective here is to keep the dialogue open between Washington and Beijing, and it's been strained by the accidental attack on the *Bush* and the situation in Pakistan—"

"And their deployment of these ASAT bases and submarines," Phoenix cut in.

"I said hold on, Ken." The president paused reflectively, then went on: "As you all know, as SECNAV, I disagreed with President Martindale's executive order about U.S. space policy—I didn't think it was necessary to, in effect, plant a flag in space and dare other nations to try to knock it down. As SECDEF and president following the American Holocaust, I didn't want to reverse any policy decisions that might make us look weak in the eyes of the world.

"But that horrible event was eight years ago now. We may still be weaker than we were before the Russian attacks, but I believe we're leaner and meaner, and it's time we take a leadership position in the world again rather than sit in a corner, lick our wounds, and glare at the rest of the world with suspicion. And I'm not going to play that Cold War game of building more and more weapons because the other side fields some new weapon."

He turned to Secretary of State Barbeau: "Stacy, you may communicate with the Chinese foreign ministers and tell them that I am forming a policy review panel to examine the U.S. National Space Policy executive order. Our purpose of the study will be to rewrite the order to make it clear to the world that the United States wants nothing more than free access to space by all nations, and that we will do nothing to jeopardize that. We want a policy that makes the deployment of antisatellite weapons, either in space or on the ground, unnecessary and detrimental to world peace and security."

"Sir, you're not suggesting we *give up* Armstrong Space Station and its defensive weapons . . . ?"

"I think the antiballistic-missile interceptors are valuable for national security and for the protection of friends and allies," the president said, "and I think any military unit or base should have a means of defending itself, and that includes Armstrong. Plus, all of the Earth and space imaging, reconnaissance, surveillance, and communications stuff is absolutely essential.

"But I'm willing to reconsider the notion of putting land-attack and antisatellite weapons into orbit, or at least drastically decreasing how many are in use so we don't create an arms race in space. If we can get countries like China and Russia to agree on limiting deployment of antisatellite weapons, we can show the rest of the world that disarmament and cooperation is possible."

"I agree with that idea, Mr. President," Secretary of State Barbeau said. She glanced at Vice President Phoenix furtively, then added, "In fact, I think it would have that much more impact if you made it a unilateral decision: The United States will as soon as possible remove all antisatellite weapons from service, including those in Earth orbit and from ships at sea, and we call on all other nations to follow suit in the name of peace, security, and freedom of the use of outer space." She glanced again at Phoenix long enough to see his shocked expression, then said, "I'm sure the Chinese and Russians will enthusiastically receive that proclamation, and then we can proceed with a formal arms-reduction treaty that will seek to eliminate all space weapons."

"Why in the world do you think any nation would give up its antisatellite weapons and enter into a treaty banning such weapons if the United States unilaterally gives them up *first,* Madam Secretary?" Phoenix asked, obviously fighting to keep his emotions in check. "China is furiously setting up antisatellite missile launchers all around the world because we're so far ahead of them on space-based weapon technology. If we give those up, they have a chance to catch up. They could have years of development time before any formal treaty is signed and ratified and a verification regime put in place."

"I'm spinning ideas here, Mr. Vice President, that's all," Barbeau said gaily, waving a hand at Phoenix dismissively. "As always, the devil is in the details, of course. But isn't it easy enough to load those containers or garages or whatever you call them up again with missiles in case a fight breaks out?"

"I don't think it's easy at all, Madam Secretary," Phoenix said. "It means using rockets or spaceplanes to lift them back into orbit, and astronauts doing space walks to load them into their launchers. Shipborne antisatellite missiles may be easier to redeploy, but it still takes a ship several days or even weeks to return to port for—"

"Well, as I said, Mr. Vice President, it's all in the details, of course," Barbeau interjected, "but I really don't see any stumbling points to prevent this from being accomplished over time, do you, sir?" Phoenix only stared at her. She smiled back. "Neither do I. After all, we do it with nuclear weapons, nuclear laboratories, and strategic weapon systems every day."

"Yes, but—"

"I'm sure the Chinese and Russians realize that removing the antisatellite weapons from the garages already in orbit will take some time and effort, a lot more than it would take from the land-

or sub-based launchers," Barbeau went on, "but we would commit ourselves to do it, and also to setting up a verification system on all sides to be sure it's being accomplished to everyone's satisfaction." She looked at Phoenix, gave him another smile, then looked at the president. "Perhaps you would consider naming the vice president to chair the review panel concerning the National Space Policy, Mr. President?"

"Excellent idea, Stacy," President Gardner said, looking carefully at Phoenix with a thin smile. "Although he has committed to being out on the campaign trail a lot more often, I don't think the review panel would take up too much more of his time, and he does like to keep up on the latest technology. What do you say, Ken? Interested?"

"I think there are many better-qualified folks to take on this task, Mr. President, like Conrad or Miller," Phoenix responded after a brief but clearly uncomfortable pause. But then he nodded and said, "But I'd be happy to do it for you, Mr. President."

"I know you wanted to lead a commission to get congressional support for the Space Defense Force stuff, Ken," the president said, "but I don't think the two run at odds with each other—in fact, I think they could be complementary: You want the force brought up to speed as quickly as possible, but you also want to demonstrate America's willingness to cooperate with the world community on eliminating the offensive use of space. Sounds like a win-win to me. What do you say?"

It was obvious Phoenix knew he was being railroaded, but he still nodded enthusiastically. "I'm your guy, Mr. President. Thanks for trusting me to do the job."

"Very good," the president said. "Progress reports regularly, get together with Walter to get your board members cleared and seated. Stacy, you can tell the Chinese that the vice president himself will chair the policy review board. Ask that it be kept confidential for now—that'll guarantee it'll be leaked right away."

OFFICE OF THE MINISTER OF
NATIONAL DEFENSE, BEIJING,
PEOPLE'S REPUBLIC OF CHINA

DAYS LATER

"Welcome, welcome, General," Chinese National Defense Minister Zung Chunxian said as General Hua Zhilun entered his office and bowed respectfully. The minister of defense extended his hand, and Hua shook it. "You've had a most impressive week I see. Come in and tell me about the test."

"*Xie-xie,* Minister," Hua said. Zung showed him to a seat as an assistant brought tea and served it for both of them. "I am very proud of my operations staff and the crew of Submarine 483. They executed the test perfectly. I wish to nominate Captain Han and his crew for a distinguished service award. The submarine's position had to be precise and the launch perfectly timed, and the crew performed well."

"It shall be done, General," Zung said. "The submarine was under way when the missile was launched, I understand?"

"Yes, sir, at about ten knots. For optimal results, the submarine had to launch when inside a five-kilometer area at a certain time— almost no margin for error was permitted. In operational use, the timing is not as critical, but we wanted the best possible conditions for this demonstration."

"The Central Military Commission and the president are pleased, General," Zung went on. "Foreign Affairs Minister Tang tells me that he has received word that the Americans were so surprised—and intimidated, I should think—by the test that they are forming a panel to review their space policy, including a global reduction or ban on antisatellite weapons. What do you think of that?"

Hua looked a little surprised and disappointed. "Ban all antisatellite weapons? That would put us even further behind the Americans in research and development. Is the president considering it?"

"Of course not, General," Zung said, waving a hand dismissively. "But if the Americans want to do it, we would not discourage them. If we did sign such a treaty, we would continue research and development and prepare to deploy the weapons in the case of any hostilities." Hua looked relieved. "No, General, the commission was very pleased with the test, and they are taking a very hard look at expanding space and counter-space-weapon technology. Nothing China has done in recent years has riveted the attention of the Americans as much as that launch."

"That is good to hear, sir."

"In fact, the president advises me that our other proposal has been approved by the commission," Zung said. "They want risk-reduction operations to be accelerated so they can request additional funds to expand the antisatellite program before negotiations begin to shut them down. Did you bring the data I requested?"

"Yes, sir," Hua said, opening his briefcase and extracting a single piece of paper. "The Americans have thirteen Kingfisher weapon satellites in orbit—about half to a fourth of the proposed constellation, we do not know precisely. All but four are fully operational, based on data transmissions we intercept. One satellite makes almost no transmissions, although it appears to be responding to positioning commands. We believe this one's weapon functions have malfunctioned and were shut down. The Americans will probably send an astronaut from the Armstrong Space Station to attempt repairs soon."

"That sounds like a good candidate, General," Zung said. "Will it be in position soon?"

"The timing could not be better, sir," Hua said. "In five days the American satellite will be within range of our newest DF-21 installation in Taunggyi, Myanmar. That base has the most up-to-date version of the tracking and guidance software, and an improved missile and rocket motor. The launch window will be open for three hours once a day for approximately three days, and then will close for several days again before reopening, so we have a little leeway in case of other unforeseen complications."

"Excellent," Zung said. "Operation *Shan-dian* begins in six days. We will coordinate your operation to coincide with it. Hopefully the Americans will be too distracted by *Shan-dian* to pay attention to your test."

"We will be ready, sir," Hua said.

"Will the Americans detect the launch from Myanmar?"

"Yes, sir, most assuredly," Hua said. "The Americans have two very good launch-detection systems: the Defense Support Program satellites, or DSP, and their replacement, the Space Based Infrared System, or SBIRS, satellites. SBIR has two components, high and low. DSP and SBIRS-High are designed to detect rocket launches almost everywhere on the planet with great precision and have a modest tracking capability. SBIRS-Low is designed to accurately track rockets and even fast-moving aircraft in flight, predict impact areas, and cue other space, sea-based, or land-based antimissile systems. Fortunately, SBIRS-Low is not fully deployed, so the chance of the Americans tracking a missile with it are extremely low."

"I do not understand most of what you just said, General," Zung said, rising to his feet and smiling, "but I trust the Americans will eventually determine that it was one of ours. The president and foreign minister must have an acceptable explanation ready for them. But we are hoping that Operation *Shan-dian* will distract them enough. Have your forces ready for the final execution order, and good luck."

ARMSTRONG SPACE STATION

SEVERAL DAYS LATER

Kai Raydon was on his last mile of his twice-daily thirty-minute exercise routine in the daily-room module, which was a combination galley, entertainment center, gymnasium, and computer and crew communications room. He was strapped to an exercise bicycle, which used electric magnets to simulate resistance while pedaling, while at the same time he pushed and pulled on a rowing-style machine that also created resistance for upper-body toning. A vacuum vent above him sucked loose droplets of sweat into the station's recycling system.

A crewmember from the day shift was waiting his turn to use the machine. "You're hitting that thing pretty hard this morning, sir," he commented.

"I'm scheduled to return to Earth in a few days for re-acc," Kai said. "Re-acc," or reacclimation, was required of all astronauts who performed long-term tours in space. It consisted of four weeks of rest, along with several medical exams to document any changes in the body resulting from long periods of zero-g such as loss of bone density, muscle deterioration, reduced lung capacity, or radiation exposure. "I'm determined to knock the docs on their butts in surprise."

"Go get 'em, sir."

Kai wore a pair of monitor glasses that allowed him to privately watch and listen to television while he exercised, and he usually watched American, British, and Asian news channels. It seemed the news was all about China these days—but, not surprisingly, there was nothing about the sub-launched antisatellite-missile test. China seemed to be on a public-relations and foreign-affairs blitz, especially in the United Nations General Assembly. Trade, energy,

military concerns, economic development, peace initiatives—
whatever the focus, China had a representative discussing it and
investing huge sums of money in improving whatever they thought
needed improving. Chinese money and Chinese projects were
springing up everywhere, especially in the Middle East, South
America, Africa, and even Russia, along with its traditional spheres
of influence in Asia.

It was certainly not the traditional China, no longer isolated and
low-key; and yet, Kai thought, it was still the same in many ways:
China was still secretive, still inscrutable. Even though the news
seemed to be "all China, all the time," no one had any idea of any
of the fundamental questions about China: What were their strategic goals? Who were their allies? In what direction did they want
to go?

When Kai finished his routine and chalked up his scores on
the exercise equipment for others to try to beat, he showered
in the vacuum shower, put on a clean flight suit, and floated back
into the command module. He found Hunter Noble at Valerie
"Seeker" Lukas's console, flipping through various sensor downloads. "What are you doing here?" he asked. "Aren't you flying
in a couple minutes?"

"Postponed," Boomer replied. He hit a few keys and pulled up a
live video feed of the New Mexico Spaceport at Roswell, New
Mexico. "Major snowstorm at the primary landing site. They
might move it somewhere else, so I'm waiting for word." He looked
at Raydon. "What are *you* doing up?"

"Couldn't sleep."

Boomer looked at Kai's fingers, which always seemed to be
twitching or tapping or fiddling with something—did this guy
ever sleep? he asked himself. He must be a bundle of raw nervous
energy. "Even with all this circadian-rhythm nonsense going on in
here?" Boomer commented. He waved his hand around the command module. The lights had been dimmed because it was "night-

time," the same as Washington, D.C. "Whose idea was it to create a daytime and nighttime on a space station anyway?"

"They've done numerous studies on crew performance in long-duration jobs like submarines as well as space travel," Kai said, "and they all agree that humans need to keep a circadian rhythm— there has to be a day and night, and it has to be the proper seasonal length, or humans start to mentally malfunction."

"Sounds like bull to me."

"Try it sometime—when you're on leave and not flying my spaceplanes."

"I do it all the time," Boomer said. "I play cards at night in Vegas because the dealers and pit bosses on the graveyard shift are usually less experienced. I can play, fly, and work whenever."

"Cardplayer, huh?" Kai realized that he had been working off and on with Hunter Noble for the better part of four years, and he knew very little about the guy. "Are you any good?"

"I probably would make a decent living playing poker if I kept at it," Boomer said. "It's a numbers game, and I'm pretty good at numbers. My problem is, I can't concentrate on cards too long. I see a pretty girl or start turning over an engineering problem in my head, and I get distracted. Not a good thing for the bottom line. You like cards, General?"

"I don't even *know* any card games."

"What do you like? Craps? Slots? Horses?"

"I think I've gambled a grand total of five hundred bucks in my entire lifetime, mostly pro football and basketball office pools," Kai admitted. "And Vegas is just too intense. It's just a huge waste of electricity if you ask me."

"So what do you do for fun?"

"I keep a little fishing boat in Long Beach, cruise up and down the coast, sometimes to Mexico, scare some fish every now and then. If I go to Nevada, I'd rather go out into the mountains with a backpack and camera and do some photo-hunting."

"Photo-hunting? You hunt for photos?"

"Real funny. No, I bring back photos of wild game centered in crosshairs, critters I *would've* bagged if I had a gun. I have photos on my wall instead of animal heads."

"Why don't you use a gun? And why bother hunting if you're not going to kill anything?"

"I've been hunting since I was fourteen," Kai said. "I used to go out with my grandfather and uncles a couple times a season—pheasant and deer mostly. But I remember trudging back to the camper one cold snowy weekend without seeing one bird, and one of my uncles was so frustrated that he put the muzzle of his shotgun up to a little bird sitting on a fence and pulled the trigger. That little bird disappeared in a puff of feathers. Never killed another animal after seeing that."

"How very PETA-friendly of you, General," Boomer said.

"But I missed being out in the wide open, especially after becoming an astronaut, so I decided to use a camera instead of a gun."

"Sounds weird. But the boat sounds nice."

"Haven't been on it in a while."

"Married? Kids?"

"Divorced. The ex tolerated the Air Force, disliked Houston and NASA politics, and hated the boat. Three strikes and she was out. No kids."

"Any lady friends?"

Kai glanced at Boomer, obviously not comfortable talking about himself or about subjects like this. Perhaps, he thought, Noble was just realizing the same as he was a moment ago: They'd worked very closely together for years but knew very little about each other. Despite his discomfort, he resigned himself to answering anyway: "Plenty of ladies . . . no friends."

"Copy that."

The two fell silent for several moments; then Kai asked, "So did Seeker show you how to use her console?"

"Yeah. I peek into a few places now and then—the Strip, my condo complex, Hainan Island. The Chinese are sure acting restless, like they feel the need to show they won't be pushed around, especially by us."

"Agreed." Kai punched in instructions into his console and studied the responses. "Hmm . . . no recent reports on the Chinese convoy heading to Tanzania." He punched in more instructions. "They should be off the coast of Kenya by now, a couple hundred miles north of Mombasa. Let's get an updated image . . ." Now the info he was getting made him look worried. "No recent reconnaissance patrol sightings? Do they have weather problems out there, too?"

He motioned for Boomer to switch seats with him so he could use Seeker's console, then called up positions of all the reconnaissance satellites available in his system. "Twenty-six minutes to a TacSat-3 overflight; there's a NOSS satellite in the area, but the Navy hasn't let us get access to its data yet." NOSS, or Naval Ocean Surveillance System, was a satellite that could locate ships at sea by collecting and tracking radio signals. "Now, why can't we get any manned or unmanned recce photos?" In a separate window he made several queries for status information . . . and his jaw dropped in surprise. "Datalinks inactive off the southern coast of Somalia—no one's been able to make radio or satellite contact in the past two hours."

"Sunspots?"

"Might be, but I think solar-flare activity was supposed to be normal this week," Kai said. He punched in still more instructions. "I'm getting stuff from the Gulf of Aden and Djibouti, but the Combined Task Force reports nothing from patrols in the Indian Ocean, with occasional outages and unreliable datalinks, so UAV overflights were postponed."

"The eccentricities of electromagnetic propagation, no doubt."

"The what?"

"Something a buddy once told me. His explanation of the unexplainable."

"Whatever the hell it is, I don't believe in it," Kai said. "We'll have to wait for the TacSat overflight."

It was a long twenty-six minutes. Kai was so concerned about the alarm bells ringing in his head that he called several members of the day shift into the command module, including Seeker. He quickly filled her in as she checked her sensors and computers for any sign of malfunction. "All our equipment is fine, sir," she reported. "We're picking up UAV imagery from the Gulf of Aden, but nothing farther south. That's not right."

"Any contact from that Chinese convoy of ships heading to Tanzania?"

"No, sir," she replied after checking the CTF status messages, "but the rest of the Combined Task Force is staying away from that convoy because the Chinese have all three of their ships and a couple planes guarding it—in fact, there are *five* Chinese ships in the area right now because they were in the process of patrol changeover. There are two destroyers, two frigates, and a supply ship escorting that convoy."

"Pretty good timing—all that firepower arriving exactly when the convoy did."

"It could explain the week delay in Pakistan," Seeker offered. "Wait a week and get twice as many escorts."

"Maybe. But I hate guessing and assuming." He had to wait another two minutes until the TacSat-3 flew over where they expected the Chinese convoy to be. "Put in a call to the CTF-HOA operations center and ask them to—"

"Look!" Seeker exclaimed. The TacSat-3 hadn't reached the proper viewing area off the coast of Kenya yet, but it didn't need to . . . because the eleven-ship Chinese convoy was about forty miles off the coast of Mogadishu, Somalia! "That looks like the Chinese cargo-ship convoy! What are they doing so close to Mogadishu? They couldn't *all* have been hijacked!"

"I'm no Marine, but if I didn't know better, I'd say that was an amphibious invasion," Kai said. "Get Camp Lemonier on the line, fast!"

"Nauert, AFRICOM, secure," the NCOIC of AFRICOM responded after Seeker made the secure connection.

"Raydon, Space Defense Force, secure. Sergeant Major, are you getting reports from off the coast of Mogadishu?"

"We've had reported UAV datalink disruptions, so overflights in that area are grounded for now, sir," the NCOIC of U.S. Africa Command in Ethiopia replied. "We've got several task-force ships and patrol aircraft in the area, but they've reported ops-normal for the past couple hours. We were going to launch a patrol plane to cover the area until we figured out what's going on, but the Chinese say they'll handle it. Why?"

"Are the task-force ships and aircraft in that area all Chinese?"

"Affirmative. What's going on, General?"

"We just downloaded a TacSat-3 image of the area," Kai explained. "TacSat is a small purpose-built satellite, launched just a couple days ago to help surveil the East Africa region. It operates on a discreet datalink frequency—you can't get the imagery until we're networked together." He thought for a moment, then added, "And the Chinese might not have known about it, since it was launched recently and they don't have access to it, so they couldn't have had a chance to jam its datalink."

"I'm not following you, sir."

"Sergeant Major, we've detected eleven Chinese ships, including four warships, less than forty-five miles from Mogadishu, heading west at eleven knots. It looks like the Chinese convoy and the task-force ships guarding it are all heading straight for Mogadishu."

Kai was very surprised at the sergeant major's rather muted reaction—he said simply, "Please stand by, sir," and the line went dead. "Alert Space Command and Air Force," Kai said, "and put out a general warning to all MAJCOM headquarters in the clear, reporting a line of warships off the coast of Mogadishu heading west."

A few moments later, General Thomas Greene, commander of U.S. Africa Command, came on the line himself. "Greene, AFRI-COM, secure," he said breathlessly, as if he had run a very long distance to answer the phone. "Raydon?"

"Raydon, Space Defense Force—"

"I don't give a damn who you are!" Greene thundered. "Did you tell my sergeant major there was a convoy of Chinese warships heading for Mogadishu?"

"Affirmative, sir. I just put out a warning to Space Command and—"

"Who the hell do you think you are spouting off with that nonsense?" Greene cried. "I'm looking at the CTF reconnaissance reports, and there's nothing out there! You'd better goddamned explain yourself, and quick!"

"Sir, you have no reconnaissance reports from the area because all of the patrol planes were grounded due to radio interference and poor datalink," Kai explained. "The only other CTF vessels out there are Chinese, and they're reporting ops-normal—because they are engineering this whole diversion."

"What diversion?"

"Whatever the Chinese are up to, sir, they've managed to blank out all reconnaissance in the area, turn the convoy west, and are closing on Mogadishu," Kai said.

"If there's this big blackout like you said, how can *you* see it?"

"We used a small tactical satellite launched just days ago, which operates differently from other reconnaissance assets," Kai said. "I think the Chinese didn't know about it, or couldn't do anything about it if they did. We just spotted the convoy minutes ago."

"I want to see those pictures, *now*!"

"I'm going to have to route them to you through Space Command, since you're not on our network. That'll take a bit—"

"'Not on your network'? What in hell does *that* mean?"

"It means my higher headquarters has to give you the pictures—I can't do it directly," Kai said. "But until then, may I suggest you get some eyes up there to verify this sighting, sir. If the Chinese are still jamming all transmissions in the area, they may have to—"

"I don't need your suggestions, Raydon!" Greene shouted. "I want those pictures, and I want them *now*! And don't be blabbing about this contact to anyone except your bosses until I get it confirmed! That's an *order*!" And the connection went dead.

OFFICE OF THE PREMIER, BEIJING, CHINA

THAT SAME TIME

"You asked me to notify you when China is about to act," Premier Zhou Qiang spoke.

"This Operation Lightning you messaged us about earlier?" asked Russia president Igor Truznyev, speaking on the secure direct "hotline" between each president's office.

"Yes. It is under way. We have another mission under way as well. A clever officer in our Strategic Defense Forces corps calls it Operation *Zu-qiu*—Operation Soccer, what the Americans call 'football.' "

"May I inquire as to what you intend to do with this Operation Soccer?"

"You will learn more soon, Mr. President," Zhou said. "But I will tell you this: We shall see how the Americans take a kick."

"Very clever."

"We anticipate that Operation Lightning will be on station for seven days," Zhou said, "after which time they will cycle in to Aden for refueling and replenishment."

"We will be ready."

"Very well. It is nice to be working with Russia again, Mr. President."

"I would feel better about our new relationship if you would give me more details about this Operation Soccer," Truznyev said.

"It is merely another attempt to dissuade President Gardner from expanding this space-weapon constellation," Zhou said. "You will detect more shortly. Oh, and Mr. President?"

"Yes?"

"Please disregard any launch warnings coming from central Myanmar. Classify it as a petroleum plant explosion and fire." He terminated the connection, then dialed another number on a different secure phone. "Minister Zung, you may give the order to proceed with Operation *Zu-qiu*."

FIVE

Your dream is not big enough if it doesn't scare you.

—Matthias Schmelz

11th Strategic Defense Forces Operations Center, Hainan Island, China

A short time later

General Hua Zhilun picked up the phone himself. "Operations."

"Are your forces ready, General?" Minister of National Defense Zung asked.

"Yes, sir, we are ready."

"Status of the target?"

"The launch window is open for another eighty-seven minutes, sir," Hua replied. "No change in orbital path."

"Operation *Shan-dian* is under way," Zung said. "Based on radio traffic, we believe the convoy has been discovered, but the attacks are already under way. You are authorized to proceed with Operation *Zu-qiu*. Good hunting, General."

"Yes, sir, thank you," Hua responded. He hung up the phone, then put on a headset and keyed a button at his console: "All stations, this is *Yi,* authorization received, operation will commence immediately, repeat, authorization received, commence operation."

Eight hundred miles west of Hainan Island in the nation of Myanmar, also known as Burma, a petroleum-gas storage tank located outside a refinery near the city of Taunggyi suddenly exploded, creating a massive fireball that ignited several other tanks and pipes and eventually became so hot that some trees in the nearby hardwood forest began to sway from waves of heat washing across them. Pipes containing pressurized petroleum gas with open check valves continued to feed fuel to the inferno.

At the very same time, three miles away, a rocket shot from an upraised launch tube, flew on a cushion of compressed gas for a dozen yards, then ignited its solid-fuel motor and streaked into the sky, heading almost straight up. Compared to the hot glow of the petroleum-gas fire, the DF-21's motor exhaust plume was a tiny dot, and because the rocket continued to climb straight up, it did not create a very long streak in the sky when viewed from above. The first stage burned out within three minutes, and the second stage accelerated the rocket to ten times the speed of sound. A protective nose cap prevented any heat damage to the sensitive seeker in the nose as it rose through the atmosphere.

At Mach 10 and an altitude of 150 miles, the second stage burned out and the payload section began its hypersonic unpowered cruise, following its inertial guidance commands with refinements provided by datalinked steering commands from a Chinese radar site in Myanmar. The payload section continued its climb to 400 miles altitude.

Soon, the chase would be on.

ARMSTRONG SPACE STATION

THAT SAME MOMENT

"Nuts to that, General Greene," Kai said half aloud after he broke the connection to AFRICOM. "Seeker . . . ?"

"A warning has gone out to Space Command and U.S. Strategic Command with all the pics, sir," Seeker said, "and a general alert has gone out via secure instant message to all major commands' ops centers on our list, including AFRICOM. The alert reports detection of a convoy of Chinese ships apparently bound for Mogadishu, Somalia, escorted by four Chinese warships, detected by TacSat-3 but not backed up by any other electronic or visual data."

"Good enough for now," Kai said. "How's our sensor coverage of the area around that convoy?"

"Stand by, sir." Seeker entered numerous requests into her console; then: "Averages only eleven minutes per hour, sir. High of eighteen minutes. Look angles are no better than nominal."

"That's better than anyone else, but still pretty poor," Kai said. "Weapon-status report?"

"Stand by." A few moments later: "Self-defense interceptors on all garages and Armstrong are all reporting green except for Kingfisher-Eight, which is reporting a launcher continuity failure," Seeker said. "ABM interceptors are reporting in the green except for Eight and Four, whose ABMs were downloaded for routine maintenance. All Mjollnirs are reporting in the green on Kingfishers Two, Four, Six, and Ten, still down on Eight until we can restore continuity. That'll take an EVA."

"I want Eight back up and running right away," Kai said. "Boomer . . ."

"My Stud can be ready to go in one hour once I swap out the payload, General," Boomer said.

"Seeker . . . ?"

"I'm getting it now, sir," Seeker said, again typing furiously on her console. This took a bit longer than the other calculations, but soon: "If we can position in thirty minutes, we can rendezvous with the fuel load already on the Black Stallion. It'll take three orbits in the transfer to catch up with Kingfisher-Eight. If we miss it, it'll take another twenty hours to get into position from Armstrong."

"Boomer . . . ?"

"We can leave the payload in the bay, suit up, and do an EVA from the Stud's cockpit," Boomer said. "As long as the tech can fit his tools in the cockpit, we can do it. He might have to strap them on his lap."

"Get on it. I'll have a tech meet you in the locker room."

"On the way." Boomer detached himself from his anchor position and propelled himself toward the spaceplane service module.

"Seeker . . ."

"Already got Lieutenant McCallum on his way to spaceplane servicing, sir." A moment later: "Sir, SBIRS reports a large thermal event in south-central Myanmar."

"Any tracking data yet?"

"None, sir. Signature is still very hot and not moving. Could be a ground fire."

"Any launch sites nearby?"

"The only known ones are considerably farther south: a Chinese antiship site at Henzada and Mergui, and a suspected Chinese antisatellite site under construction north of Rangoon."

"They could have built a new site and we haven't spotted it," Kai said. "Let's report it to STRATCOM and SPACECOM, keep an eye on it ourselves, and start surveillance of that area for any signs of new construction." He thought for a moment. A little voice in his head reminded him that he did not believe in coincidences—but Myanmar and Somalia . . . ? "Are we going to pass over that area soon, Seeker?"

"Negative, sir, not for another . . ." She entered commands into the computer, then: " . . . fourteen hours."

Kai nodded, but something was still nagging at him. "Still no track data on that event?"

"None, sir. Still large and stationary. Looks like an industrial fire—it's just as hot as it was when it was first detected."

"Did SBIRS-Low pick anything up?"

"No SBIRS-Low spacecraft are in range."

"How about our sensors?"

"The closest one is Eight, and it's shut down. Six will be in range in four hours."

"Let's get some good images of that area when Six flies by," Kai said. The little voice in his head was still bugging him, but preparing to launch the Black Stallion spaceplane, get his fleet of satellites as fully operational as possible, and be prepared to participate in whatever response the United States was going to make to the unexpected Chinese move in Somalia occupied his mind for the time being.

When Boomer arrived at the spaceplane servicing module, Air Force spacecraft technician First Lieutenant Jeffrey McCallum was already there. He was donning a Compact Moonsuit–style space suit, specially designed for working during space walks with added micrometeorite and radiation protection but compact enough to allow him to squeeze into the Black Stallion's rather tight cockpit. He was already on an oxygen mask, prebreathing pure oxygen to begin flushing nitrogen out of his system in preparation for working in space—although the entire space station was set on a lower atmospheric pressure to help purge nitrogen from the system, for safety's sake all astronauts preparing to do an EVA were required to prebreathe oxygen before suiting up.

"How you doing there, McCallum?" Boomer asked. McCallum gave him a thumbs-up and a muffled "Good, Boomer" as he continued to suit up.

Since Boomer wasn't planning to do a space walk, his suit was of totally different design. While prebreathing oxygen, he donned a suit of thick elastic material, resembling a full-body leotard, with wires leading to a small control device. The material covered his entire body except for his head. When he nodded to the tech that he was ready, the tech flipped a switch. Fine computer-controlled elastomeric filaments in the suit contracted, compressing the material. Boomer let out a little grunt as the material pulled skintight.

Boomer's suit, called an Electronic Elastomeric Activity Suit, or EEAS (which most wearers say resembles the sound they make when the filaments tighten up), was a simple but very effective alternative to a heavy, bulky pressurized space suit. Humans can actually survive in the vacuum of space, because the skin and vascular system is already pressure-tight—as long as the human has oxygen at the right pressure, no space suit is really needed. But in a vacuum, human tissue expands because the absence of air pressure causes gases in the tissues to painfully expand, like a balloon in an airliner. So a way was needed to keep pressure on the body to prevent the tissues from expanding.

Most space suits, like McCallum's, used a compressor to pressurize the breathing oxygen inside the suit to keep pressure on the entire body. A skintight rubber suit would work, but it was almost impossible to don such a suit in zero-g, and any folds in the suit would cause muscle deformation. So the EEAS was developed to allow the suit to be easily donned and then re-formed so it became skintight. The electronic control system would keep pressure on the entire body even when moving but allow the limbs to move as necessary. For spaceplane pilots, the EEAS was a great alternative to bulky pressurized suits because it was easier to move around in, easier to manipulate controls, and didn't require a tech to help strap the pilot into the cockpit.

With the EEAS on and tight, Boomer put on a special flight suit that had a locking collar for his helmet, and continued prebreathing pure oxygen. The space-suit technician then helped him into the standard flight vest, which contained pouches for survival equipment such as portable lights, carbon-dioxide scrubbers, location beacons, backup batteries, a knife, and a suit-repair kit, along with a control panel on his left wrist that showed oxygen saturation, carbon-dioxide levels, suit power, backup battery level, and EEAS control status. "How do you hear, Jeff?" he spoke into the intercom.

"Loud and clear, Boomer," came the reply. "Good flying with you again."

"Same here." Boomer was amazed at how young these new guys were—McCallum looked as if he was twelve going on nine years old. "They brief you on what's happening?"

"I was prepared to go out to Eight later on this week to fix the continuity problem. I don't know why it's been pushed up."

"We might need it soonest." He took a moment to explain the Chinese convoy headed for Somalia. "They explain the toolbox issue?"

"If I can't do it with a soft-pack, it's got more serious problems than I suspect," McCallum said. A "soft-pack" was a standard EVA toolbag, with an assortment of zero-g wrenches, screwdrivers, testers, and other commonly used tools suited for working in space, plus room for replacement circuit boards, fuses, circuit breakers, software keys, and other system-specific necessities. "But I've got a bunch of circuit boards and components to fix fifty percent of the problems. Anything else will require a cargo run."

"Very good," Boomer said. "I'll plan on staying with the Stud, but if you need me I can hop on over. Just say the word."

"I should be okay," McCallum said, "and I'd feel better if you stayed near the plane anyway."

"I hear that." They continued to go over details about the flight while they finished dressing, and then made their way to the air lock to board the spaceplane.

The S-9 Black Stallion, nicknamed the "Stud," was the smaller of America's two models of single-stage-to-orbit spaceplanes. It was never designed for extravehicular activities or even docking with a space station, so there was no way (unless a passenger module and transfer tunnel were loaded in the cargo bay—this Stud was still loaded with cargo) to get from the station to the ship when it was docked except by spacewalking to the two separate tandem cockpit hatches and clambering inside.

Boomer stepped over to the air-lock inner hatch, but the docking technician stopped him. "My watch says five more minutes for prebreathing, minimum, sir."

"My clock says I'm good to go."

"Give it five more minutes, sir."

"Time's a-wastin', Chuck," Boomer said. "China is stirring up the shit Earthside, and we need that garage back online." He could see the technician hesitate. "It's just a couple minutes shy, Chuck, and you know there's always a safety factor built into the calculations. Let's go." Reluctantly, the technician nodded and floated aside.

While McCallum waited outside—safety dictated only one crewmember could use the air lock at a time, although it could fit two—Boomer entered the air lock. While it was depressurizing, the technician extended a fabric tunnel from the air lock to the spaceplane, which was docked outside on the station's docking beam. When the air lock was ready, Boomer undogged the outer hatch, stepped into the transfer tunnel, and closed and locked the hatch behind him. "Outer air-lock door closed, ready to equalize," he reported.

"Roger. Air lock pressurizing," the technician reported.

"I wish we didn't have to use the tunnel," Boomer radioed. "I've made the jump to the spaceplane lots of times."

"Not everyone is a lean mean space-faring fool like you, Boomer," McCallum radioed back. "Besides, I don't want to go out and retrieve you in case you missed."

Boomer used handholds to effortlessly pull himself the twenty feet from the air lock to the Black Stallion's cockpit. At the end of the transfer tunnel on the side of the Stud, he could see Earth spinning below him, and he resisted the urge to sightsee—he didn't have the time to waste. "C'mon over, Jeff," Boomer said. "I'll have the aft cockpit ready by the time you get here."

"On the way, Boomer," McCallum said.

After attaching his safety line, Boomer used a lever inside a protective door on the outside of the fuselage to motor open the front cockpit canopy, reached inside, then used a switch underneath the left front cockpit sill to motor open the rear cockpit. He then went back and arranged seat straps and umbilicals. By the time he finished arranging the aft cockpit, McCallum was at the end of the transfer tunnel. "Okay, Jeff, nice and easy, just like we practiced," Boomer said as he attached McCallum's safety line to himself, then plugged his oxygen and communications lines into the Stud's rear cockpit.

"There is just no graceful way to do this, Boomer," McCallum complained.

"Just do it slowly and deliberately and you'll minimize bumps and rebounds," Boomer said.

The easiest way to get inside the cockpit and seated was the "jackknife" method. As McCallum floated above the cockpit, Boomer steered his boots inside the cockpit. As McCallum eased inside, he jackknifed his body to squeeze between the upper instrument panel and open canopy. This always resulted in bumps as the space suit hit off one surface, against another, then back and forth until the astronaut was able to dampen the bouncing out. Boomer steered his feet and legs inside the legs wells under the instrument panel until McCallum finally landed on his behind in the seat. "Not too bad that time—only one concussion," McCallum said.

"I had to do all the work, and you kneed me in the head twice,"

Boomer said. He stowed McCallum's soft-pack in the small storage container behind the seat, then corralled the seat straps floating around the cockpit and buckled him in.

"Fifteen minutes, Boomer," Kai radioed. "How's it going?"

"Plenty of time, boss," Boomer said. "Mission specialist secured. I'm strapping in now." Actually it was going to be real close to get detached in time, but Boomer reminded himself not to hurry. He checked McCallum's umbilicals to be sure everything was stowed and secure. "Okay, Jeff, give me a systems check and a thumbs-up when you're ready." McCallum made sure everything was attached properly, did an oxygen, communications, and pressurization test, and gave Boomer a thumbs-up. "Okay, I'm moving into the forward cockpit now."

Thankfully, with the EEAS space suit it was far easier to get in, almost like a terrestrial fighter jet, and in moments he was strapped in and ready. "Spacecraft commander strapped in and ready to push," he reported.

"Boomer, I don't think we can make it," Kai said. "I don't want to rush this. C'mon back in. We'll off-load the cargo bay and wait for the next transfer orbit-entry opportunity."

"I'm ready to go, General," Boomer said. "Power's coming on." He activated the ship's battery, linked the spaceplane with the mission data computer on the space station, and started the data transfer and connection with the procedural computers that would prepare the spaceplane for launch. "Countdown's under way, three minutes to go. We'll make it."

"Let's not waste the fuel, Boomer. Bring it on in."

"I can do this, General," Boomer argued. He heard no response, which he took to mean approval, so he continued his departure checklists. At exactly three minutes, with less than two minutes to go, he radioed, "Checklists complete, data transfer complete and entered. Retract the transfer tunnel, Armstrong, Stud One is ready. Clear the canopy, Jeff." As he watched the transfer tunnel retract back toward the station's docking beam, he motored both cockpit canopies closed. "Ready to undock, Armstrong . . ."

"We're showing canopies not latched, Stud One," the docking module technician reported. "Check the aft canopy."

"Jeff?"

"I'm clear back here," he said. "No foreign objects in the way."

"Clear the canopy," Boomer said. "I'll try to reclose it." He motored the canopy open a few inches, then motored it closed once more.

"Still not showing latched, Stud One."

"Disregard it," Boomer said. "It's probably just a bad contact. We're going to open it again in a couple hours when we reach Kingfisher-Eight anyway."

"Bag it, Boomer," Kai said. "Let's get it looked at while we off-load the cargo."

"General, I'll check it when I rendezvous with Kingfisher-Eight and Jeff is doing his EVA. We'll be cool. It's probably something simple. Request detaching the fuel lines and permission to push."

"Boomer, if you have to do an emergency reentry, and the canopy's not locked, you'll both be crispy critters."

"Then we just won't do an emergency reentry, General—at least, not with us inside," Boomer said. "We'll wait outside for you to pick us up."

"It's not funny, Noble." There was a brief pause; then, "Retract fuel lines, permission to push granted," he said finally. Boomer released the locks connecting the spaceplane to the docking beam and touched the thrusters, pushing the Black Stallion away from the station.

Following the computer's guidance, Boomer steered the spaceplane to the new orbital inclination, then activated the Laser Pulse Detonation Rocket System engines to accelerate into the transfer orbit. The Hohmann transfer orbit was a new elliptical orbit that touched both of the circular orbits of Armstrong Space Station and the Kingfisher-8 weapon garage. In order to minimize fuel burn and save time, the timing had to be perfect so the garage would be nearby when the second burn was over—that was the reason why the spaceplane had to either be on its way on time or wait almost another day for the right moment.

The first burn lasted two minutes and pushed the spaceplane into a higher three-hundred-mile orbit. Forty-five minutes later, Boomer turned the spaceplane again to the proper heading and fired the engines again to enter Kingfisher-8's orbit. "Transfer complete, and Kingfisher-Eight is in sight," Boomer reported. As planned, the weapon garage was dead ahead and less than three miles away. He patted the top of his instrument panel. "Good show, Stud. How are you doing back there, Jeff?"

"In the green, Boomer," McCallum replied.

It took just a few minutes to close the distance with Kingfisher-8, and soon they were orbiting within a few yards. The Kingfisher garages were cylindrical devices about the size of a Chevrolet Suburban. They had radar, electro-optical, and infrared sensor domes that allowed them to look in all directions; datalink antennas that connected them to Armstrong Space Station, to ground stations, and to other satellites and weapon garages; solar panels for power; and thrusters to point it in any direction. The business end revealed the six Trinity interceptors and Mjollnir attack reentry devices snug in their launch tubes, pointing Earthward.

"Station check, Jeff."

"Roger." A few moments later: "Station check complete, Boomer, clear to open the canopy."

"Coming open." Boomer motored both canopies open. "Here we are, Jeff," he said. "I'm unstrapping to help the Maytag repairman out." He unbuckled himself, made sure his tether and umbilicals were secure, then floated free of the Black Stallion spaceplane. Using handholds, he maneuvered himself to the aft cockpit, unstrapped McCallum, double-checked his tether and umbilicals, helped him out of the spaceplane, then retrieved his soft-pack and clipped it onto his space suit. "Have fun out there, honey," he said. "I'll be waiting."

"Kiss kiss," McCallum said. He grasped his Handheld Maneuverability Unit maneuvering gun, aimed it properly, and hit the trigger. Small spurts of nitrogen gas easily propelled him across to the Kingfisher-8 weapon garage. "Armstrong, verify Eight's radars are standby, nose is cold."

"Kingfisher-Eight's radar is in standby, nose is cold, power is off; however, be advised, continuity is not being monitored," Seeker radioed from Armstrong. "Clear to approach, advise extreme caution, sir."

"Roger that. Moving in."

Boomer checked that McCallum's umbilicals were free and clear, then returned to his seat in the Black Stallion—his suit didn't provide the same radiation or micrometeorite protection as McCallum's did, so it was safer for him to use the spacecraft for protection as much as possible. Once inside, he motored the aft cockpit canopy up and down a few times, and each time it registered closed and locked. "Looks like the canopy fault has cleared," he reported.

"We'll check it over carefully before we do the next reentry," Raydon said.

About fifteen minutes later, McCallum radioed, "I've found the bad circuit boards. Should be another twenty minutes and I'll be done."

"Holler if you need any help, Jeff," Boomer said.

"Wouldn't you feel kinda naked, coming out here in just your leotards?"

"Nah. Besides, I'm sure the family jewels are pretty much cooked already. Luckily when I started flying in space, I decided to freeze a bunch of the swimmers for safekeeping, just in case the ol' magazine starts spitting out nothing but blanks."

"Really? You did that?"

"Haven't you?"

"Don't listen to him, Jeff—that's an urban myth," Seeker said. "Boomer might be firing blanks for other reasons."

Ten minutes before impact, the payload section of the DF-21 rocket opened and ejected a single kill vehicle, a rectangular device no larger than a refrigerator, covered in thruster nozzles aimed in all directions. The nose section had a radar guidance sensor, slaved to the position of the Kingfisher-8 satellite ahead. As the Kingfisher weapon garage rose above Earth's horizon, the kill vehicle's radar locked onto it and began making its own intercept corrections.

"Okay, Armstrong, I've replaced boards T-7 and RF-15 in the continuity control module," McCallum reported several minutes later. "I'm pretty sure that should do it. If it doesn't, I'll need to replace the entire module. We'll need to bring one up. I'm heading back to the Stud." During his space walk, Kingfisher-8 and the S-9 had drifted closer to each other—the two spacecraft were in their own orbits and would eventually proceed on their own paths unless corrected—so it didn't take as long as before for McCallum to fly himself back.

Boomer exited the spaceplane, made sure the tethers and umbilicals were properly stowed, connected McCallum back to the Stud, stowed the soft-pack, got him back into his seat, and strapped him in. "How many space walks does that make for you, Jeff?" he asked.

"Three on this deployment and eleven overall," he replied. "You?"

"I stopped keeping count a long time ago, bud," Boomer said. "It's gotta be several dozen."

"Unbelievable! I never would have thought that spacewalking and going into orbit would be so commonplace."

"A lot of otherwise smart folks still don't believe it."

"To tell the truth, spacewalking made me nervous as hell at first," McCallum admitted. "I can't shake the feeling of falling."

"I got the same way at first—like standing on a tall bridge looking down," Boomer said. "You get over it. Now I just enjoy the view." Boomer climbed back into the Black Stallion, reconnected his air and communications lines, and strapped in. He maneuvered the spaceplane about a hundred yards away from Kingfisher-8. "We're clear, Armstrong," he radioed. "Clear to power it back up."

"I want you farther away, Boomer," Kai radioed. "The continuity circuits control weapon arming and safing. If it's still malfunctioning, you could get a Trinity in the face. Prepare to head to the transfer orbit."

"Interface with the transfer orbit won't be for another three hours, General," Seeker said.

"Okay. Move out to at least a mile, Boomer."

"Roger," Boomer replied. On intercom he said, "I think the boss is getting more and more cautious these days. He's starting to sound like the guys in NASA."

"Better safe than sorry," McCallum said. "The guy didn't get to be a one-star by taking too many chances."

"He's the boss. Good job out there, Jeff. Did you do an inventory of the soft-pack?"

"Yes. It's all there."

"Think it'll work?"

"I'm ninety percent sure."

"Excellent. Okay, here we go. We'll move away, let them test it, then it's three hours to wait until we can do the transfer orbit, so you can relax." Boomer used the thrusters to move away from Kingfisher-8. They lost sight of it quickly against the spectacular backdrop of Earth and stars. "We show you one mile and clear, Stud One," Seeker reported.

"I've lost sight of it, but I've still got its transponder," Boomer said, referring to the coded radio beacon used for identification and positioning.

"Roger. We're powering up Eight. Stand by."

"Roger." On intercom, Boomer said, "I used to keep a logbook of all my flights and space walks, Jeff, and I'm sorry I didn't keep it going—it would've been something to show the grandkids. Make sure you write down all these flights and missions, or maybe do a journal or something so you don't—"

And at that instant there was a tremendous flash of light off in the distance. Boomer felt several intense blows on the Black Stallion, and then everything went dark.

ARMSTRONG SPACE STATION

THAT SAME TIME

"What the hell just happened?" Kai Raydon thundered. He had almost propelled himself off his seat in surprise when the alarms activated, and he had to grasp a handhold and reapply his Velcro sneakers to stay in place. "Where's the spaceplane? What happened, Seeker . . . ?"

"I've lost datalink contact with both Stud One and Kingfisher-Eight!" Seeker replied. "Attempting to get direct sensor contact now. They should be within Thule radar contact in three minutes."

"I want the status of all Black Stallions, Midnights, Orions, and Crew Rescue Vehicles *now*," Kai ordered. "Anyone who can get a maneuvering spacecraft we can use as a rescue or tow vehicle into that orbit, I want to know about them. Communications, contact Space Command, tell them we may have had an accident, and ask them to tag any new orbital objects and send their orbital data to us so we can coordinate a rescue or recovery. Any other garages in the area?"

"Negative, sir, not for another four hours," Seeker replied after a short search.

"As soon as Thule reports something, I want—"

"Sir, terrestrial radar contact from Kingfisher-Five," one of the other sensor technicians interjected. "A flight of heavy aircraft, westbound, five hundred miles east of the Chinese convoy. Radar reports at least five formations, speed five hundred knots, altitude thirty-four thousand feet."

"Identification?"

"Not yet, sir."

"General, Midnight One is completing phase maintenance in

Palmdale, but they report they can have it buttoned up and ready to launch in four hours," Seeker said. "They'll miss the next launch window unless they can launch in two hours."

"Tell them to hurry, but I don't want another accident," Kai said. "Follow the book, but follow it *quickly*. Anyone else?"

"Still checking on Stud Two and Three. Four is deep in depot maintenance and won't be available for four weeks."

"Anyone else on a launchpad somewhere?"

"Still checking, sir."

"I want a continuously updated status board of all manned or unmanned Orbital Maneuvering Vehicles on my monitors as soon as this incident is over," Kai said. "I want to know every moment of every day where they are and what they're doing."

"Yes, sir . . . sir, Stud Two is loading up at Elliott Air Force Base. Weather is marginal, but they may be able to launch within the hour, and they can be in the launch window to rendezvous at the approximate orbital position of Stud One."

"If they can get a passenger module installed in time, tell them to do it, but if the weather allows, I want them airborne with whatever they have," Kai said. "Any visual ID on those bogeys?"

"Negative, sir. Now reporting six formations, with one of the formations containing four aircraft in trail formation."

"Report them to Central Command and Combined Task Force–Horn of Africa—I've got a bad feeling about them," Kai said. "What about Stud Two?"

"They don't have a passenger module available, but they're dropping their payload as fast as they can to make room in the cargo bay," Seeker said. "Battle Mountain can launch a tanker in twenty minutes. That's the only one available so far."

"It'll have to do. Let me know when the planners have a rendezvous schedule set up."

"Yes, sir . . . our sensors are out of range of that formation of planes, but the CTF-HOA AWACS plane should pick them up in an hour or so."

"I hope those guys are ready. How's the weather at Dreamland?"

"Reporting marginal VFR, light snow showers, forecast to remain the same for the next—"

Just then they heard, "Armstrong, this is Stud One."

Kai's eyes bulged as his finger jabbed the "TRANSMIT" button: "Stud One, this is Armstrong. What's your status?"

Hunter Noble's voice was low and strained. "No lights on in the cockpit, leopards are out, no power, no cockpit instruments, and I can't raise McCallum," he said. "I think Kingfisher-Eight blew up."

"Are you hurt, Noble?"

"I don't know," Boomer replied, sounding as if he was drowsy. "I think I'm okay. My head must've cushioned the impact."

"Sounds like he's got a concussion, sir," Seeker said.

"Then we're going to have to keep him awake until Stud Two can get to him," Kai said. On the radio he said, "We've got Stud Two and a tanker getting ready to launch within the hour, Boomer. If nothing vital got hit, you have enough air for a while. Hang on. We're sending everything we have up there to get you."

"I can't get to Jeff," Boomer said. "My canopy won't open."

"You stay in your seat and stay strapped in, Boomer, and this time it's a damned order," Kai said. "Save your strength and your air—you're going to need every bit of both to assist rescuers. We're going to bring Stud Two up and transfer you and McCallum to their cargo bay and then back here. You think of anything to help that process and let us know—otherwise, stay put."

"Yes, sir," Boomer said. A few moments later, he added, "I screwed up, didn't I, General?"

"You did your job, Boomer. Your job is to fly the spaceplane, and you did it." He took a deep breath, then said, "I pulled the umbilicals and authorized you to push. After Jeff was done, I should've had you return to the station, or at least go into another transfer orbit—if Jeff's fix didn't work, you would've had to come back anyway. There was no reason to power up Eight with you guys just a mile away. It's my fault and my responsibility, Boomer, got that?"

"Yes, sir."

"Now let's stop thinking about the accident and start thinking about survival and rescue," Kai said resolutely, as much to himself as to Hunter Noble. "You've got at least a couple hours before Stud Two can get to you. What we're going to do is start evaluating your condition, and then the condition of your ship, because we need to pass as much information to Stud Two as we can before he launches. You've got battery-powered lights on your helmet and suit, so let's get them on and take a look around."

"Roger," Boomer said. He felt as if he was underwater, perhaps in the big NASA EVA training tank in Houston—everything was moving in slow motion. But he touched the control on the side of his helmet on the first try, which illuminated two LED lamps on either side of his helmet.

"I've got a hole in my forward windscreen on the upper right side," Boomer radioed. "That's probably jammed the canopy closed. We'll probably need the 'Jaws of Life' to pry us out of here." He turned to his right and felt a stab of pain run through his neck. "Wrenched my neck, but I can move it." He let the LED light play outside the Black Stallion. "I see a white cloud surrounding the ship, so I'm probably leaking something. Not sure if it's jet fuel or oxidizer—might be both." He then noticed the Earth—it was traveling overhead from left to right. "Looks like we're slowly spinning, x-axis, counterclockwise, not real fast, maybe two revs a minute—just enough to be annoying."

"Good info, Boomer," Kai said. "Keep it coming."

"Roger." His fingers began finding their way across the forward and side instrument panels—he was familiar enough with the cockpit layout that he didn't need lights to find them. "I'm shutting off any switches that are still on, but I'll leave the battery switch on for now so we can communicate." After he made sure all switches were off, he continued his scan. "Looks like whatever came through the windscreen exited through the left side of the canopy—probably missed me by just inches."

"Lucky at cards, lucky with flying debris."

"Unlucky at love, right?"

"We haven't finished writing that chapter yet, have we?" Kai asked.

"No, we haven't, sir. What's going on with the Chinese?"

"They're still heading for Mogadishu, and now we're tracking a large formation of high-subsonic aircraft heading that way, too."

"Looks like someone's going to get clobbered down there."

"One crisis at a time, Boomer. Check your oxygen lines and fittings."

"Roger." He let his fingers travel along the oxygen lines. He felt some pain when moving his right shoulder, but it wasn't as bad as his neck. "Can't feel any breaks in the oh-two line."

"Roger that. Stud Two is taxiing for takeoff, Boomer. The tanker is airborne. They'll be with you in about two and a half to three hours. Intermediate orbit, transfer orbit, rendezvous."

"Not bad. Lucky again."

"How's your suit?"

"Stand by." Boomer raised his left arm, then winced as he reached up with his right hand to turn on the suit control panel. "EEAS is on ship's power," he said. "Battery status is one hundred percent and still being charged with ship's power. Everything else looks like it's in—"

Just then, he noticed a flicker of light off his right side—a reflection in the white cloud of gas surrounding the ship. "Hey, I see a light off to the right," he radioed. Through the stabs of pain, he craned his neck as far as he could over his right shoulder to see what it was. "Can't see any . . . wait, there it is again. It comes and goes. It's reflecting off the vapor cloud around the Stud."

"Still no cockpit indications?"

"No. I'd have to reset the master switch. Think I ought to give that a try?"

"I don't know, Boomer. If you have a fuel- or oxidizer-tank breach, powering up the ship could set something off."

"Something might already be getting ready to set off, General," Boomer said. "I can reset the master switch, check for any sign of trouble, and then shut it off again real quick."

"And if that starts a fire? What then?"

"Only one option," Boomer said. He didn't say what it was—that would've been too horrible to think about.

"If you think the risk is worth it, Boomer, do it," Kai said. "Your help won't arrive for a few hours."

He saw the flicker of light again—that decided it. *Something* was going on back there. "I'm resetting the master switch . . . now." He felt for the switch, clicked it down from the center "OFF" position, then up to "ON." The cockpit lights turned on immediately . . .

. . . and brighter than all of them were the two red-colored illuminated handles on the eyebrow panel marked FIRE NO. 3 and FIRE NO. 4.

Boomer's reaction was immediate. He pulled both illuminated handles and waited a few seconds . . . but the lights didn't go out. He spoke as calmly as he could, *"Fire in leopards three and four, evacuating!"* He then immediately shut off the master and battery switches, cutting off communications. His right hand went immediately to a selector switch under the right forward instrument panel and verified it was in the "BOTH" position, then opened a red-colored guard next to it and flipped the switch inside up . . .

. . . which blew off McCallum's cockpit canopy using cannons of nitrogen gas, followed two seconds later by Boomer's canopy.

He quickly unstrapped and floated free of his seat. He pulled the headrest off his seat, which was a small survival kit, and clipped it onto his flight suit, then retrieved his HMU and clipped it on his suit as well. Unreeling his umbilical lines behind him, he pulled himself to the aft cockpit, unfastened McCallum's seat straps, and pulled him free of the ship as carefully but as quickly as he could.

Now that he was above the Black Stallion, he could see what was going on: Debris from Kingfisher-8 had hit the two right engines and right wing, creating clouds of leaking fuel. Something inside one of the engines was creating a spark when the oxidizer made an electric arc ignite, but when the oxidizer dissipated, the spark went away. They were extremely lucky that one of those sparks hadn't encountered a cloud of leaking jet fuel and exploded. Chemical explosions in space were extremely rare, but with this much oxidizer floating around, it was certainly possible.

Making sure his umbilicals and tether were connected, he grabbed McCallum's survival kit and HMU, fastened them to his flight suit, then grasped McCallum as tightly as he could and kicked himself away from the Black Stallion. The umbilicals were several yards long, and Boomer thought he would go out to their full length, stay connected to the ship's oxygen as long as possible, use the hand jets to stay clear of the stricken ship as it continued its lazy spinning, and detach as soon as he saw any sign of . . .

. . . and at that moment he saw a bright flash of light that obscured half the ship, and a massive tongue of flame curled around underneath the right wing inside the cloud of oxidizer and jet fuel for a fraction of a second before disappearing. Boomer didn't hesitate—he unlocked and released the umbilicals from his and McCallum's suits; then, with a momentary hesitation, unclipped the safety tethers. He then used the hand maneuvering jet to propel them away from the Black Stallion.

He and McCallum were now part of the thousands of pieces of space debris orbiting Earth.

Boomer used his HMU to push them away from the ship, discarded it when it was empty, then used McCallum's HMU to push out farther and to stabilize them both until it was almost exhausted, then reattached it back to his flight suit. He and McCallum were perhaps a quarter mile away from the Stud and slowly drifting farther—that was the best he could do. They were probably safe from all but the "golden BB" piece of space debris. The Black Stallion continued to flash and flare as fuel caught fire for the briefest of moments—it looked like a shiny speckled trout washed up on shore, sparkling brightly in the sun even while it was dying.

Next order of business was to make sure the suits were plugged in, turned on, and functioning. The suits had valves to close off the umbilical lines once disconnected, so Boomer and McCallum had a good supply of breathing air. Each suit had a backup battery to power lights and a short-range single-frequency radio, and he turned that on as well. Both suits had carbon-dioxide scrubbers that should keep CO_2 levels at survivable levels for several hours—a simple pull of a tab activated the first of two canisters in each suit. That gave Boomer a chance to look at McCallum's suit control panel, and he was pleased to see his pulse light blinking—weak, but it *was* a pulse—and good oxygen-saturation levels.

"Thank God," he said aloud. "Hang in there, Jeff. If we're still alive, we've still got work to do."

Boomer thought of waiting to activate the distress beacon until Stud Two was on its way to this orbit, but just in case the CO_2 scrubbers didn't work and he was rendered unconscious, he decided to activate his beacon and use Jeff's as a backup. Another quick pull of a tab, and the beacon was on. It was meant for use after ejection when on the ground, but supposedly it would work just as well in space. He made sure his Electronic Elastomeric Activity Suit was on battery power—that was one thing McCallum didn't have to worry about; Jeff's suit was fully inflated. The survival kits had emergency oxygen bottles that would refresh the air in the suits for a few hours after the CO_2 scrubbers were saturated— rescue was imperative after that.

There was nothing left to do but float. "Hey, Jeff," he radioed over to McCallum, hoping he was listening while still unconscious, "I'm surprised that I'm so damned calm. Here we are, adrift orbiting around planet Earth and, if not rescued in time, our lifeless bodies will eventually become meteorites. I'm not scared. In fact, I'm relaxed and kind of enjoying the view. I know help is on the way, and our equipment is actually working as advertised. We're good for now."

He kept on talking, telling stories, doing imaginary interviews about this experience with beautiful and adoring news anchors, telling Jeff which landmarks he was able to see on Earth, and even remarking that he thought he saw Armstrong Space Station whiz by. "I waved my arms, but I guess they couldn't see me," Boomer deadpanned.

Sometime later, he began wondering if he had made the right decision by abandoning the Black Stallion—but at that instant he noticed a bright flash of light off in the distance. "That blast surely did her in," he radioed. "You did good protecting us, old girl. Hope to see you when you reenter."

"Are you talking to me, Boomer?" he heard a voice ask.

"*Jeff!*" Boomer raised the dark visor on McCallum's helmet and was relieved beyond words to see his eyes open. "You're awake! How do you feel?"

"Like my head's ready to explode," McCallum said weakly. He looked around. "Where are we?"

"Adrift," Boomer replied.

"*What?*"

"Easy, Jeff, easy," Boomer said. "We abandoned the Stud a little more than an hour ago. Kingfisher-Eight exploded and creamed the ship. I think the Stud just blew."

"My God," McCallum breathed. Boomer didn't need to check his respiration blinker to know McCallum was on the verge of panicking. "Are we going to die out here? Are we going to freeze to death?"

"Relax, bro," Boomer said. "We're more likely to overheat. In space, there's no air to radiate heat away from our bodies, so it all gets trapped inside our suits. Relax. They're on their way to get us."

"We have no air?"

"Just what was in our suits when I disconnected us from the ship," Boomer said. "The survival kits have emergency bottles, and if you need it I can hook you up. But the C-oh-two scrubbers will remove the carbon dioxide for hours."

"Then what?"

"We'll be rescued before then, Jeff, don't worry," Boomer said, hoping he sounded convincing enough. "The general launched Stud Two after us, and we have a locator beacon going. Another hour or two and we should be headed back to the station."

"This is insane. We're going to die out here!" McCallum cried. Just as Boomer heard him beginning to hyperventilate, McCallum reached up to the locking mechanism of his helmet. "I can't breathe, man, help me get this damned thing off!"

"Jeff, *no*!" Boomer shouted, pulling McCallum's hands away from his helmet latches—watching carefully to be sure McCallum didn't reach for *his* gear, like a panicked swimmer pulling a life-guard under. "Jeff, listen to me, *listen*! We're going to be okay. We're safe inside our suits, we're not going to freeze to death, and we have plenty of air. You've got to relax! We're going to make it!"

"Why did you do this to me, Noble?" McCallum screamed. "Why did you push me out of the ship?"

"It was going to explode. I had to—"

"Things don't explode in outer space, you idiot!" McCallum shouted. "How can something explode without air? You killed me, you stupid jerk!"

"Relax, McCallum, *relax!*" Boomer said in as calm a voice as he could muster. "We're going to be okay—"

"I can't breathe, I can't breathe!" McCallum gasped. Boomer was having a tough time keeping his hands away from his helmet lock—fortunately, the lock was very hard to remove with gloves on. "Help me, Boomer, help me, I'm dying . . . !"

"No, you're not, Jeff, you're okay, just hang on!" Boomer shouted. "Calm down! We've practiced this a hundred times. Stay calm and we'll wait for rescue together."

"That's with a full EMU setup, Boomer, not a simple suit without an air supply!" McCallum shouted. "I've got no air! I've got to get out of this thing! I can't breathe!"

"They're on their way, Jeff, just stay calm and relax! Stop struggling! Breathe steady, man, you're hyperventilating! Stay—"

McCallum's hands suddenly left his helmet collar lock and pushed right at Boomer's helmet, sending him spinning away head over heels . . . and it was only then that, because he was unconscious until just a few moments ago, he realized that in the emergency evacuation of the Black Stallion he had broken the first and most important rule of extravehicular activities: "Make Before Break," or always attach a tether to something before releasing it . . .

. . . he had never secured McCallum to himself.

"Jeff!" he shouted. "Hold on! I'll be right back to you!" He fumbled around, finally retrieved the Handheld Maneuvering Unit, and used short spurts of nitrogen to stop his tumbling. It took him several long moments to get his bearings. He remembered Earth was "underneath" him, not above him, so he reoriented himself, then used more short bursts to look around for McCallum.

"Jeff, can you see me? Use your strobe or your helmet lights to help me find you!" He heard heavy, rapid breathing sounds, and he prayed McCallum might pass out from hyperventilating. Just then, he saw him, only ten yards away. His hands were no longer trying to work the helmet lock—it appeared as if he was checking his suit's monitor on his left wrist. "I see you, Jeff!" he radioed, raising the HMU to start his way over to him. "Hang—"

But then he realized what McCallum was doing . . . because moments later McCallum had stripped off his left protective outer glove and was now working the ring latch on his left suit glove! "Jeff, *stop what you're doing*! *Stop!* Hold on, Jeff, I'll be right over!"

"I can't get my helmet off, Boomer!" McCallum shouted. "It won't come off! I can't breathe! If I get this damned glove off, it'll be easier to take the helmet off!"

"Hold on, Jeff! I'm almost there!" Boomer hit the HMU thruster. If he hit him, he might be able to distract him enough. He had to be perfect, but there was no time to aim . . .

"I'll get it," McCallum said in a high, squeaky, strained voice, almost like a child's. "If I can take these damned gloves off, I can get it." The helmet ring latch was really designed to be operated by a helper, although the wearer himself could do it with a little patience and practice, but the glove's ring latch was designed to be operated inside of an air lock by the wearer, and was therefore easier to operate with space-suit gloves on. Before Boomer could reach him, McCallum had opened the locking mechanism and . . .

. . . at that moment Boomer rammed into him. In his EEAS it was easier for Boomer to grasp and hold something, and he grasped at anything he could—McCallum's head, his space-suit material, anything to keep from rebounding back into space. He had flipped right over McCallum, but he held on. They were both twisting around after the impact, but they were together once more. "I got you, Jeff!" he shouted. "Hold on to me, Jeff, and I'll get us secured. Hold on, man, we're gonna make it . . ."

But just as Boomer began pulling his partner around to face him, McCallum twisted the ring latch another half inch, and with a puff of moisture-laden oxygen, the air began leaking out of his suit.

"No!" Boomer cried out. He fumbled for the left wrist. McCallum made a loud animal-like bark as oxygen forced itself out of his lungs. Boomer reached the ring latch, but he couldn't force McCallum's hand away in time before all of the air in the space suit evacuated. Boomer watched as McCallum started gasping for air for a few seconds, his eyes bulging in terror, and then he closed his eyes and mercifully fell asleep from hypoxia.

Boomer managed to snap the ring latch closed. He then retrieved his seat-back survival kit, found the small bottle of emergency oxygen, removed the mask, plugged it into the port on McCallum's suit, and pulled the activation ring. It was empty almost instantly. Boomer opened McCallum's survival kit, found the oxygen bottle, and drained it into the suit as fast as he could. No reaction.

Boomer checked the wrist monitor and found less than one-fourth of an atmosphere of oxygen in the suit. McCallum's pulse and respiration were almost nonexistent. His friend would be dead within a couple minutes after all the oxygen in his brain had bubbled out. It was not a horrible way to die—the body didn't explode or freeze, the blood didn't boil—and he was free of the horror of loneliness and certain death that his mind had created.

Now it was Boomer's turn to feel alone as he grasped his friend tightly, refusing to let him go again. But after a few minutes, his mind returned to the here and now. He used the last of the gas in the HMU to turn them around until they were facing Earth's horizon, where they could see both Earth and stars. He had survived a disaster and witnessed his friend's death . . . but he was alive and well, and he had an unparalleled view of his universe from which not even death itself could distract him.

A thousand things—no, a *million* things—could kill him at any moment, he knew—micrometeorites, radiation, electrical failure, or just plain fear, which did in his friend and fellow astronaut. But for now, he was just going to fall around planet Earth, enjoy the view, and wait for a ride home.

OFF THE COAST OF MOGADISHU, SOMALIA

AN HOUR LATER

The attack began precisely at six A.M. local time, just as day-shift workers were arriving at their posts, the markets and surrounding streets were jammed with shoppers and commuters, and weary graveyard-shift workers were heading home:

The destroyers and frigates of the People's Liberation Army Navy began by firing a dozen Hai Ying-4 cruise missiles from fifty miles out. The subsonic cruise missiles took just four minutes to hit their targets around Mogadishu Airport, the Old Port, and the New Port areas, destroying known gang meeting places, arms storage areas, communications centers, power substations, and security checkpoints. At the same time, the first squadron of People's Liberation Army Air Force Hongzhaji-6 bombers launched thirty-six of their own version of the HY-4 cruise missiles. The missiles had only two-hundred-pound incendiary and high-explosive warheads, but they had better than fifty-foot precision and devastated the south part of the city.

The second and third wave of H-6 bombers roared over the city at two thousand feet above the tallest buildings, dropping one-thousand-pound high-explosive and incendiary gravity bombs on main roads, highways, and intersections, including Maka al-Mukarama Road, the main highway between the capital and the airport. The strikes were organized quickly and not well planned, and several bombs hit apartment buildings, shopping centers, markets, and other businesses, but precision was not a top priority. Every building at the airport was attacked and destroyed except for the fuel storage area—the Chinese hoped it would be taken intact. The piers at both ports were left standing, although the warehouses, dry docks, and other buildings adjacent to the port that might shelter Somali fighters were flattened. Clouds of dense smoke all around the city blotted out the sun, making large parts of the city appear as twilight.

Next, three hundred Chinese marines from the naval vessels landed at Mogadishu Airport by helicopter and crew shuttle boats. Lightly armed four-man patrol squads fanned out along the perimeter of the airport. Their job was not to attack but to call in naval artillery barrages and air strikes. If even one shot was spotted coming from a nearby building, that building was quickly identified, targeted, and completely destroyed by air or naval bombardment. The bomber attacks were timed so that the destroyers and frigates were all within range of their five-inch guns by the time the bombers released all of their weapons and had to withdraw.

The combination of the devastating bombardments and the marines on the perimeter calling in more and more accurate strikes meant that the six unarmed cargo ships could safely move closer to shore, and with the help of commandeered tugboats, they quickly berthed and began to unload cargo and personnel. The original loads of humanitarian supplies and support equipment destined for Tanzania had been partially off-loaded in Karachi, Pakistan, and quickly replaced with warehoused military hardware—rifles, heavy machine guns, mortars, ammunition, communications equipment, protective devices, mines, tactical vehicles, and food and water for a battalion of Chinese soldiers for a week.

By twilight, three thousand People's Liberation Army troops aboard the six cargo ships had surrounded and reinforced defensive positions at Mogadishu Airport and the New Port districts, and scouts had directed intense naval bombardment of the Old Port district designed to suppress any counterattack attempts. Chinese hunter-killer squads began to fan out into the outskirts of the city north and west of the airport, armed with snipers, wire-guided antivehicle missiles, security troops with automatic rifles, and night-vision equipment. Any locals who congregated in any fashion and for any reason were ruthlessly attacked, even if the purpose was to collect the dead or injured. The area within a mile of the airport boundary became an instant shoot-to-kill zone, and no buildings stood within two miles of the airport.

That evening, several large transport planes began arriving, one every hour on a varying time schedule, taking extreme defensive measures to avoid being targeted by Somali rocket-propelled grenades or shoulder-fired antiaircraft missiles. Each plane carried more troops and supplies, some carrying armored vehicles or artillery pieces. The arrivals were timed with more naval artillery barrages to keep Somali heads down until right before the transports arrived on final approach, when they were the most vulnerable.

By daybreak of the second day of the invasion, over four thousand Chinese soldiers were on the ground at Mogadishu Airport.

SIX

No one can build his security upon the nobleness of another person.

— WILLA CATHER, "ALEXANDER'S BRIDGE"

THE WHITE HOUSE SITUATION ROOM, WASHINGTON, D.C.

THAT SAME TIME

Vice President Kenneth Phoenix, White House Chief of Staff Walter Kordus, and National Security Adviser Conrad Carlyle entered the Situation Room quickly and took seats. Phoenix waved at the other members of the National Security Council in the room, who had been standing anticipating the president's arrival. "Walter finally convinced the president to get some rest," Phoenix said. "He's been watching the news coverage of the Chinese invasion on TV almost continuously, and he's beat. He's going to address the American people at seven-ten this morning." The other officials and military officers shuffled to their seats, most reaching for coffee or energy drinks, all wishing they could get some rest as well. "Let's do it, Walter."

"Yes, Mr. Vice President," Kordus said. He took a sip of coffee, then went on: "This will be our last update until the full staff update at six forty-five A.M., so we can all get at least a few hours' rest as long as your deputies are fully briefed and in place. Who's got the latest?"

"Right here, Walter, Mr. Vice President," Secretary of Defense Miller Turner said. "In a nutshell, sir, we're seeing a historic, tactically well-orchestrated, and a strategically globe-altering event: the first deployment of Chinese troops across its borders in large numbers since the Korean War, and one of the largest deployments of Chinese air and naval forces in the country's long history. What we're seeing, ladies and gentlemen, is the world's largest standing army from the world's most populous country doing what the world has feared for two millennia: breaking out of its borders and massing troops elsewhere on the planet.

"To summarize: The People's Republic of China bombarded and then invaded the main airport and the area known as New Port in Mogadishu, the capital city of Somalia, in the Horn of Africa. The invasion began with air- and sea-launched cruise-missile attacks, followed by unguided gravity-bomb attacks from Chinese H-6 jet bombers and naval gun bombardment from Chinese warships that were part of the antipiracy task force. The bombardment was followed by a land invasion of Chinese marines who came ashore from the naval warships, and then followed by Chinese army regulars who came ashore aboard container vessels initially thought to be humanitarian relief supplies bound for Tanzania. The attacks were specifically planned and executed for maximum destruction and body count."

"Do we know where those bombers came from?" Phoenix asked. "Did they fly all the way from China?"

"We don't yet know, sir," Turner replied. He checked his notes, then said, "The Chinese H-6 is China's only long-range bomber. They have only a hundred twenty of them. Unrefueled, they have a range of only one thousand miles. About sixty were updated with aerial refueling probes, and approximately thirty were converted to aerial refueling tankers, so we're assuming that half of all their air-refuelable bombers and air-refueling tankers were used in this raid. If they are, they could have come all the way from mainland China."

"The Chiefs think that's highly unlikely, sir," General Taylor J. Bain, chairman of the Joint Chiefs of Staff, remarked. "China has the world's largest air force, but seventy to eighty percent of their planes are old and outdated. General Huffman says China has very little experience with aerial refueling, especially the H-6s. They're developing more of a capability to refuel tactical jets and carrier-based fighters, but the big bombers were thought to be all but obsolete."

"Unless you can explain how a plane with only one thousand miles' range made it a quarter of the way around the planet without air refueling, I'd say your information was totally inaccurate, General," Phoenix said with undisguised irritation. Bain likewise did not try to hide his displeasure at Phoenix's remark. He glanced at Walter Kordus, making an unspoken request, and the president's chief of staff picked up his telephone.

The vice president waved a hand, then massaged his temples. "I'm sorry, General, I apologize," he said wearily. "I'm tired. It's been a really long day." Bain nodded, once and perfunctorily, and said nothing. The vice president turned to the rest of those in the Situation Room. "Ladies and gentlemen, as Secretary Turner said, what we're seeing is something completely unexpected and unprecedented. Everything we thought we knew about China is wrong, do you understand? Everything we've assumed about their capabilities, strategic interests, methodology, and order of battle has to be reevaluated, and *fast*. It looks to me like we're going to have to throw out all the game plans regarding China and make up new ones—every week if necessary."

"That's exactly what we intend to do, sir," Carlyle said after he hung up the phone. "But China has always been a secretive, closed, and one-way society—they take all the data we care to give them, and give us very little in return. It's been like that in the best of years." Carlyle checked the laptop computer display before him when the terminal beeped, then typed commands into the keyboard. "You have something to contribute here, General Raydon?"

"Yes, sir," Kai Raydon replied from Armstrong Space Station. "Display number six." One of the displays on the wall-size array of computer monitors turned dark, followed a moment later by a satellite image of an airfield with a very long single runway. "This is Rajanpur Northwest Airfield, about forty miles northwest of Khanpur in central Pakistan. It happens to have Pakistan's longest runway, twelve thousand five hundred feet long. It was built to accommodate Ilyushin-76 airborne early-warning radar aircraft and air-refueling tankers purchased from Ukraine, as well as H-6 bombers purchased from China. Pakistan received four of the AWACS radar planes and twelve tankers, but the sale of H-6s was blocked by the United States after Pakistan's nuclear tests in 1998. The Il-76s were later moved to other bases, and Rajanpur Northwest became a reserve forces base and was largely abandoned. This photo was taken about a year ago."

The photo changed, this time to the same airfield but with several rows of large aircraft parked on the southeast and northeast sides of the runway. "This is Rajanpur four hours ago," Raydon went on. "We count twelve H-6 bombers, four H-6 tankers, one Il-76 AWACS, several large transports, and some fighter jets. The airfield is choked with planes and personnel. We haven't been able to identify any personnel or get any other information, but my guess is that this is a massive Chinese air deployment."

"Our buddies in Pakistan looking out for us . . . *again,*" Phoenix commented. "I think Pakistan's friendliness toward the United States is as much fiction as the one about China not training for air refueling with its long-range bombers."

"I don't see this necessarily as a betrayal, Mr. Vice President," the president's national security adviser, Conrad Carlyle, said. "Pakistan supporting China's efforts to shut down the Somali pirates? We should be thanking them."

"It's yet to be proven if that's what China is up to," Phoenix said. "We're friends with China, or at least we're *supposed* to be friends— why didn't they advise us first before this operation? And we're allies with Pakistan—why didn't they advise us they were going to support China like this?"

"Pakistan has all but closed our embassy in Islamabad," Kordus said, "because of that space attack. We're going to have to do some major sucking up to get them to trust us again."

"No one is going to be sucking up to anyone, especially the United States of America, and especially *not* to Pakistan," Phoenix retorted. "If it wasn't for that space attack, we'd probably be watching a nuclear war on the subcontinent right now. Remember that." He paused for a moment, then spoke: "What's the latest on your incident up there, General Raydon?"

"The investigation is ongoing, Mr. Vice President," Kai replied. "We saw absolutely no faults at all when we powered the interceptor garage up. It just . . . blew."

"Any guesses?"

"Sir, the system that failed previously was the Trinity interceptor safe-arm circuit, which guarantees that the rocket motors in the interceptors are safe until the system is armed from here in the station, or until the self-protection systems detect a possible incoming threat," Kai said. "We had the entire satellite shut down except for the maneuvering system, and two circuit boards in that subsystem were just replaced. If the boards were bad or the wrong boards replaced, a faulty safe-arm circuit would have closed the motor ignition circuit. When the garage was powered up, the safe circuit fault could have been interpreted as an arm command, and the motor ignition command set off one of the booster motors. But as I said, we had no indications of any faults after powering up the satellite.

We're checking all systems right now, and we still haven't found anything."

"And the astronauts?"

"They'll be evacuated later on today, sir," Kai said. "Mr. Noble is in good shape—dehydrated, possibly a broken shoulder, some sunburn on his face, but otherwise well. We're concerned about radiation exposure—he wasn't wearing a full space suit—but so far he seems to have weathered that okay."

"*He wasn't wearing a space suit?* How could he survive in space without one?"

"Mr. Noble was wearing what we call an 'activity suit'—an electronically controlled mechanical pressure suit that allows the wearer a lot more flexibility and freedom, but it doesn't offer as much radiation protection."

"It sounds like he's a very lucky man," Phoenix observed. "And the other astronaut? His family's been notified?"

"Yes, sir, his parents and siblings—Lieutenant McCallum was unmarried. Recently graduated top of his class from Stanford. The engineering college there wants to have a public service for him, and the family has accepted."

"I'd like to be there."

"I'll set it up with your office, sir."

"Thank you. How long was Mr. Noble adrift in space?"

"A total of four and a half hours," Kai replied. "When the spaceplane caught up with him, he was napping. Scared the hell out of us—we thought he had a concussion."

"Amazing," the vice president breathed. "Alone in orbit around Earth, and the guy slept through it. I'd like reports on your investigation as you have them, General."

"We'll keep them coming, sir."

"Thank you." The vice president spread his hands to the others in the Situation Room. "Okay, back to China and what they've got planned in Somalia. It's got to be more than just a punitive strike against warlords who ordered the pirate attacks, as they claim. I think China has much more in mind. They don't drop a few thousand troops on the ground just to drop-kick some pirates."

"The secretary of state is in Beijing right now and is set to meet with the premier and the minister of foreign affairs shortly and will—"

"Secretary Barbeau has been in China so many times in the past few months, we should probably get her a nice apartment across from Tiananmen Square," Phoenix said. He rubbed his temples again. "And it seems every time she's sent to Beijing, the Chinese make another move that makes me wonder even more what they have in mind."

"Diplomacy takes time, Mr. Vice President," Kordus said without turning toward him. "Do you have any doubts that Secretary Barbeau is doing all she can to find out more about China's plans?"

"What I'm saying, Walter, is that we shouldn't be waiting around for China to state its intentions before we voice our own," Phoenix said. "We as the president's senior advisers should draft a statement for the president, recommending he strongly condemn Beijing's actions, demand a halt to the bombings and shellings and an immediate withdrawal from the area except for forces involved in the joint antipiracy task force."

"I don't think that's warranted at this time, Mr. Vice President," David C. Keeley, deputy secretary of state, representing the Department of State while Secretary Barbeau was traveling. "The Somali pirates have been terrorizing the Horn of Africa for years now, and the international community has done very little proactively to stop them. China finally does something about the problem. Why do we want to lash out at China? They did the dirty work everybody else wanted done."

"Because there's a clear pattern of aggressiveness that's very troubling, Mr. Keeley," Phoenix said. "China places antiship and antisatellite weapons all around the world. Our response: announce we will unilaterally decommission our antisatellite weapons, and call on the rest of the world to do likewise. Then, when China runs out of friendly nations to place a missile site, they decide to invade an unfriendly one. Who's next—the Philippines, Taiwan, Thailand, Cuba? And what will our response be?"

"The president's statement this evening reflects his views and those of the National Security Council: The United States is very concerned about China's actions, and we call upon Beijing to do more to minimize civilian casualties," Kordus said. "You contributed to drafting that statement, sir."

"As an initial reaction to events of which we had very little concrete information, the statement was acceptable to me, Walter," Phoenix said. "That was eight hours ago, before China started bringing planeloads of troops and supplies into Mogadishu and started bedding down what looks to me like an occupation force. I'm saying we need a stronger statement. We should—"

"Do what, Ken?" President Joseph Gardner asked. He had silently appeared in the doorway of the Situation Room, completely unannounced. Everyone in the room stood; the president ignored them, instead fixing his gaze on his vice president. "What is it you want me to say to Beijing now?"

Phoenix paused for a few heartbeats. He glanced at Kordus, realizing now that the president's chief of staff had called the president and warned him that his vice president was taking control of the meeting; then turned squarely back to the president and replied, "Sir, I think we should tell Premier Zhou that the invasion is a violation of the rights of a sovereign nation; the United States condemns China's unilateral, surprise, and horribly violent attacks against innocent Somalis; that we demand that Zhou orders an immediate cease-fire and removes all ground forces offshore to their own vessels; and that all naval forces return to antipiracy-task-force operations under United Nations and NATO supervision."

"And if they refuse?" the president asked.

"Then the United States will file a protest with the United Nations and ask for an emergency meeting of the Security Council to issue a resolution condemning Chinese activities in Somalia and ordering an immediate withdrawal."

"China will certainly veto such a resolution. What then?"

"We will then ask that the full membership issue a statement condemning Chinese actions and demand an immediate withdrawal."

"China can still refuse, or simply ignore the order. What then?"

"The United States removes China from the antipiracy Combined Task Force and notifies the world that any PRC warships en route to or from Somalia will be considered hostile combatants en route to an illegal combat zone," Phoenix said. "This action prohibits Chinese warships or support vessels from utilizing certain ports that are also in use by the United States or its allies. If any nations continue to support Chinese warships, we place sanctions on *those* countries. This will stretch out China's supply lines and make it more difficult if not impossible to support blue-water naval operations. We then make it clear to Beijing that even tougher sanctions will follow if they don't comply."

The president nodded, looked Phoenix up and down as if meeting him for the first time, then nodded again. "You've given this quite a bit of thought, I see," he said in a quiet voice. Phoenix had no response. "So you want to play hardball with China, Mr. Phoenix, is that right?"

"I want to make it clear that we don't like any country bombing another country and killing innocent civilians in an area of the world under active patrol by the United States and its allies," Phoenix said. "I want them to understand that we'll act if our wishes are not met."

"And you don't think I've been clear, Mr. Phoenix?"

The vice president hesitated just for a moment—now it was getting personal. But then he replied, "In my opinion, sir, I think your last public statement regarding China was ambiguous."

"Ambiguous?"

"Yes, sir, ambiguous," Phoenix said. "You didn't say whether or not you condemned or even disagreed with China's invasion. You expressed concern, that's all. In my opinion, sir, that wasn't enough."

"And you thought you'd convey your thoughts to the National Security Council before running them by me, Mr. Phoenix?" the president asked.

"It seemed like a good time to do so, Mr. President."

"I assure you, Mr. Phoenix, it was not," the president said calmly. He looked at his watch, then at his vice president. "You're dismissed, Mr. Phoenix."

"Yes, Mr. President," Phoenix said, and he left the Situation Room without glancing at anyone else.

The president looked directly into the eyes of the others in the Situation Room. They were all still on their feet—they had not yet been given permission to sit. "Does anyone else think I've been too ambiguous in expressing my thoughts to China or anyone else?" he asked. The reply was a quiet-voiced but immediate chorus of "No, Mr. President." "Oh-six-thirty will come soon, ladies and gentlemen," the president said. "Get some rest." The National Security Council members scattered as quickly but as calmly as they could.

"Well?" the president asked his chief of staff after everyone had departed. "Insubordination? Treason? Or just popping off again?"

"I wouldn't have gotten you out of bed if it was just popping off, Joe," Kordus said. "He dressed down Bain like *he* was the commander in chief, then proceeded to lecture the NSC on how backward we were and how we should be thinking about China from now on. He apologized afterward and said he was tired, but he stepped way over the line."

"Was he right?"

Kordus hesitated a moment, then shook his head. "Doesn't matter, Joe. Phoenix is out of control, and he could take some members of the cabinet down if he continues to plant seeds of doubt in some minds about your leadership or the Pentagon's preparedness."

The president nodded, thinking hard. "In the original Constitution," he said after a few moments, "the second-place finisher in the presidential elections became vice president. He was given the meaningless job of president of the Senate in order to keep him busy enough so he didn't spend all of his time plotting to overthrow the president." He paused, longing for a cigarette and a shot or two of rum to clear his head. "I know how those early presidents felt now." He thought for a moment more; then: "I'll deal with Phoenix after I get some rest."

"He wants to go to that young astronaut's memorial service in California day after tomorrow."

"Fine, fine," the president said wearily. "Schedule some campaign stops for him and see if he squawks about doing them, and let me know who he meets with—as in any of his so-called secret presidential campaign advisers. He just might be doing more than just *sounding* like the commander in chief."

NATIONAL SPACE MEDICAL CENTER, JOHNSON SPACE CENTER, HOUSTON, TEXAS

TWO DAYS LATER

Patrick McLanahan and Deputy Undersecretary of the Air Force for Space Ann Page stepped up to the large cluster of microphones outside the entrance to the National Space Medical Center at the Johnson Space Center in Houston. Speaking without prepared notes—at least not any that the dozens of reporters could see— Patrick said, "Good morning, ladies and gentlemen. My name is Patrick McLanahan, retired U.S. Air Force lieutenant general. With me today is deputy undersecretary of the Air Force for space, aerospace engineer, astronaut, and former U.S. senator from California, Dr. Ann Page.

"We're going to visit with astronaut Hunter Noble, who was involved in the accident in Earth orbit when an interceptor weapon-launcher module apparently exploded after being serviced by Mr. Noble and his partner, spacecraft electronics technician First Lieutenant Jeffrey McCallum. Lieutenant McCallum was killed in the aftermath of the explosion, and Mr. Noble was forced to abandon his spaceplane and was adrift in space for several hours holding the body of Lieutenant McCallum until another spaceplane crew rescued them.

"Undersecretary Page will tell you that the official investigation will soon be under way and, like most aviation accident investigations, the results probably won't be released for several months," Patrick went on. "As the former commander of the nascent U.S. Space Defense Force and a frequent traveler to Armstrong Space Station, I am very concerned about the incident and the smooth progress of the investigation, and so I volunteered my services to

Undersecretary Page at the Pentagon to assist in the investigation in any way they see fit.

"I am also very concerned about the future of the space defense program, especially in the aftermath of this tragedy. With rumors circulating in the press about the cancellation or severe downsizing of the space defense program, I would like to ensure that the truth is accurately reported in a timely manner, and as a private citizen with extensive knowledge of the Space Defense Force program, I feel I'm well qualified to help. The space defense program is the cornerstone of the future of not only national defense but also global defense, and understanding and learning from tragic accidents like this are crucial for the program's success. Thank you."

Patrick stepped away from the microphones, and Ann stepped forward. "Thank you, General McLanahan," she began. "I thank you for your service to our country, and I thank you for stepping forward out of retirement with your generous offer of support, expert analysis, and leadership. I have recommended to secretary of the Air Force Salazar Banderas that he nominate General McLanahan to chair the accident investigation board on the Kingfisher-Eight incident, and we are awaiting the final decision by Defense Secretary Turner, which we expect very soon. The formal inquiry into the incident will begin when the chairman is appointed and his or her accident investigation board is chosen, sworn in, and seated.

"As the senior civilian administrator of the Air Force's military space programs, my job is to assist the Secretary of the Air Force in ensuring that we have the best equipped and trained space force in the world," Ann went on. "The constellation of Kingfisher interceptor modules in orbit have proven extremely reliable so far in their short tour of duty, and to me this incident is suspicious and troubling. I'll be following the investigation very carefully over the next several months. Most of the findings will be classified, I'm sure, but as much as I'm permitted, I'll report back to you on the board's progress." She and McLanahan fielded several questions from the few members of the press who attended the remarks, and then went inside to Hunter Noble's room.

They were surprised to see him up and moving about. His right shoulder was heavily bandaged, he wore a neck brace, and his face was shiny from the sunburn cream that had been applied, but otherwise he looked remarkably good for a guy who had been rescued from Earth orbit. "Saw the presser on TV, General," he said. "You looked good, if I may say so. Ever think about politics?"

"Yes—and then I slap myself," Patrick responded. "What are you doing out of bed?"

"Went to find that nurse who put this goop on my face," Boomer said with a smile.

"How do you feel?" Ann asked.

"A little wobbly, ma'am—I'm not as much of an exercise freak as General Raydon, so I think the zero-g and then Earth-g hit me harder."

"Not to mention your spaceplane being blasted by a weapon garage and then being forced to evacuate it."

"That, too."

"So you feel like talking a little?" Patrick asked, closing the door behind him. Ann Page looked at Patrick—she knew *he* knew he hadn't yet been approved to serve on the accident investigation board, so he wasn't authorized to ask any questions—but she stayed silent.

"Sure—it's better than playing with that lung-exerciser thingy they gave me," Boomer said, motioning to the spirometer on the table next to the bed. He sat on the side of the bed. "Shoot."

"Did Lieutenant McCallum have any problems with the repairs that you're aware of?" Patrick asked.

"None," Boomer said. "Went very smoothly."

"Was he nervous about doing the space walk?"

"I think so," Boomer admitted. "But I told him it was natural, and that I get a little illyngophobia every now and then."

"A little what?" Ann asked.

"Illyngophobia—the fear of getting vertigo."

"You mean acrophobia."

"No, that's the fear of heights. I don't have a problem with heights. I'm just afraid I might get vertigo. Pretty much the same, but different." Ann looked at him skeptically. "I'm generally a font of useless information, Madam Undersecretary," he said with a smile.

"'A difference that makes no difference is no difference,'" Ann said.

"William James, the ultimate verificationist," Boomer said. "My man."

While they were prattling on, Patrick stepped away from Boomer's bed and touched his left hand to his left ear, a signal that he was not taking part in their conversation. "Maddie?"

"Yes, General McLanahan," the voice of Sky Masters Inc.'s virtual assistant replied a moment later, heard through the resonations transmitted through his skull to his middle ear.

"Connect me to General Raydon on Armstrong Space Station."

"Stand by, General McLanahan," Maddie replied. A few moments later: *"General Raydon, this is Maddie from Sky Masters Incorporated calling for General McLanahan, not secure."*

"Is that your Duty Officer calling for you again, General?" Kai asked.

"Same operation; different names," Patrick said. "Verificationism." That got Ann and Boomer's attention.

"Say again?"

"Disregard. How are you?"

"Tired. Yourself, sir?"

"Good. Undersecretary Page and I are here with Boomer."

"How is he?"

"Up and about."

"He's a tough bugger, that's for sure."

"I'm very sorry about Lieutenant McCallum."

"Thanks. He was a great engineer and crewman. I'll be heading down for his service in a few hours."

"I'll see you there. Any more news on the accident, Kai?"

"We're not secure, General."

"I know."

There was a slight pause; then: "Are you heading up the accident investigation board, sir?"

"It hasn't been confirmed yet."

"As soon as I get the word that you're chairing the board, General, I'll pass along all the information on the entire incident," Kai said. At that same moment, Patrick received a secure instant message that scrolled across the bottom of his field of vision, thanks to the tiny electronic intraocular lens implant in his left eye. The message read: LET ME KNOW WHERE TO SEND THE FILES.

"Understood, Kai," Patrick said. "I'll drop you a line when I get the okay."

"Roger that, sir."

"I'll see you in Palo Alto for McCallum's service. Fly safe."

"Will do. Good to talk with you again, General." And he broke the connection.

"Raydon?" Ann asked, silently reminding Patrick that he was not yet part of any investigation.

"Yep. He couldn't say anything until the board is seated." Ann looked relieved, and Patrick noticed that. "You probably shouldn't say anything else to us either, Boomer."

"You're probably right, sir. But I'll start taking notes on what I remember and pass them along to the board for the record."

"Good." He extended a hand, and Boomer shook it with his left hand. "I hope you'll feel up to attending McCallum's service."

"I'll be there, General."

"We'll understand if you're not. You've been through an extraordinary emergency."

"I'll be there," Boomer assured him. Patrick nodded, and he and Ann departed.

Back in his car, Ann said, "I was starting to get worried about you asking questions and then calling Raydon, Patrick. Be careful about contaminating the integrity of the investigation before you get seated."

"Ann, I would fall over backward in a dead faint if I was appointed chair of that investigation board," Patrick said, "or any other government position except maybe in charge of beach sandals and boogie boards in Alaska. There's no way on earth President Gardner would allow Banderas to select me."

"Why not? You're by far the highest-ranking astronaut in the world; one of the best-known and well-respected military officers in the nation; you're available; you know the space systems and the hazards; and you can work for the traditional one-dollar stipend," Ann said. She looked at Patrick carefully. "I remember all that stuff about the president wanting you pulled off Armstrong after those attacks in Turkey and whatever happened in Nevada. I also remember you suddenly disappeared off the station after convincing everyone you were too sick to stand the stress of reentry, after which suddenly the pressure was off, you were retired, and the space defense program was back on track. What happened after you returned to Earth . . . or shouldn't I ask?"

"You shouldn't ask," Patrick said evenly. "In fact, you're probably in pretty deep already, since some would assume I'd already told you everything."

Ann swallowed apprehensively after hearing that. "Then maybe you *should* tell me."

"No, not yet," Patrick said. "We'll see how this plays out."

Ann fell silent for a few moments as Patrick drove; then: "So if you are so sure you won't get the appointment, why the press conference?"

"To try to put a little pressure on the White House," Patrick said. "I won't get the appointment, and folks will wonder why not. Hopefully it'll focus a little more attention on the investigation so the results won't be swept under the rug." Ann Page looked carefully at Patrick, then smiled when he glanced at her. "What?"

"Look at you—you're starting to sound like a damned political hack," she said. "You're talking about putting pressure on the White House like you probably used to talk about planning a bomb run."

"I worked in the White House for a couple years, Ann—it's no different than any other ally or adversary," Patrick said. "Elected officials, appointees, career bureaucrats, employees, consultants, advisers, all the characters who roam around the place—they all have wishes, desires, objectives, fears, and suspicions. They respond to pressure, real or perceived. Nothing wrong with letting them have a little of it." He glanced at her again. "Would there be a problem of you getting me a copy of the data from Armstrong?"

"If you're not on the board, I don't think they'd allow it, Patrick," Ann replied. "And my head would be on a platter in a New York minute if I leaked it. Sorry." She paused, smiled at him, and added, "Kind of tough just being a regular civilian again? Can't just snap your fingers and get classified data anymore—it's gotta be frustrating."

"Sure, sometimes," Patrick said. "I believe in the Space Defense Force and the advancement of military space, just like I believed in the manned bomber years ago, and I'd hate to have politics get in the way of what I believe will be the weapon system of choice in the near future."

"Good speech, General McLanahan," Ann said with a chuckle. "Let me know when you plan to deliver it—I want to be there."

THE BERING SEA, 300 MILES NORTHEAST OF KLYUCHI, KAMCHATKA PENINSULA, EASTERN RUSSIAN FEDERATION

THE NEXT MORNING

The Japanese Maritime Self-Defense Force's *Atago*-class destroyer *Ashigara* was in the first month of a three-month-long routine patrol of the Sea of Okhotsk and western Bering Sea. The destroyer was an improved Japanese version of the American Navy's DDG-51 *Arleigh Burke*–class destroyer, with Japanese-made defensive weaponry as well as American-made weapons, the AN/ SPY-1D Aegis radar system, and fore and aft vertical-launch-system cells with surface-to-air and ASROC rocket-propelled torpedoes; the big difference was its full helicopter hangar along with its landing pad. It was one of the world's most powerful warships and was well suited for the usually harsh winter weather conditions of the Bering Sea.

The Japanese navy, along with the United States and other Pacific countries, made regular patrols in the area not only to show that they were not shy about operating so close to Russian shores, but to plot and observe all the military activity and listen in to the variety of electronic signals being broadcast in the area. The Russian Pacific Fleet had a major submarine and naval aviation base at Petropavlovsk-Kamchatsky, about three hundred miles south, with Delta-III nuclear ballistic-missile submarines and Akula attack submarines, Tupolev-142 naval attack bombers, and Mikoyan-Gureyvich-31 long-range interceptors based there. In fact, the *Ashigara* had made a weeklong port call to Petropavlovsk-Kamchatsky naval base and had been warmly welcomed by the Russians. But the *Ashigara*'s objective on this part of the cruise was three hundred miles north of Petropavlosk-Kamchatsky: the Klyuchi Test Range, an isolated part of the northern Kamchatka Peninsula, heavily instrumented and used to record the accuracy of reentry warheads carried aloft by intercontinental ballistic missiles launched from western Russia.

A lot of activity had been observed in and around the Klyuchi Test Range in recent weeks. The United States made regular ship and air patrols of the test range, and the long-range COBRA DANE radar at Eareckson Air Station on Shemya Island also kept watch, but since the *Ashigara* was already in the area, it was diverted to cruise the area and observe.

Instead of reentry vehicles, the crew of the *Ashigara* were observing numerous fighter sorties in the Klyuchi Test Range. Yelizovo Airfield at Petropavlovsk-Kamchatsky had a regiment of MiG-31 "Foxhound" supersonic fighters, designed to intercept low-flying bombers and cruise missiles hundreds of miles from shore at over twice the speed of sound. The MiGs were not dogfighters, but instead used large, powerful radars to launch advanced radar-guided air-to-air missiles . . . except the MiGs in the Klyuchi Test Range weren't practicing attacking bombers, but were simply cruising out to the range, climbing steeply, then heading back to Yelizovo.

The *Ashigara* soon found out what the MiGs were up to. As the captain and combat officers of the Japanese destroyer watched in fascination, one MiG-31 accelerated to over two and a half times the speed of sound, then made a steep climb. The fighter roared to over sixty-five thousand feet at just over the speed of sound, then released a single missile slung under its belly centerline stores station.

The missile was a 50N8 Graza, or "Storm," long-range surface-to-air missile, modified as an air-launched antisatellite weapon. The Russian antisatellite missile climbed quickly on its first-stage motor for about fifteen seconds, climbing to over 200,000 feet, then coasted for a short period as it dropped its first-stage motor section.

The second stage ignited moments later, and the missile quickly climbed to five hundred miles' altitude before the second stage separated.

Because it did not have enough speed to enter Earth's orbit, the third stage began to descend. At four hundred miles' altitude, the third stage separated, leaving the kill vehicle to continue the descent. Using short blasts of hydrazine, it adjusted its course using inertial, GPS, and datalink course guidance; then, as it closed in on its target, it used its own radar for precise terminal guidance. It scored a direct hit on a deactivated Yantar-4K2 target reconnaissance satellite just minutes later.

MEMORIAL CHAPEL, STANFORD
UNIVERSITY, PALO ALTO, CALIFORNIA

LATER THAT AFTERNOON

"I'd like to conclude with these words," Vice President Ken Phoenix said. "It was found written on a slip of paper in a trench in Tunisia during the battle of El Agheila during World War Two, but it is just as appropriate here today as we honor the memory and the extraordinary life of First Lieutenant Jeffrey McCallum, U.S. Space Defense Force. It read: 'Stay with me, God. The night is dark, the night is cold: my little spark of courage dies. The night is long; be with me, God, and make me strong.' Rest in peace, Lieutenant. Job well done."

After the service concluded, the vice president followed along with the pastor and family members as the pallbearers wheeled the casket to the front of the chapel, and then the Air Force honor guard carried the casket to the waiting hearse. The family had requested that the burial at Holy Cross Cemetery in Menlo Park be for family only, so the vice president waited at the bottom of the steps as the hearse and cars for the family departed. He greeted hundreds of students, faculty, and other mourners who had attended the service, then was escorted to his armored Cadillac limousine.

Already in the car were Patrick McLanahan in the left forward-facing seat and Ann Page, Kai Raydon, and Hunter Noble in the aft-facing seats. "Thank you for attending the service, Mr. Vice President," Patrick said once they were all seated and the motorcade headed toward Phoenix's hotel in San Jose. "I know the family appreciates your visit very much."

"Thank you, Patrick," Phoenix said. He patted Patrick on the shoulder. "It's good to see you again after Iraq. I had some doubts we'd get out of there alive."

"Same here, sir." Patrick had been a private contractor working in Iraq when the Turkish army invaded northern Iraq, and he and the vice president, who was there as part of a cease-fire-negotiating team, were trapped near Mosul as the fighting intensified.

"I'd like to get my hands on whoever leaked the details of the accident and McCallum's actions to the press," Ann Page said bitterly. "McCallum was an American astronaut, but the press has been calling him incompetent and cowardly, even before the poor guy was buried."

"Unfortunately, a lot of the radio transmissions from space were unsecure and easily intercepted," Kai Raydon said, "so anyone with a big enough dish could have picked them up."

"The only other people who knew were either in the Pentagon or the White House," Phoenix said, "and if it was from either of those places, I'll find out, and then I'll let you have first crack at them, Secretary Page." Ann nodded, and her expression left little doubt that she was looking forward to that moment. "General Raydon, what's the latest on the Kingfisher explosion?"

"Nothing definite yet, sir," Kai said. "We did find a closed arming circuit, so we're going over the entire arming system to find out why that circuit was closed. The boards that McCallum replaced initially reported in the green when the garage was powered up, but then the circuits closed and the thing blew."

"You've got to find out what happened, General, as quickly as possible, if you want your program to survive," Phoenix said. "The president already wants the ground-attack weapons removed from the garages, and he's thinking about a unilateral moratorium on antisatellite weapons ahead of a global initiative to ban antisatellite weapons completely."

"Ban *all* antisatellite weapons? Even defensive ones?"

"Unless we figure out a foolproof way to distinguish defensive from offensive weapons, yes," Phoenix replied. "We've got China, Russia, and other countries like Pakistan complaining about weapons in space, and both China and Russia racing each other to test out a new antisatellite weapon. The Russians fired off an air-launched antisatellite missile earlier today, timed so that it could be observed by a Japanese Aegis warship."

"The *Kamareeniy,* or 'Mosquito,' sir," Boomer said. He shuffled uncomfortably under his heavily bandaged right shoulder, but went on: "We first saw it about three years ago; it's based on our ASM-135 ASAT from twenty-five years ago. The Russians didn't make a big deal out of it until recently, like the Chinese and their Dong Feng-21's. Fairly mature technology, a lot cheaper than directed-energy antisatellite weapons like lasers or microwaves, and easier to move and conceal. It was supposedly one of General Andrei Darzov's favorite programs when he was the Russian air force's chief of staff—the guy is a space superfreak."

"And now he's the Russian military chief of staff," Patrick said. "Truznyev is a powerful president, but Darzov may hold even more sway, especially in the military—soldiers never got along well with spies. I would guess that Darzov would never allow Truznyev to sign a treaty banning space weapons of any kind. Not exactly an opportune time to start talking about eliminating antisatellite weapons." He looked at the vice president. "Rumor has it that you are going to head up the Space Policy Review panel, sir."

"Keeping your ear on the rail once again, I see," Phoenix said. "You always did have your own little spy network running, and I see it hasn't retired." He hesitated for a moment, considering whether or not to share the results of a confidential meeting in the White House with outsiders; then decided: "Yes, I was lobbying to head up an industry leaders' commission on space technology, but it was morphed into redrafting space policy with the direct intent to prove to the rest of the world that the United States doesn't see space as a sovereign national defense domain, and that we will co-operate with other nations for free access to space."

"Seems to me we should keep the systems we have in place *until* we have a treaty ratified."

"The president is afraid of losing all cooperation with China," Phoenix explained. "He wants to use diplomacy to get back in their good graces and stop an arms race in space. The rest of the National Security Council is with him."

Except Phoenix, Patrick noted silently.

The vice president looked out the window, obviously wrestling with a tough dilemma. "I think there's a connection between the president leaking the formation of the National Space Policy review panel and the invasion of Somalia," he said finally. "China feels this is their opportunity, and they're taking advantage. But there aren't enough pieces here yet to show the picture." He looked at each of the others in the limousine with him. "Space is suddenly becoming a very big deal, lady and gentlemen. I hope the president sees it before we lose our edge. I need to know what happened to that weapon garage, Patrick."

"Unfortunately, the rumor is that Secretary Banderas is going to choose someone else to head the accident investigation board," Ann Page said.

"Yeah, I heard, too," Phoenix said. "General Walter Wollensky, former commander of U.S. Space Command."

"It was not Secretary Banderas's choice," Ann said. "Wollensky is a good guy, but he was retired after the American Holocaust because of depression—the guy lost eight thousand airmen from his command in the attacks. He got his security clearance back and was working as a consultant for some aerospace firms. He was never a fan of Armstrong Space Station or the whole U.S. Space Defense Force concept."

"So you think he's going to help the president kill the Kingfishers?" Phoenix asked.

Ann shrugged. "I don't know, sir, but I wish we had a better advocate for the program on that board."

"You're going to have to find the answer yourselves," Phoenix said. "Cooperate with Wollensky, but challenge his conclusions with hard evidence."

The limousine approached the hotel at which the vice president was staying; a small crowd of onlookers and party officials were waiting for him. "More campaign stops, sir?" Patrick asked.

"Yes." Phoenix looked weary and a little downcast. "After attending a memorial service, it's hard sometimes to gear yourself up to do campaigning, be cheerful and upbeat, and say good things about the future."

"Especially when it's not necessarily *your* future, sir?" Patrick asked in a low voice.

Phoenix half turned toward him, but his face was absolutely expressionless. He said tonelessly, "A car will take you back to San Jose. Thank you for meeting with me on the ride over, everyone," and then shook hands with each of them.

"Good luck, Mr. Vice President," Patrick said.

"I'll be in touch, Patrick. Good to see you again." The motorcade stopped, and at that, as if someone had thrown an invisible power switch, the vice president's shoulders straightened, a beaming smile emerged, his chin lifted, his eyes twinkled, and suddenly he was in full-blown campaign mode. He was already greeting party officials, dignitaries, and reporters, most of them by name, before he had stepped outside the opened door.

Patrick, Ann, Boomer, and Kai had to listen to several minutes of cheering, questions shouted at the vice president by the reporters arrayed outside, and his campaign-ready answers delivered enthusiastically and sincerely, but soon the motorcade was on the move again. The vice president's car separated from the others in the detail and went to an area behind the hotel where several unmarked cars, police vehicles, and even an ambulance were prepositioned in case of any threats against the vice president. They transferred to a standard limousine, which drove off toward San Jose International Airport.

They dropped Ann Page off first at her airline ticket counter, then headed around the field to the general aviation area to drop off Patrick. "Did you get the files I sent, General?" Kai asked after Ann had left the car.

"Yes, and Dave Luger and I have been going over them," Patrick said. "But it's all on the Kingfisher satellite. I'd like to see a dump of all your sensor data for at least two hours preceding the explosion."

"Why?"

"Two reasons: I know you guys will be closely examining the Kingfisher, and I don't really understand it that well anyway; and . . . well, other than that, I don't know, except I have a hunch," Patrick explained. "I don't believe in coincidences. We've got anti-satellite weapons flying everywhere; we've got China firing missiles, sending troops all over the place, and invading other countries; and in the middle of all that, a very reliable piece of hardware blows up for no apparent reason right after repairs are done."

"You think China had something to do with Kingfisher-Eight?"

"We won't know until we see what your sensors saw. Remember anything that happened around that time?"

"We were pretty busy—everything seemed to happen all at once," Kai admitted, his brow furrowing as he tried hard to remember clearly. "The convoy missing, then discovered heading toward Mogadishu; the Chinese bomber formations we spotted; launching the Stud on short notice to link up with Eight; the repairs; the accident. No, I can't think of anything else."

The car pulled into the general aviation terminal and was allowed onto the parking ramp, where a dozen or so bizjets were lined up. Patrick retrieved his luggage from the trunk. "Well, if you think of anything," he told Kai, "call me anytime."

"Will do, sir." He nodded toward the impressive line of jets. "Which one is yours?"

"Not there—over down that way," Patrick said, motioning way across the ramp to an adjacent parking area. "They don't park me with the heavy iron, and that's the way I like it. The blue-and-white twin."

Kai followed Patrick's motion and saw a rather small twin-engine propeller plane, sitting by itself along with other smaller planes. "That's it? The little bug-smasher?"

"It's small, but I mostly fly solo and I rarely fly with more than two other people, so it's a good size for me," Patrick said. "It's the fastest propeller-driven general aviation plane in the world."

"*Propeller*-driven?" Boomer commented. "Why don't you fly a jet, General?"

"Because they cost money, and I don't fly that often to justify the expense," Patrick replied. "Got time to take a look?"

Neither Kai nor Boomer would ever turn down a chance to look at airplanes, so they walked down the ramp. "*You* . . . worried about expenses?" Kai asked. "I thought you were a rich retired three-star general."

"Military retirees don't make that much these days; the private-military-contractor work keeps us busy but is expensive; and Jon Masters pays hardly anything except stock options," Patrick said. "This is plenty for me when I travel and Jon's not picking up the tab. Besides, Jon and I have installed a few gizmos in the plane to pick up the performance."

The airplane resembled a bullet-shaped jet fighter with a pointed nose, very short wings, large, weirdly curved propellers, and a tall vertical stabilizer. Patrick unlocked the door and opened the split clamshell door. The cockpit looked very snug, and at first Boomer couldn't figure out how to get in the back. Patrick then pushed the pilot's seat full forward, creating a narrow aisle. "We usually load the front-seat passenger first, then rear passengers, and pilot last. I took out one of the middle seats to allow a passenger to use the worktable and satellite Internet while in flight."

"What is that smell?" Boomer asked, hunting around for the source. "Dirty socks?"

"Biodiesel," Patrick said. "The turbine engines on this plane were modified by Jon's engineers to burn almost any fuel, from unleaded gasoline to synthetics. They crank out five hundred horsepower a side but burn less than twenty gallons an hour. I can get three hundred knots easily and three-fifty at redline, and its range is about fifteen hundred miles, so I can go coast-to-coast most days with one stop. It has an automatic electric deicing system on the wings, tail surfaces, and windshield, but it can go as high as thirty thousand feet and climb at two thousand feet a minute, so I rarely need it."

The cockpit was simplicity itself, with three ten-inch monitors, some small standby instruments underneath the pilot's monitor, and a small keyboard under the center monitor above the throttles. "Two primary flight displays and a middle multifunction display; side-stick controllers; computer-controlled propeller pitch; three-axis autopilot with autothrottles," Patrick said. "Full automatic digital datalink with air-traffic control—everything from receiving clearances to traffic to weather avoidance is digital. I don't talk to anyone on the radios unless I use uncontrolled airspace."

Boomer peered into the cabin. "No potty?"

"After flying bombers for so long, I've developed a pretty large-capacity bladder," Patrick said. "Everyone else . . . well, it's a general aviation plane, not an airliner. Either hold it or I'll introduce you to the kitty-litter piddle pack."

"Your little plane just lost all appeal for me, sir," Boomer said, retreating from the entry door with a smile and a shake of his head. He shook hands with Patrick. "You and your SAC-trained bladder have a nice flight."

"Thanks, Boomer." He shook hands with Raydon. "If you think of anything, Kai, let me know as soon as you can. You know how to reach me."

"Will do, sir," Kai said. He and Boomer headed for the limousine, and Patrick headed into the airport office. He paid his fuel bill, made a stop in the restroom, then headed back to the airplane.

The temperature was comfortable enough, but a light fog was

beginning to roll in. Patrick powered up the plane's avionics and started downloading flight-planning information. Weather was good for the route of flight back to Henderson, Nevada, except for the weather at San Jose. Flying direct, the flight would only take an hour and fifteen minutes, but to avoid the Navy's China Lake restricted military airspace, the FAA's air-traffic control computers recommended flying southeast to Fresno, south to Bakersfield, and east to Palmdale before heading direct to Henderson, which added another forty-five minutes. He accepted the proffered flight plan, got an acknowledgment, then shut down the system to do a pre-flight inspection.

The plane had a computerized preflight system, but this was Patrick's only opportunity to do a personal, visual check of his machine before takeoff, so he grabbed his little preflight kit—flashlight, rag, windshield cleaning kit, and fuel strainer—and got to work. The biggest areas of concern were the tires, landing-gear struts, fluid levels, and freedom of the flight controls. He had to sample a few ounces of the smelly fuel from nine different sumps—not a very pleasant task, but essential to be sure there was no water or contamination in the fuel. Because he personally supervised the fueling of the plane's four fuel tanks, he knew how much biodiesel had been pumped—more than enough for the flight home, including reserves—but he visually checked the fuel level in each tank anyway. He had to wash his own windows because fixed-base operators, afraid of costly repairs if a linesman accidentally scratched a ten-thousand-dollar heated-glass windshield, didn't do it anymore.

After completing the walk-around and satisfied that the plane was ready to go, Patrick climbed inside, strapped in, closed and locked both of the clamshell doors, and powered up the plane again. He started engines, checked the engines, flight controls, electrical, autopilot, and hydraulic systems, then tuned in the Automatic Terminal Information System frequency, which instantly datalinked local weather, active runway, and hazard notices to his multifunction display. He then tuned in the clearance delivery channel, which downloaded his air-traffic control clearance—it had changed slightly since filing it, but that was not unusual. He made sure the updated routing was in the flight-data computer, then tuned in the ground control frequency and uplinked a "Ready to Taxi" message.

At that moment he saw a commotion back at the fixed-base operator office . . . and he noticed none other than Kai Raydon, waving his arms like crazy, and Hunter Noble running out toward him, followed by a security guard and an FBO employee obviously trying to stop them from going out onto the ramp! Patrick immediately shut down the left engine—the one nearest the entry door—sent a "Cancel Taxi" message to ground control, then shut down the avionics power and right engine.

Kai reached the plane just as the left propeller stopped spinning, and Patrick popped the upper half of the clamshell door open. "What the hell are you doing, Kai?" he asked.

"I remembered something, Patrick," Kai shouted over the spooling-down right engine. He put his hands behind his back and braced for the security guard to grab him from behind. "Something *did* happen. Dammit, General, you might be *right*."

SEVEN

Nothing is so simple that it cannot be misunderstood.

—GYPSEY TEAGUE

THE WHITE HOUSE OVAL OFFICE

THAT EVENING

President Joseph Gardner had his jacket off, his sleeves rolled up, and his tie loosened—to the photographers with their long lenses able to peer through the windows of the Oval Office from across the South Lawn, he looked like he was hard at work late in the evening, an image Gardner never tired of projecting. But he still had his Navy coffee mug, with Puerto Rican rum over ice instead of coffee, handy.

"Chinese forces in Somalia number about five thousand now, sir," White House Chief of Staff Walter Kordus said, reading from the late edition of "The President's Daily Brief," which Gardner liked to have read to him before he retired for the day. "They've solidified their position at Mogadishu Airport out beyond mortar range of anything except very large emplacements, which are easier to spot from the air and take out with gunships. They've brought in more fighter jets and have begun attacking other towns farther north that are known pirate bases."

"Premier Zhou's starting to look like a real badass now, isn't he?" Gardner asked, taking a sip of rum. "He's doing the dirty job no one else wanted to do, and he's kicking butt."

"The images of the aftermath of his bombing raids are pretty horrific." Kordus shrugged, then nodded and admitted, "But yes, he's getting full credit for completely stopping pirate activity in the Indian Ocean. Zhou has said that he intends on withdrawing all Chinese forces from Somalia as soon as his transport ships arrive with their escorts. His aircraft carrier the *Zhenyuan* is en route with its escorts, replenishment ships, cargo ships for their equipment, and a couple chartered cruise liners for the soldiers. They'll stop in Yemen for refueling and resupply before meeting up with their ships in Somalia."

"Bust up the capital city for a couple weeks, then just sail away. How nice," Gardner said. "But it was a gutsy move, I have to admit. I'd never tell Zhou that, of course. It's funny: Every other nation considered the pirates a nuisance—we set up the antipirate patrols, but piracy only increased. Folks started to think it was the insurance companies' problem, part of the cost of doing business. In comes the most unlikely player, China, and bombs the hell out of the Somalis. They attacked several other locations, too, didn't they?"

"Two more north of Mogadishu and two up in Puntland province," Kordus said after checking the reports. "They're using a lot of unmanned aircraft for surveillance, picking off pirate mother ships and teams of fighters on the ground with helicopter gunships. They're doing it all from the air—ground forces are being used to secure Mogadishu Airport and the docks in New Town only. If there's a warlord or clan leader they want, they just bomb the hell out of his last known location. If the attacks kill hundreds of civilians, that's too bad."

"And no one is saying boo about it except a few human-rights organizations," the president observed. "If the United States did it, we'd be catching hell from half the known universe, including our own press; China does it, and people are either applauding or too scared to squawk about it." He took another sip of rum and looked at his watch. "What else do we have?"

"Russia is sending its *Vladimir Putin* carrier battle group into the Indian Ocean," Kordus read. "Brand-new carrier, closer in size and number of embarked aircraft to Western carriers, similar to the Chinese carrier—probably built in the same shipyard—along with seven escorts. The Russian Ministry of Defense says they're going to drill with the Chinese in resupply, joint-communications, vessel-identification, search-and-rescue, and antipiracy operations."

"It's going to get crowded," Gardner said. "I want a briefing from Conrad on what, if anything, the Chiefs want to do—observe only, ask to play, stay out of the way, whatever. Find out if they want us to participate—that'll shock 'em." Kordus nodded and made a note. "So how did the vice president sound out in California?"

"He attended the memorial service, made short and nonpolitical remarks, did all the interviews we set up, did the fund-raiser that evening, gave a rousing speech from what I've heard, raised a bunch of money, and stuck to the script," Kordus said. "He was asked several times about his own presidential aspirations and ducked the questions pretty well. He's a very good campaigner, that's for sure."

"Whom did he meet with?"

"Exactly who he said he was going to meet with as he posted on his agenda," Kordus said, "with the notable exception of four other invited guests to the memorial service: Ann Page; General Raydon from the space station; Noble, who was the other astronaut involved in that satellite explosion; and none other than Patrick McLanahan."

"*McLanahan?* Phoenix met with *him?* Where? When?"

"In the ride from the memorial to the hotel, maybe thirty minutes max," Kordus said. "McLanahan had been nominated by Page to head up the accident investigation board on the satellite explosion; Conrad asked me about it, and I advised him to find someone else, knowing how much you and McLanahan like each other's company."

"You're damned right. Christ, that guy can't stay retired. I thought he'd be done after almost getting himself blown up in Iraq. I almost had a cow when I saw him give that presser with Page the other day." His brows furrowed in deep thought. "Phoenix and McLanahan, getting together again, all these years after Iraq? What in hell are they up to?"

"The vice president is interested in military space stuff; he was surrounded by four of the most knowledgeable persons on that very subject," Kordus said. "You think it's more than that? Something political?"

"Phoenix and Page, obviously," the president said. "Raydon and Noble, those two rocket jockeys . . . no way. McLanahan?" He thought for a moment, then shook his head. "He's an aviator, a bomber puke who turned space nerd when Kevin Martindale gave him an almost unlimited budget after the American Holocaust and let him fly in those spaceplanes." Gardner took a tiny sip of rum, staring at nothing, then said, "McLanahan . . . a *politician?*"

"Generals make lousy politicians unless they've just helped win a world war," Kordus said.

"I think the American Holocaust qualifies," Gardner said worriedly. He looked at Kordus. "Start checking on him, Walter. You can't run for county dogcatcher without campaign cash, and if McLanahan has got access to any, I want to know from whom and how much."

PORT OF MA'ALLA, ADEN,
REPUBLIC OF YEMEN

THE NEXT DAY

The *Jianghu*-2-class frigate *Wuxi* of the People's Liberation Army Navy, one of seven escort ships of the aircraft carrier *Zhenyuan,* was the first of the Chinese flotilla to enter the Port of Ma'alla, a modern and bustling port on the west side of the volcanic peninsula on which the city of Aden was located. The *Wuxi,* first built in the late 1970s and on its very first voyage away from Chinese home waters, was accompanied by two Yemeni tugboats, which would assist the aging single-screw frigate in berthing at its assigned refueling dolphin. It would refuel and take on water and a few supplies, then depart and go back to escort duty while another warship entered the bay and visited the port.

Because of security concerns, they would refuel only during the day, and the flotilla would remain a few miles offshore in the Gulf of Aden; the *Zhenyuan* itself would not come in for refueling, but would take on fuel and supplies from its two replenishment ships, practicing underway refueling. Resupply helicopters made a steady stream of trips out to the *Zhenyuan* and other ships that had helicopter decks with food, spare parts, munitions, and mail slung underneath, and returned to Aden International Airport and other supply bases in the port city with garbage, unrepairable equipment, and outgoing mail. Shuttle vessels sailed back and forth between the flotilla and the port, carrying more supplies and equipment as well as a few sailors allowed to visit the city and a few visitors allowed to go out to the ships for meetings.

The *Wuxi* was almost complete with refueling when a Yemeni patrol boat with the words NAVY PORT PATROL painted on the sides in English and Arabic left a berth on the north side of the harbor and sailed toward the *Wuxi* at a moderate speed. "Watch, this is Watch Four," the starboard stern lookout on the *Wuxi*, accompanying a gunner manning a 12.7-millimeter twin-barreled machine gun, radioed. "Visual contact, Yemeni patrol boat heading south toward us, speed approximately twenty kilometers per minute, range four hundred meters."

The watch commander stepped out of the bridge to the starboard overhanging deck and got a visual contact on the approaching patrol boat himself through his binoculars. "Acknowledged," he radioed back. "Report to briefed location." He made sure the watch stander and machine gunner left their station, then went back into the bridge and said so all could hear, "Officer of the Deck, this is the watch, approaching Yemeni patrol vessel on the starboard stern, four hundred meters, closing at approximately twenty kilometers per hour."

"I acknowledge, Watch," the officer of the deck responded. He picked up the VHF radio assigned to the Yemeni navy's harbor patrol frequency. "Port Patrol, Port Patrol, Port Patrol, this is the *Wuxi* on channel one-nine," he said in English, "requesting information on approaching patrol vessel, say your intentions, over."

There was a rather uncomfortable delay in the response; then: "*Wuxi, Wuxi, Wuxi,* this is the Yemeni Navy Port Patrol on channel one-nine, say again, over."

"I say again, Port Patrol, you have a patrol vessel approaching the *Wuxi*. Say intentions, over." The officer of the deck then said, "Watch, where is that patrol boat now?"

The watch officer went back outside and spotted the Yemeni patrol boat again. "Still closing, perhaps two hundred meters away, one-five-zero-degree bearing."

"Acknowledged," the officer of the deck responded. He turned to the boatswain's mate a few paces from him on the bridge. "Boats, verify that the aft decks are ready."

"Yes, sir." The boatswain's mate made two telephone calls, then reported, "Stern decks are ready as briefed, sir."

"Very well."

At that moment he heard, *"Wuxi,* this is Port Patrol Boat Three, I am inbound with the pilot for your departure. Many apologies for not contacting you sooner, sir. May we approach? Over."

"Patrol Boat Three, this is the *Wuxi,*" the officer of the deck radioed, finally reciting his well-rehearsed speech, "please do not approach, I will request verification. Stand by, please." The captain was observing the refueling and resupply and was not on the bridge, so he picked up another radio: "Captain, this is the officer of the deck."

"Go ahead," came the captain's reply from his portable radio.

"The patrol boat is inbound to the ship."

"Acknowledged," the captain said. "Is everything else in place?"

"Affirmative."

"Very well," the captain said. "Continue. Let's hope the old sow stays afloat long enough to get the rest of the crew off."

"Acknowledged," the officer of the deck responded. He switched his radio to a second channel and keyed the microphone several times.

"Bridge, Watch!" the watch officer suddenly shouted. "Inbound patrol vessel has increased speed, heading straight for us!"

"Captain, patrol boat has picked up speed and is heading for us!" the officer of the deck shouted into his radio.

"Repel, sound battle stations, sound collision!" the captain ordered. He and the ship's chief boatswain's mate, who was with the captain supervising the refueling and resupply, began to wave crewmembers away from the stern and off the helicopter landing platform.

"Sound battle stations, sound collision!" the officer of the deck shouted to the boatswain's mate on the bridge. "Watch, repel all attackers, repeat, repel all attackers!"

The boatswain's mate reached up on the overhead communications panel and hit two large red buttons, and the earsplitting sound of horns and bells seemed to rattle every surface of the warship. He then pulled the shipwide intercom microphone up and shouted, *"All hands, battle stations, all hands, battle stations, all hands, collision, collision, collision, brace for impact, starboard side!"*

The officer of the deck grabbed his life vest and helmet and rushed out to the starboard overhanging deck as damage control teams and backup duty personnel started rushing into the bridge. He followed the watch officer's binoculars and spotted the incoming patrol boat just as the number four machine gunner opened fire. There was a helicopter with a load of supplies slung underneath still hovering over the landing pad. *"Boats, wave off that chopper!"* he shouted inside the bridge.

But it was too late. At that instant the Yemeni patrol boat slammed into the side of the *Wuxi*. At first it appeared to just bounce away, heeling sharply over to starboard and scraping along the side of the warship . . .

. . . but then the three thousand pounds of explosives packed inside the patrol boat detonated, and a massive fireball obscured the destroyer's entire stern. The *Wuxi* seemed to jump ten feet straight out of the water before being shoved violently to port. As the vessel came down, the entire stern dove beneath the churning waves, then bobbed back up . . . until the flaming wreckage of the stricken resupply helicopter, instantly engulfed in flames from the fireball, slammed down into the landing platform. The *Wuxi* was pushed into the refueling dolphin, severing fuel lines that ignited and fed even more flaming devastation on the Chinese warship.

In seconds, the entire aft half of the vessel was afire. It began to take on water from the huge hole in its aft port side and sink by the stern. An area of almost a half square mile of burning oil surrounded the *Wuxi,* dooming any sailors who decided to abandon ship or who had been thrown into the harbor by the force of the explosions. Ammunition began cooking off, followed moments later by exploding antiship missiles and their warheads, which leveled entire sections of superstructure.

Chinese Aircraft Carrier Zhenyuan,
10 Miles off the Coast of Yemen

That same time

"Sir, the frigate *Wuxi* has been hit," the communications officer reported in a remarkably calm, almost nonchalant tone. "She is on fire and is sinking by the stern. We are not in contact with the captain."

"Acknowledged," the admiral in command of the *Zhenyuan* battle group replied. He turned to the carrier's captain. "Sound battle stations, Captain." As the horns and Klaxons blared, he then ordered, "Commence launch, Captain."

On the *Zhenyuan's* flight deck, two Jian Hong-37N fighter-bombers, already in place on the forward and waist catapults, lit their afterburners and blasted off into the late afternoon sky. Lined up behind them were six more JH-37s, their wings bristling with bombs and missiles. Every ninety seconds, two more JH-37s were catapulted skyward. They did not climb high, but stayed less than five hundred feet above the Gulf of Aden, speeding northward.

The first two JH-37s were each loaded with four Ying Ji-91 antiradiation missiles, which were versions of the Russian Kh-31 air-to-surface missile. Capable of speeds well over three times the speed of sound, the missiles had been programmed to destroy particular radars protecting the area around the city of Aden. Missiles targeted the air-surveillance and height-finding radars at Aden International Airport, air-surveillance and marine radars at the naval base, the air defense radars also at the airport, and coastal surveillance radars east and west of the peninsula.

The second wave of fighter-bombers each carried four Kh-29T TV-guided missiles. They climbed a bit higher than the first wave, both because the air defense radars had already been neutralized and because they needed to get a better look at their targets before attacking. The JH-37 pilots flew precise attack courses and used time and preplanned acquisition waypoints that would guarantee they could spot their targets—air and coastal defense gun and missile sites. Once the sites were spotted, the pilots quickly locked each Kh-29 electro-optical sensor on target and released the missiles, which flew at almost the speed of sound and destroyed them in seconds.

Each of the JH-37Ns in the third and fourth waves carried just two weapons instead of four, but they were even more devastating than their brothers: KAB-1500KR guided two-thousand-pound armor-piercing bombs. They used low-light TV sensors in the nose to home in on the central telecommunications facility in the city, the TV and radio broadcasting center, and the Yemeni army and navy headquarters, allocating two of the massive bombs on each target to assure complete obliteration. Their armored structure allowed them to penetrate even hardened roofs with ease, and their fuses had been set to allow the weapons to penetrate a specific number of floors in each assigned target and then explode in precisely the floor they wanted, mostly in the power-distribution and data-storage rooms, control rooms, or subfloor command posts.

In minutes, the Yemeni civilian and military infrastructure in the city of Aden was rendered deaf, dumb, and blind, followed shortly thereafter by totally decimation.

ARMSTRONG SPACE STATION

THAT SAME TIME

A warning tone sounded in the command module, which immediately got everyone's attention. "SBIRS-High recording a thermal blossom, sir," Senior Master Sergeant Valerie "Seeker" Lukas reported. She typed some instructions into her computer and carefully read the response. "Looks like it's in the harbor at Aden, Yemen."

"Okay," the station commander, U.S. Army Colonel Alan Camerota, weakly responded. Camerota, just forty years old and looking even younger, was Kai Raydon's replacement while the general was on scheduled rest and reacclimation back on Earth. An Army strategic air defense engineer and weapons designer, Camerota had trained as a Shuttle and Orion mission specialist for three years but had never been selected for a mission. As one of the experts on the Trinity interceptor vehicle, he had supervised the deployment of the Kingfisher weapon garages, but always from Earth, not from space—but now, with Raydon grounded for at least a month, he had been selected to command Armstrong Space Station as his first and long-awaited time in orbit.

As the old saying goes: Be careful what you wish for—you might get it. Despite years of training and rigorous physical conditioning, weeks in the neutral buoyancy tank at NASA, many hours in the "Vomit Comet" zero-g training aircraft, and a careful diet, Camerota found to his great disappointment that zero-g did not agree with him—and that was putting it mildly. He was using anti-airsickness drugs, both chemical and herbal, and he also used acupressure wristbands and blood-cooling patches on the neck, but after two days in space he was still battling airsickness—his stomach would just not settle down. It was getting to the point where his performance might be affected. He was determined to overcome it, but for now his body was calling the shots.

"Can we get a look at it, Master Sergeant?" Camerota asked.

"We have Kingfisher-Six overhead in nine minutes and Kingfisher-Two within oblique view in seventeen minutes," Seeker replied. She looked at Camerota and noticed his "barf bag"—a specially designed receptacle with a one-way valve that prevented emesis from flying back out in zero-g—was out and at the ready. "You okay, sir?"

"I'm fine," Camerota said, but he looked anything but fine.

"I can get Major Faulkner up here." Former Marine Corps F-35 pilot Major Jessica "Gonzo" Faulkner was the senior spaceplane pilot on the station while Hunter Noble was back on Earth, and she had been training at the commander's console when not flying or training other pilots—she was, in Seeker's opinion, by far the best-qualified station commander if Camerota couldn't continue.

"I said I'm fine, Master Sergeant," Camerota said as convincingly as he could. "Notify me when Six is in range. What does SBIRS say it is?"

"Stationary dot, very hot burst but cooling off quickly—most likely a large explosion," Lukas said. "Could be a missile launch, but SBIRS didn't detect a track."

"Notify Space Command and STRATCOM," Camerota said. "I also want to . . ." And then he paused, gurgled a bit, then threw up in the barf bag.

"Sir . . . ?"

"I said I'm okay, Master Sergeant," Camerota said irritably, wiping his face with a towel. "Do we have any naval sensors we can tap into, or any local news coverage, some other way we can . . ." He gurgled again, fighting off another wave of nausea; he seemed to be having a great deal of trouble orienting himself, as if his seat were slowly spinning. "Dammit, if I can just hold myself steady here, I'll be okay."

"I'll try for both, sir," Seeker said. "Six should be in range in a few minutes." She tried scanning for radio or TV broadcasts, but there was nothing but static from all of the known channels. "Nothing on the civil broadcast frequencies. That's odd. You know, sir, we couldn't receive any UAV imagery from around Mogadishu or even fly UAVs out there because the Chinese were jamming all the frequencies." She turned to Camerota. "The Chinese task force reinforcing their ships in the Indian Ocean was supposed to be taking on supplies earlier today in Aden. Maybe we should . . ."

. . . and as she turned, she saw Camerota floating before her, belly up, his mouth open, hands on his throat in the classic "I'm choking!" signal, with a haze of vomit encircling his head and his face turning deep blue. She stabbed the "ALL-CALL" intercom button: "Medics to the command module immediately, emergency. Major Faulkner, to the command module immediately." She then detached herself from her console and propelled herself over to Camerota. His mouth and throat were packed tightly with nearly solid vomit. The barf bag was open and the contents were coming out—the one-way valve must have failed, and Camerota must have inhaled a throatful of vomit and passed out.

Alarms and warning beeps began sounding one after another, but Seeker ignored them as she maneuvered herself to help Camerota. As she began scooping out vomit from his throat, Jessica Faulkner floated into the command module, followed by the crewman on medical detail. "Jesus, Seeker, what happened?" Faulkner shouted as the medic took over for Lukas and got busy inserting a resuscitator tube into Camerota's throat.

"He choked on some vomit, I think," Lukas said. "My God, he's passed out. I'll help Crawford. Ma'am, get on the console and find out what all the alerts are about." She had to maneuver Camerota against the lower bulkhead and restrain him with both of their bodies Velcroed down to be able to do cardiopulmonary respiration on him.

"What in the hell is going on here?" Faulkner asked as she scanned the monitors. "A possible missile launch and explosions all around . . . where is this? Somalia again?"

"Aden, Yemen," Seeker said. "We detected a big thermal event in the harbor. Kingfisher-Six should be overhead soon."

"I got it," Faulkner said. The interceptor platform was already above the target's horizon, so Faulkner entered commands to slew the garage's imaging infrared and telescopic electro-optical sensors on the initial explosion and zoom in. "Holy cow, it's a warship!" she exclaimed. "Looks like it's sinking by the stern."

"Where is it?"

"Looks like a frigate, moored on a refueling platform in the harbor."

"I hope it's not one of the Chinese ships that were supposed to refuel at Aden," Seeker said. "What about the other events?"

"Checking." Faulkner entered commands to zoom in on the other alarms. "More explosions. Looks like at an airport. It looks like . . . *whoa,* holy cow, I just saw another explosion, and a jet just zoomed by the picture! I think it's an air raid!" She zoomed out again, then focused in on other targets. "Lots of pretty localized explosions." She looked over her shoulder at Camerota. "How's he doing?"

"He's breathing," Seeker said. Camerota's eyes were open, but they were spinning dazedly; he was badly disoriented. Other crewmembers floated over to help, so Lukas detached herself from the bulkhead and reattached herself to her seat at the sensor console. She took a few moments to study the entire area around the city, then punched in instructions on her console. An intelligence map of the city superimposed itself on the frozen sensor image, with various buildings and places identified.

Seeker adjusted the map's size until it perfectly matched the image. "I think it's definitely an air raid, ma'am," she told Faulkner. "This is a coastal defense gun and missile emplacement; this is an air defense missile site; this is where the local broadcast center is. Whoever hit these places wanted to take out all of the area defenses and shut down communications."

"And I'll bet I know who did it," Faulkner said. She used the commander's console to zoom the image out until the Chinese flotilla was in sight, then zoomed in. Taken just moments before, the image showed fighters lined up on the catapults waiting to launch and even fighters still on the arresting cables waiting to taxi clear. "Pretty freakin' incredible," she said, shaking her head. "First Somalia, and now Yemen?"

"I'll bet that ship burning in the harbor is a Chinese warship," Seeker offered, "so this might be retaliation for a suicide attack. The Chinese went after air and coastal defenses and command-and-control centers . . ."

"Softening them up for another land invasion?"

"That would be my guess, ma'am," Seeker said. "I'd better make sure SPACECOM and STRATCOM have these images."

"I need to talk with the boss," Faulkner said. She donned a headset and entered instructions into her computer to activate an encrypted voice link, then spoke: "Armstrong to Raydon, secure."

21st Space Operations Squadron, Onizuka Air Force Station, Sunnyvale, California

That same time

"Raydon here, secure," Kai answered a few moments later, after being led to a communications room by the senior master sergeant in charge. Raydon, along with Patrick McLanahan and Hunter Noble, was in a secure laboratory at the 21st Space Operations Squadron at Onizuka Air Force Station near San Jose. They had requested access to a secure facility to examine the classified-data downloads from Armstrong Space Station in the hours prior to the destruction of the Kingfisher-8 weapon garage. The Twenty-first, located in the large windowless light blue-colored building near Moffett Federal Airfield known as the "Blue Cube," maintained the Air Force's network of satellite control centers and provided satellite communications between both terrestrial and in-orbit users. Originally slated for closure in 2011, Onizuka Air Force Station—named after Lieutenant Colonel Ellison Onizuka, one of the seven crewmembers killed in the *Challenger* Shuttle disaster in 1986—was kept open to properly service and support the growing U.S. Space Defense Force satellite infrastructure.

"Faulkner, secure."

"Hi, Gonzo." Patrick was immediately on alert—Kai's face told him this was not a routine call. "What's going on?"

"The Chinese appear to be at it again, sir," Faulkner said. "This time in Aden, Yemen."

"What?"

"It's happening right now, sir. Looks like they launched bombers from their aircraft carrier off the coast of Aden and bombed defensive sites and command-and-control sites around the city. It might be retaliation for an attack on one of their warships in the harbor."

"You've *got* to be kidding me," Kai exclaimed. He turned to Patrick. "The Chinese are attacking Aden, Yemen." Patrick immediately picked up a secure phone. "Everyone's been notified?"

"Seeker is double-checking that SPACECOM and STRAT-COM got the message."

"Good. Where's Camerota?"

"He's down, sir."

"'*Down*'? What do you mean, 'down'? What happened?"

"Chronic space sickness ever since he got here, apparently passed out with a throatful of vomit," Faulkner explained. "He's breathing again but still loopy. Crawford is with him."

"You take command of the station."

"Yes, sir."

"What's your status?"

"The station is Code One," she replied. "I haven't checked all the garages yet." She scanned her monitors and studied the one Lukas was pointing to. "Seeker just put it up: Three and Seven show some kind of fault."

"Are you up, Seeker?"

"Yes, sir," Lukas responded.

"The faults on Three and Seven: Are they similar to what happened to Eight?"

"The safe and continuity circuit faults? Stand by." She called up a more detailed readout of Kingfisher-3's fault. "Yes, sir, same fault on Three."

"We're looking at data readouts for the Kingfisher constellation for the past few days before the incident on Eight," Kai said, "and we're starting to pick up a pattern: The satellites develop an error in the continuity circuits over just about the same location on Earth each time, give or take five hundred miles."

"That's almost a pinpoint in orbital terms."

"Exactly. We notice the failures at different times, and they're not exactly the same type of fault, but it's close enough to get our attention. We're trying to get tasking to set up reconnaissance over Venezuela. The Russians have two signals intelligence sites in Venezuela: Caracas and El Tigre. They're doing more than just listening at one of those sites."

"So you think the Russians are using SIGINT sites to hack into the Kingfisher safe and continuity circuits and fault them so we're forced to shut them down?" Faulkner asked.

"Exactly."

"Could they have caused Eight to blow itself up?"

"We might have a different reason for that," Kai said. "Something I remembered about the moments before the accident. Remember that industrial fire we detected right about the same time, Seeker?"

"Yes, sir. We verified it: A Myanmar natural-gas processing facility caught fire. We photographed it afterward."

"But if you take the typical attack profile of a Chinese DF-21 missile and place the origin of that profile at that spot, the missile would have hit Kingfisher-Eight," Kai said. "I think the Chinese set an explosion at that natural-gas plant to hide a DF-21 launch."

"But no other sensors detected a missile launch, sir."

"No other sensors had the capability," Kai said. "DSP and SBIRS-High did exactly what they were supposed to do: detect the thermal bloom. On a typical DF-21 attack, the missile rises almost straight up to its intercept point, which means no track develops, or the track was still obscured by the ground fire. Only SBIRS-Low or Kingfisher-Eight could have tracked a DF-21."

"Still not exactly evidence the Chinese attacked one of our satellites, sir."

"We found another piece of the puzzle, Seeker," Kai said. "We assumed that the safe and continuity circuits that McCallum replaced on Eight were faulty and caused a Trinity interceptor to explode. It turns out the safe and continuity circuits were working just fine . . . because Eight went into self-defense mode almost immediately after we powered it up."

"What?"

"Kingfisher-Eight had activated its self-defense mode," Kai said almost breathlessly. "It wasn't a fault: It was real, because Eight detected the incoming Chinese DF-21 and was trying to reposition itself to launch an interceptor when it was hit. We were looking at the data but coming to completely wrong conclusions. We assumed the satellite was still bad even after Jeffrey changed the boards, but it wasn't. Eight was trying to protect itself from a Chinese DF-21 attack."

"That's unbelievable!" Faulkner exclaimed. "The Russians damage Eight, and the Chinese attack it. Incredible!"

"But we still can't exactly prove that the Russians attacked it or the Chinese DF-21 hit it, sir," Seeker said.

"It's more than enough proof for me, Master Sergeant," Kai said. "This is starting to look like a Russian-Chinese conspiracy to saturate or shut down the Space Defense Force. Secretary Page is going to set up a meeting with SECDEF and PNSA and present all this information. We might not have proof positive, but it'll be enough for the White House to stop any plans of shutting down the program or banning antisatellite weapons."

UNITED NATIONS SECURITY COUNCIL CHAMBERS, NEW YORK CITY

EARLY THE NEXT MORNING

"This emergency meeting of the United Nations Security Council will come to order," the rotating chairman of the council, Ernesto Nascimento, said, tapping a gavel on the stone sound block before him. "The meeting has been called by the request of the delegation from the United States, with Great Britain seconding the request for an emergency meeting. The chair recognizes the ambassador from the United States."

"Thank you, Mr. Chairman," Marcus Colby said. Colby was a successful and well-respected attorney, senior partner of a political consulting group, and professor of international affairs. Although not a part of President Joseph Gardner's true inner circle, the tall, gray-haired, and scholarly-looking gentleman was known to have full access to the president and therefore carried considerable power to the Security Council chamber. "Ladies and gentlemen of the Security Council, thank you all for agreeing to this emergency session. I know the hour is early, but a grave situation has arisen that requires our attention.

"The matter of the People's Republic of China's invasion of Somalia has already been discussed by the council, and although no consensus had been reached by this body, it was generally accepted that China had been sufficiently provoked by freighter crewmembers being executed by Somali pirates into taking direct military action against the pirates' bases of operation in and around Mogadishu. However, last night's air attacks in and around the harbor at Aden in Yemen is a clear violation of a nation's sovereignty and is a serious act of aggression. The United States demands that—"

"I object, Mr. Chairman!" Ambassador Li Jianzhu, the delegate from the People's Republic of China, interrupted. "The attacks in Aden earlier were purely and simply defensive in nature. Our entire task force, which had been granted permission to anchor in Yemeni waters and use Aden's harbor, port, and shore facilities, was in danger by Islamist insurgents, obviously in retaliation for our punitive actions in Somalia. The vessel that attacked and severely damaged our destroyer and killed a dozen sailors was part of the Republic of Yemen's marine patrol police, which is headed by the navy. That means the conspiracy to attack Chinese warships had to have been made by Yemen's defense forces. That is why defense sites were attacked by our naval air forces."

"They were indeed attacked, Mr. Ambassador—attacked within mere minutes of the attack on your warship," Colby said. "That is certainly suspicious. Why did you have so many planes so heavily loaded with munitions obviously carefully selected for a specific set of targets?"

"I do not know, Mr. Colby," Li responded. "The Ministry of National Defense is occupied with rescue-and-recovery operations for its heavily damaged warship. I do know that the *Zhenyuan* was dispatched to the region to escort the Somali task force back home to China and to participate in exercises with the Russian navy; I also know that the carrier conducts many drills in preparation for diverse combat operations. And since the group was sailing into a known hostile area—"

"Indeed—a hostile area created by *China*!" Colby interjected.

"—I am sure they had an array of aircraft standing by on ready alert to respond to a wide array of threats," Li went on, ignoring the outburst. He turned to the council chairman. "Why is China being portrayed as the aggressor here, Mr. Chairman? Why is China under such examination?"

"The reason is obvious, Mr. Ambassador—Chinese forces suddenly and without warning attacked the Republic of Yemen in an undeclared act of aggression," Nascimento said. "The question before this council is whether your actions constituted a reasonable response to an apparent act of aggression against your forces, and was the act of aggression orchestrated by extremists or by the Yemeni government, against whom Chinese forces acted."

"China has a right to protect itself at all times," the Chinese ambassador said loudly. "I hear no one asserting or defending this plain and simple fact!"

"That is not in question here," Nascimento said.

"China refuses to prattle about cause and effect while Chinese sailors are still submerged and trapped in the wreckage of a severely damaged warship, as if we were philosophically discussing the nature of genocide in the midst of a bloodbath," the Chinese ambassador said angrily. "There are a dozen dead crewmembers still on the deck of the *Wuxi*. The outrage belongs with China, not the United States. This emergency meeting is useless and a complete waste of time. No one here has offered China any assistance in rescuing its sailors or investigating those responsible for attacking our warship."

"Why should we risk putting rescue workers or investigators on the ground while Chinese warplanes are bombarding Aden?" Colby asked.

"Perhaps that is what we should be discussing: the withdrawal of Chinese forces from the region," the ambassador from the Russian Federation, Boris Tarzov, a reserved and gentle-voiced young diplomat, suggested.

"Withdrawal?" Ambassador Li asked incredulously. "You mean, take our stricken vessel and our dead and just sail away? If China withdraws, the perpetrators will withdraw as well, and the dead will curse us for our lack of resolve. That is unacceptable."

"And having Chinese warplanes still attacking the city of Aden and buzzing over commercial and military ships in the Gulf of Aden is also not acceptable," Ambassador Colby said. "The United States wants to know who hit the hornet's nest with a stick, sir, but we will not sit idly by while the hornets continue to swarm around the place and sting everyone in sight."

"I shall be sure to let the families of our dead know of your clever analogy, Mr. Colby," Ambassador Li said acidly. "And then I will assure them, as I do you now, that China will not leave until the perpetrators of this dastardly act are brought to justice . . . *Chinese* justice."

"How very convenient: Chinese naval forces on both the north and south sides of the Gulf of Aden," Colby observed, "all because of supposed extremist Islamist attacks on its people and ships? If I didn't know better, Mr. Ambassador, I would say that China is inventing crises to support an imperialistic agenda in that region of the world, a vital choke point to sea traffic for the rest of the world. China has built itself a blue-water navy along with its one-hundred-million-man army, and now it intends to deploy that force wherever it pleases."

"The United States certainly knows a thing or two about imperialism, instigating violence and death, and inserting military forces in critical areas with the objective of controlling them and closing them off to any power it sees as a threat to its own national interests," Li said. "Do not seek to lecture the People's Republic of China about secret agendas and military domination—one needs to do nothing but go outside on a clear night and watch your big bright space station fly overhead to understand that the United States wants nothing more than absolute world control."

"This argument is getting us nowhere, gentlemen," Ambassador Tarzov said, his voice calm but his tone surprisingly insistent. "The matter before us is simple: We need to ensure the safety and security of the Chinese navy while they are doing rescue-and-recovery efforts, and we need to launch an investigation as to who did this monstrous deed: Was it Islamist vengeance for attacks in Somalia, as it appears, or was it some other sort of attack?"

"And China needs to ground all those warplanes before any

more innocent men, women, and children are killed!" Colby interjected.

"And leave our sailors and rescue workers exposed to yet more attacks?" Li retorted. "Whom can China trust? The Yemeni army? Has the Yemeni navy and harbor police been infiltrated by jihadists? China demands that some sort of international security force be brought in to keep our sailors safe while we continue rescue-and-recovery activities. Otherwise, our armed patrols will continue."

"That is not acceptable!" Colby insisted. "China cannot continue attacks over Aden. It is one of the most valuable and strategic ports in the entire Middle East. Insurance rates for ships transiting the area, which is almost one-fourth of all vessels on the high seas, are skyrocketing, as are oil prices. The air raids are terrifying the local residents and are fueling angry protests."

"There can be no cessation of defensive air operations around Aden until the security situation is improved enough for rescue-and-recovery forces to enter the harbor and surrounding areas," Li insisted. "I do not care about such things as insurance rates while brave Chinese sailors lie dead and injured in hostile waters. The United States will never—"

"Gentlemen, gentlemen, please," Boris Tarzov said, holding up hands both to the Chinese and American representatives, his voice even more insistent this time. "Obviously something must be done to assure Chinese rescue forces can operate safely in the harbor. The *Vladimir Putin* carrier task force is just a day or two from the area, and they have a light infantry force, approximately two marine companies, I believe, embarked. May I propose that Russian marines be allowed to land ashore and secure the harbor area so Chinese rescue-and-recovery units can operate safely?"

"Exchange Russian marines for Chinese fighter-bombers?" Colby remarked. "What kind of deal is that?"

"What exactly are you implying, Mr. Ambassador?" Tarzov

asked. "Are you suggesting that our marines would form some sort of invasion force? American Marines come ashore all over the world for all sorts of humanitarian, peacekeeping, and security missions, and no one suggests they are an invasion force. This would strictly be a security operation, with no more than five hundred or so marines and a few transport helicopters involved, which I feel should be more than sufficient to suppress any more acts of violence. Russia built the airfield and most of the modern harbor facilities in Aden, so I believe we are very well familiar with the layout of the area." Ambassadors Li and Colby glared at each other. "Then I hereby move that the Russian naval task-force commander approaching Yemen be placed in charge of an operation to provide security for Chinese rescue-and-recovery forces operating in the harbor at Aden."

"A motion has been made," Nascimento said. "Second?"

"And all Chinese so-called defensive operations cease immediately?" Colby asked.

"Cease upon arrival of Russian marines in the harbor," Li said.

"My motion is amended to include the order that all Chinese defensive and offensive operations of all kind cease upon arrival of Russian marines in the Aden harbor," Tarzov said.

"May I have a second?" Nascimento repeated.

"And China will receive assistance in conducting an investigation of the bombing of our warship?" Li asked.

"As soon as Russian marines have secured the area, Chinese forensic and military investigators may enter—"

"Multinational investigators, including U.S. Federal Bureau of Investigation and Naval Criminal Investigative Service agents, may actively participate in any investigation," Colby interjected.

"This will be a Chinese investigation, Mr. Colby!" Ambassador Li retorted.

"The fox investigating the missing chickens, Mr. Li?"

"*How dare you . . . !*"

"Gentlemen, *please,*" Boris Tarzov interjected, spitting out the word *please* with extra emphasis. "Lives are at stake here!" Colby and Li went back to glaring at each other. "The participation of equal numbers of multinational investigators is a reasonable request, to be led by a Chinese official," Tarzov went on, "and I hereby amend my motion to include it, as long as all findings made by each team of investigators shall be shared by all other investigation teams, by all participating nations including Yemen, and the Security Council. Are there any other proposed amendments?"

There were none, so Nascimento asked, "May I have a second, please?" The delegate from France raised his hand. "Thank you, I have a second to the motion. As this is an emergency session of the Security Council, I ask that each delegation contact their respective ministries by secure telephone from their seats. I shall call for a vote in fifteen minutes. Thank you."

"This is not good," Colby whispered to his deputy as he picked up the telephone.

The White House

A few minutes later

Despite the early hour, the residence of the president in the White House was already abuzz in activity. White House Chief of Staff Walter Kordus found President Gardner in his bedroom, throwing clothes into a suitcase. "Mr. President, I told you I'd have Mrs. Line do that for you," he said. He held up a cordless phone. "The Security Council is meeting right now, and Marcus Colby is asking about the vote. Where's Mrs. Line?"

"The first lady is out of town, I can't find my lightweight suit for Arizona, and Mrs. Line doesn't know the difference between golf shoes and scuba flippers," Gardner complained. "I sent her to get me some coffee. What's the deal with the Security Council?"

"They're discussing Yemen and China," Kordus said. "The motion before them right now is about letting Russian marines set up security around Aden so China can get their men and ship out of the harbor."

"Oh, for Christ's sake," Gardner swore. "Russian marines in Yemen? How many?"

"A few hundred."

"Doesn't sound too bad to me," the president said distractedly, throwing clothes into the suitcase, then throwing them back on the bed. "What does Stacy say?"

"Her secure phone isn't working in Beijing. We're working on an alternate hookup. She might have to go to the embassy."

"Great. Perfect." Gardner was about to pick up another rolled-up pair of socks, then gave up and motioned for the phone. "Marcus?" He glared at the phone. "It's dead. Great. All the phones are on the fritz." Kordus took the phone back, hit the "HOLD" button, and gave it back to Gardner. The president scowled at him before speaking: "Marcus?"

"Yes, Mr. President."

"What's going on?"

"The motion offered by the Russians is to allow Russian marines into the port of Aden to secure it," the United Nations ambassador responded. "China is to stop all offensive and defensive operations as soon as the Russians arrive. Russia suggests a force of five hundred marines, about half of what they bring in their carrier battle group. The U.S., Russia, China, and Yemen can send an equal number of investigators to find out who attacked the Chinese destroyer, to be led by a Chinese official, and everyone has to share information with the others and with the council. France seconded."

"What do you think?"

"It'll stop the Chinese from bombarding the city," Colby said. "That's a start."

Gardner looked over to Kordus, who was on the house line, motioning to him. "Hold on, Marcus." He covered the mouthpiece and nodded at Kordus. "What?"

"The vice president is in the Situation Room and wants to know if you want him to come up."

"Doesn't that guy ever sleep?" the president asked. He thought hard for a moment; then: "Tell him I'll talk with him in the Oval Office before I leave." On his phone he said, "Marcus, I'm getting ready to leave for a campaign swing out west. What's the bottom line here?"

"Five hundred Russians on the ground in Yemen backed up by a carrier task force, together with a Chinese carrier task force, all within a few miles of each other in one of the world's most strategic sea choke points," Colby said. "Our closest carrier battle group is about five hundred miles east; we have components of an amphibious ready group in Djibouti, just a hundred miles away or so. The upside: China stops bombing Yemen."

"That's it?"

"They took us by surprise, sir."

"That seems to be the norm around here these days," the president muttered, directing his remark sideways at Kordus. "What's the council looking like?"

"China is definitely the victim here so far, sir," Colby said. "Everyone believes it was Islamist retaliation for the Chinese attacks against the pirates in Somalia. They're surprised and maybe dismayed at the Chinese air attacks in the city, but I think everyone will give China the benefit of the doubt as long as the attacks cease right away. The Russian ambassador is popular and seen as a neutral arbiter."

"What's the bottom line, Marcus?" the president asked impatiently.

"You'll have to veto to defeat the measure, sir," Colby said. "Everyone else except Great Britain will vote in favor, and I don't think they will veto. You can abstain or vote no, but if it passes it'll look bad that the measure passed without the United States' concurrence."

"Swell." The president caught Kordus looking at his watch—he had to leave right away to keep to the campaign schedule. "Okay, Marcus, go ahead and vote in favor. I'll be airborne in thirty minutes—you can update me then."

"Yes, Mr. President."

Gardner tossed the phone back to Kordus. "I told Marcus to vote in favor. As long as China stops their little hissy fit, I don't care if a few Russian marines look tough in Yemen."

"Yes, sir. I'll brief Secretary Barbeau and Conrad on the way to Andrews. The vice president is in the Oval Office."

"Let's go." The president made sure his golf clothes were in the suitcase, closed it up, and strode out—the staff would bring anything else he needed for the other events, but as long as he was ready for a half round of golf with the Arizona candidates and the photo ops that followed, he was satisfied.

Vice President Ken Phoenix met him in the hallway outside the Oval Office. "Good morning, Mr. President," he said, looking far too chipper for Gardner's mood. He followed the president into the Oval Office. "The Security Council meeting . . . ?"

"The Council moved to allow Russian marines to set up security in the city to allow China to get their ship and casualties out," Gardner said, checking messages on his PDA, leaving a few messages for his secretary, then straightening his tie in preparation for greeting onlookers before heading for the South Lawn to board Marine One. "I told Colby to vote in favor."

"In favor of allowing armed Russian marines in Yemen?" Phoenix asked incredulously.

"In favor of getting China to stop bombing the city, getting their sailors out, and putting everything back to normal," the president said impatiently. "The council was pretty solid for the measure."

"The Russian marines are from that *Putin* carrier task force in the Gulf of Aden?"

"I guess."

"So the Russians and Chinese will have carriers in the Gulf of Aden, with troops on the ground in both Somalia and Yemen, and the closest counterforce we have is in the Arabian Sea?"

"The chopper's waiting, Ken. What's the problem?"

"We could have stalled the vote until we moved the *Reagan* carrier group closer," Phoenix said.

"Why would we do that? There's already too many freakin' carriers in the Gulf of Aden already."

"The United States controls the world's oceans, sir—you've said that a thousand times," Phoenix argued. "But right now there are two foreign aircraft-carrier battle groups in a very strategic location, and we have *none*. We've lost the advantage out there."

"We haven't lost anything, Ken. What we did was stop China from bombing Aden."

"China was running out of legitimate targets with their fighter-bombers anyway—they were going to have to stop on their own," Phoenix said. "We could have vetoed—"

"I don't like overusing the veto, Ken. You know that."

"At the very least we could have voted no and registered our disapproval."

"But I don't disapprove," the president said. "It's a couple hundred Russians—hell, they were probably going to be in Aden anyway on shore leave."

"Except now they'll have guns and a mandate from the United Nations Security Council!"

"I don't see a problem, Ken," Gardner insisted. "We'll keep an eye on them, and if they step out of line, we'll slam them."

"Perhaps sending some other forces out there would show everyone we're watching," Phoenix said. "Maybe an Air Force bomber to overfly the Russian and Chinese fleets, take a few pictures, show the flag?"

"Like that mysterious B-1 bomber squadron that attacked that base in Turkey?"

"Mysterious? I understood you ordered the attack on Diyarbakir; I briefed you on the mission myself. Next thing I knew, it was over."

The president didn't want to tell Phoenix that he ended up taking responsibility for the mission, even though he did not order it—another end run around the law and the chain of command performed by none other than Patrick McLanahan, with help by his secret mentor, former president Kevin Martindale. "Never mind. Yes, that squadron. I'll ask Conrad and Miller to make some suggestions. What else is going on?"

"We'll have a draft of the new space policy drawn up by the end of the day," the vice president replied. "I'm still not for a unilateral ban on antisatellite weapons, but all the other provisions you were looking for are in there."

"Excellent. Fast work," the president said. "I'm willing to discuss the unilateral ban, but I think it'll send the right message to other space-faring nations—America is not out to control space." He noticed Kordus nodding at him, motioning toward the door.

"I've got to go, Ken. I'll talk to you on the staff conference call." He shook hands with Phoenix, turned on a heel, and departed without another word.

On board Marine One, the helicopter that would take him from the White House South Lawn to Andrews Air Force Base, the president fastened his seat belt, then checked his secure PDA again for any messages. As they lifted off, Chief of Staff Kordus held up a note. "We found something."

"On what or whom?"

"McLanahan," Kordus said. "We knew that McLanahan was a director for a nonprofit think tank and education foundation called Progress for Space and Military Future Policy. McLanahan has given several unpaid speeches around the country to industry and civil-military advocacy groups on behalf of this group, touting increased awareness and funding for military space programs, acceleration of military space development, blah blah."

"So?"

"One of my clever staffers noticed that the initials of the organization could stand for 'Patrick S. McLanahan for President.'" Gardner rolled his eyes and gave a short chuckle. "I know, I know: pretty thin. So I checked some more on the organization. Turns out they aren't a nonprofit—they're more like a not-for-profit."

"They're the same thing."

"True, but they never registered as a charitable or educational organization."

"So monies they take in aren't distributed to shareholders but stay in the organization, like an—"

"Exploratory committee," Kordus finished for him. "So we took a peek at the group's bank-account balance . . . and it's huge. We then looked at their filed list of officers and directors. All the big-time military and political players of the last decade, including Page, Goff, Venti, Morgan, Busick; even Thomas Thorn is on there, the list goes on and on."

"Sounds like a new Trilateral Commission."

"You bet it does. At the very end of the list—"

"Phoenix?"

"No. He would have had to disclose that and resign from it, but he never belonged as far as we know. The big name on there: Martindale."

"*Kevin* Martindale?"

"The one and only," Kordus said. "The guy is a Washington institution—two-term vice president, two-term president, connected up the ying-yang. You can't have a more powerful ally. It's practically a ready-made cabinet."

McLanahan and Martindale's names were popping up more and more in the White House these days, Gardner thought—way too much for comfort. "You said Ann Page is on there?" Kordus nodded. "Did she report that on her prenomination questionnaire?"

"I don't remember."

"Check. If she didn't, it's cause to terminate her, if we need to." Kordus nodded and made a note to himself on his ever-present PDA. "So Patrick McLanahan is turning to politics, huh?"

"If he is, he's showing how amateurish he is," Kordus said. "There's only six months to their party's nominating convention. He hasn't campaigned at all except for a few speeches and pressers here and there. I'm not even positive what political party he belongs to, or if he intends on running as an independent, like Thomas Thorn."

"He doesn't need to build up national name recognition like senators and governors do—he's already got plenty," Gardner said. "All he has to do is show up with a slick well-oiled organization behind him, and he'll wow the delegates. If he's been talking with the other candidates, he might be able to avoid a floor fight and snatch the nomination."

"What do you want to do, Joe?"

"Start building a file on candidate Patrick S. McLanahan," Gardner said. "Start digging for dirt. That shouldn't be too hard— the guy's been tossed out of the Air Force twice."

"I wish we could tell *all* the stories we know about the guy," Kordus said.

Gardner shook his head. "The information would sink me and a lot of other folks as well, and McLanahan might not even take any heat himself—he's definitely a loose cannon, but he gets the job done, and the folks really like that. No, use open-source and verified info only. And start a file on this not-for-profit group, too."

"Maybe let Treasury take a look at them?"

"Of course—all aboveboard and routine, but let's see what they forgot to report or filed incorrectly," the president said. "That's the problem with not forming an out-and-out exploratory committee— the IRS can look at you and it's not considered a political attack. And let them take a look to make sure McLanahan paid all his taxes, paid his housekeeper's payroll taxes, reported income on limo rides, all that stuff."

"I'm on it."

"I don't want to body-slam the guy, unless he's *really* doing something criminal," the president said casually. "He's still Patrick McLanahan, aerial assassin and genuine all-American hero. I just want to give him a taste of what it's like playing in the D.C. big leagues. He thinks working in the basement of the White House gave him enough exposure—hell, he doesn't know the half of it."

EIGHT

Justifying a fault doubles it.

—French proverb

Office of the Vice President, Eisenhower Executive Office Building, Washington, D.C.

Later that morning

Although many past American vice presidents had an office in the West Wing of the White House, Joseph Gardner had completely banished Kenneth Phoenix to the Eisenhower Executive Office Building across the street from the White House, along with the National Security Council and other top advisers, preferring to have his chief of staff orchestrate the schedule and bring the staff to him rather than have them always hovering around. Phoenix took advantage of the gentle snub and greatly expanded his suite of offices, making it a true working office while retaining its traditional ceremonial uses.

Representatives from the president's national security adviser, secretary of defense, State Department, attorney general, Central Intelligence Agency, and other federal departments got to their feet when Vice President Phoenix entered his conference room. "Thank you, ladies and gentlemen, thanks for being here," he said. He took a few minutes to shake hands and exchange pleasantries with the panel members. They were all young assistant deputy directors or lower rank—this panel didn't rate any higher-ranked representatives. Phoenix took his seat at the head of the table, and the others took their seats as well. "Our goal today is to finish the draft of the revised National Space Policy and prepare it for review, and my goal is to get a draft in the president's hand by the time he returns from his West Coast campaign swing. But before we begin: Any thoughts about the Chinese attacks in Yemen?"

"I think it's still too early to tell for sure, sir," the representative from the State Department, Annette Douglass, the highest-ranking member of the panel, said. "I understand the Security Council met about it early this morning, but I haven't heard the outcome."

"They authorized Russia to set up security at the port in Aden until the Chinese could remove their casualties," Phoenix said. "Then China is going to lead a multinational investigation, including FBI and NCIS."

"They must believe it was Islamist terrorists, maybe some sort of retaliation for Chinese attacks in Somalia," Douglass said. "It fits. Yemen has been battling al-Qaeda-related insurgents for years. With Russians on the ground, things should quiet down quickly."

"Let's hope so," the vice president said. He cast his eyes around the conference table. "Anybody else?" No one answered. "It might be a little early to say for sure, but I think it's a little suspicious myself." His eyes rested on the youngest member of the panel, the representative from the CIA, who seemed to perk up a bit at the vice president's remark. "Mr. Dobson? Something?"

Tim Dobson looked a little disheveled and rumpled; his tie was a lot off center, and his dark hair was tousled a bit too much to be considered stylish, but Phoenix always found the young CIA assistant deputy director's views insightful and his breadth of knowledge amazing. "Uh . . . yes, sir, there's a few things I found fishy, too, sir."

"Like what?"

"The . . . uh, the Chinese casualty count."

"What was it . . . twelve?"

"Reportedly went up to twenty-one, sir," Dobson said.

"Seem low to you?"

"Yes, sir," Dobson said. "The ship was hit in the right rear quarter in the engineering spaces, close to crew quarters and a chow hall. Late afternoon, day shift on their way for the evening meal, brand-new port of call, and helicopter resupply ongoing—I would have expected more men on deck, more casualties."

"Interesting," Phoenix mused. "What else?"

"The ship itself," Dobson said. "The *Wuxi* was one of the oldest *Jianghu*-2-class frigates in China's fleet—almost forty years old. It was in poor repair and had never been away from Chinese home waters before—in fact, it had spent most of the last five years in port, not even making any routine patrols. On more than one occasion it had been observed being towed by an oceangoing tug that had accompanied the *Zhenyuan* battle group—it had to go into Aden Harbor for refueling because its steering mechanism was too sloppy to attempt underway refueling that the rest of the task force was practicing. The rest of the *Zhenyuan* group is made up of much more modern designs." Dobson was talking faster as he started to get excited about voicing his observations—apparently few others at Langley were willing to listen to him. "But all of a sudden there it is, thousands of miles from home."

"So what?" the national security adviser's representative asked. "The Chinese wanted to put together this task force. Maybe that ship was the best available."

"What are you saying, Tim?" the vice president asked. "That it was old and expendable?"

"Yes, sir," Dobson said confidently. "It was sacrificed."

"Why?"

"To give China the excuse it needed to bomb the city," Dobson said very matter-of-factly, as if he had calculated this theory aeons ago.

"That's nuts," Douglass muttered.

"China's version of the Gulf of Tonkin incident?" the vice president asked. The two supposed attacks on American destroyers by North Vietnamese torpedo boats in the Gulf of Tonkin in what was then North Vietnam prompted the Gulf of Tonkin Resolution in the U.S. Congress in 1964, authorizing President Johnson to take any steps necessary to protect Southeast Asian nations from Communist aggression—it became the main justification for expanded U.S. involvement in Vietnam. The second of the two torpedo-boat attacks was later proved not to have occurred.

"Exactly, sir," Dobson said. "We already wondered about how the Chinese could have put that air raid on so soon after the *Wuxi* was hit—"

"We know that the *Zhenyuan* was already doing exercises with its air wing at the time."

"Exercises . . . with live ordnance?" Dobson asked. "Doesn't make sense."

"So you think the whole thing was staged so China could attack Aden?" Douglass asked incredulously. "Why?"

"Maybe they wanted to invade Aden, like they did with Somalia," Dobson said. "Then they'd have a presence on both sides of the Gulf of Aden."

"But they didn't invade. No one invaded."

"No one invaded . . . but this morning Russia got permission from the United Nations Security Council to set up security in the harbor area," the vice president said. "They're going to send in five hundred marines to provide security so China can get its casualties and ship out of the harbor."

"But that's not an invasion, sir," Douglass said. "It's a prudent security move, especially for China. And Russia has history in Aden. It makes sense."

"But it also gives China and Russia bases in the Gulf of Aden," Dobson said.

"China doesn't have a base in the Gulf of Aden."

"If they consolidated their hold in northern Somalia, they would," Dobson pointed out.

"But they're getting ready to leave. They're bringing in cruise ships to take their troops out . . ."

"I haven't seen any evidence of them leaving," Dobson said, "and after this incident—real or contrived—in Yemen, I don't think they'll be in any big hurry to leave the region. In fact, they attacked a suspected pirate base at Butyaalo in Puntland autonomous region on the Gulf of Aden, and reportedly kept a three-hundred-man garrison there in the pirates' walled compound."

"So you think Russia and China want to set up bases around the Gulf of Aden, Tim?" Phoenix asked.

"Five hundred marines in Aden and three hundred in Butyaalo so far from home need a lot of support, sir," Dobson replied. "And if there are more so-called terrorist acts, they may need a lot more marines in both places."

"So you're saying that China conspired with Russia to set up this phony terrorist act, using an old and broken-down ship and making sure they didn't have too many casualties, so China could bomb Aden, which prompts the United Nations to have Russia send in marines in an overarching plot to take over the port and eventually control the Gulf of Aden?" the State Department representative asked. She shook her head. "I think you've been reading too many cheesy techno-thrillers, Dobson. Why would Russia conspire to do anything with China? They may not be enemies, but they're far from being allies."

"Okay, okay, I think we've gotten way off topic here," the vice president said, holding up his hands in mock surrender, smiling broadly. "I enjoy these exchanges, and I'd like you to put your thoughts down in a memo to my national security team later on, but let's get back to finishing the space-policy draft, shall we?" He glanced at the agenda for the meeting. "The big issue at the end of the last meeting was the question of the space policy violating or abrogating any existing treaties or alliances. What did we—" And at that moment the phone rang. The vice president rolled his eyes in mock exasperation. "I promise, we *are* going to finish that draft this hour. Excuse me." He picked up the phone. "Yes, Denise?"

"Mr. Kordus for you, sir."

"Put him on."

"Mr. Vice President?"

"Hi, Walter."

"Conrad got a call from Miller at the Pentagon, something about the space station," the president's chief of staff said. "Said it was urgent. The president's getting ready to touch down in Arizona and asked me to ask you to find out what's going on."

"I'll take care of it." The line went dead. Phoenix hung up the phone, then pressed the intercom button. "Denise, give Mr. Carlyle a call for me, will you?"

"Mr. Carlyle is on his way to the Situation Room with Secretary Turner, sir. He should arrive in the next few minutes."

The vice president's eyes narrowed, and he picked up the phone. "Right now, Denise? What's going . . . ?" He listened for a moment, then hung up and said to his panel members before him, "I lied, guys—we won't finish the draft today. I'll e-mail you all to reschedule." He got to his feet, and the others jumped up as well. As Phoenix dashed for the door, he said over his shoulder, "Mr. Dobson, you're with me."

The two walked quickly to a staircase, were met by a plain-clothes Secret Service agent, hurried down to the first basement floor, and then entered the tunnel connecting the Eisenhower Executive Office Building to the White House. It was a short walk upstairs to the White House Situation Room, where Phoenix found National Security Adviser Conrad Carlyle, Secretary of Defense Miller Turner, and Secretary of the Air Force Salazar Banderas. On the large computer monitor in the front of the room was an image of Brigadier General Kai Raydon and Undersecretary of the Air Force Ann Page, on a secure videoconference link. Phoenix pointed to Dobson. "Tim Dobson from CIA, helping me on the space-policy review; I asked him to come along. What's going on, guys?"

"It's possible the Space Defense Force weapon garages are being attacked, Mr. Vice President," Turner said.

"What?"

"General Raydon, run it down for the vice president," Miller said.

"Yes, sir," Kai began. "Mr. Noble and my engineers and staff carefully studied data from the Kingfisher interceptor garages, along with other sensor data, and discovered two things: The same faults occurred on all the affected garages; and the faults occurred in virtually the same spots over the Earth."

"Someone was shooting at the weapon garages?"

"Yes, sir, but not with a kinetic weapon, but with data. We believe the Russians are bombarding our satellites with viruslike data that enters the garages' computer system through their digital radar sensors and causes certain systems to shut down or crash."

"How do you know it's the Russians, General?"

"The faults occur shortly after the satellites pass over Russian signals intelligence and space surveillance sites," Kai replied. "Specifically, sites in Venezuela, the Kamchatka Peninsula in Siberia, Socotra Island off the coast of Somalia, and Murmansk."

"Can you verify that?"

"They proposed modifying the weapon garages with signal-gathering packages that can collect any intrusive outside signals and send them to the space station for analysis, sir," Carlyle said. "Their engineers are working to devise a suitable package."

"But as of now . . . ?"

"No, sir, we can't positively say the Russians are doing the damage."

"Can you jam or block the outside signals?"

"Not yet, sir," Raydon said. "We're working on defensive software for the garages—basically antivirus software. Our only other option right now is to shut down the digital active electronically scanned array radars whenever they come within range of a Russian site, but then we'd be letting them know we know what they're up to."

"Seems to me you have no choice—it's probably costing a ton of money to repair those things," Phoenix said. "What about the Chinese?"

"We believe the cause of the explosion of the Kingfisher-Eight garage was the result of a successful Chinese DF-21 antisatellite-missile attack," Raydon said.

"I'll ask it again: Can you verify that?" the vice president asked after a stunned pause.

"No, sir, we can't," Ann Page said. "The satellite that could have done so, Kingfisher-Eight, was already damaged—due to the data attack by the Russians, we believe—and shut down when the missile was launched."

"But we can detect missile launches with other satellites, right?"

"We believe the launch was hidden from heat sensors by a decoy: A large fire near the launch site obliterated the rocket launch."

"So you're not sure there *was* a DF-21 launch."

"It *could* have been launched from there, but no, sir, we didn't actually see it," Ann admitted.

"But we did learn that the weapon garage hadn't malfunctioned—it actually detected the incoming ASAT missile and tried to launch an interceptor," Kai said. "We interpreted the sudden, uncommanded arming as a fault causing an explosion, but it was actually the garage detecting the attack and maneuvering to try to defeat it."

"Unbelievable," Phoenix said, shaking his head. "But you have no proof of any of the attacks, right?"

"The signal gatherer will tell us if the Russians are trying their own version of netrusion on our garages, and we'll have to shut down the AESA radars until we find a way to block the harmful data," Kai said. "As far as the Chinese DF-21s are concerned: Every malfunctioning weapon garage and every unprotected satellite in low Earth orbit is a target, and the more sites the Chinese build, the more satellites will be at risk."

"So you're saying we're completely on the defensive here?" the vice president asked. "We can't stop the Russians from injecting viruses into our satellites, and we can't stop the Chinese from building ASATs all over the world? I don't buy any of that for a second. The president is going to need more options, gentlemen. Let's start putting some plans together." He picked up a telephone on the conference table as the others left the Situation Room, leaving the vice president with Dobson and the images of Raydon and Page still connected on the secure videoconference line. "Get me the president, please."

A few moments later: "Hi, Ken," President Gardner said. "Did you get the briefing?"

"I did, sir. It's staggering. None of our satellites are safe."

"I wanted you to get that info to show you how important my proposed global ban on antisatellite weapons is, Ken," the president said. "The arms race in space is on. And as soon as we figure out a way to stop one form of attack, another one will pop up, and then we have to pay to find a way to defeat *it*. It's nothing but a treadmill, Ken, and I want to get off. The revised National Space Policy is the first step. If we have to do a unilateral antisatellite-weapon ban to show the world how serious we are, then so be it."

"But what are we going to do now, sir?" Phoenix asked. "Russia and China didn't just demonstrate their antisatellite capabilities—they actually *attacked our satellites*!"

"And they got our attention, too, which I believe was their intention all along," the president said. "But we don't have real proof they did anything, do we? We have a lot of circumstantial evidence, but nothing definite. There's nothing we can do."

"An American airman died in space because of what the Russians and Chinese did, sir."

"And as an attorney, you know that you need a lot more than circumstantial evidence to prove murder beyond a shadow of a doubt. I'm just as angry as you over the death of that officer, and it probably would not have happened if the attacks hadn't happened—"

" 'Probably,' sir?"

"—but in the absence of concrete proof," the president went on, apparently ignoring Phoenix's remark, "there's nothing we can do except work to make sure such weapons are banned forever. We'd look foolish confronting the Russians or Chinese with unprovable accusations." The president paused, but Phoenix said nothing. "Am I correct, Ken? Or do you have some suggestions?"

"I like the idea of dropping a CID onto one of those Russian space surveillance sites or Chinese DF-21 missile sites and seeing how much damage it could do," Phoenix said. A CID, or Cybernetic Infantry Device, was a ten-foot-tall piloted composite-shelled robot with superhuman strength, greatly enhanced speed, and self-protection features, and which carried advanced sensors and weapons—it was, in essence, a one-man infantry platoon. Although still experimental and not produced in great numbers, it had proven itself in battles ranging from America's borders to Iraq and Persia, once known as Iran. "Maybe they'll think twice about test-firing one of their weapons at an American satellite."

"Been talking with McLanahan again, have you?" the president asked.

"No, sir, that was my idea. I've seen those things in action."

There was a long pause from the president's side of the connection—Phoenix did not know that the president, too, had seen McLanahan's futuristic infantry weapons systems in action, up close and personal, and not in a good way. Finally: "Listen, Ken, I know those manned robots are cool and tough, and it would be fun to see one use a DF-21 missile like a punching bag, but it's not going to happen," the president said. "The days of Patrick McLanahan sending these high-tech toys around the world in search of self-aggrandizing retribution are over. Hell, where do you think Russia and China got the idea of the so-called operational test? McLanahan did it all the time."

"I don't like the idea of accepting these attacks as part of the new status quo."

"I told you what we're going to do, Ken: We're going to rewrite the National Space Policy to make it more inclusive and less hostile, and we're going to work to ban antisatellite weapons around the world," the president said. "I need your help on this. Am I going to get it?"

Phoenix hesitated as long as he dared, then replied, "Of course, Mr. President."

"Good. Looking forward to reading that draft. Oh, I ran the idea of sending some long-range bomber muscle in and around the Chinese and Russian fleets, and the staff seemed to like the idea. Stacy spoke with the Russian and Chinese foreign ministers, and—"

"You told the Russians and Chinese we were going to shadow their fleets with a bomber, sir?"

"You didn't think I was going to send a bomber out there without telling them?" the president asked. "This is peacetime, Ken, remember? Everyone agreed to be cool. We maintain radio contact, we don't spook anyone, we go in unarmed, we take a few pictures, that's it. A show of force, but no pressure."

"Doesn't sound like a show of force, sir. More like a photo op."

"No use in stirring the pot any more out there. Gotta go, Ken." And the line went dead.

Phoenix hung up the phone, then turned to face the videoconference screen and Dobson. "The president sees this as all the more reason to rewrite the National Space Policy and negotiate a ban on antisatellite weapons," he said heavily. "He doesn't want to do anything else."

"But if we get positive proof . . . ?" Ann Page asked.

"I don't think he'd authorize any direct action," Phoenix said. "I think that's that."

"I'm all in favor of the CID idea, sir," Kai said.

"Are those the manned robots I saw on television, the ones that fought in Persia with the Iraqi army?" Dobson asked. The vice president nodded. "Those things are cool. But I thought we didn't have any of them, that they were all destroyed in Iraq?"

"As far as I know, that's the case," Phoenix said. "Patrick McLanahan used them in Iraq—he'd know."

"Want to ask him, Mr. Vice President?" Ann asked. A few moments later, Patrick appeared on-screen beside her.

"I didn't know you were sitting there, Patrick," Phoenix said perturbedly. "You know better than to have unauthorized persons on a secure videoconference, Madam Undersecretary. You, too, General Raydon."

"Patrick's expertise was crucial to discovering both the DF-21 and Russian netrusion attacks, sir," Kai said.

"So he's seen the data from the Kingfisher satellite, too?" the vice president asked incredulously. "That's classified, too, if I'm not mistaken."

"You have the authority to raise my security clearance level or adjust the classification level of the data, sir," Patrick said. "It's been done before."

"Don't be a smart-ass, Patrick," the vice president said. "I also have the authority to send you to federal prison without charges in the interest of national security. Want me to do that?"

"Sorry, sir. But you realize just as we do that although we might not have court-of-law evidence, we do have more than enough information to show Russia and China are conspiring to degrade or destroy the Space Defense Force. They might not stop at shooting at interceptor garages next time."

"I think the president expects that the Russians and Chinese want a sense of parity with the United States, and this antisatellite stuff is it," Phoenix said. "Just like nukes during the Cold War, they'll build up a credible enough force and claim military-superpower status."

"The difference is, sir, that the United States didn't do away with its nukes once we found out the Russians and Chinese were building them," Ann Page said. "We built more, and then we started to design an advanced antiballistic-missile system to protect ourselves. China gave up the nuke race, and Russia went bankrupt trying to keep up. But this time, President Gardner wants to do away with our antisatellite weapons in the hopes of convincing all nations to do the same, which gives our adversaries the advantage. It doesn't make sense."

"He's the commander in chief, Madam Undersecretary," Phoenix said. "It's his call."

"What do *you* think, sir?" Patrick asked.

"Doesn't matter, does it, General McLanahan?" Phoenix replied stonily.

"So . . . that's *it,* sir?" Ann asked, shaking her head. "We found information that points to Russian and Chinese active attacks on our space systems, including an attack that caused the death of an

American astronaut, and the president will do nothing?" She sat back in her seat, then put her hands on the edge of the table at which she was seated, as if bracing herself. "I . . . I can't work for this administration, Mr. Vice President. I am going to submit my resignation to the secretary of the Air Force today."

"Think about it first, Dr. Page," Phoenix said. "Look at the incredible accomplishments you've made in the Space Defense Force over the past three years. Despite the president's and Congress's decision to rely more on carrier-based naval power, you've managed to build a robust satellite-based strategic defense, communications, reconnaissance, and strike force. You didn't expect it to be smooth sailing each and every year, did you?"

"I dealt with the politics for years in the Senate, and I know that politics and not the real world are influencing the president's decisions now," Ann said. "When being a globalist and appeaser is more important than even a single American life, I don't want to be part of that administration. Good day, Mr. Vice President." And at that, Ann Page stood and walked out of camera view.

"I'll talk to her again, Mr. Vice President," Patrick said.

"Do that, but I don't think it'll make any difference," Phoenix said, shaking his head. "Thanks for the information, guys. Keep me informed, and I'll let you know if anything changes from the White House. When do you go back to the station, General?"

"Not for about three weeks, sir," Kai said. "Mandatory Earth reacclimation."

"Let's hope nothing else happens before you get back," the vice president said. "How about Mr. Noble?"

"He's grounded for at least six weeks, sir. He'll take a couple weeks off for leave, then come back and work in ground control, instruct in the simulator, help the engineers work on propulsion and other technical problems, that sort of thing."

"Well-deserved rest for both of you. Thanks again." He terminated the videoconference, sat thinking for a few moments, then turned to Tim and asked, "Your thoughts, Mr. Dobson?"

"I'll have to study up on this netrusion technology," Tim said, "but the Russians have been hacking into U.S. government computer networks for years. The CIA alone probably gets a thousand serious attempts every day just from Russia, and I know most are either sponsored, directed, or actually undertaken by the FSB." The FSB, or Federal Security Bureau, was the new name of the *Komitet Gosudarstvennoy Bezopasnosti,* or KGB, the Union of Soviet Socialist Republics' internal and foreign spy agency—but in fact their activities had hardly changed from the darkest days of the Cold War. "So they definitely have the technology. I didn't know you could do it over the air from such long distances, but if we can do it they probably can, too.

"The sensor on the weapon garages would be the best way to collect the intrusion signal, especially if it's a narrow focused beam aimed directly at the satellite," the young CIA administrator went on. "But we might be able to collect the signal from the ground with a sensor placed on the transmitting dish. Murmansk and Kamchatka would be hard to penetrate; Socotra Island and Venezuela would be easier." He smiled and added, "Of course, if you could get a couple of those Cybernetic Infantry Devices or the other armored infantry guys General McLanahan was using—"

"The Tin Men."

"That's it, sir. One of those guys could probably do the job. Bring one Tin Man and one CID robot and you could probably set up a spy sensor on the top onion dome of the Kremlin."

The vice president fell silent again; he then nodded, and his eyes had a new fire in them. "I have a new project for you, Mr. Dobson," he said, a mischievous smile growing on his face.

Tim smiled in return. "Yes, Mr. Vice President," he said. "I'm in."

"Good." Phoenix picked up the phone, and a few moments later Patrick McLanahan's image reappeared on the videoconference monitor. "Where are you, Patrick?" he asked.

"Sunnyvale, California, sir."

"More importantly: Do you have any CIDs and Tin Men available?" He noticed Patrick glancing at Dobson, then said, "This is Tim Dobson, CIA, on my space-policy-review panel; I just enlisted him to plan a few other projects for me."

"As you know, sir, all but one of the CIDs were destroyed in Iraq, and the survivor was badly damaged," Patrick said after a slight hesitation. "It was confiscated by the Army, including all remaining weapon packs and the electromagnetic rail guns. They also took possession of all of the remaining Tin Man suits, including battery packs."

The vice president smiled. "Mr. Dobson is okay, Patrick."

Patrick still didn't look convinced, but after a few additional moments of consideration, he said, "Jon Masters has a number of operational Tin Man outfits and a few more in various stages of completion. He's made a few design changes, incorporating what he learned working with the CID units."

"What about the CID units, Patrick?" the vice president asked. "Is anyone building them anymore?"

"I don't believe Dr. Masters has any CIDs—that wasn't a Sky Masters creation," Patrick explained. "The Air Battle Force bought the last remaining units, the ones used in Iraq."

"If the Air Force bought them, General McLanahan, how did Scion Aviation International, the contracting group you headed, get them?" Dobson asked.

Patrick glanced at Dobson, hesitated again, then decided to ignore the question. "I know Colonel Jason Richter and Lieutenant Colonel Charlie Turlock at the Army Transformational Battlelab were in charge of what remained of the CID project now at Aberdeen Proving Ground," he said, "but I haven't been in contact for some time."

"You had some other pretty interesting devices, if I recall," Phoenix went on. "In particular, a way to insert commandos into enemy territory from long distances and fly them out again?"

"What exactly do you have in mind, sir?" Patrick asked.

"Just brainstorming here."

Patrick's expression slowly changed from distrust, confusion, and caution to one of curiosity and finally to pleasure. "I believe you're referring to the MQ-35 Condor, sir," he said with a slight smile. "We could load up four commandos and their gear and drop them from a stealth bomber, and it could glide up to two hundred miles. If it survived the landing without much damage, it could take off again and fly out again."

"That's the one."

"That was a Lake project," Patrick said. Even on a secure link, most veterans of the High Technology Aerospace Weapons Center hesitated to use the term "HAWC" or the other common names, "Dreamland" or "Groom Lake," because of the intense security surrounding America's most secure military aerospace testing facility. "I haven't had top-level security clearance for some time, so I don't know if the Condor is still active."

"Jon Masters would know, wouldn't he?"

"I don't know, sir. Everything is pretty compartmentalized out there."

"We'll check."

"I don't know if *I* have the security clearance for that place," Dobson said, "if it's the place I think you're referring to."

"You will," Phoenix said, "and you will, too, Patrick, if it's necessary."

"They don't do much on air-combat systems these days out there, sir," Patrick said. "They concentrate on more support services, intelligence, unmanned aerial vehicles, and tactical transport. I believe Brigadier General Martin Tehama is still commanding."

"Not a friend of yours, if I remember correctly."

"We have different leadership styles and unit philosophies, yes, sir."

"What about that other group you know, the ones that helped us out over Turkey?"

Patrick's smile disappeared, and his mouth dropped open ever so slightly as he looked at Dobson again. "Sir, are you certain you want to bring that up?" he asked.

The vice president turned to Tim Dobson. "You're standing at the edge of the river Rubicon, Mr. Dobson," he said seriously. "The point of no return. You will learn things that could mark you as a legitimate threat to persons who wield great power, persons from whom even my office might not be able to protect you. You could say no and your life and career will be unaffected, I guarantee that. But if you say yes, your life will change in ways even you could never imagine."

"Sir, I don't think we should be pressuring Mr. Dobson like this," Patrick said. "He's in the White House Situation Room sitting next to the vice president of the United States. Do you really expect him to say no to anything you ask him?"

"Excuse me, General McLanahan, but I think I'm capable of making that decision," Tim said, with a determination in his voice that surprised the others. "I've been in the CIA since I graduated from Rutgers fifteen years ago. I voted for President Gardner, but I know this is the most uncomfortable I've felt about the future of the United States since President Thorn. The vice president is asking me questions about things I hoped I'd been asked about years ago." He turned to Phoenix. "I say yes, Mr. Vice President."

"And how do you know you can trust Mr. Dobson, sir?" Patrick asked. "He's on your space-policy-review panel, but maybe he would find a way to use this information to advance his career faster."

Ken Phoenix looked at Dobson carefully, then nodded. "I don't *know* I can trust him, Patrick . . . but I *feel* I can," he said finally. "I had the same feeling about *you,* back in President Martindale's White House, and you haven't let me down." He looked at his watch. "I've got fifteen minutes before my next meeting. What are you up to today, Patrick?"

"I'm available for anything you need me for, sir."

"Good. The president agreed to send the Seventh Air Expeditionary Squadron out to the Middle East to shadow the Russians. I don't know where they'll be based, but they're going to put on a little show of force to the Chinese and Russians."

"Good idea, sir," Patrick said.

"That might make them available for other missions," Phoenix said. "The president is getting too open and chummy with the Russians and Chinese for my liking, so I'd like to think up some options. Let's go back to my office and we'll get hooked up again there. I'll get you started, and then you can take over, Patrick. You've got your old security clearance back again, General."

"Thank you, sir," Patrick said.

"You, too, Mr. Dobson—you're going to wear the supersecret decoder ring from now on," the vice president said. "Whatever you thought your future looked like, it doesn't anymore." Both he and Patrick could see Dobson do a nervous swallow, but he still nodded determinedly. "Patrick, tell Mr. Dobson what we need and find out how we can get it; draw up a plan, and I'll brief the president. Let's see how serious the president is about getting to the bottom of Russia's and China's plans against our satellites."

Over the Gulf of Aden, 400 Miles East of Aden, Republic of Yemen

Days later

"Attention unidentified aircraft, attention unidentified aircraft," the stern, heavily accented voice said in English on 243.0 megahertz, the international UHF emergency frequency, "approaching the fiftieth meridian, flying west at thirty-five thousand feet, this is patrol aircraft of the navy of the Russian Federation Southern Fleet on GUARD. You are on course to approach a Russian navy aircraft carrier task force. If you do not alter course, you will be intercepted, and if your identity or stores cannot be verified as peaceful, you will be forced to alter course. The use of deadly force is authorized and you may be fired on without warning. Respond on UHF GUARD frequency, please."

"Our friends are calling," Lieutenant Colonel Gia "Boxer" Cazzotto, aircraft commander of a U.S. Air Force EB-1C "Vampire" bomber, said on intercom. Beside her in the cockpit of the highly modified long-range strategic bomber was Major Alan "Frodo" Friel, the mission commander. Boxer was the commander of the 7th Air Expeditionary Squadron, a small bomber unit based at Air Force Plant 42 in Palmdale, California. Originally organized to flight-test refurbished B-1 bombers taken out of storage, the 7th AES—being one of only a handful of American heavy bomber squadrons still in existence—was occasionally tasked for real-world missions.

The EB-1C Vampire bomber was one example of a state-of-the-art refurbished design. To date, fifteen airframes had been taken out of flyable storage, modified, and upgraded to perform a dazzling array of missions, making it a true "flying battleship." Although originally designed for four crewmembers, this EB-1C bomber was so computerized and automated that all attack and defensive functions could be performed by just two—or, operated as an unmanned attack aircraft, with *none*.

"All countermeasures in 'PASSIVE' mode, Boxer," Frodo responded. Friel definitely resembled the character from whom his call sign was derived—he was much shorter than Cazzotto, with big round eyes, thick curly brown hair under his flight helmet, and light skin. All of the bomber's defensive systems—electronic jammers, decoys, and active antimissile emitters—were not operating, only listening for threats. "He sounds pretty belligerent to me. I thought this was all worked out in advance? What's that about?"

"Maybe it's for practice, Frodo," Boxer said.

"Fracture Two-One, this is Armstrong," Major Jessica "Gonzo" Faulkner radioed via satellite from Armstrong Space Station. "We've got two bandits at your twelve o'clock, one hundred miles, four-eight-zero knots, definitely heading your way."

"Roger, Armstrong," Boxer replied. "Nice to know you're watching over us."

"We might have spotty coverage here and there, but we'll be watching as best we can until you're back on the ground."

"Thanks, guys." She switched to the secondary channel and spoke: "Russian fleet patrol aircraft, this is Fracture Two-One on GUARD, we read you loud and clear. Over."

"Fracture Two-One, switch to fleet reserved frequency two-two-nine-point-zero."

"Switching," Boxer replied. On the new frequency: "Two-One is up."

"Fracture Two-One, squawk mode three-two-two-seven-one, mode C normal." Frodo set in the new transponder codes. "I have you radar-identified, Fracture. Do not approach any Russian warships. Be advised, we will intercept you at this time for positive visual identification. Do not change altitude or airspeed. Over."

"Fracture Two-One, roger."

"I don't understand why we're doing these flights," Frodo complained. "Just public relations?"

"I'm sure it started out as a real surveillance mission," Boxer replied, "but then someone got nervous that there might be another accident, like the *Bush*-carrier episode, so the diplomats huddled and changed the rules of engagement. Now it's just pictures and a flyby."

"We can't do anything anyway," Frodo said. "All we're carrying are the AMRAAMs." The forward bomb bay carried a rotary launcher fitted with eight AIM-120 AMRAAM radar-guided air-to-air missiles; in addition, the aft bomb bay carried a three-thousand-gallon auxiliary fuel tank. "Ever do an intercept with the Russians?" Frodo asked.

"Just at 'Red Flag' and other exercises," Boxer said, "and never with a Sukhoi-33, although it's similar to the Su-27, which I have played with before. This is the first time the Russians have put together a carrier battle group of this size. But these things are usually not big deals. It's all been cleared diplomatically."

"Diplomatically?"

"Legally we can fly near their ships out in the open seas, and they can intercept us in international airspace," Boxer said. "But no one wants something to happen like what happened with the carrier *Bush,* so some diplomat sends an e-mail or fax to his counterpart in Moscow and gives them a heads-up. Everyone plays nice. We don't do anything stupid or sudden to get anybody spooked. Let's get a LADAR snapshot and see who we got."

"Roger." Frodo activated the Vampire's LADAR, or laser radar, which "drew" a high-resolution picture of everything within four hundred miles on the ground, on the ocean's surface, in space, and even several dozen feet underwater. The LADAR was on for only a few seconds, then set back in "STANDBY." "And the winner is: a pair of Sukhoi-33 Flanker-Ds," Frodo reported. "Closing at four hundred eighty knots, about eighty-five miles away. The carrier group is at two hundred sixty miles."

"Armstrong, this is Fracture, we're tied on," Boxer reported.

"Roger," Gonzo replied, "we've got a good datalink. We're look-ing for any trailers, negative contact so far."

"Thanks, Armstrong." Boxer pulled back the throttles and set a speed of 360 knots—slower airspeeds made any aircraft less threat-ening. "I'll wake up home plate," she said to Frodo. She made sure her communications panel was set up, then spoke: "Control, Frac-ture Two-One, bandits, tied on."

"Two-One, roger, stand by," the air-component commander at Central Command headquarters at MacDill Air Force Base, Flor-ida, responded via satellite. The commanders at Central Com-mand could receive all sensor data from almost all sources in its entire theater of command, so they could see what Boxer and Frodo saw on their large multifunction cockpit displays. In addi-tion, they could tap into any other data source anywhere in the re-gion, whether from ships, other aircraft, or on land, and put it all together in a big tactical picture. "Fracture Two-One, proceed as briefed," the air commander radioed a few moments later.

"Two-One copies." Boxer shrugged. "Sheesh, no pep talk, no 'go get 'em, guys,' no enthusiasm? 'Proceed as briefed'?"

"What do you expect? He's ten thousand miles away in a nice comfy command center."

Aboard the Russian Federation Navy Aircraft Carrier Vladimir Vladimirovich Putin

That same time

"Aircraft is slowing to six hundred seventy kilometers per hour, Captain," the radar technician reported. "Still at ten thousand meters."

"Very long-range, very high, very big plane, too fast for an unmanned patrol plane—it has to be an American bomber," the tactical action officer said. He and the rest of the battle management team was in the Combat Information Center aboard the *Vladimir Vladimirovich Putin,* steaming westward toward Aden, Yemen, in the Gulf of Aden. The Combat Information Center was filled with computer monitors; a team of fifteen enlisted and two officers manned the *Putin's* radars and optical sensors and controlled the ship's weapons. "The fighters should intercept in a few minutes."

"I'll notify the admiral," the commanding officer of the *Putin* said. He picked up the "Red Phone," which tied directly to the flag bridge. "Inbound patrol plane from the east, Admiral. We will intercept in a few minutes. Probably an American long-range bomber."

"Not one of their Global Hawks, Captain?" the admiral asked.

"We will have visual identification shortly, sir. It appears to be traveling faster and at a lower altitude than the Global Hawks, and faster than a naval patrol plane."

"Very well. Let me know if they do anything unusual. All defensive systems ready?"

"Yes, sir."

"Very well. Carry on."

"Yes, sir." The captain hung up the phone. "I am surprised they can spare any bombers to harass us," he said. "Gryzlov blew most of them into hell, and Gardner canceled the American Next Generation Bomber program in favor of more carriers. Yet here they are."

"Standard procedures, sir?"

"Yes, standard procedures," the captain said. "Radar silent, passive sensors only, plenty of videotape so we can complain about being harassed once again. Let the Americans have their fun. I am going topside to take some pictures."

The admiral in charge of the Russian navy task force in the Gulf of Aden lit up a cigarette, then lifted another telephone before him on the instrument panel of the flag bridge. He had three watertight computer monitors, showing him radar images.

"This is Central," a voice on the other end of the line said. "Admiral?"

"I was ordered to report when the American patrol plane approached the task force," he said.

"And?"

"We do not have positive visual contact, but it appears to be flying faster and lower than the unarmed American Global Hawks."

"You are talking in circles, Admiral," the voice said curtly. "What is it?"

"I believe it to be an American long-range bomber," the admiral replied. "The Americans have a few B-1 and B-2 bombers stationed in Diego Garcia and occasionally in Bahrain and the United Arab Emirates."

"Very well. Stand by." And the line went dead.

The senior controller turned to General Andrei Darzov, who was in his command post at his headquarters in Moscow. "The task force has made contact with a large patrol plane to their east, believed to be an American long-range bomber, sir," he said.

Darzov nodded, then picked up a telephone before him. "Mr. President, the Americans are sending their air patrols in. It does not appear to be an unmanned plane, but a bomber."

"A bomber?" Russian president Igor Truznyev exclaimed. "Do they mean to attack the task force?"

"No, sir. I believe it is a typical show-of-force tactic. The typical profile is a high pass, followed by a low-altitude flyby."

"And what are we doing while the Americans are allowed to do this so-called typical routine, General?"

"Well . . . very little, sir," Darzov said. "We do not want to show any capabilities to the Americans. We usually turn off all radars except for standard search radars. Since the carrier *Putin* is part of the task force, we will scramble fighters to intercept, but they stay radar-silent. We usually photograph the intercept, but allow the plane to inspect the fleet. As part of our agreement, the Americans transmit air-traffic control codes and talk with our controllers."

"And what is the American plane doing while we do nothing?" Truznyev asked, surprise in his voice.

"They fly around, take photographs and radar images, try to record any electromagnetic emissions," Darzov said. "It is what the Americans call a 'photo opportunity.' The plane will probably make a showy pass near the carrier, wag its wings, and be gone. It is all for show, sir."

"I do not understand any of this," Truznyev said. Then, after a short pause: "And I do not allow it. Keep that bomber away from the task force, General."

"But, sir . . . this has all been agreed in advance," Darzov said. "Our air attaché in Washington coordinates all this with their Pentagon. One plane, air-traffic control codes, a simple flyby, no overflight, no visible weapons, no open bomb doors, no supersonic flight, no electronic jamming—it is all very routine—"

"I do not care, General," Truznyev said. "I do not like pretending we accept or allow the Americans to fly attack aircraft near our fleet. If it is confirmed as an attack plane, I want it kept away from the task force . . . by any means necessary."

"Including deadly force, sir?" Darzov asked incredulously.

"Including deadly force, General," Truznyev insisted. "What is the range of an American air-launched antiship cruise missile?"

"Uh . . . uh . . ." Darzov had to struggle to recall the information: "The American Harpoon antiship missile has a range of about one hundred kilometers when launched from low altitude—"

"Fine. If the bomber comes within *two* hundred kilometers, use any means necessary to chase it away."

"But, sir, free navigation of the skies and seas never prohibits an aircraft from flying that close unless—"

"Two hundred kilometers away if it is an attack aircraft, General," Truznyev said finally. "No nation flies near our task force with impunity. The Americans believe they can fly their spacecraft and bombers anywhere they wish and it is all just a 'photo opportunity'? I *will* teach them differently."

Just as the captain finished his logbook entries and turned to head topside, the Red Phone beeped. He snatched it up immediately. "Yes, Admiral?"

"Change in procedures, Captain," the admiral said. "Keep weapons tight, but full tactical engagement procedures, air and surface. Repeat, full tactical engagement, weapons tight. If it is a bomber, keep it two hundred kilometers away from the task force. Advise me as soon as visual identification is made."

"Excuse me, sir, but you want to radiate with what is probably an American bomber coming at us?" the captain asked. "If it's a bomber, they can probably analyze our signals."

"Orders direct from Moscow," the admiral said. "They say they anticipated a patrol plane such as a Global Hawk. The bomber is a serious provocation, and they want to hit them with everything. Acknowledge my orders."

"Understood, sir," the captain said after a moment of shock. "Weapons tight, full tactical engagement air and surface, keep bomber aircraft away two hundred kilometers from the task force." The admiral rang off, and the captain hung up. "TAO, weapons tight, full tactical engagement procedures, air and surface."

The tactical action officer turned to the captain in complete surprise. "Sir?"

"You heard me, Commander," the captain said. "Acknowledge and report by all stations that weapons are tight. If it is a bomber, it is to be kept at least two hundred kilometers away from the outer ships of the task force."

The TAO swallowed, then said, "Weapons tight, full tactical engagement, air and surface, two hundred kilometers if it is a bomber," he repeated. "All stations, all stations, this is the TAO, check weapons status and report."

After Truznyev hung up the phone with Darzov, he dialed another number himself. When the private secure line was answered, he said without preamble or greeting, "I have just decided to twist the tiger's tail in the Gulf of Aden, Premier Zhou. Alert your task force that there is about to be some activity out there."

Aboard the EB-1C Vampire Bomber

That same time

A yellow triangle appeared on the nose of the Su-33's icon on the display. "Bandit's radiating," Frodo said. "He'll be locked on in three minutes."

"American patrol aircraft, we are tracking you on radar at this time," the Russian pilot said a few minutes later. "Be advised, you are approaching a Russian military naval task force at your twelve o'clock position. Unidentified aircraft are not permitted to fly near Russian warships. You must alter course at least thirty degrees immediately or you may be fired upon. Acknowledge."

"Russian patrol aircraft, this is a routine patrol mission," Boxer said, shaking her head in confusion. "We intend to do a visual inspection of your ships in international waters. We're complying with your communications requirements."

"Fracture, Armstrong," Gonzo reported from Armstrong Space Station, "bandits are speeding up, five hundred . . . six hundred . . . seven hundred knots . . . going supersonic. Intercept in about three minutes."

"They're going *supersonic?*" Frodo asked nervously. "What's going on?"

"It's all for show," Boxer said. "At that speed, they'll have us in sight for about two seconds, they'll waste fifty miles turning around to chase us, and they'll be burning gas like crazy."

"But . . . but that must mean that—"

"Fracture, Armstrong, we've got two more lifting off from the carrier," Gonzo reported.

"—that they'll have to launch more planes after us," Frodo said, finishing his thought with a slight crack in his voice. At that moment a separate window opened up on Frodo's large supercockpit display, and it showed two more Sukhoi-33 fighters taxiing onto the aircraft carrier *Vladimir Putin*'s forward catapults, with two more behind the blast deflectors, getting ready to hook up to the catapults as well. It was the data being passed down from the space station. "Is that happening right *now*?"

"Now it's starting to get interesting," Boxer said, and suddenly she didn't feel like cracking jokes anymore. "We're getting your imagery, Armstrong," she radioed.

"We'll have that satellite feed for only about sixty seconds, Fracture, and after that our sensor coverage will be spotty for the next thirty minutes," Gonzo said. "You really stirred them up. You might want to think about getting out of there. Your tanker is at your five o'clock, three hundred ninety miles in the refueling anchor."

"Not quite yet, Armstrong," Boxer said. "I think we somehow hurt their feelings—I want to see what they're going to do about it."

"X-band radar in high-PRF lock-on," Frodo reported as he watched the intercept on his passive electromagnetic threat detector. The high-PRF, or pulse-rate frequency, meant that the Sukhoi-33's radar was solidly locked onto the Vampire. "Passing off to the left. Why are they locking us up, Boxer?"

"Fracture, first formation will be passing below and to your left . . . now." Boxer didn't see anything. The threat detectors depicted the two Russian carrier jets streak past them, and moments later they felt two sharp burbles as the twin supersonic shock waves passed.

"Christ, that was *close*," Frodo breathed.

"Fracture, second formation is closing at six hundred knots, two hundred miles," Gonzo reported. "Third formation is on the catapults. We're losing full-time coverage."

"Copy, Armstrong," Boxer said. "Frodo, let's set the LADAR to intermittent."

"LADAR radiating," Frodo said, trying to keep his voice steady. In "Intermittent" mode, the Vampire's laser radar would broadcast for a second or two every ten to fifteen seconds to get a better picture of the intercept, but avoid being tracked by the Russians in case they had laser detectors. The supercockpit display clearly showed all the players now, even tracking the fighters behind the Vampire and identifying the aircraft on the *Putin*'s deck getting ready to launch and the rescue helicopters hovering beside the carrier in case of an emergency.

"We've got a real furball forming here now," Boxer commented. "These guys are serious."

"Admiral, it is an American B-1 bomber," the captain of the *Putin* said on the direct line to the flag bridge. "They are on the fleet reserve frequency and are transmitting air-traffic codes as directed by our controllers, as agreed in the Memorandum of Understanding."

"I do not want an American bomber anywhere near this task force, Captain!" the admiral shouted. "Get him away from here!"

"But, sir, are they not permitted free navigation over international waters? How can we—"

"I told you, Captain, I do not want that plane anywhere near this task force," the admiral said. "They might decide to shoot a cruise missile in our direction, like the damned Chinese did to the Americans. Get it away from here, *now*!"

"We're approaching two hundred miles to the carrier, Boxer," Frodo said, "and one-ninety to the first escort. We—"

And at that moment they heard, *"Caution, caution, target tracking mode, Sukhoi-33, five o'clock, nineteen miles."*

"Do you want countermeasures?" Frodo asked excitedly.

"Not yet," Boxer said after just a moment's consideration. "Let 'em come in. Standard play is one on each side so they can take pictures of each other with the big bad American bomber. These guys will be low on gas anyway—they'll get their hero shot, then leave and let the second and third formations take over."

A few minutes later, that's exactly what happened: The first pair of bright blue Sukhoi-33 fighters moved in, one on each side of the bomber, about a hundred feet away. Boxer and Frodo didn't see any cameras.

"American bomber aircraft, this is the Russian Southern Fleet aircraft carrier *Vladimir Vladimirovich Putin* on fleet reserve channel," a new voice announced. "You are three hundred kilometers from this task force. Combat aircraft are not permitted to approach this group. Alter course immediately and stay at least two hundred kilometers away or you may be fired upon without warning."

"Second formation of fighters are fifty miles away, slowing," Frodo said. Suddenly they heard another warning tone. "Fighter locked onto us!"

"Carrier *Putin,* this is Fracture Two-One," Boxer radioed. "Do not lock your fire control radars on us. Flying near your ships is not a hostile action, but locking missile radars on us is!"

"This is your last warning, American bomber aircraft," the controller radioed. "Do not approach! We will take immediate action."

"What do we do, Boxer?" Frodo asked. "Do these guys want to take a shot at us?"

"This is bull," Boxer said. "I thought this was just a photo op and nice peaceful flyby."

The second formation of Sukhoi-33 fighters approached, one on either side, much slower than the first formation, close enough to see fuselage lights winking on and off . . .

. . . until Boxer and Frodo heard the fast-paced drumming on the cockpit canopy and realized that they weren't lights, but cannons opening fire on them! The shells missed, but they came so close that Boxer and Frodo could feel their shock waves on the fuselage. *"Holy shit!"* Frodo shouted. *"They're shooting at us! Let's get out of here!"*

"You bastards want to play—let's play," Boxer shouted. "Get ready to go low, Frodo. Kill the freq and the transponder, get us into 'COMBAT' mode." She hit a button on her control stick and spoke: "Terrain-follow, clearance plane two hundred, hard ride."

"Terrain-follow, clearance plane two hundred, hard ride," the flight control computer responded. Boxer watched the computer's automatic control inputs on her supercockpit display as it readjusted settings for an overwater letdown, then spoke: *"Stand by for descent, now."* The EB-1C Vampire pitched over and started a twenty-thousand-foot-per-minute descent, rapid enough for bits of loose dirt to float to the top of the cockpit. Normally the bomber would automatically sweep the wings back to their maximum sixty-seven degree setting in the high-speed descent, but the Vampire's wings were permanently set to the full swept-wing position— lift and drag were controlled by mission-adaptive technology, where thousands of tiny actuators on the bomber's fuselage controlled the shape of the plane, so every square inch of the surface could be a lift or drag device.

"Fighters are staying high, twelve o'clock, twenty miles . . . no, here they come, one is heading down," Frodo reported. "Still locked on. 'COMBAT' mode engaged, full countermeasures active."

"C'mon down here, boys," Boxer said. In less than two minutes, the Vampire bomber leveled off at two hundred feet above the Gulf of Aden. Boxer watched the computer perform a self-test of the flight control system, then checked the electrical, hydraulic, and pneumatic subsystems herself.

"American B-1 bomber, this is the carrier *Putin* on GUARD channel, you are flying at an extreme low altitude and are heading directly for the Russian task-force ships," the Russian controller radioed. "This is considered a hostile action. You appear to be on an antiship cruise-missile attack. Alter or reverse course immediately. This is your final warning."

"You ain't seen nuthin' yet, Comrade," Boxer said, pushing the throttles up until they were flying at six hundred nautical miles an hour.

"One hundred miles to the first escort," Frodo said. "Search and height-finders from the ships, and fast-PRF search from the fighters, not locked on. The third formation is supersonic, heading this way fast."

"Armstrong has you again, Fracture," Gonzo reported. "Now I know what a game of 'chicken' looks like."

"They screwed with the wrong broad, Armstrong," Boxer said.

"We've got the bandit on your six, ten thousand above you, closing to twenty miles," Gonzo said. "His wingman is descending slower. The third formation is maneuvering, looks like they're staying high for now. We've reported to Central Command."

"Thanks, Armstrong," Boxer radioed back.

"First escort is fifty miles," Frodo said. "*Udaloy*-1-class destroyer. He's got search radar . . . now searching with a height-finder, not locked on.

"Coming up on thirty . . . hey, the fighters are peeling off!" Frodo said. "They're all climbing."

"Can't stand the heat, eh, boys?" Boxer said. "Too bad. It's fun down here." She peeked at Frodo and saw his eyes as big as saucers behind his clear visor. "How's it going, Frodo?"

"I'm worried about those fighters," he said. "Why are they . . . ?" He paused, then shouted, "Golf-band target acquisition radar from the *Udaloy*, SA-N-9 system! Not locked on."

"Well, well, they're turning on everything today," Boxer said. "If they want to play hardball, I'm ready to go to bat. Pushing 'em up." She nudged the throttles up until they were supersonic—the highly modified EB-1C Vampire was the only model of the nearly 500,000-pound B-1 bomber that was able to go supersonic at low altitude. "Come and get us now, suckers."

The captain of the *Putin* snatched up the Red Phone. "Admiral, the American bomber has descended to less than one hundred meters' altitude and is approaching the task force at supersonic speed!"

The admiral swore into the phone, then ordered, "Continue full tactical engagement, weapons tight."

"Acknowledged, full tactical engagement, weapons tight."

"Is he radiating at all?"

"No radars, but strong electronic countermeasures."

"Use the signal generators on him and see if he reacts," the admiral ordered, "and advise me when he reaches the task force." And he hung up before the captain could acknowledge.

"What in hell is going on here?" the captain muttered. "What in *hell* is going on?" He turned to the TAO. "Full-spectrum signal generators, weapons tight, full tactical engagement."

"Echo-Fox band target-acquisition radar, twelve o'clock, forty miles, not locked on," Frodo said. "S-300 missile, probably on the cruiser escort . . . now Golf-band target-tracking radar from the destroyer, eleven o'clock, fifteen miles, not locked on."

"American attack bomber, this is your final warning!" the Russian controller radioed. "Alter course immediately or you will be fired upon! Respond immediately!"

"I see the destroyer!" Frodo said. They were going to pass up the starboard side; Boxer nudged the stick left. It looked to Frodo as if they were going to fly right over it! Suddenly he saw puffs of smoke shooting from each side of the vessel. *"Guns . . . !"*

"Close-in weapon system!" Boxer shouted. "Think you can catch us, Comrades? Think again."

"Jesus . . . !" It looked as if they were going to fly right through the smoke from the cannons' muzzles! Suddenly a fast-paced *beep-beepbeepbepp* sounded. *"Missile guidance!"*

"It's a false signal, Frodo," Boxer said. He couldn't believe how calm she sounded. "No warning from the computer. It's a false missile-guidance signal, trying to provoke us to do something. Time for our close-up, Mr. DeMille." Just as they passed the destroyer, Boxer rolled the Vampire bomber into a ninety-degree bank left turn, darting just ahead of the destroyer. Frodo thought for sure the left wingtip was going to drag the water! Boxer strained to look out the left cockpit window and managed to catch a glimpse of the vapor cloud created by the supersonic shock wave roll over the destroyer's bow. "Have a face wash, courtesy of the U.S. Air Force," she crowed happily.

"Golf-band radar . . . Echo-Fox radar, not locked on," Frodo reported. Boxer rolled wings-level, then started a turn toward the aircraft carrier itself. "Why are they shooting at us? I thought this was all for show."

"Someone obviously didn't get the memo, Frodo," Boxer said. "But I'm not going to let the Russkies push us around. I think we'll take this pass down the port side of the carrier. Any helicopters up?"

"Yes, starboard side."

"Good. Get your cameras ready, boys."

"Echo-Fox radar has intermittent lock-on, Golf-band radar not locked on. Carrier's one o'clock, ten miles."

"Where are the fighters?"

"Six o'clock, thirty miles, fifteen thousand feet."

"We'll make the pass, then climb north to clear the fighters," Boxer said. "Any fighters on the catapults?"

"Yes, two moving onto the forward cats."

"I'll stay a little farther out in case they decide to launch them," Boxer said. "It'll spoil the picture but they should still get a nice shot."

"American attack bomber, this is the carrier *Putin*," the Russian controller radioed once again. "This is your final warning, alter course away from this task force immediately. Acknowledge!"

"I thought you already gave us your final warning, Comrade," Boxer said on intercom. "Just one more flyby and we're outta here. I expect to see the pictures on the Internet by the time we get home."

"Admiral, American B-1 bomber on the port stern quarter, eighteen kilometers, altitude less than one hundred meters, approaching at Mach one-point-one-five!" the captain of the *Putin* shouted into the phone.

"Is he radiating, Captain?"

"Defensive electronic jamming signals only. No attack radars."

The admiral paused for a long moment; then: "How close has he come to the task force, Captain?"

"He flew supersonic less than a kilometer from the destroyer *Vysotskiy* at ninety degrees bank. I thought there was going to be a collision! The *Vysotskiy* tried to warn him away with their close-in weapon system—the gun's guidance radar was completely jammed."

"What about electro-optical tracking? It is daylight, Captain!"

"The crewman manning the optical tracker took cover—he thought the bomber was going to crash right into him. Several men were injured by the shock wave."

Another pause; then: "I think the American bomber is hostile, Captain," the admiral said in a remarkably calm and even voice, as if he was reading from a script. "Sound battle stations, full tactical engagement . . . all weapons released."

The pass by the aircraft carrier was farther away, but they were still well within a half mile when Boxer made her supersonic high-bank right turn in front of the carrier. Frodo felt as if his arms weighed a hundred pounds each as the g-forces increased.

"Okay, Frodo, fun time's over," Boxer said. She started a left turn and headed away from the Russian task force, staying one hundred feet above the ocean. She pulled the power back to full military power to conserve as much fuel as possible—she knew she was already eating into her reserves by doing the low-altitude, high-speed maneuvers. "Where are those fighters?"

Frodo activated the laser radar. "Closest formation is southeast, twenty miles, fifteen thousand feet," he reported. "The other formation is . . ." He paused as a warning tone sounded. "India-Juliet-band target engagement radar active!" Frodo shouted. *"It's locked on!"*

Suddenly the threat warning computer blared, *"Warning, warning, missile guidance, SA-N-6!"*

"Here it comes!" Boxer shouted. She immediately punched the throttles into full afterburner.

"Countermeasures active!" Frodo shouted. Boxer punched the buttons on her control stick to eject decoy chaff and flares, then rolled into a hard left turn, pulled the throttles out of afterburner, and pulled on the control stick to make the turn as tight as she could. There was a bright flash of light out the right cockpit window, and both crewmembers were jerked violently to the right from the force of the exploding missile. Their supercockpit displays flickered, and the right side of Frodo's screen went blank.

Boxer rolled out of the turn before all of her airspeed bled off in the break, then selected full afterburner again . . . but then brought the rightmost throttle back. "Compressor stall on number four!" she shouted.

"Warning, warning, missile guidance, SA-N-4, four o'clock!" the threat computer blared.

"Is the active defensive system up?"

"No—all ECMs faulted. I'm rebooting."

"Hang on!" She punched out chaff and flares again, hoping the ejectors were working, then rolled into a hard right break, using the underpowered number four engine as an air brake to tighten the turn. "Can you see the missile?"

Frodo frantically scanned out his window, then shouted, *"Climb, now!"* Boxer pulled the control stick until all they could see out the front windscreen was sky, then pushed wings-level and reversed the turn. She saw a flash of light below and to her left.

"Missile guidance, SA-N-6, six o'clock!"

"Our airspeed is almost gone," Boxer said. "I can't do any more breaks or else we'll spin into the ocean. How's the ECM—"

"Coming online now!" Frodo shouted. The right side of his supercockpit display was on once again, and his fingers were flying across the touchscreen. "ADS active!" The Vampire's ADS, or Active Defensive System, was a pair of free-electron laser emitters, one atop and one underneath the fuselage. When the laser radar detected an incoming missile, the ADS lasers would slave themselves to the LADAR and attack the missiles with beams of white-hot laser energy powerful enough to destroy the thin dielectric nose cap of most surface-to-air missiles at long range. They had to fight off at least a half-dozen Russian missiles fired from the carrier's escorts.

"Airspeed's finally picking up," Boxer said. "I'm going to see if number four is back with us." She gently advanced the throttle of the number four engine, watching the exhaust temperatures to make sure the fire that was in the engine wasn't going to reignite—and sure enough, the exhaust-gas temperature in the engine began to spike, and she pulled the throttle to idle, then to "CUTOFF." "Looks like number four is dead, Frodo—a fire starts in the burner can when I advance the throttle," she said. "Let's get on the radio and see if our tanker can—"

"Bandits!" Frodo yelled. "Su-33s, three o'clock, twenty-five—"

Just then the threat warning computer blared, *"Missile guidance, AA-12, three o'clock!"* Boxer punched out chaff and flares and did another hard left break . . .

. . . but it was too slow with the lost engine, and there wasn't enough airspeed to keep the break in to defeat the missile. They felt a hard *whummp* and the entire tail section of the Vampire skidded to the left. Boxer had to fight the control stick with both hands and stomp hard on the right rudder pedal to keep the plane straight and prevent a roll right into the ocean.

"Boxer . . . ?" Frodo shouted.

"I got it, I got it!" Boxer shouted. She knew that's probably exactly what most bomber pilots said right before they crashed after being hit by a missile, but she truly believed she could maintain control. She released the control stick with her left hand long enough to raise a red-colored switch guard on her side instrument panel, raised a switch inside to the "ARM" position, then climbed slightly. "Nail those fighters, Frodo!"

Frodo activated his "MASTER ARM" switch on his side instrument panel. As soon as he did, the supercockpit display changed from a view of the Russian fleet to a three-dimensional depiction of the airborne threats around them. The laser radar detected and began tracking all of the Russian Sukhoi-33 carrier-based fighters, and the fire control computer quickly prioritized each one in order of threat. As soon as the first fighter came within range, the computer opened the forward bomb-bay doors and ejected an AIM-120 AMRAAM missile into the slipstream.

The missile descended about fifty feet as it stabilized itself. Boxer hoped the Vampire was not side-slipping too much or the missile would likely fly right into it, but it separated cleanly, its digital gyros restoring stability in the badly disturbed air around the bomber. Its rocket motor fired, and it streaked after the first Sukhoi. The missile used laser guidance signals from the Vampire bomber, so the Su-33 had no threat indications that it was being tracked or a missile was in the air until seconds before impact, when the AMRAAM activated its own terminal guidance radar. By the time the Russian pilot knew he was under attack, it was too late.

"Formation two is heading back to the carrier—they must be low on gas," Frodo reported, his voice strained. "The last guy from formation three is orbiting over his leader. Looks like we're in the clear."

Boxer looked over at her mission commander and saw his fingers shake as he tried to type in instructions on his supercockpit display. "It's okay, Alan," she said softly. "You did good."

Frodo raised his oxygen visor. He sat quietly for a few moments, staring at his lap; then: "You could have gotten us killed, Boxer," he said in a low, trembling voice.

Gia didn't know what else to say except, "Sorry, Frodo."

His head snapped over toward her, and his eyes were blazing. "Sorry? You're *sorry*? That's *it*?"

"I guess so."

"You should've bugged out when they started to lock us up," Frodo said. "We should've turned around when we found out they were serious."

"Our job was not to turn around, Frodo—our job was to probe the fleet and report," Boxer said. "I'm not the kind of person to turn tail and run at the first sign of danger."

"But why the high-speed passes? We could've flown right into one of those close-in cannons. Hell, we were flying so low they could've hit us with a damned mop stuck out a porthole!"

"They pissed me off, and I wanted to show them they couldn't scare me off," Boxer said.

"They almost shot us out of the sky! They almost killed us! I've got two sons at home, Colonel. You could've made them fatherless, and for *what*—because you got pissed? Thanks a lot, Colonel."

"Don't worry, Major—I'll tell the review board you objected to going in and recommended we turn around," Boxer said. "You won't take any flak for my actions. Just find us a place to land."

"Armstrong to Fracture Two-One."

Boxer switched her comm panel to the primary control frequency. "Two-One, go."

"Everyone all right?" Jessica Faulkner radioed from Armstrong Space Station.

"We've been better," Boxer replied. "We lost number four, lost the rudder, probably lost most of the horizontal stabilizer, and I feel a bad vibration in the tail. We'll do a controllability test before we try air refueling or landing, but I think we're going to end up ditching or crash-landing."

"We'll pass that along," Gonzo said. "Your tanker is about three hundred miles east, heading toward you for the rendezvous. We have limited coverage on you right now, but as of three minutes ago, your tail was clear. If you can't tank, the closest air base is Salalah, Oman, about four hundred and fifty miles east-northeast. Got enough gas for that?"

"Barely."

"That's your only hard-surface runway for a thousand miles, guys, unless you want to try Al Mukalla, Yemen," Gonzo said, "but the Russians might spot you and try for some payback. We'll keep an eye out for you as much as possible and pass along your information. Good luck."

It was not looking good as the Air Force KC-767 aerial refueling tanker rolled out in front of the Vampire bomber. "Rudder control is almost zero," Boxer said as she slowly, carefully pulled the throttles back. "Elevator control is about fifty percent—it looks like the mission-adaptive system is having to work overtime to compensate for the loss of the tail stabilizers." She started to bring the power back, but the vibrations increased below 400 knots, and below 350 knots indicated airspeed, the vibration almost made the plane uncontrollable. "Looks like our limit is three-fifty, Milkman," Boxer radioed to the tanker. "What's your max?"

"Our published max is three hundred," the pilot responded, "and the most I've ever done in an emergency is three-twenty. The plane gets real twitchy in pitch above that."

"And we're not too responsive in pitch ourselves," Boxer said.

"I'm willing to give it a try," the tanker's boom operator said.

"Thanks, but I think we'll divert to—"

"Bandits!" Frodo shouted. "Two Su-33s . . . no, two *formations* of Su-33s, six o'clock . . . damn, just fifteen miles, with the second formation three miles in trail! My rear LADAR array must be shot off—I picked them up on the threat receiver only!"

"Time to bug out, Milkman," Boxer said. "We'll hold them off for you."

Just then, the threat-warning computer blared: *"Caution, caution, radar tracking, Su-33."*

"He's right on top of us!" Frodo shouted.

At that moment they heard a heavily accented Russian voice radio, "American bomber, this is Russian Southern Fleet patrol aircraft on GUARD. We have you and your tanker aircraft on our radar and long-range optical sensors. We have more fighters in pursuit. You cannot escape. Your aircraft is badly damaged."

"I can't see them except on the threat receiver," Frodo said. "I can't launch an AMRAAM as long as they stay in the rear quarter."

"Can we try an over-the-shoulder launch and have the missile track on its own?" Boxer asked.

"It needs an initial bearing and distance from the fire control computer to launch—it won't take info from the threat receiver," Frodo said. "The AMRAAMs are deadweight unless they appear on the lateral arrays."

"You are trying to think of a way to escape," the Russian fighter pilot radioed. "We noted you shot down one of our brothers, so you have defensive weapons, but the fact that we have come well within missile range of you undetected means that your defensive weapons are unusable, at least right at the present moment. We are in firing position now on both yourselves and your aerial refueling aircraft. We applaud your courage and exceptional fighting and flying skills on your high-speed pass through our task force. We have a proposal for you, warrior to warrior."

"Armstrong, Fracture."

"Go ahead."

"We got intercepted by Russian fighters from that carrier," Boxer said.

"Oh God," Gonzo said. "We have limited sensor coverage of you for the next three minutes, Fracture, and you're out of range of Salalah radar. We're almost blind right now."

"Pass our situation along to Central Command," Boxer said. "Ask if there are any Omani fighters at Salalah that can chase these Russians away."

"Roger. Stand by."

"Our proposal is this, American bomber: Eject out of your damaged bomber and let us have our fun with it," the Russian pilot radioed. "If you do this, we will let your tanker aircraft stay in the area to assist in recovering you from the ocean. If you do not respond, or if we see you make any turns or see your bomb bays open, we will open fire on both of you. You have sixty seconds to reply."

Boxer angrily flipped over to the GUARD channel: "Hey, bastard, you would be a cowardly chickenshit if you downed an unarmed tanker!" she shouted.

"Ah, the woman bomber pilot," the Russian pilot said. "Greetings, madam. That unfortunately is the spoils of war, my dear. You have fifty seconds to eject."

"Let us get closer to shore, closer to Yemen."

"You are much closer to shore now than our comrade was when you shot him down," the Russian said. "Forty seconds."

"Frodo . . ."

"There's nothing I can do as long as they're directly behind us," Frodo said. "I can jam their radar side lobes with the lateral emitters, but I can't touch the main beams. Besides, they're well within heater-missile range, and even if we could decoy them with flares, they can close into gun range in seconds."

"We can turn into them, lock them up, and shoot."

"The second we turn, they'll fire. We might be able to get one before they launch, but the other three will nail us and the tanker."

"Thirty seconds, madam."

"Can the jammers protect the tanker?" Boxer asked on intercom.

"Not against heat-seekers or guns," Frodo said. He started to tighten his ejection-seat straps in preparation for bailout. "Dammit, Boxer, this is all your fault! If you hadn't gone down after that task force, we'd all be safe! Now we have no choice but to punch out to save the tanker!"

The Russian fighter pilot radioed, "Twenty . . ." But at that instant Boxer saw an incredibly bright streak of light shoot across the sky coming from directly above, and the transmission was cut off. Another streak of light erupted seconds later, this one seemingly aimed directly at them but passing behind them, missing by what seemed bare inches.

"*What just happened?* What were those things? It looked like they came in from *above* us!"

"The lead fighter in the first formation disappeared!" Frodo said. "The wingman isn't transmitting yet."

"*Nail those bastards, Frodo!*" Boxer shouted, and she threw the Vampire bomber into a tight left turn, flying between the fighters and the tanker. As soon as she did so, the lateral laser radar emitters locked onto all three Russian fighters, the forward bomb-bay doors opened, and in fifteen seconds three AIM-120 AMRAAM missiles were in the air. At the same time Boxer popped chaff and flares to decoy any missile launches that might be aimed at the tanker.

Two of the Vampire's AMRAAMs hit their targets . . . but the third missed. The surviving Su-33 fighter accelerated and fired two missiles at the KC-767 tanker. Both radar-guided missiles were decoyed away from the tanker by the cloud of chaff billowing through the sky and by the Vampire's heavy jamming . . .

. . . but when they detected the jamming and the chaff, they automatically switched to infrared guidance and locked onto the biggest heat source in their line of sight: the EB-1C Vampire bomber. The two missiles exploded above the exhaust nozzles of the number one and two engines, blowing the left wing completely apart. The stricken bomber cartwheeled several times vertically through the sky, flipped upside down, then spiraled into the sea.

NINE

Half the failures of this world in life arise from pulling
in one's horse as he is leaping.

—Julius and Augustus Hare,
"Guesses at Truth"

The White House Situation Room,
Washington, D.C.

Later that evening, eastern time

"This is just freakin' unbelievable," President Joseph Gardner said. He had just received the initial report on the engagement in the Gulf of Aden. Now he was watching a computerized three-dimensional holographic replay of the incident as reported by the aircrew and verified by Armstrong Space Station. "We *told* them we were coming, and they said as long as we followed international law, they were fine with it."

"That's the part we can't figure out, sir," National Security Adviser Conrad Carlyle said. "There should have been no surprises. The aircrew did as the Russians told them: They changed to their radio frequency and put in a transponder code that made it easier for the Russian radar controllers to track them. The Russians engaged anyway."

"Our guys did it by the book, Mr. President," Secretary of Defense Miller Turner said.

"Oh, no, not quite, Miller, not by a long shot," Gardner said, shaking a finger at him. He entered commands into a keyboard to speed up the holographic animation floating above the conference table. "The Russians repeatedly warned the crew away; they kept on coming, which in my view wasn't a smart move."

"Legal, perhaps," Secretary of State Barbeau said from a secure videoconference link from Beijing, China, "but we don't know what was going on with the Russian fleet. They could have had some other sort of emergency, or were under some other kind of attack, and they warned our plane away thinking it was part of the other emergency."

"That's speculation, Stacy," Turner said. "We don't know that."

"In any case, Miller, the smart thing would have been to reverse course and get out of there," Barbeau said. "Why risk your life unnecessarily? It was a stupid move on that pilot's part."

"Exactly right," the president said, pointing at the hologram. "And then look at what she does—"

" 'She'? " Barbeau exclaimed. "A *woman* bomber pilot?"

"Colonel Gia Cazzotta, the squadron commander," Carlyle said, glancing at his notes. "Veteran bomber pilot, engineer, unit commander, lots of flying hours, experience in Desert Storm, Iraq, and Afghanistan."

"Sounds like a cocky type A jet jockey," Barbeau commented. She thought about her last encounter with a type A but laid-back jet jockey, Hunter Noble—he was actually a spaceplane jockey— but then remembered how *that* encounter ended, and quickly dismissed the memory.

"Friend of Patrick McLanahan's, too, I heard," White House Chief of Staff Walter Kordus said.

"What?" Barbeau asked, her eyes flashing in complete surprise. "Well, *that* explains a lot."

"Here's where the fighter attacks, sir," Secretary of Defense Turner said, pointing at the hologram. "Our guys didn't do a thing wrong, but they were shot at!"

"She should've bugged out and gotten out of there," the president said. "Instead . . ." He stared at the holographic replay in amazement. "Look at this—she's diving out of the sky, fighters on her tail! Now she's skimming over the water . . . now she's supersonic, for God's sake, heading right for this destroyer. More warnings on the radio. The ships are trying to lock her up, but she's too low and fast and jamming them . . . Jesus, no wonder they thought they were under attack! Somebody tell me what in hell she had in mind here, please!"

"Sir, without having interviewed her myself yet, I believe Colonel Cazzotta was conveying to the Russians that she and all American forces weren't going to be intimidated by hostile actions in open and free airspace," Chairman of the Joint Chiefs of Staff General Taylor Bain said. "There's no reason for the Russian fighters and then their ships to engage the bomber—it was on a routine and legal patrol, one sanctioned by the Kremlin. There may or may not have been some other sort of emergency that the Russians were dealing with, but it doesn't matter—Colonel Cazzotta had every right to fly there—"

"But what gives her the right to buzz those ships like that, General?" the president asked incredulously. "She is going *supersonic* and heading right for those ships! If it was me, I'd definitely think I was under attack!"

"Sir, international law prohibits overflying any vessel below one thousand feet altitude," Bain said. "The bomber didn't overfly any of those ships."

"Don't give me that crap, General—she may not have overflown them, but crossing in front of them at supersonic speed close enough to spray them with water kicked up by her shock wave? I'll bet the law says something about flying close to a ship in a careless, reckless, or dangerous manner. The Russians were obviously spooked and opened fire." He pointed again. "The Russian cruiser fires missiles but are either jammed or . . . what? What happens to the Russian missiles here? They just stop flying. Why?"

"The bomber has an advanced self-protection system that fires lasers at incoming missiles," National Security Adviser Carlyle explained, "that are hot enough to destroy the missile's guidance system."

"But one gets through?"

"Yes, sir, one gets through," Carlyle said. "An AA-12 radar-guided missile. A copy of our AIM-120 AMRAAM missile, fired from one of the Russian fighters. It explodes near the bomber's tail, severely damaging it."

"But the bomber not only keeps going, but *shoots down* the Russian fighter? How does it do that? With the laser?"

"The bomber is an EB-1C Vampire, a highly modified version of the B-1B Lancer bomber," Carlyle said. "It can carry a variety of weapons, including air-to-air missiles."

"McLanahan's magic bombers," President Gardner said, running a hand through his hair wearily. "I should have known. The guy could be thousands of miles away but still somehow involved." He turned to Chief of Staff Kordus. "Didn't you say McLanahan is personally involved with that bomber's pilot?"

"Yes, sir," Kordus said. "They've been seeing each other for a few years."

"Maybe McLanahan *was* involved in this," the president said. "Find out where McLanahan is; see if there's enough reason for the Pentagon or the FBI to question him." Kordus made a note to himself on his PDA to follow up with Defense and Justice. "This whole incident could have been invented by McLanahan to goad the Russians into attacking one of our planes. Then he can go on the campaign trail and complain that I'm not being tough enough on the Russians."

"The campaign trail?" Secretary of State Barbeau exclaimed, looking up from her notes in surprise. "McLanahan? What's he running for, Mr. President?"

Gardner realized he had way outspoken himself, so he waved a hand dismissively at the videoconference camera. "I meant lecture circuit, Stacy," he said. "But I wouldn't put it past him to do something crazy like that." Judging by the blank expressions on their faces, many of the president's advisers obviously didn't agree, but no one said anything. The president turned their attention back to the holographic replay. "The bomber meets up with the tanker; they get jumped by *four* fighters from that carrier, and then one is taken out . . . *how*?"

"By one of those Thor's Hammer interceptor projectiles from a Kingfisher weapon garage," Carlyle said.

"Direct hit, too," General Bain said, a boyish grin on his face. "Blew that plane into pixie dust—*literally*. Obliterated by a guided rod of tungsten steel traveling at fifteen thousand miles an hour!"

"And who gave the order to launch one of those things?" the president asked. "You, General?"

Bain quickly wiped the smile off his face. "No, sir."

"I know *I* certainly didn't! Miller?"

"The interim commander aboard Armstrong Space Station, a Major Jessica Faulkner, gave the order, sir," Turner said.

"We may set an all-time world record for the number of persons whom I am going to shit-can, kick in the ass, or both!" the president thundered. "A *major* ordered the destruction of a Russian fighter, and it wasn't in self-defense? What's next—an airman one-striper is going to sink their aircraft carrier? I thought I ordered that those Thor's Hammer things not be used and be removed from orbit? Include the space-station personnel, Ann Page, and the Secretary of the Air Force in the incident investigation."

"Undersecretary Page resigned her post, sir."

"I don't care. I want her included in the investigation."

"Yes, sir."

"What about the crew from that Vampire bomber, Miller?" Vice President Phoenix asked.

"Still listed as missing, sir," the secretary of defense said. "The *Reagan* carrier group is heading west and launching a rescue mission as we speak."

A phone buzzed, and Kordus picked it up, listened, then put the call on hold. "What the hell is it, Walter?" the president asked.

"President Truznyev of Russia on the line for you, sir."

He motioned for everyone at the conference table to pick up their dead-extensions, then punched the "HOLD" button again. "Put him on."

A moment later: "Mr. President, this is President Truznyev, via an interpreter."

"Hello, Mr. President. This is about the incident in the Gulf of Aden, I presume?"

"'Incident'? Three Russian airmen are dead and one is missing," Truznyev said. "In addition, several sailors were injured due to your bomber's provocative high-speed pass near our vessels, which also sustained some damage. This is more than just an 'incident,' sir—it is an act of war!"

"What it is, Mr. President, is a terrible misunderstanding, a complete lack of communication, and the case of a bomber pilot who far exceeded her authority and performed in an extremely careless and reckless manner," Gardner said. "But that doesn't excuse you sending four more jets out there and attacking the bomber and its tanker."

"I understand that you would choose to forget about the Russian pilots killed by missiles launched from that very same bomber," Truznyev said. "But I have another grave concern to ask you about, Mr. Gardner, and I hope you will be truthful with me, because tensions are already high in that region, and lying would only make matters worse."

"Lying? Mr. President, I'm not in the habit of lying. What is it that—"

"It is our finding that one Russian airman was killed at the very same time that one of your space-based attack weapons was detected deorbiting in the same area," Truznyev interjected. "We have not been able to extensively interview the surviving pilot yet, but it appears to us that an American space-launched interceptor weapon destroyed one of our planes. Is this true, sir?"

"Stand by, please, Mr. President," Gardner said, hitting the "HOLD" button again. "Shit, he knows about the Hammer thing taking out one of his planes! How could he know that?"

"Russia operates space surveillance and intelligence-gathering sites from an island off the coast of Somalia, from India, and from ships that can be deployed anywhere, sir—they might even have one in their task force out in the Gulf of Aden," Director of National Intelligence Gerald Vista said. "I'm sure they carefully track any of our spacecraft in range, especially the weapon garages."

"Well, what the hell am I supposed to say now?"

"Mr. President, if you tell Truznyev that Major Faulkner acted without authorization," Vice President Ken Phoenix said, "it'll appear as if the entire U.S. military is out of control."

"It *does* look like it's out of control, Ken!" Gardner snapped.

"Colonel Cazzotta and Major Faulkner were doing their jobs, sir—Cazzotta had been ordered to inspect and report on the Russian fleet, and Major Faulkner was ordered to protect American interests with their space-based weapons."

"I didn't tell the bomber pilot to race around the ships as if he—I mean *she*—was getting ready to attack them, just fly nearby and show the damned flag!" Gardner exclaimed. "And I ordered those Thor's Hammer things not to be used, and I was in the process of doing away with them."

"Sir, I recommend you use this opportunity to challenge Truznyev," Phoenix said. "This whole thing started when the Russians gave us permission to inspect their task force, then engaged the bomber offensively with radar and verbal challenges, acting as if they were ready to attack. If the Russians had simply allowed the plane to fly by, none of this would have happened. It's not our airmen's fault they reacted aggressively—they were only doing their jobs."

The president thought for a moment. Finally the expression of confusion and doubt lifted, and the rest of the president's national security team thought they were going to watch the commander in chief get tough with the Russians. Gardner hit the line button: "Mr. President, I . . . apologize for what has happened today," he said. Most of the national security team looked as if they tensed all at once—even Barbeau's surprised expression on the video teleconference screen was evident. Ken Phoenix's expression was utterly blank. "The actions of the bomber crew were uncalled for and provocative at the very least, and were possibly a violation of orders punishable by a court-martial. As for the downing of one of your fighters . . . yes, sir, a weapon was fired from space by our Space Defense Force."

"So you admit it." Truznyev crowed. They could hear the Russian president's angry, incredulous voice in the background, even though the translator delivered it in his usual even monotone.

"Mr. President, it underscores the absolute necessity of instituting a ban on offensive space-based weapons," Gardner said. "The space-station crew felt it was necessary to help defend the bomber and tanker, and so they acted. If such weapons are banned, such actions will not occur."

"So you ordered this attack from space to induce Russia to agree to a ban on the very weapons you used to kill our airman?" Truznyev asked. "How dare you, sir! It is bad enough holding a gun to our heads by placing those monstrosities in orbit and then asking for a ban on such weapons, but then you dare try to increase the pressure by killing a Russian with one!"

"That was not my intention, sir," Gardner said. "I did not sanction either action—the bomber crew and the space-station crews acted without my prior permission. They thought that their actions were part of their standing orders. They should have asked . . ."

The Russian president's incredulous voice in the background completely drowned out the translator's: *"Vy ne odobrjaet ikh dejjstvija?"* Truznyev shouted. The translator quickly cut in: "You did not approve their actions, sir?"

"Of course not!" Gardner said. "Things happened too fast." He realized he had just about lost control of this entire conversation, so he quickly added, "We told you we were going to patrol your task force, sir, and you engaged us anyway. Why was—"

"No, sir, do not attempt to place the blame on Russia," Truznyev said. "Your airmen and Space Defense Force troops' provocative and warlike actions resulted in the deaths of perhaps four Russian airmen and a dozen injuries."

"And I deeply regret the loss of Russian life, Mr. President," Gardner said. "But we are still confused as to why you would grant permission for a simple patrol overflight of your fleet, and then attack it. Were you trying to instigate a response, or—"

"Do not change the subject, Mr. Gardner," Truznyev said. "You promised the world you would not employ those space-attack weapons and you called for a ban of such weapons, then you proceed right along and use another to shoot down a Russian aircraft. You simply cannot be trusted any longer, sir. You are a liar. And if you seek to pretend that you did not give the order to employ those weapons, you are not only a liar but a coward."

"There is no need for such language, sir," Gardner said.

"This is Russia's demand to you, Mr. Gardner," Truznyev said. "All patrols by aircraft within strike range of our task forces will cease immediately. We will consider any such aircraft hostile and engage it immediately and without warning. Do you agree, sir, yes or no?"

"We are allowed freedom to navigate the sky as well as the sea, sir. We will not—"

"I said, Mr. Gardner, do you agree?"

Gardner hesitated, but only for a few moments: "Agreed, Mr.

President," he said. "In the interest of mutual peace and trust, the United States will fly no patrol aircraft within one hundred miles of any Russian warship." His national security advisers looked aghast as they listened in on the conversation; Phoenix still wore the same stony expression.

"And you must deactivate all of the Kingfisher interceptor satellites immediately," Truznyev went on, "and they must be allowed to burn up in the atmosphere."

"*Excuse me,* Mr. President?"

"Russia has the capability to monitor signals between those weapon satellites, Earth satellite control centers, and your military space station," Truznyev said. "Those signals must cease. With prior permission, you will be allowed to maneuver the weapon satellites to deconflict with other satellite traffic or pick a safe reentry crash area, and you will be allowed to approach the satellites to recover sensors or other valuable equipment, but otherwise you may not alter their orbital path or activate any systems on board. They will be allowed to crash in the atmosphere."

"Mr. President, those satellites perform a function over and above attack," Gardner said. He glanced at his advisers around him and their shocked expressions—all but Phoenix's. The president didn't know enough about the Kingfisher satellites to defend them; no one at the table really did, except perhaps for Phoenix, and the president wasn't about to ask him. "They are used for . . . for reconnaissance, uh, and communications . . ."

"Mr. Gardner, we both know that their primary function is to destroy satellites and attack targets on Earth, apparently now including aircraft," Truznyev said. "You can prattle about this and that as you please, but we all know that they were designed to kill, and have now done so many times. They must be deactivated, immediately, or Russia has no choice but to respond in kind."

"What do you mean, Mr. President?"

"The United States and China are deploying antisatellite

weapons—Russia shall start deploying them as well, in great numbers," Truznyev said. "China is placing long-range hypersonic antiship missiles all over the world in strategic locations—Russia will do so, too. America depends on Russian cargo spacecraft to supply the International Space Station and to boost it in its proper orbit—perhaps Russia's resources can best be used to help another nation's space program."

"So you're threatening to start a new arms race?"

"The race began when you began deploying these armed satellites in orbit two years ago," the Russian president said, "as well as engaging in this rapid buildup of aircraft carriers. You seek to dominate space like you dominate the world's oceans. This will not stand. You will agree to stand down your space weapons and leave our fleet in peace, or you will begin encountering more and more antiship and antisatellite weapons arrayed against you all across the planet."

"America is not Russia's enemy," Gardner said, his undertone almost pleading. "What happened over the Gulf of Aden will not be repeated. We have no designs on your task force, and we agreed to let Russia secure Yemen against further terrorist acts."

"Mr. Gardner, words mean very little right now as we pull bodies and wreckage out of the Gulf of Aden," Truznyev said. "Actions show your true intent, not words. Prove to Russia that you want peace and freedom of the seas and skies: Remove your armed patrols so our ships can move without fear, and remove the satellites of war so we can look up into the night sky again without fear of an artificial meteor streaking down on our heads. Then we shall see who is the enemy and who is a friend. Until then, you will find no cooperation from Russia." And the line went dead.

The president hung up the phone, as did the rest of his national security team, then sat back in his seat, staring at nothing on the conference-room table. He looked utterly deflated, like the home football team's coach suffering a bad defeat in the Homecoming Day game.

"I wouldn't agree to anything that bastard says, Mr. President," Ken Phoenix said after a few strained moments of silence. "He attacked without warning. We should demand—"

The president held up a hand to silence the vice president. "I'm not demanding anything, Ken," he said. "Right now, I'm ordering: *All* patrol planes stay at least a hundred miles away from the Russian and Chinese fleets. Our radar planes can still keep an eye on them from a hundred miles." He took another deep breath, then went on: "I'll have to have a talk with the congressional leadership, explain what happened." He paused for a moment, then looked directly at Vice President Phoenix and said, "And I'm ordering the Kingfisher satellites deactivated."

"What?" Phoenix exclaimed. "Sir, you can't do that!"

"They're not worth the aggravation, Ken," the president said wearily. "Truznyev is right: They are fearful weapons. An aircraft-carrier battle group is intimidating when it's parked off your shore, but when it sails away and disappears over the horizon, it's not anymore. The satellites are overhead each and every day. If we completed the constellations, there'd be *six* overhead every *minute* of every day. How can we expect any sort of friendship or cooperation from any country who's facing something like that?"

"Sir, Truznyev created this incident, provoking us to react, just so he could accuse you of belligerence and make unreasonable demands of you," Phoenix said. "He's hoping to get you to accept full responsibility for this to force you to pull our forces back from engaging or even monitoring them. Then they'll be free to sail anywhere they please, conduct any operations they care to, completely without supervision."

"There won't be any more provocations, Ken," the president said, "because we *will* pull back. We kept an eye on the Russians just fine without flying supersonic bombers around their carriers, and we sure as hell won't shoot down any more Russian fighters with a space weapon. We've protected the nation and the world just fine before Kingfishers and hothead bomber pilots arrived on the scene. No more. I want them shut down immediately." He turned to Secretary of Defense Turner and added, "I want all other military and intelligence operations in the area to stand down for a couple days. The tension level is getting ratcheted up too high. Keep our carrier away from the Chinese and Russians and let's everybody just cool down."

"The intel mission on Socotra Island . . . ?" Director of National Security Vista asked.

"I said *all* missions," the president snapped.

"Mr. President, that mission to Socotra Island is meant to provide positive proof that Russia is actively attacking our satellites with damaging streams of data," Phoenix said. "If we call off the mission, we won't have proof. I recommend we—"

"We don't need any proof if the Kingfishers are all shut down."

"So what will prevent Russia from doing the same attacks to other satellites?" Phoenix asked. "Will we shut down our intelligence satellites next because the Russians don't like them, or just wait for the Russians to attack them, too?"

"Ken, I said I want to ratchet down the tension level, and any ops against a Russian base will just create more headaches and force everyone's finger closer to the red button," the president said. "Everyone just back off, and let's hope things quiet down." He lowered his head for a moment, then said, "Keep me up-to-date on the search for the bomber crewmembers, Mil. Thank God we didn't lose the tanker, too."

DIEGO GARCIA, INDIAN OCEAN

A SHORT TIME LATER, EARLY EVENING

"Mission's been scrubbed, guys," U.S. Army Reserve Lieutenant Colonel Jason Richter said. "No plans to go in the foreseeable future." Richter was young, tall, and dark, but the stress of this hastily prepared mission had spread concern across his handsome features. He was sitting in the air-conditioned briefing room of the expeditionary bomb wing stationed at the military airfield on Diego Garcia, a former British navy base located 450 miles south of the southernmost tip of India.

Jason Richter was the commander of the Army Infantry Transformational Battlelab at Fort Polk, Louisiana, designing, building, and testing new devices for future Army infantry forces. He was in charge of developing and fielding a specialized weapon system he had designed years earlier called the Cybernetic Infantry Device, a creation that would eventually change the entire face of land warfare—if anyone could ever find money to fund it.

"I had a feeling it would be," former U.S. Army Reserve captain Charlie Turlock said. Charlie—her real name, not a call sign or nickname—was slim and athletic, but the heat and humidity of the central Indian Ocean had drained a lot of her natural energy, as well as taken a lot of the bounce out of her short strawberry-blond hair.

"I hate getting dressed up for a party and having it canceled," former U.S. Air Force major Wayne Macomber said. The former Air Force Academy football star and special operations commando always looked angry and on edge, as if he was expecting trouble to start any second. Patrick McLanahan's private military contracting company, Scion Aviation International, had hired Macomber and Turlock to manage some very special assets for the company—

several Cybernetic Infantry Devices and Tin Man commando units Patrick had absconded with from his former command, the Air Battle Force. Most of the CID units had been destroyed in the brief skirmish between Turkey, Iraq, and the United States two years earlier, and the rest had been returned to the U.S. Army and Jason Richter.

"Let's get our stuff out of the Condor," Charlie said.

"I'm not going out there until I get this poopie-suit off," Whack said. He was referring to the full-body gray suit he wore. Nicknamed "Tin Man," the suit was composed of a material called Ballistic Electro Reactive Process that kept it flexible until it was struck by any projectile or object, when it would instantly harden into composite armor that was impervious to even medium-caliber cannon fire. The Tin Man commando system also used an exoskeleton of microhydraulic actuators and limb braces that gave its wearer almost superhuman strength and abilities, and a helmet with several advanced sensors and communications equipment that made him a one-man infantry squad.

It took Whack several minutes to wriggle out of the Tin Man armor and put on athletic shorts, shirt, and shoes, and loop his ID card on a chain around his neck, and then he, Charlie, and Jason walked out to a nearby aircraft hangar. He was bathed in sweat during the short walk across the tarmac, even though it was almost dark, and then instantly chilled again in the air-conditioned and humidity-controlled hangar. "She's a beauty," Whack said after their IDs were checked by an Air Force Security Forces officer.

"Are you canceled, sir?" the officer asked.

"Yeah, Casone—my first flight on a B-2, and it's nixed," Whack said. "We'll get to fly in it someday." He was referring to the B-2A Spirit stealth bomber inside. The bat-winged composite long-range strategic bomber and its five sisters composed virtually all of America's long-range air-breathing strike forces after the B-2's lone base, Whiteman Air Force Base in Missouri, had been destroyed in a

Russian nuclear sneak attack eight years earlier—four of the six survivors had been forward-deployed to Diego Garcia as part of an Asian bomber task force, and two had been airborne.

"She's pretty, that's for sure," Charlie said. She touched the almost completely smooth dark gray skin. "Smooth, like a baby's bottom."

"Yeah, but flying in the Condor is just plain loco," Jason said. They walked over to the open bomb bays. The left bomb bay had a rotary launcher with two RAQ-15 StealthHawk reconnaissance and strike cruise missiles, designed to loiter for several hours, transmit images and data back to the Spirit bomber, detect and analyze possible targets, then attack with small guided missiles if directed. The missiles were meant to neutralize any area defenses or patrol ships and make it easier to extract commandos on the ground.

The right bomb bay held something entirely different: an MQ-35 Condor air-launched commando insertion and extraction air vehicle. The Condor could carry up to four commandos and their gear. The commandos entered through the Spirit's bomb bay, and the Condor was dropped like a bomb. The Condor could glide for up to two hundred miles and had a retractable landing gear for landing on a hard surface. If undamaged, the Condor had a small turbofan engine that allowed it to take off again and fly up to two hundred miles to safety.

"Almost as loco as flying in space stuffed in the back of those little spaceplanes," Whack said, "but we've had the opportunity to do that, too."

The three waited as a weapon-loading crew arrived and downloaded the Condor from the bomb bay. After it was placed on its storage cradle, Charlie opened a hatch on the left side, and the three dragged a large dark gray rectangular box resembling two refrigerators bolted together—but considerably lighter in weight—out and set it on the glossy polished hangar floor. "Hey, Carlo," Charlie called out to the security officer. "You haven't seen this thing in action yet, have you? C'mon over here."

"I'm on duty, ma'am," Sergeant Casone said. "I'll watch from here."

"Rog." Charlie turned to the box and spoke, "CID One, deploy."

At that, the box began to move. Sections of it shifted and popped out, quickly replaced by other moving pieces, until the box became a ten-foot-tall two-legged robot.

"Awe*some,*" Casone exclaimed.

"This is the best part," Charlie said. "CID One, pilot up."

The robot squatted down, its left leg and both arms extended backward, and a hatch popped open on its back. Charlie used the outstretched leg as a ramp and the arms as handrails to climb up and wriggle inside the robot. The interior surface was composed of a soft electroconducting material that completely surrounded her entire body, cushioning her from shock and picking up neural impulses in her body for transmission to the robot's haptic control computers. Her head fit into a helmetlike device with a breathing mask, communications gear, and an electronic wide-angle multifunction visor.

Moments after the hatch closed, the robot stood up—and it moved as lithely and naturally as a human. "All systems in the green," Charlie spoke, although her voice was heard as a male electronically synthesized growl. She ran around the B-2 bomber to Casone, curtsied before him, and extended a massive armored hand, its fingers moving as realistically as her own. "Nice to make your acquaintance, Sergeant Casone."

"All right, Charlie, stop screwing around," Whack said. "Put the CID away and—"

Jason's secure cellular phone rang, and he answered it immediately. "Richter here . . . who? . . . General McLanahan . . . you mean, General *Patrick* McLanahan? Excuse me, sir, but how did you get this number?" The name got everyone's attention instantly. Jason looked at Whack, then said, "Stand by, sir." He held out the phone to him. "It's Patrick McLanahan. He wants to talk with you."

Whack smiled ruefully and shook his head. "I should have known he'd be involved with this," he said, reaching for the phone. "If it has to do with the Tin Men, the CIDs, or big bombers, McLanahan's got to be behind it, civilian or no." He took the phone. "Hello, General. Fancy talking to you."

"Hello, Whack," Patrick said. "Listen up. We lost a B-1 bomber over the Gulf of Aden. Gia's plane."

The smile was instantly replaced with a scowl. "Where and when?" he asked.

"About ten minutes ago, approximately four hundred miles southwest of Salalah, Oman. The *Reagan* carrier group is en route; fixed-wing searchers should be on scene within the hour."

"Any 406 signals?"

"No." A 406-megahertz locator beacon with a GPS receiver built into each crewman's survival harness automatically sent a survivor's identification code and position digitally via satellite to rescue coordinators. "She missed the first manual-activation window." To reduce the chance of location signals being picked up by enemy forces, survivors who could manually activate their beacons were instructed to do it for short periods of time at specific times every hour, based on Greenwich Mean Time. "I heard your mission was scrubbed."

"*You* heard? How could you hear that? We just found out a couple minutes ago ourselves!"

"I had a little to do with planning your mission onto Socotra Island."

That explained a lot, Whack thought—and it was probably a *lot* more than just "a little." "We've got a badass bomber with four cruise missiles, plus a CID and Tin Man, all dressed up with nowhere to go," he said. "What do you need?"

"I'm trying to get clearance to press forward with your mission," Patrick said, "but the White House shut down all air intel and surveillance ops in the region. We have a backup plan to get two of you onto Socotra. A plane's on the way to take you and your gear to

Dubai. You'll meet up with a CIA guy who'll get you the rest of the info."

"You know, General, I'm just a shooter here—you'd better speak to the boss," Whack said. He handed the phone back to Richter. "McLanahan's got a backup plan."

Jason took the phone. "Richter again, sir."

"Backup plan in progress, Colonel," Patrick said. "A plane will be taking Macomber, Turlock, and the CID unit to Dubai."

"How did you know who and what we have here, sir?"

"The same way I got your secure cellular number and codes, Colonel," Patrick said. "That's not important right now. The plane will be there in about eight hours."

"I can't tell Macomber what to do, sir," Jason said, "but Turlock is an Army officer under my direct supervision, and she's not going anywhere without proper orders."

"It's just a plane ride to Dubai, Colonel," Patrick said. "Her orders will be waiting for her there."

"Sorry, sir," Jason said. "I don't know how you're involved with this—and I'm sure I don't have a need to know—but until I get orders in my hands, Turlock stays put. You can come get Macomber anytime—the sooner the better."

"And the equipment?"

Jason thought for a moment: "The Tin Man stuff isn't the Army's, so Macomber can take it and wear it for Halloween if he wants to," he said finally. "The CID unit belongs to the U.S. Army, and I need a valid transfer order before it leaves my hands."

"Understood," Patrick said. There was a slight pause; then: "I studied your work with Task Force TALON, Colonel—tough, fast, gutsy, a lot like the Air Battle Force ground teams," he went on. "And of course I've had a chance to work with the CID units on a number of occasions. Fantastic technology. Good work."

"Thank you, sir," Jason said, "although it's never been fully explained to me how *you* as a civilian managed to get them."

"I'd like the opportunity to explain it to you, Colonel," Patrick said. "Perhaps we'll have a chance to work together in the very near future."

"Apparently we already have been, except I didn't know it," Jason said. "Exactly what is it you do, sir?"

"Oh . . . a little bit of this, a little bit of that," Patrick said. "I help out when and where I'm needed." And Patrick hung up.

Socotra Airport, Socotra Island, Republic of Yemen

Days later

The Yemeni customs inspection official looked surprised and more than a little indignant as the tall, beefy, white-skinned man carried an enormous blue-and-white nylon bag, a briefcase, and a backpack over to his inspection station. Although this Felix Air flight had originated in the Yemeni capital of Sana'a, visitors to Socotra Island, an oval-shaped, rocky island two hundred miles east of Somalia in the Indian Ocean, were required to have their bags and travel documents reinspected. *"Salam alaykum,"* he said in his rough, low voice reserved for European visitors, holding out his hand. *"Jawaz as-safar, min fadlak."*

The big man fished out travel documents from his backpack and handed them over. The customs officer was pleased to see the man wore a long-sleeved shirt and long pants—they were not as strict about Muslim clothing customs on Socotra Island because it depended so much on tourism, and shorts and short-sleeved shirts were allowed near the water and on hotel properties, but in public, even men and especially women had to cover their heads and bodies. He expected courtesy and respect for Muslim customs from every visitor—at least until they got to the hotel and beaches, where he enjoyed watching scantily clad Western, Asian, and African women just as much as the next guy.

"Wa alaykum as-salam," the man said in extremely clumsy and heavily American-accented Arabic. He was tall, with closely cropped blond hair, blue eyes, and a light complexion. Socotra was a remote but popular destination for European tourists, so the customs agent played his favorite game and tried to guess the man's nationality—German or Scandinavian descent, he figured, al-

though the accent was definitely American, maybe Canadian. At least he gave Arabic a try, the customs officer thought.

"I speak English," the agent said with a slight thank-you bow for giving his language a try. The passport was American. He had flown to Yemen aboard Emirates Airlines via London and Dubai; the tags on his backpack and large duffel bag verified all the previous destinations. "I am required to inspect your bags, Mr. . . . Wayne Coulter," he said.

"They told me you might have to do that," the man named Coulter said.

"It is required." His documents were all in order, with a visa procured in Washington—getting three-month tourist visas at Yemeni airports was not always reliable, especially with the current hostilities. Flipping through his passport, he found a folded twenty-dollar bill stuck inside. The customs officer locked eyes with the man, then held out the open passport. "That is not necessary here," he said disapprovingly.

"Sorry," the man named Coulter said, although he certainly didn't sound apologetic. He took the bill and stuffed it into his pocket. "I don't know how that got there."

"Of course." The passport was a couple years old, a few trips to Europe and Asia—this was his first trip to the Middle East. "Your occupation, sir?"

"Mechanical engineer. I design industrial robots, you know, to build cars, trucks, things like that. I'm demonstrating a robot to help fishermen."

"I see." If this man was an engineer, the agent thought, the sun would certainly set in the east tonight. He was definitely military. Everything looked in order, but he still did a couple of suspicious double takes at the photograph and a few of the pages to see if the man would react. He did not—a very cool customer indeed, he thought, a man trained and experienced in keeping cool. "How has your travel been, sir?"

"Fine," the man said. "I had to sleep in the airport last night. They canceled a couple flights because of the Chinese and Russians in Aden and because of the weather."

"I am sorry you were inconvenienced. The monsoons have come early this year, and of course the trouble with the Chinese . . . *ma sha' Allah*. God's will be done."

"I hope I can still get some diving in."

"I think so." He flipped through the passport. "May I ask the purpose of your visit, please?"

"Demonstrating a machine for the Yemeni Fish Company Limited," Macomber said. "I want to do some diving, too. I'm told it's like the Great Barrier Reef of the Indian Ocean."

"God has indeed blessed our island with great beauty, especially under the sea," the customs officer said idly. He kept the documents in front of him on his desk as he unzipped the big duffel bag. It appeared to contain a gray scuba diver's wet suit, weight belt with weights, gloves, and boots. "Such thick wet suits for the Indian Ocean? I am afraid you may be most uncomfortable in our warm waters."

"I did some diving in the Irish Sea before coming here, demonstrating my technology," Coulter said. "This equipment allows me to dive deeper and stay underwater longer."

"I see." The customs officer knew the equipment had come from the United States via London, so the Irish Sea story could have been real, but his interest was piqued—these were not typical visitor's scuba equipment. The last item was even more curious—it looked like a cross between a full-face motorcycle helmet and a deep-sea diver's helmet. "And this is?"

"My diving helmet."

"It is very unusual. I have never seen one like it."

"It's the latest thing," Coulter said. "I can wirelessly talk to other divers or to surface crews while underwater, and it gives me readouts of air supply, dive depth and duration, water temperature and current, and even gives my location."

"Quite remarkable," the customs officer said, examining the helmet closely. Inside it did seem to have rows of tiny light-emitting diodes aimed at the visor, as well as microphones and earphones. Despite the fact that all this had to have been already inspected and approved in Sana'a, he knew he had to report it to the National Security Organization, or NSO, Yemen's foreign intelligence service—this equipment, as well as this man who claimed to be an engineer, had to be checked out further. He did declare all this equipment, so he was not trying to hide anything.

Still, the agent was getting more and more suspicious and decided to give this man several more minutes of attention, so he carefully and deliberately repacked the odd diving gear, then started to go through the man's backpack, again being slow and deliberate. The backpack contained clothes and toiletries, including some cold-weather clothing, giving further credence to the Irish Sea story, plus spare battery packs and a pair of binoculars, all listed on the declaration form. The briefcase had a laptop computer, cellular phone, power adapters, more spare battery packs, a personal digital assistant, pens, and other typical businessman travel things—no pornography, alcohol, or prohibited items, everything properly declared. He checked his papers and found permission letters to use a house owned by the Yemeni Fish Company in Hadibo, along with vouchers for scuba trips and island tours, all arranged online fairly recently through a tourist agency in Sana'a from a hotel in London using an American credit card. All very touristlike.

He really didn't have anything to detain him here legally, the customs agent thought, but he had to be reported. The officer had recently received some advanced training in how to spot foreign agents and insurgents, and this guy definitely looked like a fighter, not an engineer. "You are aware of the pirate trouble in the region lately?" the customs agent asked. "The Chinese navy has successfully suppressed much of the pirate activity to the south, but it is still active in the Gulf of Aden and northern Indian Ocean."

"Oh yes," the man named Coulter replied. "I've already got some dives scheduled with Captain Said's tour group, and the tourist agency told us he runs a very secure operation."

"He does indeed," the agent said, "but any business on the high seas that attracts the attention of wealthy Western or Persian Gulf customers attracts the attention of pirates. Traveling very far off-shore is not recommended, and be sure to advise your consulate in Sana'a by phone where you will be and your expected time of re-turn."

"I will," the man said. He locked eyes with the agent for a mo-ment, then added, "Good advice," in a tone that sent a chill down the agent's spine. He had a feeling this American would like noth-ing more than to have an encounter with a Somali pirate.

The customs agent again took his time repacking the man's bags, but the line was already getting long, and there was only one other inspector working this afternoon, so he quickly finished his paperwork and returned his travel documents to him. "Welcome to Socotra Island," he said. "Please enjoy your stay."

"Salam alaykum," the man said, and the customs agent immedi-ately thought that his Arabic was much better the second time— had he intentionally stumbled over his Arabic pronunciations to appear more like a tourist, and forgot to do so again now? The man collected his belongings and headed for the taxi area.

The agent processed several more visitors who had come off the Felix Air flight, got a cup of tea, then went to the cargo inspection area to find the man he wanted badly to speak to. He soon found a familiar white face, casually looking around, a cup of tea in his hand. The man noticed the customs officer and stepped over to him. "Greetings, Sergeant Dhudin," he said in Arabic but with a very heavy Russian accent. "How is your family?"

"Very well, Captain Antonov," Dhudin said. "And yours?"

"Everyone is fine," the Russian replied. "Helping with the cargo processing?"

"No, I wanted to mention something to you, Captain," the customs agent replied. He had known Antonov for about two years and they were friends, as much as any Arab could befriend a Russian. The Russians had provided a lot of upgrades and support for the airport since they had started using it more often—Dhudin had received security and firearms training from Antonov about a year ago.

Dhudin looked around and noticed a small pile of wooden crates, being watched by another white man—a Russian guard. Antonov and undoubtedly the guard were from the *Glavno'e Razved'vatel'no'e Upravleni'e,* or GRU, the Russian Federation's military intelligence unit. As before, when southern Yemen was known as the Democratic People's Republic of Yemen and actively supported and manned by Soviet troops, in the past few years the Russians had become much more active in Yemen in general and on Socotra Island and on Barim Island in the Bab-el-Mandeb waterway between the Gulf of Aden and the Red Sea. Since the terrorist incident against the Chinese navy, the Russians were back in Aden once again.

"What did you want to talk about, Sergeant?" Antonov asked.

Dhudin nodded toward the guard and the crates. "Bringing in more electronics for the facility?"

"Not today—mail, payroll, probably some un-Islamic beverages and reading materials," the Russian said. "Anything I can interest you in?"

"Russian vodka is always appreciated in my family."

"Very well." Dhudin was known to be an honest Yemeni government employee, but he was definitely not above taking bribes or tip money from infidels. "So. Something interesting today?"

"An American," Dhudin said. "He claimed to be an engineer."

"Claimed to be? You do not believe him?"

"He looks like a commando," Dhudin said. "Big, muscular, and cool as a crocodile."

"Few commandos would travel to their target on commercial airlines," the Russian said.

"You asked me to be on the lookout for something unusual, Captain," Dhudin said.

"Of course. My apologies." Dhudin also wasn't above passing along useless tips just to get his hands on Russian vodka or pornography, but he seemed genuinely suspicious this time. "Anything else?"

"His papers said he had a large case in the cargo hold, to be picked up by the owner."

"Let us take a look," Antonov said. After a few minutes of searching, they found a large fiberglass case, very high-tech-looking. Antonov stooped down and inspected the customs seals—they were secure, official, and the registration numbers agreed with the manifest. "Have any more seals, Sergeant?" he asked.

"Of course."

Antonov pulled a multipurpose tool from a belt holster, cut off the customs seal, and opened the case. Dhudin hurried to sign the manifest indicating that he had opened the case. The case contained flexible tubing, some solid tubes and rods, and what appeared to be hydraulic actuators. There was a small stack of color brochures inside, printed in both English and Arabic. "What does it say?" he asked.

"It is apparently a machine that crawls along the ocean bottom and autonomously collects shellfish from traps, then returns to shore," Dhudin said. "Ingenious."

"A walking fish trap, eh?" Antonov commented. He searched through the contents more carefully but was unable to find any hidden compartments or anything that looked like spy gear. "This looks like spare parts perhaps."

"He is scheduled to get another large container tomorrow."

He would definitely like to take a look inside that container as well. "All signed off by inspectors in Sana'a?" the Russian asked.

"Yes."

"His papers were in order?"

"Yes."

"What else alerted you?"

"He was carrying his diving gear—not the usual warm-water tourist stuff, more like professional underwater construction gear. He said it was for long-exposure deep diving—definitely not recreational, although he did say he wanted to do some recreational diving."

"How interesting," Antonov commented. Dhudin could see that the information was raising the Russian's suspicions, just as it did his own. Antonov took out his cellular phone and took a few pictures of the equipment with the phone's camera. "Staying at a house in Hadibo, you say?" he asked the Yemeni.

"Actually, it is between Qadub and Hadibo, the old Ottoman lighthouse owned by the Yemeni Fish Company. All vouchers and other papers checked."

Antonov knew that the Yemeni Fish Company had been investigated in the recent past for being involved in smuggling—this was getting interesting indeed. "And you say he looked military?"

"Very much so."

"Did you notify the NSO yet?"

"I was going to do it right after inspections."

"Do it now. Also give the Yemeni Fish Company a call and find out when this demonstration will be. I want to visit this one while he is out of the house."

"Should I keep this case for now?"

The Russian thought for a moment, then shook his head. "Go ahead and release it," he said. "I do not want to alert the American yet, if he is not who he claims to be."

As Wayne Macomber waited near the taxicab stand—a pitiful-looking place surrounded by trash, cigarette butts, and donkey droppings—a newer-looking Range Rover drove up and honked its horn. That, of course, got every local's attention around the entire airport terminal, something Whack was hoping to avoid.

The driver jumped out. "Mr. Coulter?" he said in pretty good English. "*Salam alaykum*. Peace be upon you."

"*Wa alaykum as-salam,*" Whack responded for the um-hundredth time on this trip. "And upon you peace."

"Very good Arabic, sir," the man said. "I am Salam al-Jufri from the Yemeni Fish Company. *Al-Hamdu lillah al as-salama.* Thank God for your safe arrival." Whack knew that was a common salutation, even when someone just came across town to visit. "I am here to take you to your house." He produced a business card, and Whack gave him his in return. "Yes, the robot maker," al-Jufri said. "Very good." He looked at the large fiberglass case. "I am sorry, but this must be strapped up." Whack lifted the case up, and al-Jufri produced three tattered bungee cords and a length of rope. Whack would have felt more comfortable with the case inside and *himself* on the roof, but after two or three tries, it looked secure enough.

It was easy to see why the case couldn't go inside: The back of the Range Rover was filled to the brim with every kind of article—fishing gear, miscellaneous items of clothing, spare fuel cans, a bicycle, and sacks of something. There was barely enough room in the backseat for the big duffel bag and backpack. Whack squeezed himself into the front passenger seat and took a few moments to try to roll the seat back, finally giving up.

They departed the airport down a dusty rock and dirt road, then turned east along a two-lane paved highway. Whack knew that his objective was west along the same highway, but certainly asking the driver to turn in the wrong direction would have attracted more attention. The highway twisted toward the Gulf of Aden, and he saw the spectacular blue-green waters and thought of McLanahan's friend Gia Cazzotta, and of the three navies vying for position out in those peaceful-looking waters.

The highway was on a sandstonelike shelf about a hundred feet above the ocean, with a thirty-foot cliff to their right, so there was little to see except for the ocean. Whack checked behind them every few moments, not only to look for any sign of surveillance but to make sure the fiberglass case hadn't fallen off the roof.

"You are well, sir?" al-Jufri asked after a few minutes.

"Aiwa, shukran," Whack replied.

"Your Arabic is very very good," al-Jufri said, nodding appreciatively, showing a mouthful of stained and rotting teeth. "You build robots, no?"

"Just drive," Whack growled.

"Mish mushkila, mish mushkila," al-Jufri said, swallowing nervously and taking a better grip on the steering wheel. "No problem, sir."

It was only about six miles down the highway until they came to a wide, short peninsula where the cliffs to the right disappeared, so the highway twisted away from the ocean. They turned left down a short dirt road, past a three- or four-foot stone wall with a crumbling wooden gate, then across a yard of dirt and stone and a few scraggly trees to a whitewashed stone building with a flat roof, and another building beside it with what appeared to be a tapering cylindrical lighthouse with four windows on the top floor, crowned with a Muslim crescent. Beyond the lighthouse Whack could see a covered outdoor patio with a fireplace, and beyond that there appeared to be a stable.

"Here we are, sir," al-Jufri said. He parked the Range Rover beside the lighthouse, then took Whack's bags to the house. He unlocked a green metal door that had six circles of multicolored glass in it, probably the most colorful thing Whack had seen in all of Yemen except for the Gulf of Aden. "This is the old Turkish lighthouse and its caretaker's home. It is now my boss's weekend house. You will enjoy."

The house was small but remarkably modern, and Whack

thought this would be a nice place to vacation. The view of the ocean was spectacular from every room in the house. There was a small patio off the kitchen, and a long flight of stone stairs had been carved into the cliff down to a pink sand beach, with sailboats and fish boats moored alongside a short pier.

Whack went outside and helped al-Jufri untie the fiberglass case from the roof. "Shall I drive you somewhere, Salam?" he asked after he lifted the case free.

"La, shukran," al-Jufri said. "No, thank you." He opened the back of the Range Rover and retrieved the battered bicycle, then stood beside it proudly, smiling at Whack—he did everything but hold out his hand. Whack took twenty U.S. dollars from his pocket—about four thousand Yemeni riyals, about a month's wages for most working-class Yemenis—and gave it to him.

The man's eyes almost popped out of their sockets. *"Shukran, shukran jazilan!* Thank you, sir!" he said over and over. "Please, if you need anything whatsoever, call. My sons will be by later in the evening and in the morning to look after the horses, and my wife and daughter will come to light the outdoor stove and lanterns." He bowed several times, clasped Whack's hand in thanks, then rode off.

Whack wished no one would come during the day, but for the mission he had to continue to accept the hospitality of the Socotra manager of the Yemeni Fish Company. Fortunately, the real robotic trap was coming in a separate shipment tomorrow, so his planned meeting and demonstration would take place as scheduled the day after tomorrow. That gave him a couple days to look around.

First things first. Whack took one of the laptop battery packs from his briefcase and the binoculars from his backpack, put on a Bluetooth earset, and went outside. He made it appear as if he were looking the place over, but he was checking to see if any of al-Jufri's family members were already here. The place appeared deserted except for two Yemeni ponies in a stone stable. His last stop was the lighthouse. Although the outside looked original, it had obviously been extensively reinforced with steel inside. There was a ladder to the top, with a metal grate as the floor of the top story, and it was an easy climb up. He found some toys, a battery-powered radio, and a nice German telescope up there—obviously the owner's grandkids liked coming up here.

He used his binoculars to scan the compound and the highway, then scanned the coastline and the nearby waters for any sign of surveillance—nothing. He then took the battery pack out of his pocket, flipped a hidden switch, and hid it as best as he could on the floor. The battery pack was actually a powerful ultrasonic motion detector that could detect any type of motion for several hundred yards in all directions, even through walls. Ignoring the soft beeps in his ear set, indicating his own movements, he went back down the ladder and to the house.

Whack brought his laptop computer and AC adapter to the patio outside the kitchen, booted it up, then selected an application from a hidden and password-secured menu. It showed a satellite image of the compound, along with red dots that indicated motion. He rotated the image until the dots representing the horses' movements in the stable was aligned with the image of the stable. When he stood up, he saw the dot corresponding to his own movement on the patio, so he knew the image was properly aligned. Now he would receive a warning beep in his ear set when the motion detector saw something, and he could see where the movement was on the laptop. He was able to squelch out the movement of the horses in the stable from alerting him, knowing but accepting the fact that anyone else moving in that same area wouldn't trigger an alert.

Perimeter security done, he opened his e-mail application. Armstrong Space Station and the Space Defense Force's network of satellites provided most of the world with free wireless Internet access, and although in this part of the Middle East it was not high-speed access, it was still impressive service. Just in case the Russians were able to tap into satellite e-mail services, he sent an e-mail address to his phony home office's address, then one to a phony colleague's address. He knew if the Russians could beam damaging data to American Kingfisher satellites, they could probably pick up wireless data broadcasts for hundreds of miles around, so he had to make this look realistic.

He then opened a Short Messaging System chat window with a phony girlfriend, but writing messages took much longer than normal because he used a mental encoding routine he had learned in Air Force special operations. Every commando learned a system of messaging to be used on unsecure transmissions based on a twenty-five character alphabet, arranged in a five-by-five grid. The date of the message told which of six possible encoding grids was to be used, and the first word in the main message would indicate the sequence to pick letters out of words to use to compose the coded message.

He then mentally used the grid and the sequence to compose a regular-looking message, filled in this case with standard boyfriend-girlfriend chat, remarks on the trip so far, and a few sexually suggestive lines. The recipient would use the same grid and sequence to pick out characters to form the message. All special ops guys had to learn this system by heart and be able to execute it without using pencil or paper to encode or decode, which took time but was a very effective poor man's secure telephone.

The phony girlfriend's e-mail address actually went via several secure servers directly to Patrick McLanahan. OK HERE he wrote. Those six letters took an entire 160-character SMS message to write.

McLanahan had a computer that would do the encoding and decoding for him, but he knew to keep the messages short because Whack had to mentally do the decoding. Patrick replied, GUARDS

24. That was a doubling of the known number of Russian guards at the facility, a sign that the mission could be compromised.

Whack sent: Gia.

Patrick replied: No word.

Damn, Whack thought, it's gotta be tough on the old guy. He wrote: Gia OK.

Patrick: Customs.

Whack: Curious.

Patrick: Gear.

Whack: All here.

Patrick: Assembled.

Whack: Visitors.

Patrick: Cops.

Whack: Maids.

Patrick: Luck.

Whack: Gia OK, then Later.

Check-in done, he prowled around the house and the grounds. He found plenty of Irish whiskey, Scotch, bourbon, and tequila semihidden in the kitchen, got out a bottle, dumped a little in the sink to make the bottle look used, poured himself a half glass of water, and strolled outside—just in case he was being observed, it hopefully would look like he had fixed himself a drink and was settling in for the night. He then went back to his laptop and reviewed the information on the robotic fish-trap thingy he was supposed to demonstrate in a couple days.

About an hour before sunset, the motion sensor alerted him to a vehicle in the driveway, and a few minutes later Salam al-Jufri's family arrived in a dilapidated Toyota pickup. Whack thought they acted as if he'd given Salam a yacht instead of a twenty-dollar tip—they bowed profusely every time they made eye contact, they brought enough food to feed a family of six, and they lit enough lanterns around the place to land a Boeing 747. The mother handed Whack a message written in broken English saying that they'd be back around seven A.M. for their morning chores, and reminded him to keep the big lantern near the front door lit so they would know not to disturb him in his bedroom as they worked. After they departed, Whack took the time to look around the compound for signs that any of the family had stayed behind. Satisfied he was alone, he got to work.

It took him just minutes to assemble the Tin Man armor exoskeleton from the parts in the big duffel bag, then hide it in the bathroom. He waited another hour until well after sunset, donned the Tin Man armor, then slipped on the exoskeleton and powered it all up using the battery packs in the duffel bag, which had been redesigned to resemble scuba diver's weights. Everything appeared normal—another big hurdle crossed.

Now using the suit's built-in secure communications system, he radioed: "Whack here."

"Good to hear your voice," Patrick McLanahan responded.

"Same here, General. Anything on Gia?"

"Navy helicopters have been on station for about two hours. They found wreckage but no survivors. No beacons. A destroyer from the *Reagan* carrier group will be there in a couple hours to assist."

"She's okay, General. They'll find her."

"Head back in the game, Whack. You copy the message about the guards?"

"I'll be ready for twice that number."

"You think customs suspects something?"

"The inspector didn't look like your run-of-the-mill Jamaican glorified skycap-turned-customs-agent, General," Whack said. "He made me as military right away. I'd be surprised if he didn't drop a dime."

"Then maybe we'd better wait another night or two," Patrick suggested.

"They won't be expecting a Tin Man, General," Whack said. "I assume the Russians are watching the house, and I assume they'll be watching to see if I take off in the Range Rover—I'm a good six miles from the airport and to town at least. My tails will stay with the car, and I'll be out and back in no time while they twiddle their thumbs. I say we press on."

Patrick hesitated, but only for a moment, before replying, "Okay, Whack. Press on."

WENCHANG SPACEPORT, HAINAN ISLAND, PEOPLE'S REPUBLIC OF CHINA

THAT SAME TIME

Riding an immense column of fire, the Chinese Long March-5 booster rocket lifted off from its launchpad on Hainan Island into the chilly, clear early morning sky. The massive rocket, China's heaviest-lifting model, had a three-stage, fifteen-foot-diameter core, with four ten-foot-diameter strap-on boosters, for a total of almost a million tons of thrust.

The launch window was very narrow for one reason: The payload for this mission was Shenzhou-10, the next component of the Chinese military space station, which was to link up with Shenzhou-7, already in orbit. Like the earlier spacecraft, Shenzhou-10 comprised three modules: the orbiter section, where most work was done; the command module, which was designed for reentry and had accommodations for the three-man crew; and the service module, which had all of the systems and equipment to support the spacecraft and also provided storage space. The payload also contained a docking module.

The launch was a complete success, and Shenzhou-10 entered its orbit in perfect synchronization with SZ-7. It would take just two orbits to close the distance between them, and then docking would commence. That would double the size and personnel aboard China's first military space station, Tiangong-1 . . .

. . . which happened to be in precisely the same orbit as Armstrong Space Station.

TEN

*The most rewarding things you do in life are often the
ones that look like they cannot be done.*

— ARNOLD PALMER

SOCOTRA ISLAND, REPUBLIC OF YEMEN

A SHORT TIME LATER

Whack waited until two A.M. before venturing outside via the back
patio and roof of the house. He made careful scans of the area with
the Tin Man suit's millimeter-wave radar, infrared sensor, and
sound amplifiers. Sure enough, there was a car parked about thirty
yards east of the driveway, tucked behind a tree, with a view of the
Range Rover parked at the base of the lighthouse.

"One tail on the main highway," he radioed to Patrick McLanahan via his secure satellite transceiver built into the Tin Man
armor.

"How many observers?" Patrick asked.

Through his telescopic low-light sensor he could see a lone
white-skinned occupant in the vehicle, smoking a cigarette and

reading a newspaper, with what appeared to be a camera with a long lens on a monopod. "One. Distracted. Good time to leave."

"Roger."

Whack dropped off the house, then down the embankment to the shore. He ran until he saw lights from a fishing boat, then climbed back up the rocky ledge and scanned again. He was out of the line of sight of the surveillance car, and the way was clear, so he went south of the highway, scanned again, then started running west toward Socotra Airport. The terrain was rocky and barren, with few places to hide, but it would make it easy to spot pursuers or locals. The land rose steeply at first, then dropped into narrow crevasses and then smoothed out to vast wastelands. Running and jumping would've been easier closer to the ocean, but he wanted to avoid fishermen and patrols.

"It's getting more rugged farther west," he radioed. Northeast of the town of Qadub, he found himself running up a large plateau that rose precipitously a thousand feet above him to his left. He stopped to scan the area and check battery levels. "Damn, I'm already down to fifty percent," he radioed, "and I'm only halfway there."

"You got the second set of batteries?" Patrick asked.

"Yes, but I might have to risk returning via the coastline and avoid this terrain on the way back if I'm burning watts like this."

"We might need a third set of batteries?"

"I thought of that, but I also thought it might arouse suspicion— that's an awful lot of weights for a beefy saltwater diver. I'll be more careful."

From his premission target study, he knew he had to cross the highway east of Qadub, because the plateau dropped quickly south and east of town. Locals in Qadub seemed to be having some sort of festival or mass gathering. The town was actually split into three neighborhoods, divided by the highway and by the dirt road leading from the main part of town to the sea: the fishing village near the ocean, the town itself south of the highway, and a cluster of farms and orchards to the west. South of town was impassable— the town sat at the base of two sheer plateaus. The only way around was a narrow strip of sand north of the highway and south of the fishing community.

Whack knew he was in trouble the minute he scanned the area around the town. "I don't friggin' believe it," he radioed.

"What?" Patrick asked.

"It looks like they're having a fiesta or something down there," Whack said. The townspeople were actually holding a procession from town to the fishing community along the dirt road! "I just got reminded again of the commando's 'Six Ps': Proper Planning Prevents Piss-Poor Performance."

"Abort and try tomorrow night," Patrick suggested.

He was 3.4 miles to his objective and still on time. "The procession looks like it's just getting started," Whack radioed. "It's the middle of the night, for Christ's sake. Don't you people sleep?"

"It's a weekend-long party celebrating the beginning of the fishing season," Patrick said. "I just Googled it. They'll be out there tomorrow night, too."

"Great." He could see lights being carried by townspeople, but through his infrared sensors he could see that not everyone was carrying lights, so the procession was quite long—probably a couple hundred people in all. There was absolutely no place to hide north of the highway.

"I'm going to go for it," Whack said. "I'll pick a gap in the procession, jump over the dirt road, and hope to get lost in the darkness."

"Too risky, Whack," Patrick said. "If someone sees you, they'll certainly alert the police, who would alert the Yemeni army border patrol, who would undoubtedly alert the Russians. Better off not pushing a bad situation. You got a couple more nights to—"

"Wait!" Whack exclaimed. At that moment the skies to his

right over the ocean erupted in a shower of rockets and sparkles. "Fireworks! They're having a friggin' late-night fireworks show at the fishing village!" The people on the dirt road began running toward the sea, and in minutes the road was clear. A quick scan showed the area clear for two hundred yards in all directions. "How about that, boss? Looks like it's clear." He didn't even need to jump the highway—that would have highlighted him against the fireworks in the sky. He simply sprinted across the sandy marsh, across the road, and straight ahead north of the highway, halfway up a gentle sandy dune leading to the highway. There were a few homes on the crest of the dune overlooking the ocean, but if anybody was home, they'd probably—hopefully—be looking up at the fireworks, not down toward the beach.

Another three-mile run, and soon he was at Socotra Airport. "I made it, boss," he radioed. He made his way east of the airport and up a gentle rise to just outside a very large rectangular fenced compound situated on a rocky plateau overlooking the airport. During World War II, this compound had been a British prisoner-of-war camp, and then became a British military headquarters and radar site after the war until they withdrew from Yemen in the late 1960s. When the Soviet Union was invited by the Communist Democratic People's Republic of Yemen to use port facilities in Aden in the 1970s, the Soviets took over the Socotra facility, enlarged and modernized it, and turned it into first an observation post, then a sea- and air-scanning radar facility, and finally into a combined space tracking facility and intelligence-gathering site, listening in on transmissions from space and from ships transiting the Gulf of Aden and Indian Ocean. It was again modernized and enlarged two years ago, when the United States started expanding its Space Defense Force satellite network.

The twelve-foot-tall perimeter fence was brightly illuminated. "Just as our intel said," Whack radioed. "Roving patrol on the west side, guard towers at the corners. The objective is in sight." It was right in the center of the compound, mounted near and below a large radome: a 150-foot-diameter steerable open latticework dish antenna, pointed almost straight up.

A lot of times, the first sight of the objective made commandos anxious and excited, and it was vital to squelch that feeling and stick with the plan. The most important thing was not to alert the Russians to the point where they would shut down the transmitter or inspect the antenna. They were already alerted to Whack's presence by the inspector at the airport, and they had probably assumed this was his objective.

He moved to his planned entry point on the east side of the facility, the farthest away from the airport, then took a few moments to study the guard towers on the corners. They were the farthest apart here and, being away from the airport and the highway, the least busy. His telescopic TV sensor showed two men in one cab and one in the other, so he chose the area closer to the tower with two men—the odds were better that the one guard in the other tower wouldn't be looking in his direction. Whack also changed batteries—the first set was down to 15 percent. He would enter the facility with fresh power in case he needed to bug out fast.

"Here goes nothin', boss," he radioed.

"Good luck, Whack," Patrick said.

Taking a running start, he jumped just at the very edge of the illuminated area outside the fence, clearing it with ease. He rolled as he hit the sandy hard-packed dirt inside the compound, leaped to his feet, and dashed as fast as he could to the closest spot of darkness at the inner edge of the illumination area he could find. He stopped and listened for any sound of alarm or pursuit. His escape plan was to jump out of the compound to the north, run downhill toward a riverbed about a mile away, then hide in a small cluster of farms if necessary. But so far he didn't need that plan.

"Made it, Muck," he radioed. "No sign of alarm."

"Don't get cocky, Whack," Patrick said.

"I know, I know," but he knew that, except for the exit jump, the hard part was over.

The inside of the compound was almost completely dark except for pole lights mounted near fire hydrants or outside entrances to some of the buildings, and it was easy enough to avoid those areas. His sensors tipped him off to any personnel or patrols nearby in plenty of time to take cover. There were guards everywhere, but no one seemed especially vigilant. That was often the case: When the number of guards increased, everyone tended to relax a bit more, assuming that the added numbers made everyone more secure.

Whack reached the antenna within two minutes of jumping the fence and found the service ladder. He carefully and quietly popped the lock off the protective gate, opened it, extended the ladder, and started climbing. His armored feet barely fit between the rungs, so he just used his arms to crawl up the ladder, going about three times the normal climbing rate. He made the twenty-story climb in about sixty seconds. Once on the bottom of the dish, he identified the framework structure that also attached to the transmitter-receiver module in the center of the dish, climbed onto it, and was on the rim of the antenna dish in no time.

The antenna had four long arms holding the large transmitter-receiver module in the center of the dish. In the Tin Man armor, it was easy to climb across the arm to the module. Hanging by one arm, he retrieved the signal analyzer-transmitter box from his backpack and attached it to the side of the center module. It would pick up any signals broadcast by the antenna, store them in digital memory, and then burst-send them to a waiting CIA satellite for downloading and analysis.

He reversed his direction, climbing back down the pedestal service ladder. He closed the gate, then pressed the hasp of the broken lock down into the lock with his microhydraulically powered fingers until the hasp jammed in place. Hopefully no one would notice the deformed lock until many days and at least one netrusion attempt from now—the first flyby of a Kingfisher weapon garage was in just eighteen hours.

Almost home free. He made his way carefully to his planned exit point on the north side. The terrain dropped away on the other side of the fence a bit more steeply, which might make it harder for pursuers to locate him. He also knew that there were probably motion or vibration sensors on the ground outside the fence, so he had to jump as far as he could past the fence and hope he didn't set anything off. He lined up, took one last scan around for any sign of guards, dashed for the fence . . .

. . . and cleared it with plenty of room to spare. He landed a little inside the illumination zone, but he quickly rolled away, got to his feet, and dashed for the ravine. He ran all the way down the slope for about a half mile before he dove behind the biggest rock he could find and lay still, scanning for any sign of alarm or pursuit.

Nothing. Dead quiet. "Holy cowbells, boss, I think I friggin' made it," he radioed.

"Congrats, Whack," Patrick radioed back. "Now concentrate on getting back to the lighthouse. Check your power level—it looks low from here."

Whack checked and was surprised to find the second and last set of batteries already down to 40 percent. "There might be a glitch in the armor," he radioed. "I think I'll try staying nearer the shoreline to avoid all the steeper terrain."

"Take time to do more scans," Patrick suggested.

"Roger. On the move." Whack made his way down the ravine to the freshwater stream that led to the Gulf of Aden, then started heading east.

It was easy going until Qadub. The fiesta and fireworks were over, but now the fishermen were working on their boats, getting ready to put to sea. Staying away from the lights from the wharves and piers meant moving closer to the highway, and it was getting a bit busier as dawn neared. Whack had to drop prone several times to avoid what he thought were people staring in his direction, and he considered digging a hole in the marshy sand a few times because he thought someone might come out for a closer look at what they thought they saw.

It took much longer than during the fireworks show, but soon he was at the eastern edge of the fishing community, almost clear. He was in a prone position once again. He listened, heard nothing, and then raised his head a few inches to let his sensors get a better look. Still nothing. He was at the edge of a baby-powder-soft sand beach at the eastern end of the fishing community. The highway curved rather close to the beach here, but it was empty right now. All he had to do was run about five hundred feet across the beach to the other side to a formation of huge boulders right at the ocean's edge and he would be home free—after that, just an easy four-mile jog back to the lighthouse. Like a sprinter in the starting block, he crouched low, gave himself a countdown, yelled "Go!" to himself, and dashed off . . .

. . . and after four steps, he tripped over something lying in the sand.

"Ahhh!" a man shouted. Whack hadn't seen the guy, sleeping nestled in the sand, covered in a rug, a bottle of something lying beside him. The man sat up, and Whack could see his eyes grow as wide as dinner plates. *"Ma bifham la afham!"* he shouted. He started to crawl away, still staring at the apparition in front of him in absolute terror. *"Imshi! Imshi! Al-bolis! Al-bolis! Sa-iduni!"*

"Crap!" Whack swore, and he sprinted away down the beach as fast as he could. He didn't stop for about a half mile until he heard an approaching car on the highway, then found a good hiding place.

"You okay, Whack?" Patrick radioed.

"I tripped over some guy sleeping on the beach," Whack said.

"Did he see you?"

"Yes. He looked like he was sleeping one off, and it's real dark out, so maybe he'll think it was the booze."

Whack took his time making his way back along the shoreline, and was extra careful as he approached the lighthouse. A different surveillance car was in the same spot as the first. He hadn't received any warnings from the motion detector, so no one had approached the house since he left it. He climbed back up the escarpment onto the patio and went inside.

Carefully and quietly, without using any lights, he signed off with McLanahan, undressed, cleaned the Tin Man armor and exoskeleton as best he could, and repacked it. The signals analyzer, disguised as a spare laptop AC adapter, was missing now, but hopefully the customs inspectors wouldn't notice, or he could say it was lost or forgotten somewhere. Whack set all the Tin Man armor's batteries in chargers in case he needed it again for an escape. He checked his path to make sure he hadn't dragged in anything from the beach, took a sip of Scotch whiskey to settle himself down, and then went to bed about an hour before dawn. Mission successfully accomplished.

Whack was awakened by the sounds of low, hushed female voices outside in the kitchen. He looked at his watch—a little before seven A.M., right on time. The voices seemed to be getting nearer his door. The note from al-Jufri had said that if the lantern was still on, he wouldn't be disturbed by his family preparing the house for the day, and he hadn't extinguished it, so he wondered if it had blown out or was—

Suddenly the bedroom door splintered apart from its hinges and flew across the room. Whack had already thought about what he would do: He rolled away from the door onto the floor, lifted the bed up, and flipped it toward the door to screen his next move. But just before he was going to leap through the window, it exploded as a three-round burst of bullets fired upward into the ceiling . . . from the *outside*. Whoever it was, they had anticipated his attempt to jump out the window and were waiting for him.

"Stay where you are and raise your hands, Mr. Coulter," a man with a thick accent—a *Russian* accent—said in English. Whack looked out the window and saw two men in black combat suits, helmet, web gear, and balaclavas, with AK-74 submachine guns aimed at him. The mattress and bed were pushed aside, and two more men similarly outfitted had weapons trained on him. They pulled him out of the bedroom into the living room, shoved him to the floor facedown, yanked his arms behind his back, secured his wrists with plastic handcuffs, then sat him up.

"What the hell is going on?" Whack yelled.

The toe of a boot came out of nowhere and landed on the left side of his head. Whack hit the floor hard, his vision completely blurred out, and he tasted blood and felt a loose tooth in his mouth.

"That will happen every time you speak out of order, Mr. Coulter," the voice said. He was pulled upright by his neck. "Nod if you understand." Whack nodded, slowly and carefully, fighting off nausea. "Very good. We were planning on meeting with you later today to ask some questions, but we received a curious report this morning from a local citizen about a sea creature that came out of the sea and tried to eat him. The police dismissed the citizen as a hallucinating drunk, but then I remembered something."

Whack looked up and focused through the pain. The Russian, dressed in a white short-sleeved shirt, black tie, and light brown trousers, was holding his Tin Man helmet. "An American carrying unusual scuba-diving equipment came through customs yesterday afternoon. Could this be what the man saw?" He paused, then gave the helmet back to one of his men. "You may answer now, Mr. Coulter."

"I don't know what you're talking about," Whack murmured.

"So you are saying it was not you, Mr. Coulter?" the man asked. "You are saying you did not go out for a swim in your fancy diving gear last night?" Whack said nothing. "Mr. Coulter? You may answer now."

"I wasn't out swimming last night," Whack murmured. "I'm hurt. I can't see straight, and I feel dizzy. I think I need a doctor."

"You were not?" the Russian asked. "Now I am confused. You are an engineer and builder of undersea robots, according to your Web site. You are scheduled to demonstrate a robot to the Yemeni Fish Company tomorrow afternoon. If you decided to go for a swim in your gear, I completely understand, and it makes perfect sense. All you need to do is tell me you went for a midnight swim, and this whole unfortunate matter can be cleared up immediately."

"But I didn't go for a swim," Whack said. "I didn't do anything. I need a doctor. Help me, please."

"We will take you to a doctor right away, Mr. Coulter," the Russian said, "but this matter must be cleared up first. A citizen reported seeing a man dressed in this outfit on a beach not far from here. It is, of course, not a crime to be out on the beach late at night. I believe the man saw you dressed in your fancy diving gear. All we want to do is straighten this matter out. There has been no crime committed. You can clear all this up by admitting that it was you that the man saw on the beach. Does this make sense to you, Mr. Coulter?"

"I swear to you, sir, I don't know what you're talking—"

Whack saw the boot coming this time, but he couldn't move anywhere near fast enough to dodge it. Another tooth came loose, and he choked on a fresh mouthful of blood.

When he could see again, he was sitting upright, looking into the face of the English-speaking Russian with the nerdy-looking black tie. He shook his head. "You do not look so well, Mr. Coulter. I will summon a doctor for you right away, but first you must tell me that it was you that was on the beach early this morning. If you tell me this is so, you will be treated by a physician and released. If you do not, we may be at this for quite some time."

Whack's vision blurred. He didn't try to clear it, but instead let his mind drift. His vision, and then his conscious mind, went dark.

To Wayne Macomber, darkness meant solitude, escape, rest, superiority over an adversary, and safety, and so he allowed his subconscious mind to expand and embrace the darkness. The pain was still there, but it was now tolerable, as if he were falling asleep on rocky ground.

"Mr. Coulter, are you still with us?" he faintly heard the Russian ask him. Whack could feel an eyelid pulled open, but his consciousness remained dark. The Russian said something in Russian, sounded like a curse; then, in English: "I have seen this before, Mr. Coulter. It is a technique that only the best field intelligence operatives and special forces commandos have mastered. Some men are able to shut down their conscious minds to such an extent as to block out pain and fear and thus make the muscles almost impervious to physical torture. So which are you, Mr. Coulter—an intelligence operative, or special forces commando?" Whack chose not to answer.

"Of course," the Russian went on, "if the mind is even partially conscious, eventually a combination of physical and chemical torture will break down even the most disciplined and well-trained mind—break it, or destroy it, in a most painful and twisted manner. Can you hear me, Mr. Coulter? If you can, you are minutes away from the worst pain any man has ever experienced. You can save yourself the agony, Mr. Coulter, by telling me who you really are, and what this equipment really does, and what you were really doing out there last night."

Whack's eyes were partially open and partially rolled back in his head, his blue tongue hung loosely out of his mouth between partially clenched bloodstained teeth, and his breathing looked as if it had stopped. Antonov stood up and shook his head. "A real old-style warhorse, this one," he mused. He opened his cellular phone, dialed a number, waited, then spoke in Russian: "It is me, Gennadiy. We found him; he tried to run, but we got him. He can hear us, but he shut down his body to resist interrogation . . . no . . .

just shut up for a minute . . . yes, I said he shut down his body to resist physical interrogation . . . no, I am not making up a story, it can be done, and this one has done it. I have done all I can here. He will have to be evacuated to headquarters in Sana'a or to the carrier *Putin* to continue chemical interrogation."

He noticed a splotch of blood on his boots, knelt down, and began to rub it off as he went on: "Oh, and one more thing, Gennadiy: Go over and talk to the commander of that new Strategic Defense Force unit at the radar facility . . . yes, you need to go over there and talk with him in person, because you need to impress upon him the importance of shutting his operation down and doing a thorough security sweep before . . . I know those bastards do not like the GRU and do not allow us routine access to do proper security checks. That is why you must convince them to do their own sweep to be sure everything is normal. I will . . . yes, I will call him first, but you must go over there and . . . just do it, Gennadiy. I do not care how stuck-up you think those Strategic Defense Force guys are . . . Me? I will be analyzing this man's equipment. If it is who I think it might be, we may have stumbled upon the espionage event of the decade."

In the Gulf of Aden

Early the next morning

Seventy-five miles west of its nest, the *Arleigh Burke*–class destroyer USS *Rourke,* the SH-60 Seahawk helicopter continued its search grid for the downed bomber crew. The *Rourke* had been detached from its duties escorting the aircraft carrier *Ronald Reagan,* which was about two hundred miles to the east, to help in the search. At the beginning of its third full day of searching, the outlook was not promising, although the weather was cooperative and the seas rather benign.

For the surface search-and-rescue mission, the Seahawk was equipped with a forward-looking infrared sensor on the nose and a rescue hoist on the starboard door, along with its usual APS-124 search radar. The enlisted aviation-systems warfare officer, trained in searching the surface of the ocean, was in the starboard-side-door station, while a rescue swimmer manned the port-side door. Since there had been no radar contact with the bomber except for an approximate position given by Armstrong Space Station operators, and the bomber had skipped through the sky uncontrollably after being hit, there was no precise location for the crew, so it was a hit-or-miss job, and so far the results had been a miss.

"Coming up on bingo fuel, guys," the Seahawk's copilot/airborne tactical officer reported. He entered instructions into the flight computer, which would catalog their grid pattern search and automatically relay updated grid-search instructions to the follow-on crew. "Station check, secure your gear, and—"

"*Contact,* port side, nine o'clock, one mile!" the rescue swimmer in the port-side door shouted on intercom. He immediately formed a gunsight with his left hand around what he saw so he wouldn't lose contact as the pilot turned. "Clear to turn." The pilot didn't turn the full ninety degrees, but only forty-five degrees left, so the observer could maintain contact with what he saw out the door while giving himself a chance to spot it, too.

As they closed in, they could see why it had been so hard to spot: The orange life raft was covered with oil, obscuring the bright color, and it was partially submerged because it appeared both crewmembers were aboard a single one-person raft. That was not a good sign.

"I've got contact," the pilot reported. "Swimmer, get ready." The rescue diver began donning mask, snorkel, and fins.

"We're coming up on emergency fuel, boss," the copilot said. "Not enough fuel for a hoist. The destroyer's too far away."

The pilot thought he was going to go for it anyway—bingo and emergency fuel figures always had an extra margin included "for the wife and kids"—but there was another helicopter already en route, so why risk losing a helicopter if they screwed up the fuel flow and quantity numbers? "Paul, looks like you're going to go swimming for a while," the pilot said. "Feel up to it? Three-Two is only thirty minutes out. Last water temp was sixty-seven."

"No sweat, Lieutenant," the rescue swimmer, Petty Officer Paul Malkin, said. He wore a twelve-millimeter one-piece cold-water wet suit, which would keep him safe in water down to forty degrees. He sat on the open door's sill, removed his headset, put his mask and snorkel in place, and gave the copilot a thumbs-up.

"Stand by on the rescue container," the pilot said. He maneuvered over to the raft. "Now!" The sensor operator threw the orange-and-white fiberglass container overboard out the starboard door. When it hit the water, it automatically opened and deployed a four-person covered life raft with water, survival, and medical equipment secured inside. The pilot translated slightly, getting as close as possible to the survivors without flipping their raft or the rescue raft over with his rotor wash. When he was sure he was clear of both rafts, the rescue swimmer jumped out the door, holding his mask firmly in place.

"Swimmer in the water," the sensor operator reported on intercom. A moment later: "Swimmer signaling okay, heading for the survivors."

"Emergency fuel," the copilot reported.

"We are outta here," the pilot said. "Radio the *Rourke,* have them make a ready deck, we're going to be on fumes."

The rescue swimmer Australian-crawled over to the buoy attached to the lanyard of the four-man rescue raft, attached the ring to his waist, then swam over to the survivors, towing the bigger raft behind him. One crewman was atop the other, and the one on top looked pretty messed up—maybe a broken neck. He felt for a pulse and didn't feel anything, but survivors' bodies immersed in seawater for long periods of time were known to shut down so much that a pulse was undetectable, only to be revived later. He rolled the crewman on top off the other one, letting him float by himself faceup using his own still-inflated personal flotation vest.

The one on bottom definitely had a pulse. He still wore his flight helmet, gloves, and survival vest, but he was sitting in seawater that had mostly filled the little raft. "Sir, this is Petty Officer Malkin, USS *Rourke,* United States Navy," the rescue swimmer shouted. "Can you hear me?" The crewman's head moved, he coughed, and his eyes fluttered. "If you can hear me, sir, listen up, I'm here to rescue you," Malkin said. "You're going to be okay, buddy. I'm going to get you and the other guy in my raft. My chopper will be back in no time. Hang tough and do what I tell you, okay? Are you hurt? Any broken bones? Do you feel any pain?"

The survivor coughed, spitting up a mouthful of water, then actually tried to sit up. He looked at Malkin . . . and it wasn't until then that he could see that the *he* was really a *she*! Not only that, but she was an Air Force *colonel,* the equivalent of a captain in the Navy! She was by far the highest-ranking person he had ever rescued! The name on her badge below her command pilot's wings read CAZZOTTA. "Can you hear me, Colonel Cazzotta?" he shouted.

Cazzotta coughed again, rolled to one side, then looked at him. "Thank you for rescuing us, Petty Officer Malkin," she said, "but can you please stop yelling now?" Malkin couldn't help but chuckle—here they were, bobbing in the Gulf of Aden hundreds of miles from help, and this zoomie colonel was cracking wise. She looked around. "Where's Frodo?"

"Frodo?"

"The other crewmember—Major Alan Friel."

Malkin looked at the other crewmember's flight suit and verified the name. "He's right here," he said, "but he looks like he's hurt bad. Let's get you into the big raft first. Can you move? Are you hurt anywhere?"

"My neck and back are killing me," Boxer said, "but I think I can move." As Malkin pulled the big raft over, she tried to sit up and was rewarded with a shot of pain that sped through her neck and zapped her all the way down to her legs. But she was still able to get up far enough to grab the other raft, and with Malkin's help she rolled herself off her raft and into the other, suppressing a cry of pain but thankful not to be lying in a raft full of water.

"Those cases on the side of the raft have bottles of water and survival blankets, ma'am," Malkin shouted. "Can you reach them?"

"Get Frodo," Boxer said. "I'm okay."

Malkin returned to the second crewmember to do a more thorough examination. "I'm afraid he's dead, Colonel," he said a few minutes later. He brought the body over to the raft, climbed aboard, pulled him inside, then pointed out his injuries to Boxer. "I'm very sorry, ma'am," he said. Boxer was too exhausted and dehydrated to cry anymore. Malkin had her drink a tiny bit of water, checked her over carefully for any injuries, wrapped her in a survival blanket, then covered the body with another survival blanket.

About twenty minutes later he heard on his radio: "Sierra, Trident Seven-One, standing by to authenticate."

"This is Sierra," Malkin responded. He looked at the code card secured to the radio and mentally computed the proper challenge based on the current time and the daily authentication code. This was a standard challenge-and-response security procedure for communications on an unsecure channel. "Authenticate tango-mike."

"Seven-One authenticates 'charlie.'"

Malkin computed the response on his card and came up with a matching answer. "Good copy, Seven-One."

"Roger," the helicopter copilot replied. "Sierra, authenticate yankee-hotel."

Malkin did the reverse on his card and responded, "Sierra authenticates 'bravo.'"

"Good copy, Paul," the copilot of the second Seahawk radioed. "We've got a good DF steer and it checks with the GPS coordinates, about two minutes . . ."

Suddenly Malkin saw two streaks of white flash across the sky overhead . . . and a second later he saw a bright burst of fire in the sky to the east. *"What the hell . . . ?"*

"That was a *missile*!" Boxer croaked through salt water–coarse lips. "Someone fired a missile!"

"I think the helicopter got hit!" Malkin shouted. "For God's sake, who would shoot down a *rescue helicopter*?" Seconds later he saw a jet fighter fly high overhead, but he couldn't identify it. With shaking fingers he keyed the microphone button on his radio: "Seven-One, Seven-One, this is Sierra, how copy?" No response, even after several more tries. His face was a frozen stunned mask of confusion. "Holy crap . . . !" He keyed the mike again: "Mayday, mayday, mayday, any radio, any radio, any radio, rescue helicopter down, possible hostile antiaircraft fire, any radio, please respond." He then reached over and activated the raft's satellite EPIRB, or Emergency Position-Indicating Rescue Beacon, which would broadcast location information via satellite to rescue coordination centers around the world.

"I think we're going to have company, Petty Officer," Boxer said. "Keep trying to raise someone on the radio." Boxer found her personal satellite locator in her harness and saw that it had not automatically activated upon ejection—because she'd been flying near possibly hostile forces, she did not want it to automatically activate—so she activated it now, and activated the beacon on Friel's vest as well. She then started to drink as much of the water as she could without throwing up, and she stuffed nutrient bars from the survival rations into her flight suit.

The thing she feared showed up about fifteen minutes later: a Russian-made Ka-27 naval helicopter. This one was fitted with pylons carrying antiship missiles, a machine gun in a turret in the nose, and machine gunners in the side doors. Neither Malkin nor Boxer could see any other flags or markings. With guns trained on the Americans in the raft, two black-suited divers dropped into the water, swam over to the raft, and climbed inside. They wore black balaclavas; neither could tell if the men were black or wore black camo paint on their faces. They motioned for Malkin to raise his hands.

"What the hell do you think you're doing?" Malkin shouted. He raised his hands but kept the mike button on the portable radio keyed. "Who are you?"

"Don't resist, Petty Officer," Boxer said. "They'll gun you down just to save weight." Again, neither American could see any insignia on the uniforms, and they said nothing so it was impossible to identify them by their voices or accents. While the first commando pushed Malkin over on his front and secured his arms behind his back with plastic handcuffs, the second removed Boxer's survival harness, ignoring her cries of pain, wrapped Malkin's radio and the EPIRB in the harness, and dropped it into the ocean; the weight of the radio pulled everything underwater. A rescue basket was lowered, and in just a few minutes both Americans were aboard the Ka-27.

Before being hoisted back aboard the helicopter, the last commando punctured all of the air chambers of both rafts and Friel's life vest with a knife, and in seconds Frodo had disappeared beneath the waves of the Gulf of Aden.

Russian Military Headquarters, Moscow, Russian Federation

That same time, early morning

"General Darzov here." The chief of staff of Russian defense forces spoke.

"General, the site is ready to radiate," the commander of the special intelligence unit on Socotra Island, Yemen, said. "Overflight will be in five minutes."

"I received a message from the GRU, reporting a possible security breach of the facility," Darzov said. "But I found nothing in your daily reports about it. Explain."

"Sir, the military intelligence branch from Sana'a detached to Socotra Island arrested an American engineer here, claiming he was a spy," the commander said. "They advised us to shut down all special intelligence operations and do a complete search of the facility."

"And did you?"

"Yes, sir. We found nothing."

"Did you interview the suspect?"

"We could not, sir—the GRU beat the man senseless. He is probably a vegetable."

"Where is he?"

"They said he was to be transferred to GRU headquarters in Sana'a or to the *Putin* for further medical tests."

Darzov knew full well that meant chemical-induced torture— the guy was certainly going to disappear after the GRU was through with him. "Did you look at the files on the suspect?"

"I did, sir. He checked out. He builds robots. He was scheduled to demonstrate some sort of robotic fishing device to the local fish company here. We looked at the device—it's a robot that walks in the ocean and checks fish traps. All his other papers were in order. He flew in the day before on Felix Air from Sana'a. We checked his entire itinerary and background. Clean."

"So what was the GRU suspicious about?"

"I do not know, sir," the commander said. "They said his dive suit was unusual. I looked at it: It was fancy, very high-tech, made for long and deep underwater missions, but it was a dive suit. I think the GRU mouth-breathers got a little too overexcited on this guy and beat the hell out of him, and now they want to deflect attention from themselves."

"And your facility checked out?"

"Completely, sir. Nothing out of the ordinary."

Darzov thought for a moment. Something was not right. The GRU regularly used a heavy hand in their operations, but they did not target foreign civilians without plenty of reason. But there was no time to waste on this matter now. "Very well, Commander," he said. "Proceed with the operation."

"Yes, sir," the commander said, and the connection was broken. He turned to his operations officer. "We are cleared to radiate, Major."

Minutes later, 260 miles above Earth, the Kingfisher-3 orbiting interceptor spacecraft rose above Socotra Island's horizon. The space tracking facility immediately locked onto it, and steering signals were transmitted to the adjacent parabolic antenna, which also began to track it. When the spacecraft was thirty seconds from its highest point above Socotra Island, sensors detected digital radar emissions from the satellite, and the special intelligence unit's computers synchronized on the digital data stream and began transmitting corrupt digital data instructions that would be received and processed simultaneously with the radar returns.

The corrupt data stream lasted only tenths of a second, but in that span of time Kingfisher-3's targeting and identification computers received millions of lines of computer code from the Russian computers on Socotra Island. Ninety percent of the code was rejected as corrupt or irrelevant data, but 10 percent was accepted and processed as valid commands. The commands ran the gamut: Some were orders to shut down, power up, reboot, or do all three at the same time; others were for repositioning and realignment with unrecognizable or illogical references such as the moon or some other celestial body instead of with Earth; others were for immediate engagement of nonexistent targets.

Within minutes of trying to sort out all of the contrary or unexpected commands, the spacecraft simply rejected *all* commands, safed and locked all of its weapons, reported itself as out of service, and shut itself down.

THE WHITE HOUSE OVAL OFFICE

A SHORT TIME LATER, EARLY EVENING
WASHINGTON TIME

"What the hell is it now?" the president asked as he strode into the Oval Office. He drank a full glass of water—he had been in a dinner meeting with his reelection campaign staff, celebrating another primary win, and had a couple glasses of wine, and he hoped the water would dilute some of the alcohol.

"The *Reagan* carrier group went on battle stations in the Gulf of Aden, sir," National Security Adviser Conrad Carlyle said. "One of its escort ships, the destroyer *Rourke,* was participating in a search and rescue for the bomber that was shot down a couple days ago. They found a survivor, but couldn't pick him up because of low fuel, so they put a rescue swimmer in the water and dispatched another helicopter. The destroyer lost contact with the second helicopter shortly after detecting an unidentified high-speed aircraft heading east toward it."

The president shook his head in confusion. "So the carrier came under attack?" he asked.

"No, sir," Turner said. "They lost contact with the second rescue helicopter. The captain of the *Reagan* must have assumed the helicopter was shot down or collided with the unidentified aircraft and went to battle stations."

"Did they see this plane attack the helicopter?"

"No, sir. They were out of range. The carrier's Hawkeye AWACS radar plane detected both the aircraft and the helicopter but did not pick up any distress or warning calls and can't say for certain what happened. The Hawkeye did pick up some radio traffic between the second chopper and the rescue swimmer, and also detected another helicopter from the west of where the survivor was located."

"One of ours?"

"No, sir, but by the time a patrol plane from the carrier *Reagan* got on station, it was gone. The patrol plane searched for it until it got within a hundred miles of the Russian carrier battle group, then turned around."

"Thank God for that," the president said. "The last thing we need is for the Russians to shoot down another of our planes. But I still don't see what the emergency is about. A rescue helicopter went down, and the carrier's captain suspects something with this unidentified aircraft and goes to battle stations? Does he think the chopper was shot down? Why would anybody shoot down a rescue helicopter?"

"I don't know, sir," Carlyle said. "It's preliminary word, a lot of guesstimates. But I asked that the Navy notify the White House anytime one of their battle groups in the vicinity of the Russian or Chinese carrier groups goes to battle stations for real, so they did. I thought you'd like to know."

The president nodded, then burped uncomfortably—the sudden flurry of excitement was dumping stomach acid atop the fine dinner and wine he had partially finished, and now it was all turning into sour junk in his guts. "That's okay," he said. "Keep me advised." At that moment the phone rang, and he picked it up, listened, then grunted something in reply. "Phoenix wants a quick word."

"What about?"

"Wouldn't say." He picked up the phone again. "Ask Mr. Kordus to join us in the Oval Office. He's upstairs in the residence with the reelection team. Thanks." Just as he hung up, there was a knock on the Oval Office door, and Vice President Ken Phoenix walked in. "What's going on, Ken?" the president asked.

The vice president held up a folder. "I have information that proves that the Russians have been sabotaging our Space Defense Force satellites, sir," he said.

The president's eyes narrowed with suspicion. "*You* have information? How did *you* get it, and *I* didn't?" He turned to the national security adviser. "You hear about this, Conrad?"

"No, sir, I haven't."

Phoenix ignored the question. "Just a few minutes ago, the Russians sent netrusion signals into a Kingfisher weapon garage, causing it to shut itself down a short time later. The signals were detected originating from a Russian space tracking and intelligence site in the Gulf of Aden, off the coast of Somalia."

"Answer my question, Ken—how did you get this information? Who is it from?"

"Apparently a nongovernmental group investigating Russian activity in the Gulf of Aden."

"A 'nongovernmental group'? Care to elaborate?"

"That's all I was told, sir."

"Does this have to do with the commando insertion plan you concocted on that island in the Gulf of Aden . . . what was it, Socotra Island?"

"You canceled that operation, sir."

"I canceled *all* operations in that area, Mr. Phoenix," the president said. "How did *this* one come about?"

"I don't know, sir," Phoenix replied. "But the results are conclusive: The Russians are definitely targeting Kingfisher weapon garages, causing them to shut down."

Chief of Staff Walter Kordus entered the Oval Office, and he motioned to National Security Adviser Carlyle that he had a phone call waiting for him. While Carlyle took the call, the president motioned for the papers Phoenix had and quickly flipped through them. "It's all unsubstantiated stuff, Ken," the president said, giving the file back to him. "It's hearsay. No specifics. I think someone is feeding you information you wanted to hear. Besides, it's moot: I'm shutting down those Kingfisher satellites anyway." Carlyle hung up the phone loudly enough to get the president's attention. "What, Conrad?"

"More information on that incident in the Gulf of Aden." When he noticed Vice President Phoenix's quizzical expression, he explained quickly: "The *Reagan* went to battle stations after one of its search-and-rescue helicopters went down."

"*What . . . ?*"

"Go on, Conrad," the president ordered irritably.

"Soon after the second helicopter went down, three emergency satellite beacons were detected. One belonged to the life raft dropped by the first helicopter. We assume it was activated by the rescue swimmer when he saw the second chopper go down."

"Makes sense. What about the others?"

"They belonged to the crewmembers of that bomber that was shot down."

"So there *were* survivors!" Phoenix said.

"The rescue swimmer could've activated the beacons on the victims' life vests," Carlyle pointed out. "There's more. The position of the three beacons stayed constant for about fifteen to twenty minutes, and then they were lost . . . at approximately the same time as the *Reagan*'s radar plane detected the unidentified helicopter come in from the west."

"*An unidentified helicopter . . . ?*" Phoenix exclaimed.

Gardner ignored him. "Lost? You mean, shut off?"

"Military locator beacons are designed so they can be shut off, to avoid crews being tracked by enemy searchers in an escape-and-evasion situation," Carlyle said. "But EPIRBs carried on ships or life rafts are designed to stay on until the battery runs out, which could be for several days. It's seawater-activated, waterproof, and designed to float, but if it's submerged deeper than thirty feet, the signal can't be heard."

"So the beacons came on and stayed steady until an unidentified helicopter came in from the west," Phoenix summarized for himself, "when at that time the beacons were cut off? Sounds to me like whoever was in that helicopter had something to do with that. Was anything found at the last location of those beacons? Rafts? Bodies? Wreckage? Anything?"

"No, sir, nothing," Carlyle replied. "When the Navy patrol plane came back after turning away from the *Putin* carrier group, it orbited the last position for an hour until the first rescue helicopter came back, but found nothing."

"A patrol plane flew toward the *Putin*?" Phoenix asked. "You mean, chasing the unidentified helicopter?" He looked at the president with a stunned expression. "It was a *Russian* helicopter?"

"We don't know that, Ken," the president said, rubbing his eyes wearily. "We're making a lot of assumptions here, and we could be screwing ourselves up. We don't know the identities of any of those other aircraft except our own."

"What other aircraft, sir?" Phoenix asked.

"The Hawkeye tracked a fast-moving aircraft in the area just before the Navy rescue helicopter went down," Carlyle said. "No idea what it was, where it came from, or where it went."

"It sounds like the Russians attacked the rescue helicopter, then sent one of its helicopters to pick up the survivors," Phoenix said. "That's madness! That's an act of murder and piracy!"

"We don't know shit, Ken," the president said. "All this happened within the last thirty to sixty minutes half a world away. The story will change a dozen times in the *next* sixty minutes."

"Sir, we've got to confront the Russians with what we know and what we suspect," the vice president said. "Lives are at stake. Those bomber crewmen and the Navy diver could be in the hands of the Russians."

"It's being handled, Ken," President Gardner said, longing to get back upstairs to the victory party. He looked at his vice president, thought for a moment, then: "Maybe you're right, Ken," he said, nodding. "I'll meet with the entire national security team in the morning, get the latest updates, then rattle Truznyev's cage. We'll get to the bottom of this."

Phoenix nodded. "Yes, sir. I'll make a few calls to the *Reagan* commander and get up to speed. Sorry I wasn't here for the briefing."

"That's okay," the president said. "But if I'm going to chair this status meeting tomorrow, I'm going to need you to fill in for me."

"Fill in, sir?"

"I have three campaign stops scheduled in Chicago and Milwaukee for tomorrow," the president said. "I'll stay in Washington, get the update, and brief the Press Corps myself on what happened and what we know. I'll have you fill in for me in Wisconsin, then we'll blow the doors off the place by appearing together in Chicago." He nodded to his chief of staff. "Set it up, will you, Walter? I'm heading back upstairs. Good night, all. Thank you."

The president, chief of staff, and national security adviser departed the Oval Office, leaving Ken Phoenix by himself. He stood motionless for several long moments; then, as if accepting an unwelcome fate he had seen coming for quite some time, he went over to the president's desk and picked up the phone. "This is the vice president," he spoke. "Get me President Truznyev of Russia immediately."

The president and chief of staff strode through the outer office of the West Wing, heading for the stairs to the residence. As they passed the chief secretary's desk, she put her phone on hold and called out, "Excuse me, Mr. Kordus?"

He stopped and looked quizzically at her. President Gardner called out over his shoulder, "I'll meet you upstairs, Walter," and continued on with a wave of his hand.

Kordus went back to the receptionist. "What?" he asked impatiently.

"Sir, the vice president is still in the Oval Office," she said, "and he just asked to speak with the president of Russia!"

Kordus's face went blank, and then his mouth dropped open in shock. "Call the president, *now,* and cancel Phoenix's request to talk with Truznyev!" he shouted, running back to the Oval Office.

President Gardner strode into the Oval Office a few minutes later, finding the vice president and Chief of Staff Walter Kordus standing next to the president's desk. "What the hell is going on here?" he asked. "What are you still doing here, Ken?"

"The vice president put in a call to President Truznyev from the Oval Office, sir," Kordus said. "I canceled it."

"What?" Gardner thundered. "You asked to speak with the president of Russia, without my permission, *from my office?* Are you insane, Ken? That's a criminal offense! You can be impeached for that! What—"

The phone rang, and Kordus picked it up. "Yes . . . ? Oh, Christ . . ." He put the call on hold and turned to Gardner. "President Truznyev. Wants to know why the vice president called him and then canceled the call."

"Tell him it was a mistake."

"Insists on talking to you, sir."

Gardner's furious eyes impaled Phoenix with burning lances of anger, and he snatched the phone out of Kordus's hand and hit the "CALL" button. "President Truznyev? President Gardner here . . . it was a mistake, Mr. President, a miscommunication . . . no, it was not some sort of tactic . . . yes, I mean to find out right now." He put the call on hold again. "Well, Phoenix? What the hell were you going to talk with Truznyev about?"

"I was going to tell him that we know about the netrusion activity from Socotra Island that damaged a Kingfisher satellite," the vice president said.

"Dammit, Phoenix, I told you I was going to confront him with that tomorrow . . . !"

"I was also going to tell him that we know the Russian military intelligence bureau captured the operative that planted the sensor that discovered the netrusion activity," Phoenix went on, calmly and very matter-of-factly, "and I was going to warn him that if he didn't release the operative, the bomber crewmembers, and the Navy rescue swimmer that he captured today immediately, certain powerful nongovernmental groups were going to start destroying Russian bases and ships around the world."

"What the hell did you say?" Gardner shouted.

"I was also going to tell him that we know he has been conspiring with Premier Zhou of China to neutralize American space and seaborne military systems," Phoenix went on, "and similar attacks would commence against Chinese assets."

"Are you *insane,* Phoenix . . . ?" Gardner shouted. "He's not going to believe any of this. *I* don't believe any of this!"

"It's true, sir," Phoenix said. "You can explain it to him, or I can." He held out his hand for the phone.

Gardner gaped in astonishment, first at Phoenix, then at Kordus, then at the phone, then numbly handed the phone to his vice president. "I can't friggin' wait to hear this," he murmured.

Phoenix took the phone and pressed the "CALL" button. "President Truznyev? This is Vice President Kenneth Phoenix," he said. "As I just explained to President Gardner, I know about the netrusion attacks against our Kingfisher satellites, the Chinese antisatellite-missile attacks, and Russia shooting down an unarmed rescue helicopter and capturing the bomber crew and rescue swimmer . . . no, don't bother denying it, sir, it won't matter.

"I told the president that I am in contact with certain powerful nongovernmental groups that demand you release the captives immediately," he went on. He listened for a moment, then interjected: "Sir, I'm not here to debate the matter. This group is already on the move. The first attack will be against the space tracking site on Socotra Island. The entire facility will be destroyed in"—he glanced at his watch—"well, any moment now. The second attack will occur shortly thereafter against your marine detachment in Aden. The third attack will be against the aircraft carrier *Putin* in the Gulf of Aden and its escort ships. The attacks will continue until the captives arrive unharmed at the American embassy in Sana'a."

Phoenix listened for a moment to the translator's words. At that moment Kordus's cellular phone rang, and he answered it. "President Truznyev, this is not a joke," Phoenix said. "The group is not under anyone's control here in the White House, I assure you, including myself . . . yes, sir, I do know the leader's name." Gardner's eyes grew wide. "His name . . . is Patrick S. McLanahan."

"McLanahan . . . ?"

"Sir, the consulate in Aden reports a massive ground attack at the harbor," Kordus said excitedly. "They are saying those manned robots, the Cybernetic Infantry Devices, are tearing the Russian marine detachment facility to pieces! And AFRICOM is reporting a massive air attack near the airport on Socotra Island! The place is getting plastered!"

"We have just been advised that the attacks are under way in Yemen, Mr. President," Phoenix said on the phone. "I would get those captives to the embassy right away before your aircraft carrier is hit." He paused to listen, then said, "I'm just a messenger here, sir—I have no control over retired general McLanahan."

Phoenix listened again, then looked directly at President Gardner, put on a slight smile, and said, "No . . . no, sir, I don't have a responsibility to stop this, because . . . I hereby resign as vice president of the United States. I have a duty to uphold the Constitution of the United States and perform my duties under the law, and I find I cannot do either for this president, so I have resigned." He pulled a letter out of a jacket pocket and dropped it on President Gardner's desk. "Good day, Mr. President." And with that, Kenneth Phoenix hung up the phone and walked out of the Oval Office without another word.

WASHINGTON, D.C.

JANUARY 2013

"You *are* going to be there, aren't you, Patrick?" Ken Phoenix asked. He was in a limousine driving down Pennsylvania Avenue heading toward Constitution Avenue in the nation's capital on a surprisingly temperate January morning, talking on a secure cell phone, holding his wife's hand, his two children watching the sights of the capital from the front of the passenger compartment. "You said you would."

"I said I might, sir," Patrick McLanahan corrected him. "But we looked at the situation and decided against it. Sorry. Besides, I think I'm the last guy you'd want to be seen with right now."

"Nonsense . . . but I understand," Phoenix said. "You did say you'd try. How's Gia?"

"Out of the hospital and right here with me," Patrick replied.

"And Macomber?"

"Still in the hospital, but if he doesn't leave the nurses alone, they're likely to toss him out no matter what the doctors say."

"Still wish you could be here for this thing, General," Phoenix said.

"It wasn't going to happen," Patrick said. "The last thing anyone expected was for Truznyev to go public with the whole thing. I became public enemy number one in an instant. President Gardner had no choice but to indict me."

"It's going nowhere, believe me," Phoenix said. "We've got the best defense attorneys waiting in the wings, but their services won't be needed."

"We'll see."

"In the meantime, not a hell of a lot else has changed," Phoenix went on. "China has practically taken over Somalia—they've made a basing deal with the northern Somali province of Puntland to improve port facilities on the Gulf of Aden in exchange for missile-basing rights. Both Russia and China are building aircraft carriers like crazy. Russia stopped supporting resupply missions to the International Space Station and are resupplying the Chinese Tiangong military space station instead. Allies are either arguing with us or turning their backs. It's a mess. And I don't have my favorite general by my side advising me."

"I'll always be there, sir," Patrick said.

"But you should be where you deserve to be—right up there with me," Phoenix said.

"I thought about it and talked it over with Gia for a long time," Patrick said, "and we decided what I knew all along: I'm just not a politician. I couldn't make it as a lobbyist, private military contractor, defense-contractor exec, or industry advocate either. I guess I'll always be just a flyboy."

"You're a leader, that's what you are, my friend," Phoenix said. "Always will be. That's what we need in Washington."

"I don't know, sir. Lots of fun things happening at Sky Masters again, and my son likes his school."

"I know, Patrick," Phoenix said. "But Bradley is a tough Air Force brat, and Washington is good for kids. I have a feeling you'll be back soon. When things settle down, let's sit down and talk."

"Roger that, sir," Patrick said. "Good luck, sir."

"Thanks, Patrick. You take care, General. See you soon." And he hung up.

A short time later, the limousine arrived at the East Portico of the Capitol Building, amid tight security keeping back thousands of cheering onlookers. Phoenix and his family were met by Dr. Ann Page, and they embraced, which only energized the crowd even more. "You ready to do this thing, Madam Vice President?" Phoenix asked.

"You bet I am, Mr. President," Ann replied. "Let's do it." Taking each other's hand, with Phoenix taking his wife's hand and Ann taking Phoenix's daughter's hand, they ascended the east steps of the Capitol.

Once through the Columbus Doors and into the Rotunda, they met with several of the distinguished guests who would be in attendance for the oath of office on the West Portico of the Capitol: several former defense secretaries and chiefs of staff, plus former vice president Les Busick and former presidents Thomas Thorn and Kevin Martindale and their families. After they greeted each other, they proceeded across the Rotunda to the West Portico.

Ann embraced Ken one last time before she walked out. "I'm so scared," she admitted as they embraced.

"I am, too, Ann," Ken said. "But we're it now."

She stepped back and smiled. "Damn right we are, Mr. President," she said. "Damn right."

Phoenix took his wife's and son's hands while his wife held their daughter's, and they waited for their cue to emerge onto the West Portico. They could hear the roaring crowd outside and feel the unusual January warmth through the doors.

Holy God help me, he thought as he smiled at the sunshine and listened to the cheering crowd . . . I'm it.

HENDERSON, NEVADA

THAT SAME TIME

Patrick McLanahan put his arm around Gia, and she snuggled closer to him—until he tightened his arm too much across her back, causing her to wince in pain. "Sorry, sweetie," he said. "Didn't mean it. Still sore, huh?"

"That's okay, lover," Gia Cazzotta said. She snuggled closer, and he kept his arm safely on the back of the couch. Patrick's son, Bradley, looked over at his dad's girlfriend in concern. "That was Ken?"

"Yes." They were watching the inauguration of Kenneth Phoenix on television from McLanahan's condo south of Las Vegas. "He still wants me in Washington."

"You just talked with the new president, Dad?" Bradley asked.

"Yep."

"Cool."

"He wants to talk about going back to Washington, Brad," Patrick said. "How about it? Feel like going back to Washington again for a while?"

"I don't know, Dad," Bradley said. "I'll be on the varsity squad next year, and . . . and . . ."

"You forgot about Heather, Dad," Gia reminded him with a smile.

"Who?"

"*Dad . . .*"

"The cheerleader?"

"No!"

"That was last month, Patrick," Gia said.

"She's my lab partner," Bradley said. "We're building that telescope. Remember? Can we leave after the school year's out?"

"We'll talk about it," Patrick said.

At that moment Central Intelligence Agency senior scientific programs analyst Timothy Dobson came into the room, his face wearing a smile but his body language saying otherwise. "Hey, Timothy," Gia greeted him, "come to watch the inauguration with us?"

"Sure," Dobson said.

But Patrick studied his face and immediately got up and walked him into the kitchen. "What's up, Tim?" he asked.

"The FBI picked up on another team that came through McCarran International today," the CIA assistant director said in a low voice. "Both Ukrainian nationals. Registered in the consulate as employment and training consultants for the Ukrainian government, but verified by the CIA as Russian Federal Security Bureau agents. It's the second team to come through this area in a week." Patrick looked over at his son with Gia, enjoying the pageantry of a presidential inauguration. "I'm sorry, General, but the Agency says it's a high probability you've been targeted by the FSB. We've got to relocate you."

"When?"

Dobson took in a long breath, then let it out quickly and said, "Yesterday, sir." He saw Patrick's shoulders slump. "President Phoenix has been advised, and he'd be as pleased as punch if you came back to the Washington area. President Martindale wants to meet with you, too. He says he'll set you up any way you want."

Now Patrick realized what Phoenix had meant by "I have a feeling you'll be back soon"—he'd already had the briefing and was suggesting an alternate home. As much as Patrick thought he knew the inner workings of Washington, he reminded himself, he found he actually knew very, very little.

Just as Ann Page was beginning to recite the oath of office, Patrick came back into the living room and pressed the "MUTE" button on the TV remote. Gia and Bradley turned to him, but they both looked at his worried face and didn't say a word.

"We have to talk about the move, guys," Patrick McLanahan said somberly. "We have to talk."

ACKNOWLEDGMENTS

A major source of information on living and working in space was from the book *Sky Walking* (New York: Smithsonian Books, 2006), written by four-time Shuttle mission specialist, fellow B-52 veteran, Fox News space commentator, and friend Thomas D. Jones. Thanks for your great work, TJ.

As always, the mistakes are all mine.

Your comments are welcome at readermail@AirBattleForce .com! I read all e-mails and respond to as many as I can. Please visit my Web site at www.AirBattleForce.com for the latest info on my novels, upcoming interviews and events, and my occasional rants about flying, geopolitics, foreign affairs, and almost everything else under the stars!